on the other side shiny and happy. Overall, this is another great addition to the Paradise Romance series.

-Bookvark, *NetGalley*

All the Reasons I Need

One of the reasons I love *Three Reasons to Say Yes* so much is that Clevenger wrote such strong secondary characters in Kate and Mo. I fell for them almost as much as the main characters, so to have them get their own book I was excited. This is a story about two best friends since college that have a ton of chemistry but have never done anything about it. ...If you are looking for a well written, angsty romance, look no further. This is an easy romance for me to recommend. I think with this series, Clevenger is at the top of her writing game and I can't wait to see what she puts out next.

-Lex Kent's Reviews, *goodreads*

This book is the second installment in Clevenger's Paradise Romance series. It's not necessary to read the first book, *Three Reasons to Say Yes*, to enjoy Kate and Mo's story ...*All the Reasons I Need* is a thoughtful summer romance full of emotion. It let me imagine myself on a tropical beach, napping in a hammock, and sipping an exotic drink with a little umbrella in it. There's just something about beautiful sunsets and waves crashing on the beach that make falling in love seem easy.

-*The Lesbian Review*

Three Reasons to Say Yes

This is without a doubt my new favourite Jaime Clevenger novel. Honestly I couldn't put it down from the first chapter. ...All in all this book has the potential to be my book of the year. Truly, books like this don't come around often that suit my reading tastes to a tee.

-*Les Rêveur*

...this one was totally my cup of tea with its charming relationship and family dynamics, great chemistry between two likable protagonists, a very convincing romance, some angst, drama and tension to the right extent and in all the right moments, and some very nice secondary characters. On top of that, the writing is technically very good, with all elements done properly. Sincerely recommended.

-Pin's Reviews, *goodreads*

This was a really easy story to get into. I sank right in and wanted to stay there, because reading about other people on vacation is kind of like taking a mini vacation from the world! It's sweet and lovely, and while it has some angst, it's not going to hurt you. Instead, it's going to take you away from it all so you can come back with a smile on your face.

-*The Lesbian Review*

Party Favors

This book has one of the best characters ever. Me. Or rather you. It's quite a strange and startling experience at first to be in a book, especially one with as many hot, sexy, beautiful women in it who, incidentally, all seem to want you. But believe me, you'll soon get used to it. ...In a word, this book was FUN. It made me smile, and laugh, and tease my wife. I definitely recommend it to everyone, with the caveat that if you don't like erotica you should probably give it a pass. But not only read it, enjoy it, experience it, also find a friend, or a spouse, or even a book buddy online to talk to about it. Because you'll want to, it's that great.

-*The Lesbian Review*

I've read this book a few times and each time changed my decisions to find new and inviting destinations each time. This is a book you can read time and time again with a different journey. If you're looking for a fun Saturday night read that's sexy and hot as hell then this book is 100% for you! Go buy it now. 5 Stars.

-*Les Rêveur*

The story is told in the second person, present tense, which is ambitious in itself—it takes great skill to make that work and for the reader, who is now the narrator, to really connect to the thoughts and actions that are being attributed to them. Not all of the scenes will turn everyone on, as we all have different tastes, but I am pretty sure there is something for everyone in here. And if you do as you're told and follow the structure the author uses, you can dip into this book as much or as little as you wish. An interesting read with some pretty hot interactions.

-Rainbow Book Reviews

UNDER THE STARS WITH YOU

JAIME CLEVENGER

Books by Jaime Clevenger published by Bella Books

The Unknown Mile
Call Shotgun
Love, Accidentally
Sign on the Line
Whiskey and Oak Leaves
Sweet, Sweet Wine
Waiting for a Love Song
A Fugitive's Kiss
Moonstone
Party Favors
Three Reasons to Say Yes
All the Reasons I Need
Just One Reason
One Weekend in Aspen
Over the Moon with You

Published by Spinsters Ink

All Bets Off

About the Author

Jaime Clevenger lives in a little mountain town in Colorado. Most days are spent working as a veterinarian, but time off is filled writing, reading, swimming, practicing karate, and goofing off with their wife and kids (both two and four legged). Jaime loves hearing a good story and hopes that if you ever meet, you'll share your favorite. Feel free to embellish the details.

UNDER THE STARS WITH YOU

JAIME CLEVENGER

BELLA
B O O K S
2023

Bella Books, Inc.
P.O. Box 10543
Tallahassee, FL 32302

Printed in the United States of America on acid-free paper.

First Edition - 2023

Editor: Heather Flournoy
Cover Designer: Sheri Halal

ISBN: 978-1-64247-439-8

PUBLISHER'S NOTE

Acknowledgment

After writing *Over the Moon with You*, I realized there were so many more veterinary stories I could share. But while *Under the Stars with You* contains a vet school plotline, it is more about what I have learned from a lifetime of loving and learning from horses. This story would not have been mine to tell had I not been gifted with years spent riding and caring for horses, nor without the opportunity I had to crew on the Tevis race. There are many people and horses I could thank, but most of all I want to thank my mom who first put a brush in my hand and taught me how to groom a horse. The horses I have loved changed my life, and at times, kept me alive.

Thank you to all my writer friends for your help and encouragement. It is amazing to know other storytellers and to share in the ups and downs. Thank you to my beta readers, Laina Villeneuve, Aurora Rey, and Alix Wandesforde-Smith. You all rock and I so appreciate your feedback! A special thank-you to my wife, Corina, for reading my story first, and second, and last. I don't know why you are so patient with me, but I know I am truly lucky to have you in my life. Last, but not least, thank you to my editor, Heather, for understanding that I need one more editing round or I won't sleep, and thank you to everyone at Bella for your help giving all the stories a happy ever after.

CHAPTER ONE

"Ty." Zoe banged on the bathroom door. "How much longer are you going to be in there?" More banging. "Ty?"

Ty Sutherland pulled on a clean T-shirt and opened the door. "You know there's another bathroom in this house."

"I don't have to use the bathroom." Zoe smiled. "Hi. How was your shower?"

"Fine." Ty cocked their head. "Why do I feel like you're about to ask me to do something I don't want to do?"

"You're going to want to do this. It involves cookies. And a hot realtor." Zoe waggled her eyebrows.

"No thanks." Ty picked up the scrubs, socks, and boxers they'd stripped out of earlier. The stench of the sick horse they'd worked on all morning rose up again. "All I want to do is start a load of laundry and put my feet up."

"You haven't even heard what type of cookies."

Ty tried to step out of the bathroom, but Zoe blocked the doorway.

"Double chocolate chunk. The realtor bakes them in little batches so they're warm and fresh out of the oven all day."

"How do you know this?" Ty shook their head a moment later. "Actually, I don't need to know."

"I met the realtor this morning. She was putting up the open house sign when I was getting our mail—which no one's checked all week."

"It's your job to get the mail."

"Not the point. The point is double chocolate chunk cookies, and all we have to do is walk through an open house. Also, I'm pretty sure she's queer."

"Who's queer?"

"The realtor." Zoe gave them a frustrated look. "Who else?"

"I thought this was about a cookie."

"Well, yeah, but I figured the hot lesbian part would get you to say yes."

Usually hot and lesbian in the same sentence would convince Ty to leave the house but it wasn't enough today. "I just got home from work. Can't you go by yourself?"

"No one would believe that I'd have enough money to buy a house."

"But they'd believe I do?"

"You're older at least." Zoe pursed her lips. "If you put on nice clothes for once it would help." She reached up and patted down their tousled hair. "And you could do something with your hair."

"I'm broke, Zoe. I don't need to pretend I can afford a house." Ty mussed their hair. "I haven't eaten all day—or sat down once—and I still have to go to the barn tonight to take Polaris out on a run. Plus muck the stalls."

Zoe dropped her shoulders and stepped out of the way. "It's killing me not to be riding Polaris myself."

"It's not worth screwing up your knee. That doc said one full week off riding."

"I know," Zoe grumbled. "How was she yesterday?"

"A little hellion. Like usual." Polaris was fun to ride even if she spent half the time yanking the reins out of Ty's hands. She loved to let loose and fly down the trail—as much as Zoe did—which was what had gotten Zoe injured. They'd been racing around a narrow turn when a mountain biker appeared. Zoe had made a split-second decision that squeezed Polaris to the side of the trail and smashed her knee into a scrub oak.

"I'm going with you to the barn tonight even if I can't ride." Zoe followed Ty down the hall, snagging her notebook as they passed through the kitchen. "I spent the morning working on my Tevis checklist and mapping the sections I want to ride before the race."

"As long as you don't push it like last time. It's too close to take dumb chances now."

Zoe stopped at the doorway to the laundry room. "Weren't you supposed to have today off? You were gone before the dogs even woke me up."

Said dogs were in the backyard happily barking at the squirrels now. Ty made a mental note to bring them back inside before a neighbor complained. "I got called in to help with a colic surgery." At five in the morning. "A little Arab mare with a twelve-centimeter enterolith."

"Ouch." Zoe scrunched up her nose. "Bet you could use a cookie after working all morning."

Ty chuckled. "You're desperate."

"I'm PMSing and we have no chocolate in the house. And I'm stressed about Tevis and not being able to ride my horse. Or run."

"You can handle a few days off." Ty opened the washing machine. Someone had started a load of laundry and hadn't moved the wash to the dryer. "I bought Oreos last week. They're on the top shelf in the pantry."

"Jenna found them." Which meant they were now gone. "Holly was pissed because she didn't share."

Jenna was the third housemate and Holly was the fourth. Four students living in one house meant the junk food disappeared as fast as the beer.

"Oreos aren't the same as a homemade cookie anyway. Think about it—warm, chocolatey, chocolate cookies. Mm. And the open house is right next door. It'll take ten minutes. Tops. We look around, grab a cookie, and leave. Did I mention the realtor was hot?"

"You did." Ty smiled. "I'm impressed you talked to her."

Zoe shrugged. "We talked about cookies. Who wouldn't have that conversation?"

Six months ago Zoe would have avoided any conversation with a random stranger. It was progress at least. "You promise it will only take ten minutes?"

"Tops."

Ty sighed. "Fine."

"Yes!" Zoe's face lit up as she cheered. After a beat, she added, "Can I pick out a different shirt for you to wear?"

"Why?"

"So the realtor thinks you're legit."

"Legit what? I'm not going to tell her I have money to buy a house." Ty tipped the laundry detergent to get out the last drop. One more thing to buy. They looked over the container at Zoe. "I'm a broke vet student. I'm not gonna lie."

"And you shouldn't lie."

Was touring an open house when you only wanted a cookie ethically wrong? Ty turned over the question. "The realtor invited you to come get a cookie, but you didn't tell her you were really interested in buying, right?"

"No." Zoe bit the edge of her lip.

"But?"

"I may have said that my cousin wanted to buy a house." At least she had the decency to look guilty.

"Zoe, why would you do that?"

"She seemed so eager. And she was so friendly. I wanted to help her out."

"By lying?"

"It's not lying if I convince you to buy a house from her." Zoe batted her eyelashes. "Someday you'll have money."

Ty stopped in front of the open house sign and tugged at the buttoned collar of their shirt. "You know, I could loan you five bucks and you could buy a dozen cookies."

"Not a dozen homemade cookies. Besides, you'll need a realtor eventually and this one's pretty. Think of it as an interview." Zoe tugged them toward the house. "Would it make you feel better if I told you all the reasons why you should be in the market to buy?"

"Zoe, I'm worse than broke. My student loans are—"

"Only going to get bigger by the time you graduate. Which is why you should buy a house and add the mortgage payment to your loan."

"I'd have to have a down payment to buy a house."

"Details." Zoe made it to the front door and rang the bell, then motioned for Ty to stand next to her.

Ty grabbed one of the open house flyers and scanned for a price. "Holy shit. Do you know much they're asking for this place?"

Zoe glanced at the price and shrugged.

"I bet our landlord is gonna raise our rent."

"Another reason why you should buy a home. Also, we could have as many pets as we wanted." As the door opened Zoe whispered, "I can smell the cookies already."

The realtor's smile didn't falter as she glanced from Zoe to Ty. Ty was used to long looks from people trying to fit them into a gender box, so it wasn't a surprise to feel the realtor sizing them up. They straightened, pulling back their shoulders on reflex. *Go ahead and judge.* People always did.

"Come on in." She opened the door wider. "It's hot out there and lovely and cool in here." As soon as Zoe and Ty were inside, she closed the door and said, "Don't tell anyone, but it's nice to have some Family show up. I've had nothing but straight couples touring this house."

Ty instantly regretted their initial assessment. They were the one who'd judged and the realtor confirming she was queer made it even harder to think about lying to her.

"You must be the cousin Zoe told me about," the realtor said. "I hear you worked your way through college training horses and now you're in vet school. With a scholarship for this next year. Congrats. That's impressive."

Ty felt their cheeks get hot. What was true on paper wasn't nearly as impressive in reality. "Uh, yeah."

"And you're hoping to stay in the area after you graduate which is why you're thinking of buying now? It's a great idea if you can swing it. And as you already know, this is a wonderful location."

Instead of glaring at Zoe for putting them in an impossible spot, Ty found themself nodding. The realtor's smile widened, making her even more attractive. Tan complexion, wavy brown hair, petite frame but generous curves in all the right places. All that with a strong femme vibe meant there was no chance of resisting her charm. And from the confident way she held Ty's gaze, she knew all about her charm.

It was true, at least, that staying in Davis after graduation was the plan. Maybe they could buy a home. Could student loan money be used as a down payment? If that was possible, wouldn't everyone be doing it?

No, there was no way. The mentioned scholarship only funded a portion of next year's tuition and the student loans would continue stacking up. As much as Ty hated to say it, the truth had to come out. "I don't think I'm financially ready to buy."

"But it's important to know the market, right?" Zoe nodded at Ty, reminding them to play along. "Those cookies smell amazing. I want to stand right here and just take a deep breath."

"That's my goal." The realtor laughed. "I hope they taste as good as they smell." She turned back to Ty. "I've got a financial planner I can put you in touch with. Sometimes things that seem impossible are actually doable with the right planning." She paused, then added, "I forgot to introduce myself. I'm Leslie Brandt."

Ty felt the room tip. *Leslie Brandt.* They'd promised to forget the name but of course it was embedded in their brain.

Leslie extended her hand and Ty had no choice but to clasp it. Her skin was smooth as silk and her palm cool against Ty's. Her fingers settled into place in a perfect fit. The rush that followed was overwhelming. Hormones mixing with adrenaline. How was it possible they were meeting now? After everything?

"It's nice to meet you," Leslie said. "I don't get to meet nearly enough cool people."

Ty searched for a response. *Me neither? We know each other?* After a moment, they managed, "Nice to meet you too."

Leslie's grip loosened and Ty had to let go. When Leslie smiled, Ty's heart floated up in their chest. Had Leslie held on longer than necessary, or was it only their imagination?

Zoe cleared her throat. "This entryway is nice. I love the raised ceilings and how open the space feels. Ty, what do you think about the living room?"

"It's nice. Yeah." Belatedly, Ty realized they ought to at least look in the direction of the living room. Subdued gray walls, a gray sectional, and a modern-looking darker gray coffee table. "It's...a lot of gray."

Zoe tilted her head, clearly expecting them to say something more. Unfortunately, the only thought in their head was how unbelievable it was that Girl-Monday was standing in front of them.

"I'm sorry, Leslie. I dragged Ty out of the house without giving them time to eat lunch." Zoe gave Ty a what's-wrong-with-you look and added, "They got called into work early this morning for a colic surgery."

"I have no idea what that is, but it sounds serious," Leslie said. "I hope things went well?"

Ty nodded.

"I'm sure you're exhausted after doing surgery."

"Oh, I didn't do the surgery. They don't let first-year vet students touch anything that isn't already dead."

Zoe's expression made it clear Ty had said the wrong thing. She covered with, "Ty's also a vet tech." Then, turning to Ty, added, "But in a few years you'll be the one doing the surgeries and you'll want a nice place to come home to."

"Why don't you two take a look around? If you like open floor plans, I think you'll really appreciate this one." Leslie glanced at her watch as an alarm beeped. "I've got to get the next batch out of the oven. I'll have warm cookies waiting for you when you come check out the kitchen."

"Nice." Ty smiled and Leslie's return smile warmed them through. She headed to the kitchen and Ty followed her with their eyes till she rounded the corner.

Zoe swatted Ty's shoulder and whispered, "What's wrong with you? I thought I was the one with anxiety. Is this how you always act around hot queer women?"

"No. Well, sometimes."

Anyone with a pulse would think Leslie Brandt was hot, but this went much deeper. Before Ty could figure out how to explain, Zoe said, "Just try and act cool, okay?"

That wasn't going to be easy. Ty followed Zoe through the living room and into the first bedroom, their thoughts spinning. When Zoe poked her head in the closet, Ty said, "I know her."

Zoe pulled back, brow furrowed. "You sure? She didn't seem to recognize you."

"We met online."

Zoe made an O shape with her mouth. "On that dating app?"

"No. It's…complicated." The dating app and all the women they'd met on it had come after. The site where they'd met Leslie was specifically not a dating site. No one was supposed to disclose their real identity. Everyone used a code name and avatars.

"She doesn't know my name, but I found out hers." Ty shifted so they could see through the bedroom door into the hallway. No sign of Leslie. Now that she wasn't standing in front of them smiling and going on about financial planning, the gravity of the situation settled in.

Ty kept their voice lowered as they continued, "I don't want to do this. I don't like lying. Even to a stranger. But lying to someone I know is worse."

"She really doesn't act like she knows you."

"Yeah, well, she knows me." Ty glanced again down the hallway. "Maybe we could slip out the front door?"

"No way. That would be rude."

Zoe was right, of course, but Ty's stomach clenched in a knot.

"It doesn't matter if she knows you online—she doesn't recognize you in real life."

It mattered. The only woman from the TryItOnce group who they'd connected with, the only one they'd imagined a real-life relationship with, and the only one who didn't want anything to do with them, happened to be in the kitchen, baking cookies.

Zoe half dragged Ty through the two rooms on the main story and then upstairs. At the first landing, Ty caught sight of Leslie in the kitchen. She was lifting cookies off the pan onto a platter and managed to look entirely sexy doing so.

"You're ogling," Zoe said.

Ty didn't even bother with a response. They knew Girl-Monday lived locally—or was from the area—because of the phone number she'd called from, but that she was in the same town, in the same house, now? It didn't seem possible.

"Ty." Zoe glared down from the second landing. "Snap out of it."

Ty headed up the rest of the stairs. "You sure we can't leave when she's not looking?"

"I'm sure. Quit asking. You're making me stressed when I finally think I've gotten my meds right." Zoe walked into one of the rooms and then turned to Ty. "Okay, what's the deal? Did you ask her out and she turned you down?"

"No."

"Then what happened?"

"I can't talk about it." Ty knew from Zoe's crossed arms that they'd have to explain more or the questions wouldn't stop. "We were in an online group that was supposed to be anonymous, but I found out Leslie's name and she freaked. That's all I can say."

"You weren't stalking her, were you?"

"Hell no. It was an accident. Her accident."

Zoe rubbed her face. "Okay, so, you two were on a dating site—"

"Not a dating site. More like a meet-up group."

"Meet-up groups are dating sites." When Ty started to argue, Zoe held up her hand. "This is why you need a real girlfriend. An in-person live girlfriend. Things get too messy online."

Ty dropped their gaze to the hardwood floor. Things hadn't been messy with Leslie. It'd simply been fun and easy. Until they'd suggested phone sex one night instead of their usual online banter. It was late and they were maybe a little drunk when they'd messaged Leslie with their number. When Leslie called, her number appeared on Ty's phone with her full name listed. Ty had told her—knowing that keeping things anonymous had been important to her. Everything had imploded from there.

"How old is she?" Zoe asked.

"I don't know. Thirty-something?"

"You don't know?"

"We didn't talk about personal stuff." That wasn't entirely true. At first they hadn't talked about anything personal beyond what they liked in bed. But after a few weeks, they'd both started sharing more and more. Still, they hadn't exchanged details like age. Or what they did for a living.

"I bet she's older than you. She seems way more mature."

"Most people my age are more mature. The problem is who I hang out with." Ty looked pointedly at Zoe. "Anyway, it doesn't matter how old she is."

"Well, it matters if you're going to ask her out."

"Who said anything about asking her out?"

"You two definitely had a connection downstairs. You could be brave and—"

"There's no way I'm asking her out. I'd have to tell her how I know her." Considering how fast Girl-Monday had dropped them, she'd certainly already moved on. Still, Ty knew the conversation wouldn't go well. Even the idea of it made their armpits sweat. "And now she thinks I want to buy a house."

A phone rang downstairs and Leslie's muffled answer came a moment later. Ty fought the impulse to move closer to the stairwell to hear her voice better while at the same time wanting to make a break for the front door.

"I guess it would be awkward if she finds out who you are," Zoe said.

"You guess?"

"Okay, fine. We'll get a cookie and leave. I won't make you talk to her." Zoe walked past Ty into the hallway, then glanced back at them. "But this could be fate."

"Randomly running into someone who never wanted to talk to me again? Yeah, that sounds like my kind of fate."

CHAPTER TWO

Dust billowed up in the wake of the Jeep's wheels, obscuring the blue mountains on the distant horizon. Leslie tapped the brakes on her Mercedes, adding another car length between her and the Jeep. Passing on a one-lane gravel road was dumb to consider, yet that didn't stop her from swerving to the left to see how much clearance there was around the Jeep. The answer: not enough.

She eased her grip on the steering wheel and resigned herself to her fate. The road split at the halfway point, one way going to her friends Seren and Paige's ranch and one way leading to a water tower with only an access road for the fire department. People used the access road for off-roading fun even if it wasn't legal. No doubt the Jeep was headed for the water tower. As she contemplated how much farther it was to the halfway point, a paved section of the road came and the Jeep sped up. A rock ricocheted off the Jeep's back tire and struck her windshield.

"Dammit." Leslie squinted at the bug-sized divot in the glass. She'd only had the car for a month and was still enjoying the new-car smell.

"Incoming call: Kaitlin."

She answered the call on the car's dash. "Hey, Kaitlin. What's up?"

"You're missing signatures for the disclosure addendum on the F Street property. The seller's agent called...and emailed."

"Shit. The buyers did sign but I didn't finalize the document. I'll take care of it." She bit back another curse as the Jeep slowed to a near stop. A moment later she spotted a squirrel dart off the side of the road into the scrub brush. Stopping for squirrels did win back a few points. "Any other fires I should know about?"

"No. Well, you got a call on the office line from your dentist. Something about a missed appointment?"

Kaitlin ran circles around all the other office staff Leslie had worked with over the years. And she was the only one Leslie counted as a friend. Which is why she said, "I overslept. I was having a dream when the alarm went off and I hit the off button instead of snooze."

"Must have been a good dream."

"It was about work."

"You work too much," Kaitlin said. "Dreaming about work is a sign of potential burnout."

Leslie wasn't sure that was true but didn't argue. Anyway, it wasn't a bad dream like Kaitlin assumed. The dream had been completely inappropriate, however, and involved her propositioning a client at an open house—which she positively never would do. She'd woken up right as her dream lover had settled in on top of her. Even without a satisfying conclusion, the dream had been the highlight of her day. Everything had gone decidedly downhill after she'd gotten out of bed.

"Have you thought any more about a little weekend getaway?" Kaitlin asked.

"I don't have time for weekend getaways." Before Kaitlin could hassle her, she said, "Can you make sure Sharon over at Title has everything she needs to close on Acacia Lane? That's happening Friday morning."

"Sure. Anything else? By the way, your connection keeps breaking up."

"I'm on my way to my friends' ranch. Kind of an emergency thing."

"Is everything okay?"

Kaitlin's concern was sincere but Leslie knew anything she told her would spread through the office. She considered what message she wanted broadcast. "I'm fine, but there was a medical emergency and I have to watch my friends' baby." Her phone buzzed and she read Seren's name on the screen. "Kaitlin, I have to go, but if you need me, I'll have my phone on me all evening."

"Good luck babysitting."

She ended Kaitlin's call and clicked over to Seren.

"Hey, sweetie. I'm almost there. I got stuck behind a Jeep that looks like something my grandpa would've owned." She also realized they'd passed the halfway point and the Jeep hadn't turned off for the water tower.

"That's probably Ty. They board their horse here."

Ty? As in the same Ty who'd been in her dream that morning? She felt the blush hit her cheeks even as she argued it must be a different Ty. "You have boarders?"

"Yeah, we took on two horses last month. Paige loves having more animals around. Honestly, it is nice seeing the barn fill up."

Had Seren actually said Ty? Maybe she'd heard the wrong name. She wanted to ask but stopped herself. It didn't really matter, she rationalized. Ty hadn't called her back and hadn't contacted the mortgage lender she'd recommended either—she knew because she'd called the lender and surreptitiously asked. Which meant they were simply a random person who'd come through an open house. A random person who'd made it into her dreams.

She thought again of how she'd held their hand a moment too long. Afterward, she'd wondered what had gotten into her. She'd worried she'd made things awkward and still wasn't sure what had made her hold on. For a moment, she'd almost asked if they'd met before. But she never forgot a face and was sure she wouldn't have forgotten someone who looked that hot and was so obviously queer. Ty's smile had rocked her and their sky-blue eyes had made her lose her train of thought. It didn't help matters that Ty's hand had felt perfect wrapped around hers.

Seren's voice broke her train of thought. "I'm hoping we won't have to ask you to stay the night, but if we get stuck in Stanford—"

"Everything in my schedule can be rearranged. Anything for you and Olivia. And Paige, too."

It was Paige's mom, Bea, who'd had to go in for emergency surgery. Some problem with a pacemaker. Seren hadn't given all the details. All she knew was that Bea had been seemingly fine that morning and then was suddenly taken to surgery after a routine checkup with her cardiologist. Seren had lost her own mom two years ago and didn't do well with medical emergencies, so Leslie hadn't pressed.

"I know you have a million things on your mind right now, but could you write down what I need to do for the animals?" She'd taken care of Olivia before, but the barn animals were more intimidating.

"You won't have to worry about that. Since Ty was coming to do some work on the barn, Paige asked them to take care of everything else too. They're a vet student and Paige has known them a long time."

Definitely the same Ty from the open house. "Are they spending the night?" She hoped the answer was no. At least mostly.

"No. It'll just be you and Olivia. Ty will come back in the morning to do the feedings if we aren't back."

Well, that settled it. She'd avoid the barn and stay in the house with Olivia. This wasn't the first time she'd had to avoid a second-chance encounter. Davis was a small enough town that everyone seemed connected to someone she knew. She glanced down at her blouse and skirt. "Could I borrow a change of clothes? I'm in a work outfit and didn't grab an overnight bag. And maybe some pajamas and a spare toothbrush?"

"Of course." The sound of a baby crying on the other end interrupted. "Paige is trying to put Olivia down for a nap. She'll be in a better mood later if she sleeps a little."

"I'm okay with her being grumpy. We'll be a good pair."

"You seemed a little out of sorts when I called you earlier. You sure you don't mind babysitting?"

"I'm sure. I've just had one of those days." She looked at the divot on her windshield and noticed a thin line already spreading out from the spot. "Olivia will help get me out of my funk. See you in a minute."

Seren and Paige's barn came into view around the next turn, newly painted red with white trim. The Jeep veered toward the barn and Leslie pulled up in front of the brown ranch house.

Seren came out the front door, her expression more tense than the call had let on, and Leslie felt her stomach tighten. She pushed away her own day's baggage—which really had been more ridiculous than awful—and worked up a smile as she headed up the walkway. When she opened her arms for a hug, Seren stepped right up.

"You have no idea how much it means to me for you to drop everything and come over." Seren pulled back and squinted at Leslie's blouse. "That stain's going to be hard to get out. Coffee?"

"I had a heck of a morning." Made worse by not having enough coffee.

"What happened?"

"You don't want to know." When Seren put her hands on her hips with a "tell me" look, Leslie sighed and said, "I missed a seven a.m. dentist appointment because I was dreaming about work. Then I tried to squeeze in a cycling class but showed up without my workout clothes. So I went to the donut shop to get coffee and donuts for our morning meeting but forgot the donuts. I seriously walked in, ordered coffee for me and Kaitlin, and left. With no donuts. Who does that?"

"Someone who's trying to do too much." Seren's look was full of sympathy. "And then you spilled the coffee?"

Leslie picked at the front of her blouse. "I had a scarf covering it up at work, but I figured you could handle the real me."

"Always. You sure watching Olivia isn't too much?"

"Not at all. She got me off work early."

Seren smiled. "Good point. If you want more coffee, Paige started a fresh pot after Bea's doctor called. And I set out some clothes for you in the guest room."

"How's Bea?"

"We haven't heard anything after the first call from the doctor," Seren said. "Paige keeps saying Bea's tough as nails, but that's what I used to say about my mom."

The catch in Seren's voice made Leslie's chest tighten. She clasped Seren's hand. "I know this is hard, but I'm siding with Paige. Bea *is* tough as nails. Roofing nails. You know those ones that are like two inches long and twice as thick as regular nails?"

Tears welled in Seren's eyes, but she nodded. "You're right. And I should only be thinking good thoughts. Come on inside."

As soon as they stepped into the house, Paige came down the hall with a look as strained as Seren's. "Hi, Leslie. Thanks for coming."

"I don't hear any crying," Seren said. "Success?"

"Success." Paige glanced at her watch. "If Olivia follows her usual routine, she'll wake up around four."

"I'll be ready." Leslie wanted to hug Paige too, but she seemed like an even bigger ball of stress than Seren.

"I wrote down the schedule and bedtime routine in case we aren't back. It's all on a notepad in the kitchen." Seren looked to Paige, then they both looked at Leslie. "You sure you're up for this?" Paige and Seren said at the same time.

"The fact that you two said that in stereo should bother me but it doesn't. Have a little faith in Aunt Leslie."

"We have more than a little faith, and Olivia loves you, but it's still a lot to ask last minute," Seren said.

"Bedtime can be hard," Paige added. "She might not sleep much without us."

Seren nodded at Paige, her lips squeezed together in a tight line.

"I'll cuddle her all night if that keeps her happy. You two have someone else who needs you tonight."

"You're right." Paige wrapped an arm around Seren and brushed a kiss against her cheek. They'd been together a little over a year and were still the sweetest couple.

"Ty's at the barn if you want to talk to them before we leave," Seren said to Paige.

"Great." Paige looked back at Leslie. "Ty's in charge of all the animals so you won't have to worry about that. I hope Ollie's good for you."

"She'll be an angel."

Paige hefted an overnight bag and glanced at Seren. "See you outside?"

As soon as Paige was out the door, Leslie said, "I really could have taken care of the pets and Olivia. If you're not back tonight, at least let me do the morning feeding so you don't have to pay someone."

"It's more work than you'd think. Two heifers, three horses, eighteen chickens, all the barn cats—not to mention the house cats—and Olivia?"

Leslie pursed her lips.

"Besides, Ty's working off their horse board. But if you're worried about having a stranger here when you're alone with Ollie—"

"It's not that." How could she explain? Definitely not by referencing the sexy dream. "Ty toured an open house last weekend and it's fine seeing them again, but I don't feel like being in work mode."

"Are you sure it's the same Ty?" Seren's eyebrows bunched together. "Paige offered to let them board here because their last barn raised prices and they couldn't afford it. I can't imagine they have money to buy a house."

"Maybe they only came for the cookies." It wouldn't be the first time. And it would make sense why Ty hadn't followed up with the lender.

"I'd come for your cookies," Seren said, smiling. "How have you been doing, by the way? You sounded so stressed when I called earlier."

Leslie knew Seren's concern was sincere but she wasn't the one with a sick mother-in-law to worry about. "I'm fine. Work's been maybe too busy but, hey, I'm making money."

Seren squeezed Leslie's shoulder. "You've been working too much."

"You're right. When you called, I realized how much I wanted the afternoon off. I need a break from peopling. Adult people, I mean. Babysitting Ollie will be a good change."

"I'll tell Paige that you can take care of the house cats so Ty won't need to come in. Then you can have an adult-free and work-free evening."

"Perfect."

"Oh! I almost forgot. You need the baby monitor." Seren hurried down the hall and returned with the monitor. An image of a sleeping Olivia blinked on the screen. Nature sounds played in the background. "She won't wake for a while, but this way you can go enjoy the sunshine and not worry. The garden exploded this past week. If you want tomatoes or green beans, pick as many as you like." Seren paused. "Do you think I'm forgetting anything?"

"I can always call you."

Seren nodded. "Okay. Good luck."

Hopefully she wouldn't need to count on that. Luck had not been part of her day. "Everything will be fine here. You go take care of Paige and Bea."

CHAPTER THREE

Ty hefted the boards over one shoulder and unlatched Nellie's gate. Brown velvety ears twitched at the sound.

"Easy, girl," Ty murmured. "You okay if I pass through?" They held out their free hand and the mare sniffed their fingers. "Hey there. How are you?"

After one sniff the mare turned her head pointedly away, staring at the plank walls of her stall.

"You don't want to talk. I get it. Sometimes I don't feel like talking either."

Paige had mentioned that the previous owners of the ranch had gotten the mare as a rescue and no one knew exactly how old she was. Or how much training she'd had. At this point, she was only a pet—who, Paige admitted, didn't get enough attention.

Ty walked through the stall, maneuvering the boards carefully so they didn't bump into anything. The mare swished her tail with obvious annoyance. "I'm here to fix your paddock gate so no cows get in. You should be thanking me."

The heifers shared a big pen next to Nellie's paddock and had managed to take down several boards and bust a gate. Typical cow mischief.

Ty set the boards in place and got to work. After a few minutes, Nellie came over to inspect, sniffing the wood first and then Ty's hair. At first, Ty pretended not to notice. When Nellie pushed her muzzle into their back, they looked up and smiled. "Now you want to be social?"

Nellie seemed to consider the question. Ty clicked to her and got a half-hearted ear flick. "I think I could win you over."

The mare tossed her head and snorted. Horse snot sprayed Ty's hands and face. Laughing, they brushed off the snot. "That's what I get, huh?"

If a horse could smile, Nellie had one on her face when Ty looked up at her again. "Fine. But go on. I don't need a supervisor today."

Nellie stubbornly settled in a few feet away, and Ty only shook their head. "Mares."

When Ty had moved Polaris and Archer to the ranch a month ago, Paige had hoped to pasture Nellie with the other horses. So far, though, Nellie had refused to leave her stall if Polaris and Archer were in the front pasture. Every night she'd squeal and kick when the other horses were led past her stall and Paige worried one of the three would get hurt if forced together.

"You might like the others if you try getting to know them," Ty said. "Archer's my boy. He's a sweetheart. Polaris is wild—like my cousin, Zoe. But you get used to her energy and she's kind of a jokester. Maybe someday you'd want to hang out with them?"

Nellie met Ty's gaze as if considering it, then swung her head side to side.

"Suit yourself."

Once the new boards were in place, blocking access from the cow pen, Ty went to get Nellie a treat. She didn't balk as they came into her stall the second time and only studied them for a moment as they held out a horse cookie. A second later she snagged the cookie and even allowed a head rub as she chewed.

"You warm up quick. Maybe later I'll grab a brush and give you a good grooming." But there was more work to be done.

Paige had left a to-do list along with instructions for care of all the animals. Ty had to laugh at the details Paige had included— as if taking care of a barnful wasn't second nature at this point. The note, though, was more a testament to how much Paige loved every animal in the barn. There was a line about how the heifers liked to be sung to in the mornings and an added mention about the chickens preferring ice cubes in their water. Nellie got a whole paragraph explaining her dining regimen.

Ty finished reading the last line when the barn door swung open. A woman burst in, close to tears.

"Do you have a key to the house?"

Ty stared at her for a moment before realizing it was Leslie. *Leslie Brandt.* What the hell was she doing here and why did she look so panicked?

"I went out to the garden and the door closed behind me." Leslie's voice cracked. "I didn't realize it would lock."

"I don't have a key."

"Fuck. Olivia's awake. What am I going to do?"

Leslie was the babysitter? Paige had mentioned a friend of Seren's would be watching Olivia but they hadn't thought to ask who. Because what were the chances? "Did you try all the doors?"

"Of course I tried all the doors."

She choked back a sob and held up something Ty recognized as a baby monitor. The sound of crying came through loud and clear. "I can't even call Seren—or Paige—because I left my damn cell phone in the house." She shook her head. "I can't believe this happened. Except I can. Because today has sucked since I got out of bed."

"I can call Paige." Ty reached for their phone and quickly hit the call button.

"Do you have Seren's number? Paige is the one driving and I don't know if she'll answer."

"I don't have Seren's number," Ty said, listening to the ringing. They couldn't help looking again at Leslie. Did she recognize them from the open house? The call went to voice mail after the second ring. "No answer. Should I leave a message?"

Leslie glanced down at the monitor again and groaned. "I don't know. She probably won't check the message until they get to the hospital. Seren makes Paige set her phone to Do Not Disturb when she's driving after that accident last month."

"Maybe Seren would check Paige's phone?"

They looked at each other and both knew it was unlikely. Ty left a quick message for Paige to call them then ended the call.

The drive to Stanford took two hours with good traffic. Too long to wait.

"Let me go back to the house with you," Ty said. "There's gotta be some way we can get inside. Maybe the door's not locked—maybe it's just a tricky handle or something. Is that one of those monitors that you can talk through?"

Leslie nodded.

"Tell her everything's okay. We only need a few minutes to double-check the doors."

"She's nine months old." Tears welled. "She won't understand."

"She'll understand if you sound calm. Maybe sing to her?"

Leslie swiped at her tears and took a shaky breath. She hit a button on the monitor and seemed to force a cheerful tone as she said, "Hi, Ollie. It's Auntie Leslie."

Ty headed to the house with Leslie following right behind. They tried to focus as they jiggled the door handles and not on Leslie or the fact that she had a sweet voice when she sang. But Leslie's earlier panic returned when Ty confirmed that the front and back doors were definitely locked. They checked under the doormats for a key and then hunted for any open windows. No luck.

Fortunately, by the time they'd circled back to the locked front door, the baby wasn't crying. Leslie's singing had calmed her at least. Ty motioned to the intercom. "Good job."

"Good job?" She switched off the intercom voice connection and added, "Are you fucking kidding me? I locked my best friend's baby in the house. *Alone.*"

"But she's not crying."

Ignoring Ty, Leslie reached for the handle, tested it for a third time, and let out a guttural sound. "What are we going to do? Should we call 911?"

"We could, but it's not exactly an emergency yet. I can call Paige again and hope Seren answers. Or I can leave another message and hope she gets to the hospital soon and checks it." Not the best option, especially if there was no spare key.

Leslie shook her head. "We can't wait that long. God, I'm such an idiot."

"You're not an idiot. You didn't know the door was gonna lock." Ty glanced at the baby monitor. They'd only seen Olivia a few times at the barn—usually in either Paige or Seren's arms. She liked the horses, but that's all Ty knew. Now her image on the monitor was hard not to sympathize with. She wasn't wailing anymore but she certainly didn't look happy sitting in one corner of the crib hugging a stuffed Pooh Bear.

"You don't think we should call 911?" Leslie asked.

Ty eyed the narrow window next to the front door. It wouldn't take much effort to break, and it'd be faster than waiting on Emergency Services to show up. But then the glass would have to be replaced. "Let me try checking all the windows one more time. Maybe I can find one that isn't latched. Why don't you check the potted plants? Maybe there's a key hidden in one of those little fake rocks."

"And if we don't find anything, then we call 911?"

"Or break a window."

It wasn't much of a plan, but Leslie seemed resolved to it. She went right to the begonias and Ty left her peeking under the leaves with Olivia's cooing baby voice back on the monitor.

The kitchen window opened two inches and then stopped. Not enough to squeeze more than a hand through and likely a rod prevented it from opening it any farther. The only other window that opened wasn't a great option. The bottom ledge was about six feet up from the ground and the opening was narrow. Fortunately, it was the one window missing a screen. Ty pushed it as far as it would open and then stepped back and stared at the space.

"You found one that wasn't latched!"

Ty startled at Leslie's voice, suddenly only a foot away. "It's open, yeah, but I don't think I can fit through."

"I can."

Ty glanced from the window to Leslie. Now that Olivia had stopped crying, and with hope replacing her panic, an expression of confidence on her face changed everything. Up until that moment, Ty had done a good job separating Leslie from the woman they'd gone down on a dozen times. *Virtually.* But with Leslie's eyes locked on theirs, Ty was struck again by how gorgeous she was. And how much they missed their times together.

"What, you don't think I can fit?"

"I think it'd be...tricky." Tricky? Ty groaned inwardly. Tricky was better than tight. The truth was, the opening wasn't big. They looked from Leslie to the window and back again. Leslie did have a petite figure compared to Ty's stocky build, but she had curves. Ty studied her hips, trying to ignore how good it would feel to hold her there, then cleared their throat. "I think it'd be tight for anyone."

"Well, I think I can fit." Leslie was a few inches shorter, but when her gaze locked on Ty's, chin jutted up, hands on her hips, there was no doubt she was calling the shots.

It was impossible to ignore the pulse of arousal, however poorly timed. Ty looked her over again, fighting down the urges in their body. Her waist was smaller than theirs and her shoulders weren't broad either. But still. She looked as if she'd come straight from a business meeting. Heels, skirt, fancy blouse—stained with something brown right between her breasts—and her dark brown hair pulled back with a clip at the low of her neck. Certainly not the attire to crawl through a window. "What if you get stuck?"

"Then you'll have to shove me in."

Ty checked to see if she was serious. No smirk. No raised eyebrow. "You're serious?"

"Completely."

Determined Leslie was sexy as hell, but Ty felt like they had to be the voice of reason. "What if you fall getting down on the other side and break something?"

"The real problem will be getting myself up there." She scanned the area under the window before glancing back at the garden. "We can drag one of those planting barrels over here and I can use it as a step stool."

"Those barrels weigh a ton as soon as you fill them with dirt." Not to mention all the water that was likely soaking the plants growing in the barrels. "We also don't know what's on the other side of this window. Maybe we should call 911."

Leslie squared her shoulders. "That's what I said before."

"Well, I didn't want to do that if there was another way."

"Neither did I, and you found us another way." Leslie motioned to the window, her earlier curt tone returning. "Olivia's happy now, but that isn't going to last long. It's killing me not being in there. What if she tries climbing out of her crib?" She held up the monitor as if that could happen at any moment.

Ty glanced from the window to Leslie. She probably weighed about the same as a young foal and they had no problem lifting one of those. Not that comparing a woman to a horse was something they'd ever admit out loud.

"I used to do cheer. I won't have any problem tucking and rolling. Can you get me up there or not?"

Her direct gaze, along with the implicit challenge in her words, hit Ty right in the chest. "I can get you up. But if you fall and break your neck—"

"I'm not going to fall."

Ty shook their head but moved into position. With fingers interlaced and back against the side of the house, they braced for Leslie's weight. "There's no shame if you get up there and change your mind."

Leslie kicked off her heels and then stepped forward, facing Ty. "Four years of cheer and ten years of gymnastics says I'm in Olivia's room in under two minutes."

Ty couldn't help smiling. "All right, Cheer. Bring it on."

She arched an eyebrow. "Consider it brought."

Leslie was fast. Her hands had barely settled on Ty's shoulders before her bare foot was in Ty's palm. She vaulted upward like Ty was a trampoline, then hung, halfway in and halfway out of the window. Her hips were the catching point. Ty tried to steady her legs without thinking about how smooth her skin felt.

"I'm going to try something." Leslie shimmied her body, and a moment later her legs slipped out of Ty's hands and through the window. A crash sounded but she called out, "I didn't die. That was only the shower curtain rod. I might have bent it."

"As long as you're okay."

"I'm going to get Olivia. Mind bringing the monitor and my shoes around to the front?"

Ty stooped to pick up the heels and the baby monitor, grinning when Leslie appeared on the screen cooing to Olivia. The baby immediately held up her arms. Leslie scooped her up, hugging her and showering her with kisses. Leslie turned then to face the camera and held up two fingers.

Ty pressed the talk button on the monitor. "Yeah, yeah, go ahead and brag."

Leslie smiled, squeezing Olivia tighter. "Thank you."

Her voice crackled through the speakers but it warmed Ty all the same. They pressed the talk button on the monitor and said, "Any time."

Why or how Leslie would need their help again Ty couldn't imagine, but at least now they were equal after the whole open house cookie thing. As for the other part, Ty wasn't sure if they were more in the right not mentioning that they were Hitch or if that truth should come out. But telling the truth had been the reason everything had gone wrong.

CHAPTER FOUR

Kaitlin answered on the first ring. "I was just about to call. You got a second call about those missing signatures on the disclosure addendum."

"And another email. Two nasty-grams two hours apart." Leslie sat down on the floor across from Olivia, who was carefully reviewing the contents of her purse. Sunglasses, keys, pens, a container of Altoids, and lip gloss had already been assessed, shaken, and then discarded. "That agent needs to chill the hell out."

"Would you like me to tell him that? I'd be happy to do so."

"No. I've got it." Leslie couldn't hold back a smile. Both that Kaitlin was more than willing and that she'd even suggested it. She'd officially used up all of her patience for the day. To think she'd considered it a bad day even before she'd had to ask a potential client to throw her through a bathroom window.

"All the documents are finalized now and it'll be my pleasure to call Mr. Antsy-Pants and tell him to calm the eff down. We had until midnight anyway."

"I'd love to hear that call." Kaitlin laughed. "How's the babysitting gig going?"

Olivia had found her wallet and plucked out all the contents. Bank cards, membership cards, receipts, and cash were scattered in every direction. Fortunately, she didn't carry coins. Seren had warned that she tried to eat those.

"Neither of us have died yet." At that, Olivia picked up the purse and held it over her head like an umbrella. When she stared up at the paisley-patterned inside lining, Leslie had to smile. "I know I always say I don't want kids—and it's true—but they are pretty cute."

"That's how they lure you in." Kaitlin had two of her own. "Be careful. The baby disease is catching."

"Speaking of, why are you still in the office? It's after five."

"The workaholic is telling me to go home? That's funny. I'm almost done. Just one more question."

Leslie eyed Olivia, half dreading whatever Kaitlin had to ask. How many more problems could she tackle today?

"I'm adding a block to your schedule for the first weekend in August. You have no meetings scheduled and I'm going to be very upset with you if you add anything. So. Would you like me to schedule you an Airbnb at the beach or at the mountains?"

"Kaitlin, you know I can't take a weekend off in the summer."

"The other agents do it all the time. And I looked back through your planner. You haven't even taken a sick day in over a year. Not one day off."

"I don't get sick."

"Not the point." Kaitlin started listing the dangers of burnout.

"I get it. Lowered productivity and all that."

"Please leave the block in your schedule. If you don't leave town, fine. Take yourself to the spa."

Leslie sighed. "If I say I'll think about it, will you go home for the night?"

"Yes. And thank you."

Leslie ended the call and looked back at Olivia. She had the purse down on her head like a hat and peeked up with a mischievous grin.

"Dang, you're cute." Leslie tickled her chin, which got a round of baby belly laughter.

Despite the rough start, she'd managed to change Olivia's diaper, get her fed, and had entertained her for the past half hour.

Fortunately, she seemed to have no memory of having been alone for a half hour in her room.

"What were you thinking trying to crawl out of your crib?" When she'd gotten to Olivia's room, she'd found her hanging precariously with one leg over the top edge of the crib. "You could have fallen and broken something."

But she'd gotten there in time. That was what mattered. Thanks to Ty—who she still had to figure out a way to thank. Would it be weird to bring them a beer as a thank-you even if it wasn't her beer to give? She could bring a case the next time she was over to replace it... Except what if Ty didn't like beer?

"I'm overthinking this, aren't I?"

Olivia ignored her. She'd found Leslie's license and was studying the picture. Recognition seemed to hit and she looked up and smiled. "Yep, that's my dorky picture. I was having a bad hair day. Not that you'd know about that because your hair is perfect." She leaned forward and ruffled her wispy blond locks. "You know who else has nice hair? Ty."

And she'd completely embarrassed herself in front of them. "I can't believe they were in my dream and then...here."

Seeing Ty again had made her attraction all the more undeniable. The moment she'd locked onto their eyes and reached for their shoulders, ready for a boost through the window, she'd imagined what it'd be like to kiss them. Arousal had raced through her and it was a small miracle she'd been able to keep her wits as she placed her foot in their hands. She pictured the tattoos on each of Ty's forearms and the defined muscles tensing under her. She hadn't had time to study the tattoos closely, but she'd recognized them as a pair of constellations. Nothing fancy, but definitely intriguing. And sexy.

"Maybe I need to go on a date even if I don't have time for a relationship," she said. "It's probably a sign if I'm feeling this horny thinking about someone's forearm tattoos."

Olivia made a sound like "uh-huh," and she realized she'd voiced her thoughts aloud. "Thank god you don't understand what horny means." She wagged her finger and Olivia nodded, the purse-hat rocking back and forth on her head.

"The thing is, it's been a year and a half since I've gone on a date, and it's been a damn good year." At least professionally.

She thought of the online sex group she'd joined and then dropped out of. Even that had taken up too much time. Partly, though, that was because she'd gotten a little too involved with one of the people in the group. *Hitch.* Hitch was a code name. Everyone in the group had to have a code name because it was all anonymous. Which meant that the last person she'd "dated," if having regular online sex could count as that, was someone whose real name she didn't even know. She wasn't sure if that was ironic or just pathetic.

Not wanting to lapse into full existential crisis mode, she got out her laptop and emailed the agent who'd wanted the disclosure addendum signed, then scanned the emails she'd missed since leaving work.

Ty's face to came to mind, angular and androgynous. Ty's body was just as androgynous. No visible breasts, no clearly defined hips. Ty was taller than she was by three or four inches but they weren't distinctly tall. If she'd had to describe them, she'd say medium build, medium height, well-muscled and with the look like they'd have no problem throwing someone through a window. She smiled. Having felt the strength in Ty's body made her attraction harder to ignore. But it was really Ty's smile and those sky-blue eyes…

"Gah, I'm clearly not focusing on work." She closed her laptop and eyed Olivia. "Do you like lemonade?"

Seren had mentioned having too many lemons, and the overflowing bowls on the counter attested to that fact. Also, lemonade seemed like the best way to pave over what she knew had been an unprofessional interaction. She could bring the lemonade to the barn, chat for a while, and maybe ask if Ty had any questions about home buying. If she refocused on the real estate part of how and why they knew each other, maybe they could both laugh about the rest.

With Seren's fancy juicer, it took no time to make the lemonade and Olivia kept herself entertained sorting through the items she'd dumped from the purse. Leslie filled two glasses and one sippy cup. "Hey, Ollie, want to try it?"

Olivia looked up at her nickname but shook her head. She had a container of Altoids and was trying to squeeze it open.

"I don't think you can open it, sweetie."

She strained, grunting as she did and then shifted her chubby thumbs. The lid popped open, startling both her and Leslie. In her surprise, she dropped the container and Altoids scattered across the floor.

"Oh, shit." Leslie ran to her, but not before she'd picked up something. "Please, can I see what you have?" she pleaded, then tried to pry open her fist, which only made her clamp down harder. "What if we trade?" She picked up the now empty Altoids container and held that out. "This was fun, right?"

Olivia raised her hand to her mouth.

"No, no, no!"

One mint fell out of her grip as she hurried to smash her whole hand into her mouth. A second later, a look of smugness confirmed she'd gotten at least one.

"That's too small for you to choke on, right?" Pulse pounding, Leslie stared at Olivia. Seconds ticked by. If it lodged in her throat, could she actually do the Heimlich on a baby? Should she run outside and call for Ty?

"Ahh!" Olivia opened her mouth and started swatting at her tongue.

Leslie snagged the mint. "Spicy, huh? That's why we don't put random things in our mouth."

When she started to cry, Leslie scooped her up and kissed her forehead. "I swear this just isn't my day."

Maybe Ty wouldn't leave until Olivia was in bed. She hated admitting she wanted babysitting backup, but it was the truth.

CHAPTER FIVE

With the big items on the list checked off, Ty knew they could round up the hens and head home for the night. But they didn't want to leave without talking to Leslie. If they didn't fess up to being Hitch, they worried they'd regret it forever. The question was, what would she say in response?

Ty's phone buzzed and they pulled it out of their back pocket, leaning their shovel against a rail. Zoe's name flashed with a text: *How's Polaris? I took her on a long run this morning.*

She looks good. She's chasing Archer around in the pasture. Ty debated for a moment and then added: *You know that realtor we met last weekend?*

Zoe texted a little devil emoji. *How could I forget? Double Yum.*

She'd been referring to Leslie as Double Yum all week along with comments about how Ty should have asked her out so they could all have more double chocolate chunk cookies. Ty had chalked the whole thing up to a small bizarre world and resolved to forget it'd ever happened—hoping Zoe would soon do the same. But now it was impossible to dismiss what felt like fate.

I helped her break into Paige's house. It's weird that we'd bump into each other again, right?

You helped her break in?? WTF?

Ty imagined Zoe's horrified expression and couldn't help smiling. *She's babysitting Paige's kid and got locked out.*

Oh. OK. Why is she babysitting?

She's friends with Seren and Paige. Paige's mom had a problem with her pacemaker and had to have an emergency surgery.

Shit. Is she okay?

No word yet. Ty had considered texting Paige but decided to wait. No news was good news. Usually. *Should I tell Leslie about the online connection?*

Zoe didn't respond for a moment and Ty realized they were hoping she'd say yes, while at the same time dreading it.

You said she never wanted to talk to you again.

Yeah. Ty stared at the text for a long moment. *But it feels like a lie of omission not telling her.*

Well it is.

What would you do?

Not tell her. A moment later Zoe added: *Unless you plan on asking her out, let it go.*

It was probably good advice. It even sounded like the right thing to do. Still, disappointment welled up.

Zoe: *You could still flirt.*

She's up at the house with the baby and I'm mucking stalls. I'm not going to go knock on the door to flirt.

Why not?

First, because of their history. Second, because of their history. Too much had passed between them for casual flirting.

You're alone at a ranch with a hot woman who owes you a favor. A licking emoji followed.

She's babysitting. Plus she's not going to have sex with me just because I helped her.

Ty pocketed the phone and reached for the shovel. They caught sight of their calloused, dirt-smudged hands and the memory of Leslie's foot in their palms came back with a sudden rush. Leslie's hands had rested on their shoulders and her face had been only inches away.

"Hey there."

Ty looked up from the shovel. Leslie stood five feet away, a curious smile curving her lips.

"Oh. Hi."

Leslie had changed out of the blouse and business-suit-style skirt and into a pair of shorts and a white V-neck T-shirt that looked entirely too sexy. Olivia was in one arm, balanced on her hip, and she had a glass of something in her other hand.

Olivia gestured to Nellie and made a gurgling sound. When Nellie turned to look, Olivia went wild, flapping her chubby legs and windmilling her arms.

"Whoa, slow down, sweetie," Leslie said.

Ty quickly stepped forward, grabbing Leslie's glass before it spilled. The sippy cup went flying. It landed upright, but only a foot away from a pile of horse poop.

"Olivia loves visiting the horses," Ty said, picking up the sippy cup. "She does that same thing when Paige brings her out here too."

"Now you tell me." Leslie seemed to still be struggling to keep Olivia in her arms.

"Want me to take her?"

"No, I've got her." She shifted Olivia to her other hip and gave an exasperated sigh. "I've had a day. The last thing I need is to drop my best friend's baby."

"I think they bounce at this age."

Leslie narrowed her eyes.

"I was joking," Ty said quickly. They looked at Olivia, who was still wriggling to get closer to Nellie. "Think Nellie wants a sip of your juice?" Ty clicked to the mare and held out the sippy cup. She sniffed the cup and snorted, making Olivia laugh.

When Ty handed the sippy cup back to Olivia, Leslie's lips pursed. Ty barely held back from saying, "A little dirt is good for kids." They held the other glass out to Leslie but she shook her head.

"That's for you."

"Oh. Thanks." Ty glanced at the lemonade.

"I made it with some of Seren's lemons. Olivia says it isn't terrible." She distracted Olivia with a dandelion. "How's it going out here?"

"Good. I'm almost done with the chore list."

"So you won't be here much longer?"

Ty cocked their head. "Not too much longer, no." Did Leslie want them to leave? "If you need me to go—"

"Oh, no. Not at all. That came out wrong." A blush hit Leslie's cheeks. "I was only wondering…you know what, never mind." She met Ty's gaze and shook her head. "I've had a crazy day but I really wanted to thank you for your help earlier. I don't know what I'd have done if you hadn't been here."

"After seeing how fast you got in that window, I bet you could have figured it out without me."

"I don't know about that. Not only did I lock her in the house alone, she tried to choke on my Altoids. I don't think I'm cut out for babysitting." She motioned with her chin to the lemonade. "Do you not like lemonade?"

"Oh, no. I like it." They took a sip, very much aware of Leslie's gaze on them. "This is good." It wasn't a lie. The ice-cold combination of sweet and tart hit the spot.

"I may have been tempted to add tequila," Leslie admitted. "But I decided it was better to not get tipsy while I'm still in charge of this girl." She kissed Olivia's forehead. "As soon as she's asleep, though, I'm going for the adult juice."

Ty laughed and their pulse kicked up a notch when Leslie smiled at them. They recalled some of the times Leslie had admitted to being tipsy and the fun they'd had together on those nights. But it'd been fun every night. That was the hardest part. Everything had felt so perfect and easy and fun. Until it wasn't. "In case you're worried, I won't tell Paige or Seren about you getting locked out. There's no reason to—Olivia's fine."

"I'm planning on telling them myself. As soon as they get home and I'm no longer the one in charge. I don't like secrets. Not that type anyway. It feels too much like lying, you know? And I can't keep things from Seren."

Ty's stomach turned. "I don't like secrets or lying either."

Leslie grimaced as Olivia chomped on the stem of the dandelion she'd been holding. "No eating weeds, Ollie. Even pretty weeds."

Ty watched Leslie with Olivia and the weight of what was unsaid was too hard to ignore. "I'm not sure if you remember or not, but my cousin and I toured an open house you had last weekend and—"

"I remember. Sorry. I interrupted you." Leslie paused. "I figured you probably recognized me too. I was debating how to bring it up. You've officially seen me in my least professional moment."

Ty swallowed, knowing that was definitely not the least professional moment they'd shared. "We all have those moments. Well, maybe not the part about climbing through bathroom windows."

"Blame my cheer coach." Leslie's smirk was distractingly attractive.

Ty wanted to give in to the urge to flirt but instead said, "The thing is, I'd really like to use you as a realtor, but I have no idea when, or if, I'll be able to buy a house. A financial planner would laugh if they saw my bank account. I really only went to the open house for Zoe."

"So she could get a cookie?" Leslie guessed.

"Well…yeah." The words seemed to fall flat. "The thing is, it was about more than a cookie. Zoe has anxiety about doing new things—especially alone. Even going to a new grocery store is hard for her. People-never guess it because she seems so outgoing and talkative when she's some place she feels comfortable. Or with people she feels comfortable. Or with horses." Ty knew they were rambling. "Anyway. She was so excited about going to the open house. I didn't want to say no."

Leslie nodded like she was taking it all in. "So you went because it was something your cousin wouldn't normally do and you wanted to be supportive."

"And we wasted your time. I'm sorry."

Leslie studied them for a moment. "It's sweet that you did that for her."

"But I lied about wanting to buy a house."

"You told me you weren't financially ready. I maybe hoped you'd call me up to look at other properties, but I completely understand not having the money for a down payment."

"You're not mad?"

Leslie smiled. "No."

Ty felt so much lighter getting the house thing cleared up they half wondered if they should stop there. The next part probably wouldn't go as well.

"What do you have in your mouth, Ollie?" Leslie asked. "Shit, where's the dandelion?"

Ty glanced at Olivia and then at the ground. The dandelion was gone and the baby's lips were squeezed tight while she worked something in her mouth.

"It's definitely in her mouth," Ty said.

"Are dandelions toxic?" Leslie asked, panic making her voice catch.

"Not to horses. Or cows." For once Ty wished they knew something about kids.

"Olivia, open your mouth right now." Leslie's sharp tone surprised even Ty. Olivia looked startled, then started to cry. As soon as her lips parted, Leslie snatched out the crumpled flower. A loud wail followed.

"I'm not sure I'm going to make it through this day," Leslie said, trying to soothe Olivia and looking miserable.

Probably adding how Ty was the person she'd had online sex with and never wanted to hear from again wouldn't make her day any better. As Olivia's cries got louder, Ty set down the lemonade and dusted off their hands.

"I can take her to see Nellie. It'll get her to stop crying."

"I don't know. If she gets hurt—"

"She won't. I promise she'll be safe with me."

Leslie met their gaze and a buzzing feeling made it hard to forget all the things they'd done together. A moment later Leslie looked back at Olivia, then raised her voice above her cries. "Do you want to see the horse?"

The wailing stopped almost instantly. Olivia gulped down a breath and nodded. Leslie started to hand her off but paused midway. "For the record, one scratch and you're dead."

"Totally fair."

As soon as Ty had Olivia, it occurred to them that holding a baby wasn't something they had any clue how to do. They decided to pretend she was like any other baby animal. *Only this one has arms.* And Leslie would kill them if she got dropped.

Ty opened the new gate to Nellie's paddock. She nickered and happy baby squeals followed. There was no question the two were well acquainted when Nellie lowered her muzzle for Olivia to pet.

Olivia was surprisingly gentle, reaching her tiny hand to brush the dark brown velvet and then laughing as the horse's whiskers flicked over her skin. "Horses are pretty cool, aren't they?" Ty asked.

When Nellie snorted, Olivia tried to mimic her, then laughed again. Leslie laughed then too, and the sound filled Ty's chest. They glanced over their shoulder and caught Leslie's smile. All those nights of wondering what Girl-Monday looked like, forming a picture of her based on the few details she'd shared, and she was more beautiful than Ty had ever dreamed. The things they'd done together seemed almost unbelievable now.

Olivia took that moment to smack Nellie's nose. She'd clearly meant to only pet her but got overexcited. In response, Nellie only closed her eyes and lowered her muzzle another inch. Ty shifted quickly when Olivia tried again.

"All right, say goodbye to Nellie." Ty passed Olivia to Leslie, briefly meeting her gaze. "No scratch. That means I get to live, right?"

"I wouldn't have really killed you."

"You sure?"

"Good thing you won't have to find out."

Leslie's flirty tone took all the thoughts from Ty's mind. They watched Leslie bounce Olivia—who was all smiles now—in her arms.

"Thank you," Leslie said. "That's clearly what she needed."

When Olivia pointed to the far pasture where Polaris and Archer were grazing, Leslie shook her head. "No more horses today. We're going to stop while everyone's still alive."

Ty expected Leslie to say goodbye then, but she lingered, walking from Nellie's stall to the chicken coop and pointing out different things to Olivia. She repeated the words for random items and congratulated Olivia when she gurgled in response. Ty tried to focus on mucking the stalls but made slow progress sneaking glances every minute or so at Leslie. The question of whether to bring up TryItOnce gnawed at their conscience. They still hadn't decided when Leslie stopped in front of Nellie's stall again.

"I'm taking Ollie back to the house. I think she's getting hungry."

"Right." Ty's pulse thumped fast as they considered simply blurting out, *By the way, I'm Hitch.*

"You probably have other plans—and it's totally okay to say no—but I was wondering if you wanted to join Olivia and me for dinner." She paused for a moment before adding, "It's only going to be pizza and salad. Nothing fancy. But it'd be nice to have company. I can tell Olivia likes you and I wouldn't mind having another responsible adult around." She gave Ty a look like they already had a private joke going.

Leslie was asking them to stay for dinner? Ty realized their mouth was hanging open and promptly closed it. "Sure. Yeah. I could stay. I mean, I'd like to stay for dinner."

"Great. I promise I won't sneak in a lecture about financial planning so you can buy a house from me someday." Leslie laughed as Olivia waved goodbye. "Guess we're leaving. See you in a half hour or so?"

Ty nodded, their smile straining their cheeks. They couldn't seem to rein in the happy. It wasn't until Leslie and Olivia had gone that it hit them that they'd be having dinner with the woman they'd fantasized about for most of the past year. The same woman who'd broken their heart. And Leslie still had no idea who they really were.

CHAPTER SIX

Leslie finished chopping the last of the cucumber and added it to the salad. The pizza was still in the oven staying warm, which meant the kitchen smelled amazing. Dinner wouldn't be fancy, but it sounded perfect. More than the food, she was looking forward to the company.

She'd surprised herself inviting Ty, but as soon as she thought of it, she couldn't not make the offer. It felt too right. And Ty's response—surprised but definitely happy—had convinced her it was the right decision.

She pictured Ty's wide smile again and couldn't help smiling in response. It'd been a long time since she'd truly been excited by a dinner date. Not that this was a date. It was only a shared dinner. With someone she found attractive. And sweet. And…

Would Ty think it was a date?

"No. They'll think I'm babysitting and I wanted company. Which is true." Besides, Ty helped her out and a glass of lemonade really wasn't much of a thank-you. She looked over at Olivia, who was studying her bowl of Cheerios.

"You like Ty, right? People say babies and dogs can tell good people."

Olivia's brow furrowed. Instead of answering, she offered a Cheerio.

"Is that a yes?"

Olivia ate the offered Cheerio with an adorable baby shrug.

"Not that it matters since I'm not looking to date anyone," Leslie continued. "Although if I were going to date, I wouldn't mind someone like Ty." She ran her hand through her hair, then wondered if she had time to run to the bathroom to check her reflection before Ty showed up. "Dammit. This is how I feel before a date." It'd been a long while since she'd felt that intoxicating mix of excited and nervous and happy.

"But I don't feel anxious and I'm not worried about screwing up like I usually do. Maybe that means it isn't a date? Maybe it's only dinner. With a baby." She blew out a breath. "I need to chill out. That's what you're thinking, right, Ollie?"

Olivia grinned, showing off her pair of teeth. Two. Right on the bottom.

She smiled back. "At least Paige and Seren know Ty and wouldn't mind that I invited them to have dinner with us. They trusted them to take care of all the animals. That says a lot, right? Then again, Seren trusted me with you. I can't believe I locked myself out of the house with you in your crib. God, what a day."

The worries of getting through the evening with Olivia had definitely motivated her to ask Ty to stay. But she'd be lying if she claimed that was all of it. There was something about Ty that made her want to get to know them better. Was it because they reminded her of Hitch? She'd tossed the same question around after Ty had shown up in her dream that morning. Both of them were nonbinary which of course didn't mean they'd be alike in other ways. But still.

After months of trying to keep them out of her mind, she let her thoughts wander to Hitch. Instead of bringing up the last night they'd talked, however, her brain went to the first. She'd flirted with Hitch in the group chat room. Why she'd connected to them more than anyone else, she couldn't say exactly. But when she'd suggested a more private conversation, Hitch hadn't hesitated to send her a message. From there, things went from flirting to sex so fast she hadn't wanted to blink. It had all felt daring and freeing and amazing. She'd told Hitch things she'd never told anyone else. Done things with them she'd only dreamed about. But the whole relationship—if she could even call it that—had been online and never felt completely real.

Just an online fantasy with a stranger who'd let her imagination run wild. "In real life, I'd probably never do half of those things." She paused, thinking of Ty now and wondering if they were anything like Hitch other than being nonbinary.

Hitch had been cocky and full of sex appeal. Ty seemed more understated. Attractive, for sure, but not over-the-top, making her feel like she had no chance. Definitely kissable, but also comfortable. "Like a nice hoodie you know you're going to like before you even put it on." She laughed and shook her head. "I clearly need to get laid."

Olivia gave her a curious look and she was glad she didn't have to explain "laid" to a nine-month-old. When Olivia went back to her Cheerios, Leslie pictured Ty again—cowboy hat pushed back on their head, short tufts of reddish-brown hair sticking out and sky-blue eyes that crinkled at the corners when they smiled.

"And then there's the sweet part." She thought of how Ty had danced around the real reason for coming to the open house. All to help out their cousin.

"Definitely kissable. Not that I need to think about kissing anyone." Leslie handed Olivia a bowl of finely chopped cucumber and tomatoes to go along with the Cheerios. Olivia took one look at the veggies and immediately dumped the bowl.

"Seren told me those were your favorite."

Olivia poked one of the cucumbers on the not-clean-at-all linoleum floor, looked up with a wide smile, and then popped it into her mouth. Leslie pressed her lips together, barely suppressing an "eww." As she watched, Olivia pushed one of the tomato chunks in a semicircle around her and then added it to the cucumber in her mouth.

"You like it with extra dirt, huh?"

"They say it's good for the immune system." Ty stood on the other side of the screen door, cowboy hat still on and a little bouquet of dandelions that had all gone to seed. "Knock, knock."

One look and the word kissable danced in Leslie's mind again. "Come on in."

"Smells amazing in here."

"It's not delivery, it's DiGiorno."

Ty grinned. "I've heard that line somewhere. What can I do to help?"

Before she could say help wasn't needed, Olivia clamored for attention. From Ty.

Ty squatted down in front of her, holding out the bouquet. "So, I looked it up, and dandelions aren't toxic to kids. But we're gonna talk about not eating them. It's way more fun to blow on these things and make a big mess."

Ty blew on one of the dandelion puffs and as the seeds flew across the room Olivia clapped her hands together, mouth gaping. "Pretty cool, huh? Wanna try?"

Olivia grabbed the bouquet and huffed.

"No eating, okay?" Ty looked from Olivia to Leslie. "I promise I'll watch her."

She smiled at Olivia's attempt to blow on a dandelion. "This is why I can't be a parent. I'd just ban flowers forever."

"You might be smarter than me." Ty coached Olivia on blowing dandelions for another minute and then straightened up. "How can I help with dinner?"

"You can set the table if you'd like." Leslie pointed at the dishes and utensils. "But maybe you want to wash up first?"

"Good idea."

Ty washed up at the sink and Leslie nearly laughed at the rivers of dirt that came off their hands. Positively never had she felt an attraction to someone who not only smelled like they'd been working around horse and cow poop all day but also looked like it. *First time for everything.*

After Ty set the table, they filled two glasses with water and took those to the table. Leslie finished with the salad, stealing glances when it wasn't too obvious. Ty's body was hard not to look at. Fit but not scrawny, and solidly sexy. They walked the line between masculine and feminine perfectly. Add a few sexy tattoos and she wanted to convince Ty to spend the night.

What am I thinking?

Apparently, she wasn't thinking. After everything that had happened with Hitch, she should have learned her lesson. Sex with someone who was practically a stranger was a bad idea. Usually a terrible one. She cleared her throat and went to open the oven. "If you don't mind getting Ollie in her high chair, I can get our food."

It took Ty a few tries but soon Olivia was in the high chair. Leslie half expected Ty would ask for help when Olivia immediately cried to get out of the seat. Instead, Ty found a bucket of toys and distracted her with a couple of plastic horses.

In between entertaining Olivia, Ty took off their cowboy hat and finger-combed their short hair. Leslie hid her smile carefully. The finger-combing did little to help the messy look, but the fact that Ty had tried making themself presentable managed to be both sexy and endearing.

She brought a bowl of yogurt to the table for Olivia and without a word, Ty set to feeding her. "You can stay as long as you like."

Ty grinned. "If you're feeding me, I just might."

That easy, huh? She resisted saying the words aloud and instead focused on slicing the pizza. When she brought the platter to the table and sat down in the seat opposite Ty, she felt herself relax for the first time all day.

"Thanks again for inviting me." Ty pretended to feed one of the plastic horses some yogurt and Olivia clapped her hands together.

"It's nice to have company." She took a slice of pizza and then gestured for Ty to do the same.

Ty ate while entertaining Olivia. They polished off their first slice of pizza, then the salad, offering every bite to the plastic horses first, much to Olivia's glee. When they reached for a second slice of pizza, they hesitated, hand hovering over the platter as they eyed Leslie's plate. "You eat a lot slower than me. You probably chew your food instead of inhaling it, huh?"

Leslie laughed. "Usually, yes. But don't slow down on my account."

Ty picked up the second slice. "I didn't have time to eat lunch today and I had to come straight from work to here, but I think I've trained myself to eat too fast."

"No time for breaks at your job?"

"Most techs eat while they work." They took a bite of pizza, then caught Olivia's bowl of yogurt right before she pushed it off the tray.

"Good save."

Ty nodded, mouth full. They made Olivia's spoon dance before dipping it in the yogurt. Olivia took the offered bite, clearly fascinated.

"You're good with babies. Did you babysit when you were younger?"

"No, but my cousin's twelve years younger than me and I helped raise her when she moved in with us. And baby humans don't seem that different from other baby animals."

"Do you generally entertain other baby animals with dancing utensils?"

Ty looked down at the spoon and chuckled. "It seemed like a good idea?"

"It's working." A lot of things were working. Like her libido. Leslie felt a flush when Ty met her gaze. A flush that felt entirely too good. She wondered if Ty had a girlfriend and if she should ask. She turned the question over as she watched Ty entertain Olivia. There was something about them that felt...comfortable. That word again. But also maybe familiar?

"Have you ever met someone and felt like you already know them?" She shook her head. "Never mind. That sounds weird." And it wasn't exactly what she meant. She was certain she'd never met Ty. She would have remembered them.

Ty set the spoon down and then their half-eaten slice of pizza. "I need to tell you something."

Leslie knew instantly what was coming. Ty had a girlfriend. Had they broken some rule having dinner with her? Maybe they weren't monogamous? As the questions and doubts flew round in her mind, she realized—belatedly—that her cell phone was ringing and Ty was looking at the counter where she'd left it.

"You can answer that if you need to," Ty said.

"It might be Seren." If so, she had good-terrible timing. Leslie got up to get her phone, wondering if she'd put Ty in a bad spot asking them to stay. She'd hate to come between anyone and their girlfriend, even if her own attraction was distractingly strong.

The caller wasn't Seren or Paige but one of her nervous first-time buyers. Unfortunately, it took more than a minute to calm him down. Fears over an issue with a sewer line had spiraled and he was ready to back out of the whole deal. She got out her laptop, pulled up the inspection report, and read through the part that had him freaked, while distractedly watching Olivia put dandelions in Ty's hair.

After promising to review the entire report that night and send recommendations for plumbers, she reminded the client there was still plenty of opportunities to get out of the deal. When she ended the call, she realized Ty had Olivia on their lap.

"Sorry about that. Work call. Want me to take her so you can finish eating?"

"No, I'm done. Besides, she's happy."

Olivia did look happy. She was sorting the dandelions and holding each one up for Ty to see. When she found one she liked, she set it on Ty's head. Ty held perfectly still as Olivia pushed another and then another dandelion into place. The gentle way Ty had with Olivia, along with their being willing to put up with a baby's antics, made her heart feel squishy. Of course Ty had a girlfriend.

"How do I look?" Ty asked, meeting her gaze with a half-smile.

"It's a statement." An adorable, yet also sexy, statement. She snapped a picture, then held her phone out to Ty.

Ty squinted at the screen. "I look like a flower girl tried to take out a ground squirrel."

Leslie laughed. Then Ty laughed, brushing a hand through their hair to dislodge the dandelions. They set Olivia down to collect the flowers and stood up, meeting Leslie's gaze. "You get work calls late."

"I do. But I stop answering the phone after nine every night."

"Every night? Meaning you work seven days a week?"

She nodded.

"Do you like the job?"

"I do. Mostly." She wondered if Ty was asking about her work hoping she'd forget they'd been about to tell her about their girlfriend. She decided to hold off on any more flirting. Or maybe Ty was poly? Plenty of people were, but it wasn't for her.

"What are the parts you don't like?"

It took her a moment to realize Ty was still on the subject of work. "Well, I don't like the late calls or the long hours. I don't like feeling like if I take any time off, I'm missing a sale or disappointing someone who expects me to be always available. But there are parts I truly love."

"Like?"

"Like finding the perfect home for someone. We spend so much time in our houses—it's important for it to be the right place. And I love the final walk-throughs when all the papers are signed and the client gets to unlock the door to their new house. Knowing I've helped make someone happy makes me happy."

"I love that answer. I guess I hadn't really thought about how important a good realtor is."

She shook her head. "I'm no brain surgeon."

"What you do is important. You help people make big life decisions."

She hadn't expected that response. It was sweet and genuine. Which seemed to sum up Ty. But did they have to be sexy, too? She cleared her throat. "So, do you like your job?"

"Some days I love it, others not so much. I always feel like I'm helping—people and animals—but being a vet tech is a hard job."

"Do you think being a veterinarian will be easier?"

"No, but I'll make more money." Ty smiled. "Mostly though, I'm ready to be the one making the treatment calls. I want to be the one in charge instead of the one following orders."

"I bet you'll be a good vet. Nellie seemed so comfortable with you and you're clearly calm under pressure."

Ty nodded, seeming almost distracted. They glanced at Olivia and then at Leslie. "That thing I was going to tell you earlier…"

"Are we done stalling?"

Ty dropped their chin. "You noticed." They took a deep breath. "You know how—"

Her phone interrupted with a loud beep. She'd turned up the volume so she wouldn't miss a call or a text from Seren. "It's only a text. Go ahead."

Ty glanced at the counter when her phone beeped again. And again. "I can wait if that's important."

She couldn't make Ty talk, but the more they held back, the more she wondered if it was more than a girlfriend. Wouldn't they simply come out and say that? Unless it was a poly arrangement that they felt had to be explained. Her phone beeped a fourth time and she finally went to check the texts, fully expecting more sewer line concerns. The news was worse. She sobered quickly as she read the words. "Shit."

"What's wrong?"

"Bea's out of surgery but it sounds like things didn't go so well. Seren said there was some problems under anesthesia…"

"Paige and Seren are probably staying down there tonight?"

Leslie nodded, scanning through the multiple texts Seren had sent.

Ty reached into their back pocket and pulled out their own phone. "I'm gonna tell Paige it's no problem for me to come back to do tomorrow's feeding."

Leslie tapped out a reply to Seren, promising again that she could stay as long as was needed. She set down her phone and looked at Olivia. "Seren says I've gotta get you in bed before you turn into a pumpkin."

"Paige told me to remember to get the chickens in bed too," Ty said.

"Does that mean I have to wait till tomorrow for whatever you were going to tell me?"

Ty met her gaze and her heart skipped a beat. Did they have a girlfriend or not? She felt ridiculous for how much she wanted the answer.

Olivia grabbed hold of Ty's jeans and yanked on the material, then held up her hands.

"She likes you." Olivia wasn't the only one.

Ty scooped her up, smiled at Olivia, and then sighed. "I wish I could just say it. But it's something that...well...Could we maybe talk after she's in bed?"

"Sure." She stretched out her arms and Ty handed over Olivia. It had to be that Ty was poly. She half wished that wasn't a deal-breaker for her.

Ty helped clear the table, but when Olivia started to fuss, Leslie told them she could finish the cleaning after Olivia was in bed. She wanted to simply ask if Ty was poly, but the more she considered it, the more she questioned what she'd say in response.

"Thanks again for dinner," Ty said, putting their hat on as they paused in the doorway. "Should I come back to the house after I finish in the barn?"

"I'll come find you in the barn. I don't know how long it'll take to get Ollie asleep."

"Okay." Ty stepped outside but glanced back at her as the screen door shut. "See you in a bit."

The almost wistful smile on Ty's face sent a tingly warmth through her. If only she didn't need to consider what weighed on Ty's conscience.

CHAPTER SEVEN

"Now that's a gorgeous sunset."

Ty looked up from the nesting box with the newly replaced hinge. "Yeah. Guess it is."

"You guess?" Leslie gestured to the view out the back side of the barn.

The mountains were blue in the distance and the setting sun brought streaks of orange and pink and purple to the sky. Ty couldn't see much past Leslie, though, and when she gave them a curious smile, their chest clenched. They'd spent the past half hour thinking of a delicate way to break the news about being Hitch. But no matter how they said it, there was a good chance Leslie would hate them as soon as the secret came out.

"It is beautiful," Ty said.

Leslie held out a beer she'd already popped the lid on. "When Paige and Seren first bought this place, I thought they'd be lonely. A ranch ten miles from town with no one around…But the views are hard to beat. I'm even starting to like how quiet it is."

"I grew up in the country. I've always liked being able to hear myself think." Ty took a sip of the beer and then glanced at the label. "I also like friends who buy fancy IPAs."

"I don't think any beer qualifies as fancy. Even overpriced IPAs." Leslie took a sip of her own beer and rocked her head. "This does taste good, though."

"Mm-hmm. Fancy." Ty grinned when Leslie rolled her eyes. "Thanks for including me in your party."

"It's more fun drinking with company." The baby monitor was hooked on the front pocket of Leslie's shorts and she had to unclip it to sit down on the bale of hay opposite where Ty was working. "I have to admit I'm kind of obsessing about what it is you want to tell me."

"*Want* might be a strong word." Ty set the beer on the work bench and then fiddled with the latch that didn't quite lock.

"What are you working on?"

Ty turned the nesting box around so Leslie could see. "It's a nesting box. The hens each have a cubby to lay their eggs." They opened the lid in the back with the replaced hinge. "You reach in to take out the eggs from the top. I still have to get it reattached to the coop and the latch isn't working quite right. But it can wait another day to be finished."

"You can keep working if you like." Leslie stretched out her legs, crossing her ankles. "As for me, I'm officially done with today."

Ty's libido rocketed up with Leslie's leg move, but the realization that nothing would happen between them put on the brakes a moment later. Even if Leslie didn't hate them for being Hitch—and that was a big if—Ty wasn't sure they could handle getting close again. The more they wished for it, the more warning bells sounded.

"Any trouble getting Olivia to sleep?"

"No, but I'm not trusting my luck." Leslie held up the monitor with a picture of Olivia sound asleep in her crib. "And, yes, I left the door unlocked."

"Even if you didn't, we've already established how fast you can get in through the window."

"Good point." Leslie gave Ty a coy smile. "Anything I can do to help?"

"You brought me a beer—and you're keeping me company. That's plenty." Ty picked up the nesting box and carried it over to the chicken coop. "Hopefully it won't take me long to get this reattached."

"Hopefully not as long as it takes you to open up and talk," Leslie said.

"We can hope." Ty smiled but couldn't hold it for long. They had to tell her, but still the words stuck in their throat.

After they had all four corners secured, they fussed with the latch until it finally caught. Not perfect, but it would work for the night. They stood and brushed their hands off on their jeans.

"Do you want to talk about the weather?" Leslie asked.

Ty met Leslie's gaze. They felt shaky but took a deep breath and said, "Do you remember the name Hitch-21?"

"I'm sorry, what?"

Ty knew Leslie had heard but they repeated it anyway. "Hitch-21."

She shook her head. "How do you know—" Slowly her expression morphed from confusion to realization.

Ty didn't wait for the anger to hit. "I know you asked me to forget your name, and I promise I never looked you up, but I'm not good at forgetting things."

"Fuck." Leslie stood up, hand clasped to her chest, then paced in a circle. She stopped walking and turned to face Ty. "You're Hitch?"

"I'm Hitch."

"But Hitch lives in Nevada—the number was a Reno area code."

"That's where my parents live. Where I grew up. I got my first cell phone there and kept the number."

Leslie shook her head again. "You can't be Hitch." She looked at Ty. "Tell me you're kidding. This is a joke?"

"I'm not joking. I'm not really good at jokes." Ty waited for Leslie to say something more. When she only paced, Ty added, "I didn't know how to tell you and clearly this wasn't the best way but—"

Leslie held up her hand, stopping Ty's words. A moment later she went back to the hay bale and sat down, one hand half covering her eyes as if she'd like to disappear under it. "I shouldn't have gotten out of bed today."

At least she wasn't storming out of the barn. "We don't have to talk about anything that happened—or didn't happen—but it didn't seem right I knew and you didn't. My last name's Sutherland.

Ty Sutherland. You can look me up or do whatever you want so this all feels fair."

"Fair?" She stood up but then sat down again a second later. "How is this even happening?"

"How is it possible we live in the same town? How is it possible I went to your open house? For that matter, how is it possible that your open house was right next door? How could you possibly be friends with Seren and Paige?" Ty lifted a shoulder. "I don't know."

"I didn't recognize your voice. I mean I know we only talked on the phone that one time but…"

"And you didn't let me say much." As soon as the words were out of Ty's mouth, they regretted it.

Leslie's look hardened. "You should have told me you were Hitch sooner."

"When? At the open house? I thought we'd never see each other again." Ty knew Leslie was right but couldn't help defending their choice. "Or when you came to the barn saying you were locked out?"

"I can't decide if I should laugh or scream." Leslie glanced at Ty but looked away quickly. "Okay. Damage control. Who knows?"

"No one," Ty said.

"No one? Not even your cousin?"

Ty opened their mouth and promptly closed it. *Shit.* "I told Zoe we knew each other from a meet-up group. Nothing specific. I wouldn't have told her at all but she knew I was acting funny at the open house. When I heard your name—"

"What does nothing specific mean? What exactly did you tell her?" Leslie's lips made a tight line.

Ty felt sick but had to answer. "I told her we'd gotten to know each other online—in a meet-up group—and that I wasn't supposed to know your real name but I'd found out on accident."

"You didn't tell her it was an anonymous sex group?"

"No." Ty hesitated and then added, "But she's smart. She knows I wasn't telling her the whole story."

Leslie exhaled, then closed her eyes. "I shouldn't have called you that night. I still can't believe it didn't occur to me that my number would come up with my name." She let out a string of cuss words followed by, "My entire livelihood depends on my reputation."

"I'm not going to tell anyone what we did. But plenty of people have online sex. And phone sex."

"With total strangers?" Leslie tilted her head. "And the kinds of things we did?"

Ty wanted to argue there'd been nothing wrong with anything they did. Two consenting adults could agree to do some things that might make others uncomfortable, but they'd both done everything willingly. And yet what was the point in arguing? Leslie was determined to be angry. "I'm sorry if we did anything you didn't want to do. Clearly you regret it now and if you want—"

"Stop," Leslie interrupted. "Don't apologize for what we did. I messaged you first and there was never a point where I did anything I didn't want to do." She met Ty's gaze. "I can't believe you're Hitch. And at the same time, I can."

Leslie's anger seemed to be replaced with disappointment, which made Ty feel worse. "I know it'd be weird if we ran into each other again, but it is Davis so I can promise to pretend we never knew each other."

Leslie shook her head. "Maybe you're right. Maybe I'm being ridiculous and plenty of people have online sex."

"I never said you were being ridiculous."

She held up her hand. "I'm not done. In my career, people need to trust me and see me as a professional. Not as someone who has kinky online sex with strangers."

"I get it. And I won't tell anyone. I'll even sign something if that would help."

"You don't need to sign anything. I trust you." Leslie met Ty's gaze and her expression softened. "I know we don't know each other well in real life but…you actually seem really cool. I'm just upset. And I think a little shocked." She blew out a breath. "You should know I told Seren."

"You did?" Ty couldn't hold back their surprise.

"I didn't tell her your name, since I didn't know it, but I told her what happened. That I'd met someone online and we'd done things. She told me she always thought I was wild. I'm not. I mean, I've wanted to be more wild than I am but…"

"It's easier online when you can be anonymous."

"You're not mad I told her?"

"I don't care who knows I've had online sex. Besides, Seren doesn't know I'm Hitch. Even if she did, I wouldn't care."

Neither spoke for a long minute but Leslie didn't seem to be ready to leave. Ty pointed to the hay bale next to her. "Okay with you if I sit down?"

"Go ahead. I think we're going to be here a while."

CHAPTER EIGHT

"You can ask me anything," Ty said.

Leslie took a sip of her beer, realized she'd almost drained it, and wished she had something stronger. Now that Ty was sitting across from her it was even harder making eye contact. And impossibly hard to not think about the scenes she'd had with Hitch.

Ty was Hitch.

It didn't seem possible, and yet it was. She'd recognized the possibility that someday they might come face-to-face when she'd heard Hitch's voice on the phone—which is exactly why she'd freaked out. Everything they'd done had truly felt like a game up until that point. A game with virtual players. But Hitch wasn't virtual as soon as she'd heard their voice. They went from being a cartoon avatar to a real person. Only she'd thought that real person lived far enough away that she didn't have to worry.

She considered all the questions she'd wanted to ask Hitch. She'd always been the one in charge. Always the one suggesting the things they'd done. Had Ty really been okay with everything? Had they liked playing the roles or only gone along with all of her fantasies? She wanted to start there but she wasn't ready.

She took a deep breath and said, "Tell me something about the real you."

"You know a lot about the real me already." Ty picked out a piece of hay from the bale and ran it between their fingers. "Just not the specifics."

She'd made it clear when she started messaging Hitch privately that no personal information was going to be shared on her end. So Hitch hadn't shared anything either. At least not at first. Slowly, though, they'd both started mentioning things from their daily life. And things that had happened in the past. Nothing specific like places or names or details. Nothing, she'd thought, that would lead Hitch to find her in real life. But even without the specifics, she'd felt as if Hitch knew her better than anyone.

"I don't know where to start," Ty said, shifting back on the hay bale and folding their legs cross-style. "You know that time we were going to have phone sex?"

How could she forget?

"I'd never done it before."

She was surprised and yet it made sense. Hitch—*Ty*—had been a novice at so many things. An eager, fun novice.

"Also, and I guess this makes two things, I left the group after that night."

"I knew you left," Leslie admitted. "Well, I wondered if you left or just changed your screen name."

"I dropped out. Your turn." Ty reached for their beer and clinked it against Leslie's. "Tell me something about the real Girl-Monday."

"You're the first person I had sex with online. Also the only person."

"Seriously?"

She nodded. The group wasn't meant for people who wanted to be monogamous. It was meant for casual sexy interactions with everyone in the group in a no-strings-attached way. But she'd gotten attached quickly to Hitch. "Once I started messaging you, I ignored everyone else."

"Same," Ty said. "But I figured you'd find someone new."

"I didn't go looking. Hitch was…what I'd needed. The only reason I even joined that group was because a writer friend convinced me it'd be good for me."

"You're a writer?"

"No, not really. I mean, I write. Or I did. I stopped. I was working on a novel."

Ty's brow furrowed. "Why'd you stop?"

She waved her hand like she could bat away the bad feelings that came with the question. "Lots of reasons. Not enough time, mostly. That and not feeling like I was good enough to write anything someone would want to read."

"I loved reading what you wrote to me. Some of the ways you'd tell me to do things…" Ty's voice trailed. Their eyes crinkled and their half-smile made Leslie want to ask what they were remembering. After a moment, they said, "It makes sense you're a writer."

"Wanted to be a writer," she corrected. "I was in a writing group for a while. It was a group of local writers who meet up at the café next to the bookstore downtown every month. I got to be friends with a romance writer, and she was the one who told me about TryItOnce. She'd been dealing with writer's block and had decided to try something different."

"She joined an online sex group because she had writer's block?"

"Apparently it helped her get back to writing. She had all these positive things to say about the group and the people she'd met. I thought maybe it'd help me too. And how could I not check out an anonymous queer chatroom where you could hook up with anyone?" She lifted a shoulder. "But honestly I never thought I'd do anything like what we did."

"Wait, you joined the group because of writer's block?"

"I wasn't exactly blocked. I wanted to write a kissing scene. Well, I'd tried and it was terrible. I knew I needed more practice writing sexy stuff." Ty's expression stopped her. Confusion bordering on hurt.

"You joined the group for writing practice?"

"Well, at first, yeah, but it became more obviously." Ty's expression didn't change and she tried to think of how she could explain. "I told myself it was all writing practice, which is why I felt brave enough to reach out to you. And tell you to do all those things. And why I did all those things to you. I didn't expect to connect with anyone. Not the way we did."

Ty tossed the bit of hay they'd been twisting onto the ground and stood up. They walked over to the project they'd been working on earlier, stared at the tools they'd left on the ground, then turned back to Leslie. "I'm trying not to take this personally. But…Damn. I thought you telling me to forget I ever met you hurt. Knowing we did all those things just so you could get some writing practice maybe hurts more."

She felt the beer she'd downed way too fast lurch up in her throat. "I swear it wasn't only writing practice."

Ty didn't look like they believed her. Why should they? It was a fluke thing she'd tried and she truly hadn't been serious about it at first. When had it become serious?

"I'm not going to lie to you, Ty. When I messaged you that first night, I was in writer mode and I was thinking of it all as an exercise. But I liked you and…our conversations turned into something more."

"Until you needed practice writing a breakup scene?"

Ty's tone stung. She thought of how lonely she'd felt after things with Hitch had ended. How she'd numbly looked for something to distract her from a loss she hadn't expected. Yes, it'd been her fault, but that didn't mean she hadn't suffered the consequences.

"Look, I'm not going to say our conversations didn't help my writing because they did help. A lot. I figured out how to wrangle kissing scenes and wrote a few I actually liked." She paused, hoping to catch Ty's gaze, but they were staring at the old mare who seemed to be eavesdropping. The horse flicked her ears and looked from Leslie to Ty. "I swear it wasn't only writing practice. I got attached."

She felt her cheeks get hot but forced herself to go on. "I loved our nightly check-ins. Loved how you'd always send me a good-morning note. I looked forward to every message you sent. Every time a notification beeped on my phone, I'd check to see if it was from Hitch-21."

"And yet it was easy to end things." Ty's expression was stony.

"It wasn't easy. I felt like crap for days. For weeks. But do you really blame me for freaking out? With the code names and the avatars and all that identity encrypted stuff, I never expected you'd say my real name. Ty, we did things I'd never do. Not in real life. And I suddenly felt like the whole world would find out."

"You really thought I'd track you down and tell people what you'd done?" Ty shook their head. "Or was the problem the things we did? That someone in the real world knew what you wanted?"

"I don't know." She felt the press of tears and looked up at the barn rafters, shaking her head. "Both reasons maybe? You knew things I'd never told anyone and, yeah, you were suddenly real. You were a voice on the other end of the line saying Leslie Brandt instead of Girl-Monday. I'd told you things I haven't even told my therapist. Like that stuff about what happened after my parents separated and about that guy in college."

"I thought that meant you trusted me." Ty exhaled. "I'm sorry all those things happened to you, but I'd never tell anyone. Not now, not then, not ever."

"I..." What could you say to that? "I know."

"But you thought I was going to?"

"I don't know what I was thinking. One minute I was this sex goddess who had no fear. Then suddenly my Girl-Monday alter ego was gone and I was a thirty-nine-year-old realtor from Davis who lived alone with her cats. I didn't know what to do without my magic cape."

When Ty didn't say anything, she continued, "I've never tied anyone up. I've never ordered anyone to strip and drop to their knees. I've never told anyone to behave or...or I'd sit on their face." She held up her hands. "What can I say? I didn't want the whole world to know those things."

Ty nodded but didn't look her direction.

"The day after our phone conversation, I wrote you a long apology. I got a message back saying you'd left the group. So I left too. I felt awful about how things ended." There was more she could say but she wondered what Ty was thinking, what they were feeling. Online she would have asked. In person, the questions felt off-limits. "It's kind of crazy we live in the same town."

"Completely crazy." Ty finally met her gaze. "So what happens now?"

"I don't know."

Ty began gathering the tools they'd left out. They placed the toolbox on a shelf and turned back to face her. "Maybe this is it?"

Maybe everything they'd been through—everything they'd done—was all they'd have. "Maybe this is how Hitch and Girl-

Monday say goodbye?" She felt a heaviness saying the words, but she knew it was the most likely thing. "For what it's worth, I am really sorry about the things I said that night."

"Apology accepted." Ty brushed their hands off on their jeans and came back to sit on the hay bale. "Honestly, I don't totally blame you. But I hate you'd think I'd tell anyone what we did. Or that I'd tell the secrets you told me. And I'm sorry, too. I wish I'd never asked you to call me. It felt like everything was my fault and I hated being so sad about something I'd done to myself." Ty tipped the brim of their cowboy hat and added, "But it's okay. I can be a tough cowboy."

Leslie smiled. She knew the hurt was still there, same as she felt inside her own heart. She wanted to hug Ty, but hugging would be too complicated. "I never pictured Hitch in a cowboy hat."

"How'd you picture me?"

Leslie hesitated. "Promise not to laugh?"

Ty's lips turned up. "Maybe."

"Fine. Don't promise." She wondered at how they'd gone from serious to flirty again but decided not to overthink it. "I knew you worked with horses but obviously I didn't know you were a vet tech. One time you mentioned you were sore because you'd been working with this stallion who'd reared up and somehow kicked you."

"In the chest. I couldn't take a deep breath for weeks," Ty said.

"You said something about trying to catch him after he'd taken off and I pictured that scene in *The Black Stallion* where Alec's on the beach trying to give the Black seaweed and the horse keeps rearing up. You know the one?"

"You pictured me as a teenage boy on a beach with a horse?" Ty looked about to laugh.

"No. Well...kind of? You'd said something about racing horses, too, and I didn't imagine a western thing. Also, I thought you'd be shorter."

"So either I was a teenage boy stuck on a beach or a jockey?" Ty grinned, then laughed. "Please tell me this is not how you imagined me when we were having sex."

She shook her head and laughed too. "No. Definitely not."

"You sure about that?"

"Completely sure." Though now that she knew Ty was Hitch, she couldn't quite remember how she'd pictured Hitch before. All the images in her mind had been written over. "How'd you picture me?"

"I didn't really have a clear picture in my head. That's why I wanted to hear your voice. I knew you'd never send me anything with your face and I'd gotten to the point where I really wanted to see you. To know you were real, you know?"

Leslie understood. She hadn't admitted it then, but she knew that was part of why she'd agreed to the call.

"As nice as it was to get those lingerie shots, I couldn't completely imagine you," Ty said.

"I was so nervous sending you those pictures." Two shots. One of her top half cut off at the neck and one of her bottom half, legs crossed.

"You didn't have to be nervous. I'd sent you a picture of me in a strap-on first."

She recalled that image instantly. Hitch, lying stretched out on a bed in nothing but boxers with a tan-colored cock poking out of the slit. But the picture was only from the midsection down. She'd asked Hitch to keep their face out of the shot.

"I deleted those lingerie pictures, by the way. Like you asked. But I maybe stared at the shot of your breasts for a good long while before I hit delete."

Leslie smiled. There was definitely some pride mixed in. "It took me months to delete the picture you'd sent."

"Months? Like after we stopped messaging?"

"Yep." She wondered at how easy it was to be open with Ty and enjoyed the look of pride she'd put on their face. "I did finally delete it. You can check my phone if you want."

"I don't need to. I believe you."

She wished she could have been that trusting with Hitch. In some ways, she had trusted them. In others, she'd told herself it was a game she could always get out of unscathed. No trust needed.

Would things have gone differently if they'd known the real version of each other? If Hitch and Girl-Monday had exchanged headshots? She'd thought it was better to not have Hitch's face in her mind. She'd only imagined someone indistinct, features blurred.

"What we did was okay, you know," Ty said.

"Does that mean you don't have any regrets?"

"I didn't say that." Ty smiled but there was still a sadness in their eyes. "You've really never tied anyone up? You seemed so good at it."

"Girl-Monday was good at lots of things."

CHAPTER NINE

One of the heifers let out a moo and Leslie got up off the hay bale and walked over to their pen, asking if they had secrets to admit as well. Ty wondered if she needed a break from the conversation. There were still so many things they wanted to ask. But maybe enough had been said.

Leslie chatted with the heifers about the weather. Summer was long, dry, and hot in Davis and usually conversations about the weather were short. But somehow Leslie was making this one entertaining.

"Cows don't really sweat," Ty said. They went over to the bins where Paige kept treats and picked out a few alfalfa cubes.

"They don't?" Leslie looked appalled. "So they don't mind the heat?"

"Actually, they hate the heat. But they love treats. Paige and Seren have totally spoiled them." Ty handed her an alfalfa cube.

Leslie stepped up to the closest heifer. "Is this one April or May?"

"April, I think."

Leslie glanced back at Ty. "You can't tell them apart either?"

"They're both black and white. I spent five years working in the large animal barn and I can tell you they're Holsteins?"

She raised an eyebrow. "Five years in a large animal barn and that's what you learned?"

"I learned a few other things, but I'm really a horse person."

Leslie seemed to consider handing the treat to the heifer but then tossed the cube into the trough. Ty handed Leslie the second alfalfa cube and watched her toss it to the second heifer. She dusted off her hands and then stepped back from the stall.

Nellie, in the next stall over, stretched out her neck to sniff Leslie's back. Leslie startled at the touch and spun around to face the horse, her hand on her chest.

"Don't worry. She's only hoping you have a treat for her too."

Nellie leaned over her stall rail, managing to get an inch closer, but Leslie only backed away.

"You don't have to be scared. She's gentle."

"I'm sure she is, but horses are jumpy around me. And they're big." Leslie glanced at Ty. "To a horse person, that probably sounds ridiculous."

"Horses are big. And they don't always think before they react. Nellie's scared of horses too."

"A horse who's scared of other horses?"

Ty nodded. They held out their hand and Nellie stepped forward, rubbing her chin over their fingers. "She acts like she wants company but she won't have anything to do with the other horses."

"Where are the other horses?" Leslie asked, looking around the barn.

"Archer and Polaris are out in the pasture."

"They don't sleep in the barn?"

"Not when it's nice weather. Archer's used to being out and Polaris goes where Archer goes. We make them come in to eat but then they go back out again."

"And Nellie always stays in the barn?"

"Yep. Always." Ty eyed the mare. "When I moved my two out here, Paige was hoping Nellie would realize how nice it is having a herd but she's been on her own for a long time."

Leslie's eyes narrowed. "You think she's lonely?"

"I'm sure she is. But you can't force a horse to trust. They have to figure out on their own what's safe and what will hurt them."

After a moment, Leslie took a step toward the mare's stall. Then another. She stopped before she'd reached the rails and Nellie stretched out her neck, sniffing again for a treat.

"I wish I wasn't scared of you," Leslie said softly. "The truth is, I've always loved horses. I was obsessed when I was a kid. I had horse posters all over my room and all these books about them."

"Me too."

Leslie looked back at Ty and smiled. "What do you know? Something we have in common."

"There's a few other things," Ty said.

"If you say spanking, I'm not sure I'm going to be able to keep having this conversation with Nellie."

Ty laughed. "You had to go right to that?"

Leslie winked, then looked back at Nellie. "Anyway. I'm sorry I'm scared of you. It's really not you in particular—I've had this fear for a long time."

"Something bad happen?"

Leslie seemed to hesitate but finally said, "My mom convinced me horses were dangerous. She got bucked off when she was a teenager and ended up in a body cast for months. Her spine was never right after. She wouldn't let me go anywhere near a horse—and I loved everything to do with them. I thought they were magical."

"They are magical," Ty said.

Leslie looked at them and smiled. "You're such a horse person."

"Completely."

Leslie eyed Nellie again. "After my parents separated, my dad moved up north. There was a pasture near his place with a couple horses. I used to watch them for hours…This one time I finally got up the nerve to try petting the buckskin. She was my favorite.

"I snuck into the pasture and walked right up to her. My heart was pounding and I thought I was going to pee my pants. When I went to pet her, the other horse charged. I don't know if he was jealous or if he was protecting her or what." She held up her hand and pointed to a faint line down the length of her right thumb. "I cut my hand on the barbed wire fence trying to get out of there. I've never been so scared. Well, never of an animal. After that happened, I was convinced my mom was right. Horses were dangerous."

"Some can be," Ty said. "Like some people. But most are sweet and only want to be loved."

"Like people?"

"That's really cheesy. I can't believe you said that."

Leslie laughed. After a moment, she reached out and pushed Ty's shoulder. "You."

The contact was brief but Ty felt a rush all the same. When Leslie quickly looked back at Nellie, Ty wondered if she'd felt something too.

"The dumb part is I'd still love to pet a horse. I'd like to give you a treat, Nellie. I want to even more because I think Ty's right. You look lonely."

Ty walked over to where Paige kept the horse cookies and grabbed two. The cookies were shaped like hearts and smelled like peppermint-flavored oats. Horses nearly unanimously loved them.

"You don't have to give her one. But if you want to try, I promise she won't hurt you. She's in a stall and can barely reach you." Ty held out a treat to Leslie. She took a moment but finally reached for the cookie, her smooth fingertips brushing Ty's palm.

"This might be a bad idea."

"Lots of things are a bad idea but fun anyway," Ty murmured, trying to ignore how Leslie's light touch had turned on every nerve.

Leslie gripped the treat but didn't make a move to offer it to Nellie. Ty couldn't help staring at her hand. From the manicured nails to the slender fingers, several of which had rings, to the silver bracelets clinking together on her wrist, everything about her hand seemed to beckon attention. Especially when she held the treat out to Nellie with the little heart between her thumb and index finger.

"Wait, not like that." On reflex, Ty grabbed Leslie's wrist and pulled it close. Now, body fully at attention, the mistake of that move was clear. Fortunately Leslie didn't look mad. Only surprised. "Sorry." Ty let go. "She could bite you on accident holding it like that. You have to hold it out with an open palm."

Rather than prying open Leslie's fingers, which definitely would have crossed a line, Ty placed the second treat in the middle of their palm. "Like this." Stepping closer to the stall, Ty waited for Nellie to reach for the treat. It disappeared almost instantly and Ty rubbed the horse's forehead, finger-combing the forelock, before looking back at Leslie. "Your turn."

Leslie nodded, clearly steeling herself as she stepped up and held out the treat. When Nellie's muzzle touched her skin, she squeezed her eyes closed. "Please don't bite me."

Nellie gingerly took the treat and Leslie opened her eyes. She looked from her empty hand to the horse. "Well, that happened."

"Good job."

"Thank you." Leslie exhaled. "It was easier than I thought it'd be." She looked back at Nellie. "Want to hear a secret? I'm thirty-nine years old and that's the first time I've given a horse a treat." She swallowed, looking as if she were holding back tears. "I've wanted to do that for a long time."

Ty held out their hand and waited for Nellie to bump against their fingers for a scratch.

"Can I pet her too?" Leslie asked. When Ty nodded, she took a step forward.

"Don't forget to breathe," Ty whispered.

Leslie breathed out heavily, clearly for exaggeration. "Better?"

"Better. And I'm not trying to tease. Horses want to smell everything. Especially things that make them nervous, like new people. She'll relax if you sigh."

"Can she tell I'm afraid?"

Ty considered lying. It might help Leslie's confidence. But it was better to be cautious around even old, sweet horses. "Yeah, she can probably tell."

Leslie had been moving so tentatively that Ty didn't expect her to reach right toward Nellie's face. Startled, Nellie jerked up her head. Which startled Leslie. She stumbled back, knocking over one of the grain buckets and spooking Nellie even more.

"Easy. It's okay." Ty wasn't sure if the words were meant more for the horse or Leslie. The white of Nellie's eyes shone and Ty repeated the words, glancing at Leslie. "You okay?"

"I'm fine." Leslie shook out her hands as if trying to lose the tension. "But I hate that I freaked her out."

"You didn't do anything wrong. You moved a little faster than I would've, but honestly I'm surprised she reacted like that." Ty leaned against the stall gate, pretending to ignore Nellie. She was clearly looking for a signal from them and still fearful. "I don't know her history. Now that I think about it, I've been letting her come to me."

Ty clicked their tongue and held out a hand. Nellie came forward shyly, bumping their fingers with her muzzle but still tentative. When she allowed Ty to pet her, they said, "She always walks up with her left side to me. She might've been whipped from the right. Or maybe she can't see well on that side."

"Or maybe it's me."

"I think it's a combination."

Leslie looked at the overturned grain bucket and then at Ty. "You could've lied and said it wasn't me at all."

"I'm not good at lying."

"I noticed." She looked at Nellie and sighed. "Can I try again?"

Ty wasn't sure if Leslie was asking them or the horse. Still, they said, "Sure. Whenever you're ready, tell me and I'll get out of the way."

"I'd feel better if you could stay right where you are."

Ty tried to hide their surprise when Leslie circled behind them, brushing her hand over their arm and squeezing between the stall rail and where they stood.

"Okay," Leslie said. "Coach me."

Ty took a step to the side, giving Leslie more room. As nice as it was feeling Leslie's body close, it was more important giving her space if Nellie shied again. "The biggest thing is moving slow. Or not moving at all. Especially with a nervous horse. Let them come to you."

Ty clicked to Nellie, getting the mare's attention. She raised and lowered her head like she was gauging the situation. Ty rubbed under her throat latch, and when Nellie realized she wasn't getting another cookie, she turned to check out Leslie. It only took a moment before the mare huffed a greeting. Leslie didn't move a muscle.

"Remember the breathing part?" Ty asked.

"I'm too nervous."

"You don't have to do this."

"I want to." She stood rigid but Ty didn't try telling her to relax. "What's the next step after standing still? I got that part down."

"Yeah, you're winning on that." Ty grinned when Leslie gave them a slightly annoyed smile. "When you're ready, hold out your hand like you're giving her a treat."

"I don't have a treat."

"She needs to sniff you again."

Slowly, Leslie raised her hand. Nellie sniffed, predictably, then snorted. Leslie didn't yank her hand away but she did let out a long exhale. After a moment, Nellie came back to Leslie's hand, sniffed again, then nuzzled her palm.

"You cleared the sniff test. When you're ready, go ahead and give her a scratch. But move nice and slow."

"If I wasn't so nervous at the moment, I'd make some joke about how this is a good way to approach me too."

"Nice and slow? Or the part about sniffing first?"

Leslie looked over her shoulder at Ty, a smile softening the lines of tension on her face. "Yes."

"You're supposed to be focusing on the horse," Ty said, not holding back their smile.

"I am." Leslie looked back at Nellie, then breathed out. She raised her hand and stroked down Nellie's blaze. The mare moved into her touch, and when Leslie stroked again, closed her eyes.

"She likes that," Ty said.

Leslie kept her gaze on the horse. "Horses really are magical," she whispered.

"I never thought you'd be this cheesy in real life," Ty whispered back.

"I have my moments. If you want to get to know me better, get used to it."

"Is getting to know you better an option?"

Leslie took a step back from Nellie's stall, putting a foot of space between them. She looked over at Ty. "Honestly, I don't know what would be a good idea at this point. One minute it feels like we're old friends and we can joke with each other, and the next…"

"I know."

Leslie glanced back at Nellie. "Today wasn't all bad."

"Glad you got locked out of the house?"

"On the record? No. Off-record?" Leslie rocked her head. "Maybe."

CHAPTER TEN

The sound of Olivia's crying came through the monitor, rustling Leslie from a dream. She swung her legs over the edge of the bed and pushed her toes into the slippers Seren had loaned her, then sat still for a moment, realizing the crying had stopped. A second later, Olivia was singing. Incoherent words, but singing all the same.

It was pitch dark in the room, which meant it was well before dawn, but she refused to look at the clock. Considering how long it'd taken her to fall asleep, it was definitely too early to be conscious. She kept the lights off as she made her way to Olivia's room, hoping she could quiet her and slip back to bed.

Olivia took one look at her, broke off singing, and let out a wail. "Oh, sweetie, you were expecting one of your moms, weren't you?"

Her crying worsened with the word "moms." Leslie rubbed her eyes, trying to jumpstart her brain. "How about I warm you up a bottle of milk?"

Olivia reached out her arms to be picked up. Leslie lifted her out of the crib, wondering if it was possible Olivia had gained weight overnight. More likely she was simply feeling weak from being half asleep.

She should have gone right to bed after Ty had left. Instead, she'd spent hours looking up Ty Sutherland on all the social media sites. It was weird knowing someone and not knowing them at the same time. She still couldn't completely wrap her head around the fact that Hitch lived in Davis. And that fate had seemed hell-bent on throwing them together.

Ty's account on Instagram wasn't private but she'd hesitated clicking the follow button. Finally, she'd decided that since Hitch had entered her real life, she needed to know if Ty was someone she could trust. It had nothing to do with wanting or not wanting a relationship—that's what she told herself. Unfortunately, all she learned from Instagram was that Ty was well and truly a horse person. There were hundreds of photos of horses.

She blinked at the time on the microwave but it didn't change. Four forty-five. "Olivia. You got me up before five. It's a good thing I like you so much."

After fixing a bottle, she took Olivia back to her room and settled in on the rocking chair. Olivia cuddled up against her chest, happily chugging her milk. Leslie closed her eyes. There was no going back to sleep, but holding a warm baby in snuggly pajamas and rocking in a comfy chair wasn't awful.

After poking through Ty's posts, she'd hoped to fall right asleep given how long her day had been. Instead, she'd lain awake thinking. Mostly about Ty. Then about horses. Then about sex—online and otherwise. Then, of course, about Hitch again and whether or not she wanted them in her real life.

After she'd gotten over her initial shock at Ty being Hitch, she wasn't upset so much as apprehensive. The attraction she felt was distractingly strong and there were so many ways she could screw up going forward. She'd hurt Ty once and didn't want to do it again. But she couldn't ignore their existence now—especially since they boarded at Seren and Paige's barn.

Probably the best thing to do was manage her own desire and keep Ty at a friendly arm's length. Hitch had said they didn't have time to date anyone seriously anyway. Now she knew why. Ty was juggling a job, vet school, and horses—definitely a full plate. But her own schedule was a full plate, too, and yet she'd rearrange to make room for someone if she wanted them in her life bad enough. Likely Ty would do the same. Still, that didn't mean it was a good idea.

Ty pulled up to the ranch not long after sunrise. Leslie had opened all the windows in the house to let in the cool morning air and heard the rumble of the old Jeep on the gravel road. She peeked out the kitchen window right as Ty jumped out of the Jeep. They pushed their cowboy hat on and headed straight for the barn.

"Still sexy." She sighed and glanced at Olivia who was happily gnawing on a wooden block. "Want to go outside and do some gardening?"

Being outside didn't make it any easier to stay away from the barn. She occupied herself watering the plants and keeping Olivia from eating weeds, with only furtive glances at the Jeep. She didn't want to miss Ty leaving—not that she knew what she wanted to say to them. *Hi, I've been thinking about you all night. And for about six months, off and on.*

Olivia glanced up, a fistful of dirt in each hand.

"It's not like I've been pining for Hitch. I haven't." She pursed her lips. "You don't look like you believe me, but it's the truth." She'd thought of them and hoped they were well, but that was all. Well, that and wishing she could send them a note checking in. And another note to apologize.

She set down the watering can. "Want to go see the horses?"

Olivia held up her hands and dirt fell everywhere.

She scooped her up, brushing the dirt off a no-longer-white onesie. "This might be a mistake."

Olivia cooed in response.

"I'm going to try and be my normal self and not think about all the things Hitch and Girl-Monday did together."

The barn was bright with the early morning light and smelled like wood shavings and hay. Leslie glanced around for a moment until she spotted Ty leaning against a shovel in Nellie's stall. She met their gaze and felt an immediate pulse between her legs. Yesterday seemed to have awakened a hungry monster. She couldn't remember the last time she'd felt such a strong sexual response to simply the sight of someone. But maybe it was simply because Ty was the real-life Hitch. Her body wanted the fantasy her mind had promised for so many months.

"Hey there." Ty's cheerful greeting came with a wide smile. "I was wondering if you two would be awake this early. It's a gorgeous day, isn't it?"

"You seem a little too happy to be scooping poop. Morning person?"

Ty laughed. "I love mornings."

"Hmm. So does someone else." Because she was reaching for Ty anyway, Leslie held Olivia out to Ty as soon as they came out of Nellie's stall. "Here, you two can talk all about how pretty the sunrise is or whatever morning people talk about."

Olivia was all smiles in Ty's arms and got even more happy when Ty asked if she wanted to say hi to Nellie. The horse had her head buried in a bucket but raised it when Ty clicked to her. Ty murmured something only the horse seemed to hear. Nellie stuck her head over the railing to sniff Olivia. After a once-over to seemingly confirm Olivia didn't have treats, Nellie looked at Leslie.

Although most of the night was taken up with thoughts of Ty, she'd also thought of Nellie. She felt sorry for the horse and wondered why she didn't want to be with the other two out in the pasture.

When Nellie returned to her bucket, Leslie took a step closer and squinted at the contents of the bucket. "What is she eating?" It looked like green oatmeal and the sight turned her stomach. "I thought horses ate hay. And grain. That looks like something from a Dr. Seuss book."

"Probably tastes like it too. Nellie's teeth aren't great. She has trouble chewing the dry hay so Paige makes her this mash. I'm not sure exactly what's in it. All my instructions said were six scoops and add water."

"And she likes it?"

"She seems to." Ty shrugged. "Archer and Polaris always seem jealous they don't get this special stuff." They motioned to the other two horses who seemed to sense they were being called out and both looked up.

Leslie hadn't even noticed the other stalls had occupants. She'd been too focused on Ty when she came in.

"Polaris gets a special feed added to her hay after long training rides but she doesn't seem to think it's as good as what Nellie's got here. Want to meet Polaris and Archer?"

Leslie nodded, wishing she could squelch the fear that flared up. Before she'd talked herself down, Ty was making introductions.

Archer was the brown-and-white paint in the stall on the left and Polaris was the dark bay on the right. Ty took Olivia right to Archer's stall and Leslie bit back the words of caution that spun round in her head.

Ty opened Archer's stall door and went right in, Olivia still in their arms. Olivia patted the horse and gurgled happily. After a minute or two, Leslie forced herself to step closer to the stall. The horse didn't look up from his hay, which was a relief. She studied him, quickly getting the impression that he wasn't jumpy when Olivia screeched and tried lunging out of Ty's arms to grab the mane and he didn't even twitch. He also wasn't very big.

"Is he kind of...short?"

Ty looked mildly offended but laughed. "Short but mighty. Technically, he's only one inch above a pony."

"I like the smaller size. It's less intimidating."

"Everything about Archer is unintimidating. He's the horse equivalent of a teddy bear." Ty gave Archer a pat, then stepped out of the stall and closed the door. Olivia complained loudly, but Archer didn't seem to care.

"Polaris is the opposite," Ty said, walking up to the next stall.

When Ty clicked, the dark bay immediately raised her head and flared her nostrils. She took a bite of hay, then approached the stall door, then backed away at the sight of Olivia, head high.

"Easy, girl," Ty murmured. "Come say hi."

Leslie didn't think the horse would approach, but she dropped her head and walked up to the gate. She stretched her neck far enough to nuzzle Ty's outstretched hand, all the while keeping one eye on Olivia.

Leslie held back a warning, reminding herself Ty knew what they were doing. A moment later, the horse swung her head toward Leslie. It wasn't easy remembering to breathe but she made herself do it even as the mare's dark brown eyes locked on her.

"I feel like she's sizing me up."

"She is. Polaris is a thinker. Give her something new and she always balks, then comes back and studies it for a while. She's smarter than any horse I've ever met, but that isn't always a good thing."

"What type of horse is she?"

"Half mustang, half Arab, half wild."

"Half wild?"

Ty kept their gaze on the horse. "Sometimes when Polaris looks at me I think she still remembers when horses were all wild. The funny thing is, Archer's the one who was born wild and he acts like a puppy dog."

"Does she like people?"

"Oh, yeah. She loves being groomed, loves pets, loves going on rides."

"Could I pet her?"

Ty seemed surprised at the question but nodded. "You know how to do it now."

Whether Polaris was as smart as Ty claimed or not, she was gorgeous. But the "half wild" comment was hard to get past. Still, Leslie wanted to pet her. She stretched her hand out and Polaris sniffed her fingers. Slowly she raised her hand to pet Polaris's head. Unlike Nellie, Polaris stood in place, still as a statue. "She's beautiful."

"Yeah, and she knows it."

Her cinnamon-brown coat caught the warm morning light and contrasted stunningly with her jet-black mane and tail. But it was her eyes that Leslie couldn't get over—holding her own with a disquieting intelligence. She only breathed out when Polaris broke the stare and swung her head back to her breakfast.

"Nicely done," Ty murmured.

"I want to be a horse person," she said, surprising herself. "I wish I was more confident around them."

"I could give you lessons."

She turned to look at Ty. They seemed serious about the offer. She'd only made the comment as an offhand thing but now the idea of lessons took hold. She looked from Polaris—who truly did scare her—to Archer, who wasn't scary at all. At least not while he was eating. And then she looked at Nellie. Her chest felt tight when the old mare lifted her head and met her gaze. Something drew her to Nellie but she didn't know why.

"If you decide to become a horse person, that one could really use a friend." Ty nodded at Nellie as if guessing Leslie's thoughts. After a moment, they said, "How are you after everything yesterday?"

Leslie met their gaze, then smiled at Olivia who was still in Ty's arms happily chewing on a piece of hay. "I'm…" *Adjusting to the new reality where I want horse lessons from my ex-online lover?* She shook her head. "I'm fine. How are you?"

"I feel better with everything out in the open." Ty looked at Olivia. "Want to see if we got any eggs?"

Ty walked over to the chicken coop, deftly switching Olivia to one hip as they opened the nesting box lid. "Look at all those eggs. Who's having breakfast with me?"

Leslie couldn't help coming forward to peek. Ty reached into the nesting box and plucked up an egg, then handed it to her. It was still warm, and she couldn't help thanking the chicken who clucked at her.

Ty chuckled but didn't tease. They handed Olivia the next egg and said, "Don't drop this."

"Were you serious about breakfast? I saw some frozen waffles in the freezer, and there's sausage too."

"Oh, I was joking. I don't want to impose." Ty gathered the rest of the eggs and closed the nesting box lid.

Leslie held out her hands to take the eggs. "You wouldn't be imposing. Olivia likes company."

Ty looked from Olivia, who was still contemplating her egg, to Leslie. "You sure?"

Ty seemed to be asking about more than breakfast. Did she want to share another meal? Did she want to go forward on whatever path they were heading? Or did she want to say goodbye now and close the chapter on Hitch and Girl-Monday for good?

"I'd like it if you joined us for breakfast."

Ty's nod was decisive. "Give me five minutes to finish up my chores."

Olivia refused to let go of Ty, and rather than make her cry, Ty decided to simply do the chores with her. With a baby in their arms, the chores definitely took longer than five minutes but Leslie found it entirely entertaining: Olivia mimicking Ty as they shooed the cows out to the back pasture, Olivia trying to stick her egg in the water stream while Ty filled the troughs, Olivia babbling continuously while Ty led Polaris and Archer to the front pasture.

There was something undeniably sexy about how effortlessly Ty worked around the animals. Ty didn't seem one bit thrown off with a nine-month-old in tow, and their quiet competence made her think of Hitch. In some ways, they were entirely different—

one humble and quiet, the other cocky and outgoing. But there was a layer of friendly confidence and openness to both. She thought of how Hitch had willingly let her be in charge. Not because they couldn't be, but because it was what she wanted. If only she was as sure of what she wanted now.

CHAPTER ELEVEN

When Ty had finished the barn chores, they all headed up to the house. Olivia insisted on staying in Ty's arms, which left more opportunity for Leslie to overthink everything. Breakfast definitely felt like a step down the getting-to-know-you-better path. And the truth was, that's exactly the path she wanted to take. But she didn't want to lead Ty on, and until last night, she would have argued she was solidly against the idea of a relationship with anyone. Nothing in her busy world had changed—except for Ty crashing into it.

"Any word from Paige and Seren?"

"Not yet. I was planning on calling them at nine." She held the kitchen door open for Ty and Olivia, avoiding eye contact when Ty stepped close to squeeze past her. Her cheeks got warm as she fought the impulse to touch Ty's arm. She needed a moment to think. What she didn't need was for her libido to kick into overdrive.

"I hope Paige's mom is okay."

"Me too." She'd nearly forgotten about Paige's mom being in the hospital.

Ty took Olivia over to the kitchen sink and helped her wash up. When they'd finished, Ty dried both their hands and Ollie's, then straightened up and said, "Tell me how I can help."

Her center clenched involuntarily and she felt her arousal drip between her legs. *Oh, jeez.* She cleared her throat and said, "Want to look for the waffles and the sausage?"

She washed the eggs they'd collected, while Ty poked around in the freezer. "Waffles are up there in my list of favorite foods," Ty said.

"Same. But I like real waffles. Not the freezer kind. I almost never have them—except on my birthday."

"When's your birthday?"

She was about to break open one of the eggs but paused. "Next Friday. I'm not ready."

"Success." Ty held up a box of waffles and a package of sausage links. "I love birthdays. I'm always ready for mine."

"You're still young."

Ty lifted a shoulder. "I turn thirty-six on my next birthday. Compared to most of my vet school friends, I'm ancient."

Why had she thought Ty was younger than that? Because Hitch had seemed young? Four years difference wasn't much... Leslie silently berated her mind for sliding back to the possibility of a relationship. "Why do you like birthdays so much?"

"Well, I love cake. But mostly I like having one day out of the year to do whatever I want. You know, you get to do something that makes you happy and tell people to eff off if they don't like it."

"I like that philosophy."

Ty grinned and opened the box of waffles. "So besides waffles, what else are you doing for your birthday?"

"I've got meetings all day. I was going to try to take the day off but it didn't happen."

"If you could have it off, what would you do?"

Leslie considered the question as butter melted on the pan. She added the eggs while Ty got out a skillet for the sausage. The fact that she had no plans wasn't something she wanted to admit. "I'm not really a party person. And I almost never take vacations...I guess it'd be nice to have a spa day. Play hooky from work and send all my calls to voice mail. Maybe get a massage. Or maybe take a drive to the coast and spend the afternoon at the beach. Honestly, even going to see a movie in the middle of the day sounds decadent."

"Have you ever taken your birthday off?"

"Not in a long time. Not since I've had a real job, anyway. What about you?"

"I always take my birthday off."

Leslie narrowed her eyes. "Okay, since you're the pro, what would you do?"

"If I was me, or you?"

Leslie pointed to Ty.

"Trail ride. Always."

"But you do that on days that aren't your birthday too, right?"

"Yup. And I love it."

"You win." Leslie smiled. "I don't have any plans for my birthday other than too many meetings."

"Could you do something for your birthday after the meetings?"

"I could, but I'll probably just work."

"If you had to do something to celebrate, what would it be? Pretend it's the rules. Everyone has to do something for fun."

"I don't have time for fun."

Ty chuckled. "All right, grumpy, is there something un-fun you'd like to do to commemorate surviving another year?"

Leslie rolled her eyes. "I'm not grumpy. A workaholic, maybe. Boring, also possible."

"I know you aren't boring. I've seen you vault through bathroom windows. And I know other things you like to do too." Ty waggled their eyebrows. A real waggle. Leslie couldn't help laughing, which only made them do it again. "Come on—what's one thing you'd like to do on your birthday that isn't work?"

"Hypothetically?"

"Sure. But it has to be something you wouldn't normally do. Like, no fair saying you'd have dinner and watch TV. Or go to bed early."

Leslie laughed. "Ouch."

"You're the one who said you were boring."

"Okay, fine. Something different..." She thought for a minute. "Maybe I'd go white water rafting. I've always wanted to do that." But going solo didn't sound like much fun. "Or maybe I'd be really wild and take a horse lesson."

"A horse lesson?"

Ty's surprise only bolstered Leslie's resolve. "Yeah. Why not?" She scooped the eggs from the pan and waggled her eyebrows at Ty. "Someone I know offered."

"Are you serious? Because if so, I'm in. We could even do it next Friday on your birthday. After your meetings, of course."

So much for hypotheticals.

"Archer is perfect for someone new to horses." Ty flipped the sausage onto a plate and added, "All he can do is walk, but he loves people and loves getting out on the trail."

"Why can he only walk?"

"Old injury. He can trot, but he'll come up lame the next day."

"So he wouldn't take off running?"

"Even if he could run, he wouldn't. He's like a senior dog who likes to take it slow and sniff everything."

"Does being ridden hurt him?"

"No, and it's good for his back muscles to stay in shape. You really thinking about it?"

It would mean more time getting to know Ty—which she wanted—but she hadn't figured out if it was a good idea. Still, she wanted to say yes. "Maybe it's crazy, but…why not?"

Ty's smile widened. All the things they'd said and done together and she'd never known how amazing Ty's smile was. She felt her chest tighten and had to look away. No getting caught up in thinking how nice it'd be to bring that smile out more.

"Archer's gonna be happy to get more attention."

"What about Nellie?" Leslie asked. "Could we take her out too?"

"I'd have to ask Paige. I'm not sure how Nellie is on the trail. It's hard enough convincing her to leave her paddock."

"Last night I was thinking about how you said she won't spend time with the other horses. I feel bad she's alone so much." Leslie paused. "I know Seren and Paige are busy and don't have a lot of time. She came with the barn, you know. When they bought the place, the old owner left her. I don't have time to take on a horse but…"

"But you're thinking about it? You know, that's the first step to having horses take over your life." Ty laughed. "How about we start you out with Archer and see how things go?"

"Okay."

Ty's smile warmed her all the way through. She pushed away worries about all the ways it could go wrong and settled in for breakfast.

CHAPTER TWELVE

Ty dropped into the armchair closest to the door. Dog hair darkened the cushions and one of the house cats had shredded the armrests down to the wood, but it was still comfortable. It was also the only seat available.

Friday nights were Jenna's house party night. Through the school year there'd often be a crowd of at least twenty regulars. Fortunately, since it was summer, there were fewer than a dozen. Still, Ty wasn't in the mood for a party. It'd been a long hard day, and the only thing that sounded like a party was a shower and a bed. Along with a fantasy about Leslie.

Jazz appeared, brushing against Ty's legs. "Hey, troublemaker," Ty said, scratching under the tabby's chin. "What did you destroy today?"

Jazz purred happily, probably considering all the items she'd taken out. She was only a year old and still full of mischief, which made her the bane of Calamity Jane's existence.

Calamity Jane was the border collie in charge of the household—two cats, one Chihuahua, three vet students, one college student, and fosters that came and went on a weekly basis. She was currently on cleanup duty, scouring the floor for any chips that had dropped and licking beer bottles when she thought no one was looking.

"Hey, Holly? Your dog's licking your beer," Ty said.

Holly grumbled, picking up the bottle and swiping the opening with her hand. She shook her finger at Calamity. "I love you, but you're a naughty dog."

Calamity wagged her tail low in response and then looked back at Ty as if to say, "Why'd you get me in trouble, man?"

"Turn up the volume. This is my favorite," Allie said. She teetered toward Ty's chair and handed them Penelope before climbing on top of the coffee table. Penelope settled into Ty's lap with an exaggerated sigh. The Chihuahua always seemed over the antics of the vet students she had to live with, and when Ty pet her head, she half closed her one eye.

"You sure it's a good idea for you to be dancing on the furniture?" Holly asked.

"This isn't even a dancing song," Jenna said, but she turned up the volume anyway.

"Everything by Rihanna is a dancing song," Allie argued. She was in the same class as Ty and Holly and spent enough time at the house to have a toothbrush in the common bathroom. When she launched into an interpretive dance, the others laughed.

"What makes any song a dance song?" Holly asked.

As the others argued over beat and tempo, Ty wondered if Leslie danced. Questions about Leslie had taken over their mind—even more than the fantasies, which had been plentiful. They scanned the room now, wondering what Leslie would think of the world they lived in. No doubt it was completely different from hers.

"Can you all give it a rest and agree Rihanna is not only gorgeous but has an amazing voice?" Allie swayed as she motioned to make her point. "And Eminem is damn lucky she included him on this song."

"Fine, but could you get off the coffee table before you fall and break something?" Jenna held out her hand. "We used up the last of our bandage material when Calamity got into that tussle with the raccoon. If you hurt yourself now, you'll be at the mercy of a human doc."

"Wouldn't be the worst thing," Allie said, dipping into Jenna's arms.

It was clear those two were high. Whether or not the others were as well, or just drunk, was hard to say. Most of Jenna's friends—the other fourth years—looked more exhausted than anything else. Clinics had started for the fourth years and they were all running on too little sleep and too much caffeine.

Zoe, though, was sober. Ty knew that by the fact that she had her notebook out and was intermittently flipping pages, scribbling notes, and glancing at her phone. Oscar, the cat who'd adopted the house, kept trying to get her attention by rubbing his cheek against her hand. Although he was taking up most of her lap, she hardly seemed to notice. *Three weeks till Tevis.* Ty could almost read Zoe's mind worrying over the logistics.

A new song started and Allie headed for the coffee table after a swig of Jenna's beer. "Turn it up again. This one's my favorite too."

"The last three songs were your favorites," Holly said. "You can't have that many favorites. And I'm with Jenna on this—I don't think it's a good idea for you to be dancing on tables."

Allie blinked like it took a minute to process Holly's words. Jenna only shook her head. "Who's buying the booze next week? We're almost out of beer and Holly finished off the last bottle of wine."

"I had help." Holly pointed at Jenna. "When did you last buy the booze, Jenna?"

Jenna ignored the question. "I think it's Ty's turn."

"Ty hasn't been here for the last three parties," Zoe said. Ty hadn't been sure Zoe was even listening and was surprised she'd piped up. Going against anyone wasn't usually her thing.

"I don't mind buying," Ty said, catching Zoe's eye. Was she on edge because of Tevis, or something else?

"Where have you been anyway, Ty?" Allie said, leveling her gaze on Ty like she'd just realized they'd joined the party. "I feel like we haven't seen you in months. We missed you."

"Did we?" Jenna threw a wink Ty's direction but that didn't mean the question was completely rhetorical. Things between them had been strained since Jenna asked Zoe out. Zoe had turned her down, but the fact Jenna had asked pissed Ty off. Jenna was the only one on the lease and unofficially in charge, which put Zoe in a bad spot saying no.

"Yeah, where have you been, Ty?" Holly asked.

"Work. I keep getting called in for extra shifts at the equine barn."

"And Ty's helping me get Polaris ready for Tevis," Zoe said.

Holly straightened up. "Shit, I forgot about Tevis. That's the endurance ride in the Sierras right?"

Zoe held up her notebook. "The one I'm not stressing about at all."

"This is the hundred-mile race?" Holly asked.

"In one day." Zoe sighed heavily.

"Why would anyone do that to themselves?" Allie shook her head, which only made her sway more precariously.

Zoe ignored Allie and looked at Ty. "I want to ride the section near the fairgrounds again. Could you come with me? Maybe next Friday?"

"You can't miss next Friday night's party," Jenna said. "We're renting a mechanical bull."

"Where are you setting that up?" Ty almost didn't want to ask, instantly imagining a mechanical bull taking over the kitchen.

"The garage. You and Zoe will probably show us all up since you two ride."

"We don't ride bulls," Ty and Zoe said in unison.

"Wild mustangs aren't that different, are they?" Jenna laughed.

Zoe shook her head. "It's a good thing you're on the small animal track, Jenna."

Jenna held up her beer as a salute. As much as it annoyed Ty, it didn't seem to bother Zoe that Jenna was still flirty with her. Ty wanted to confront Jenna, but Zoe swore it was no big deal and acted like the offer hadn't happened.

"We could do a ride Wednesday instead of Friday," Zoe said, tapping her pencil against her notebook.

"Sure. I can't do Friday anyway."

"But you'll be here for the bull, right?" Allie asked.

"No. I've got something else I have to do." Next Friday was Leslie's birthday and Ty didn't want to plan anything else for that day.

"You're going to miss the bull?" Holly stared Ty down from the couch across the room. "What could you possibly be doing that's more fun than a mechanical bull?"

"It's just…a thing."

"What sort of thing?" Zoe squinted at Ty.

"A horse lesson."

"Hold on." Zoe sat up straighter. "Who are you giving a lesson to?"

"I could teach a riding lesson." Allie thrust her hips, and everyone in the room groaned.

"It's not a riding lesson."

"Isn't riding kind of the point of a horse?" Jenna looked around as if expecting backup. "What else do you do with them?"

Zoe pursed her lips and Ty knew exactly what she was thinking. *A horse person would never ask that.*

"Is this someone we know?" Holly asked. "You're being weirdly suspicious, Ty."

"It's someone who wants to take lessons so she can get comfortable around horses. She's scared of them. That's all." Ty hoped that would be enough to stop the questions.

Holly gasped. "Holy shit. It's Sasha, isn't it? I heard she passed out in the middle of the equine barn when some mare reared up in front of her. Okay, I'm honestly impressed you finally talked to her."

"You asked Sasha Bertrand out?" Jenna shot Ty a look of amazement. "Nice job. She's fucking hot."

"It's not Sasha." Ty had admitted—aloud—to thinking Sasha was attractive the first month of vet school, but she had nothing on Leslie. "This is someone you all don't know. I met her when I was house-sitting for Dr. Dannenberg."

Since Paige Dannenberg often took vet students with her on farm calls, she was fairly well-known. Leslie, fortunately, wasn't a vet. Which meant no one knew her.

"I know who it is." Zoe snapped her notebook closed. "It's the realtor."

"The realtor whose card is on our fridge?" Holly asked.

"Ooh, I saw that card," Allie said. "She's pretty."

Jenna slapped Ty's shoulder. "Congrats. She's not Sasha, but I totally gave that realtor's pic a second look. She's hot."

Zoe was the one who'd jokingly stuck Leslie's business card on the fridge with a little heart magnet. Ty had thought about taking the card down but hadn't wanted to.

"I can't believe you asked her out," Zoe said. "After everything."

"I didn't ask her out." Ty's cheeks felt hot. They hoped Zoe wouldn't mention how they knew Leslie. "She wants a horse lesson and Archer will be perfect for her. I haven't really used him for lessons because of his leg, but—"

"It's not a date?" Zoe leveled her gaze on Ty's.

"No."

"You're saying you're not into her and it's only a horse lesson?" Zoe arched an eyebrow when Ty didn't answer right away.

"Ty, do you offer riding lessons on your dating profile?" Holly asked. "Maybe I could get a date if I got a horse."

Before Ty could defend themself, Jenna said, "Who's keeping count of the number of women Ty's been with in the last six months?"

"I'm in charge of whose turn it is to clean the kitchen," Holly said. "But I would like to know how Ty finds all these women."

"This isn't like that," Ty said.

"I haven't had sex since New Year's Eve two fucking years ago," Holly complained. "Throw me a bone here, Ty."

As the others laughed, Ty said, "I really don't go on that many dates."

"But you sure as hell hook up plenty," Holly returned, getting more laughs.

The hookup jab was deserved. Ty couldn't argue with that. After everything ended with Hitch and Girl-Monday, they'd set up a profile on a dating app. That was sometime in March. Two days after setting up the profile, they got an offer for a hookup. The woman was pretty and funny. Unfortunately, as soon as they met, it was clear there was no chemistry. The woman wanted to have sex anyway and Ty had gone along with it.

The whole experience had been a mixture of sad and freeing. Sex hadn't gotten their mind off Girl-Monday completely, but it'd helped. And they realized they'd learned things from Girl-Monday. They knew what to say. They knew how a woman wanted to be won over. They knew how to give pleasure. Girl-Monday had been coaching them for months.

The sex was little more than scratching an itch, but it had been good for their ego to have someone want them—even if only for that. The next match had been a little better but still no real connection. They tried again and their confidence grew with the next woman who messaged. And the one after that.

"Which dating app are you on, Ty?" Holly asked, scrolling on her phone.

"I'm not on any dating apps anymore. I got tired of having sex with people who felt like strangers." Finding a connection like what they'd known with Girl-Monday had seemed impossible. "I know most of you didn't know me when I had a serious girlfriend, but before vet school—"

"There was a time before vet school?" One of the fourth years had spoken up. He looked over at Jenna and said, "Do you remember that?"

"Nope." Jenna grinned and tipped back her beer.

"I'm not done talking about Ty's date," Allie said.

"It's a lesson," Ty argued.

"Mm-hmm. You're going to teach her all sorts of things?" Allie grabbed Jenna's beer and ran her tongue over the opening.

"Gross." Holly laughed and tossed one of the throw pillows at Allie. "I'm so horny I actually think that looks hot—which is all sorts of messed up. Ty, if you and this realtor don't hook up, want to give her my number?"

"It's a lesson. We're not hooking up."

"What I want to know is, how often does the pickup line 'Want to come ride my horse?' work?" Jenna asked, a glint in her eye.

Ty shook their head. "Can we go back to talking about the mechanical bull?"

"Just be careful, Ty," Zoe said. "I know you're into her."

Ty wanted to argue they knew what they were doing. If Leslie wanted anything at all beyond a lesson, it wouldn't be something serious. She'd been clear about that the first time she'd messaged Hitch. She hadn't said anything specific, but she'd mentioned an engagement gone wrong and never wanting to go through it again. She'd also said work was her priority and that she didn't want to make time for a serious relationship.

"It's only a lesson," Ty murmured. Penelope licked their hand and they glanced down at the Chihuahua. "What? Don't you believe me either?"

CHAPTER THIRTEEN

Leslie paced in front of the restaurant. Her Thai food take-out order was getting colder by the minute, but this particular call couldn't be avoided. It wasn't a nervous buyer, or even an exhausted seller with too much to do, but a crotchety old investor she had to shake into the new millennia. A crotchety old investor who happened to be loaded.

"I understand what you'd like to offer, but it's not going to be enough. If you go twenty grand under their asking price, you'll lose the property. And I really think we need to go for a thirty-day close." Leslie resisted the urge to check the time as the investor droned on about cutthroat deals in the nineties.

"The market's a little different now," she said. Keeping the smile in her voice was easier when her stomach wasn't growling. When the investor brought up what he'd paid for properties in the eighties, she wanted to groan.

Finally, she cut him off. "Mr. DeCosta, this is your chance to get a sweet spot right downtown—you'll have renters lining up. If you give it time, your investment could double in this location."

More grumbling. The truth was, she'd take working with a nervous first-time home buyer over the Mr. DeCostas of the world any day. She'd half decided to tell him as much when he abruptly said, "Fine. Write up the contract."

No surprise, she'd be working late. Again.

Around the edges of work, however, she promised herself she'd at least open the document with her manuscript. The story—a cozy mystery with a realtor-turned-sleuth who baked cookies—was a long way from being a novel. She'd tossed it aside more than once, vowing never to look at it again. But over the past week the story had come to mind almost daily, nudging her with plot twists when she ought to have been focused on a sales meeting, and making her smile about the realtor-sleuth's budding romance with the interior designer in the middle of a spin class.

She knew it was Ty's fault. Telling Ty about the writing group and how that'd been the reason she'd joined TryItOnce had made her wonder what her writer friends were up to. Probably they'd all finished the projects they'd been working on while hers had faltered, sputtered, and died. She wasn't sure she could resurrect the story, let alone turn it into a full-length novel like she'd once hoped, but she'd loved working on it when she'd been writing regularly. Maybe she could love it again.

After collecting her order, she drove home and opened the door to find all three cats lined up in the entryway. Walter, the big orange male, Clementine, the tortie female, and Spunk, the spry black male and the youngest of her crew. She'd had two others— Lolita and Tommy, a bonded pair she'd gotten from the Humane Society—but they were gone now. It'd been almost six months since they'd passed, both within a few weeks of each other, and yet she still sometimes looked for them, forgetting.

"Who's hungry?"

Walter let out a wail and Clementine promptly swatted him in the face. Spunk came forward to wind between her legs while the other two argued. She had to scoop Spunk up before going any farther, giving him a good chin scratch. "At least someone loves me," she murmured. Although she'd never admit it, Spunk was her favorite. His affection knew no bounds.

She went to the kitchen, set down the bag from the Thai restaurant, and fed the cats. Her phone rang before she'd finished spooning the green curry into her bowl. Seren's name flashed on the screen.

"Thank god it's you. I was worried it'd be work."

"Happy to surprise you," Seren said. "Speaking of surprises, our oven called it quits today."

"Oh, that sucks."

"Not completely. Paige picked out a fancy new one but it's going to be a week before we get it delivered. Is it okay with you if we go to a restaurant for your birthday instead of having dinner here?"

"Of course. We said Saturday, right?"

"Yeah. I'm sorry we can't do it on your actual birthday. We've got to take Bea to a recheck appointment down in Stanford."

"Saturday's better for me anyway." She wasn't quite ready to tell Seren about the horse lesson plans. "How's Bea doing?"

"Better but grumpier. Her chest hurts and she caught a cold. I still can't believe they had to replace all the pacemaker leads and she had no warning...She can't drive on the pain meds and can't teach her water aerobics classes. She asked Paige to teach after I refused."

"Is Paige stepping in again?" Seren and Paige had met at water aerobics when Bea had broken her tailbone. Leslie still couldn't imagine Paige leading the class.

"She won't do it. I told her she might pick up another hottie and we could have a threesome, but she told me one of me is all she can handle in bed." Seren laughed. "So what's this I hear about you taking a lesson from Ty?"

"How'd you hear about that?"

"Paige mentioned it. Ty asked if we'd be open to them working with Nellie—with you."

Leslie bit the edge of her lip. "Yeah."

"Yeah? That's all I get? Since when are you into horses?"

"I've always liked horses. Remember all the posters in my room?"

"I remember the poster of JT." Seren made a smooching sound and Leslie laughed. "You had such a crush on him."

"Who didn't have crush on Justin Timberlake?"

"Oh, wait, I remember you had a Clydesdale on the door of your closet. That horse always reminded me of Fabio. All hairy and muscley."

Leslie laughed. "I also had a poster of a mama horse and foal over my desk."

"That's right! But I thought you were scared of horses."

"Well, I was. I am." She took a bite of the green curry. "I've decided to get over that fear. I'm wondering if my meds are working too well."

Seren laughed. "If you sign up for karaoke, we'll know it's the meds."

"Karaoke? No way. Never. But horses are something I've always loved. You're the one who said I needed to do something besides work all the time."

"I think it's great. Really. Whatever happened to that writers' group you were in for a while?"

Leslie poked at a piece of tofu. "I gave it up. I can't write. I was fooling myself."

"That's not true. You've always been amazing at telling stories."

"Writing is different. Maybe someday I'll try again." She sighed. "Actually, I was going to make myself read over the notes for that novel I started. The one I told you about where someone gets murdered in an abandoned house and the listing agent solves the crime?"

"Where she bakes cookies and falls in love with the beautiful neighbor next door who might be the killer?"

Leslie smiled. "You were paying attention when I was ranting about how awful my idea was."

"Of course I was paying attention, and it's not awful. I can't wait to read it. I also can't wait to see you riding a horse."

"I'm not sure I'll actually ride."

Olivia's cry sounded in the background. "I've gotta get Ollie in bed. I'll text you details about the restaurant."

Leslie was happy Seren hadn't pressed her more about the horse lesson. She hadn't lied, but she'd omitted a few things. Things she wasn't ready to talk about yet. Specifically, Ty.

She pushed away the question of whether she truly wanted to get into horses or simply wanted to spend time with Ty and pulled out her laptop. She settled in at the table with the bowl of curry, and with Seren's encouragement in mind, opened the document titled, "Cozy." She still needed a good title for the story. Something with a pun about murder or cookies or open houses.

After a brief review of the titles she'd considered, she jumped to the first chapter and read the scene when the realtor finds the dead body. It wasn't bad. The tone was right—not too scary—but the character seemed flat. *What did the character want more than anything?* That's what her friend in the writing group had asked.

To solve the murder? To make a really good cookie? To sell houses? To fall in love with the neighbor lady who might be a murderer?

She sighed and closed the document, knowing she wasn't ready to write the story. If she didn't know what her character wanted, what was the point?

Work wasn't as interesting as daydreaming about her story, but it paid the bills. With a deep sigh, she reviewed the property details for the investor client. When she'd finished that, though, she didn't start on the contract. Instead, she hovered her cursor over the file named "Hitch."

After a moment of misgiving, she opened the file. Saved screenshots of conversations with Hitch popped on the screen. When she'd taken the screenshots, she'd rationalized she'd use the scenes later for writing inspiration. She wouldn't use anything Hitch had written, of course. Only her own words. But now she knew she'd been lying to herself. She'd saved the screenshots not for her writing but because they meant something to her. They were more than snapshots of two strangers having online sex—it was a conversation where two people fell in love.

She read over the first image. It wasn't from the beginning of her chats with Hitch but it was the first one she'd saved. *I've been waiting for you*, she'd written. *You're late.*

Hitch had apologized and then asked what they could do to be forgiven.

"Start by taking off your clothes. Tell me each piece you take off." Leslie murmured the words aloud as she read them. Once Hitch was naked, she'd asked them to stand in front of her. She'd described how she'd reached out to brush her hand over Hitch's cheek, rubbing her thumb over lips she'd yet to kiss. Then she'd pushed Hitch down to their knees. They'd taken things over from there, settling between her thighs and dipping their head to slide their tongue over her center.

As Ty described sucking her clit between their lips, Leslie felt a surge between her legs again. *Hitch.* Not Ty. But she closed her eyes, reimagining the scene, this time with a clear picture of Ty in place of the fuzzy nonspecific person she'd used for Hitch.

It was Ty licking her until she was well and truly swollen. Ty making her ache with need. Ty who she roughly pulled up to stand in front of her. And Ty she finally kissed.

But she hadn't kissed Hitch in that scene, had she? She opened her eyes, out of breath and disoriented. She was almost certain there'd been no kiss. She scanned the words again and then the next screenshot in the queue, trying to recall when they'd finally kissed.

She read over the next several screenshots, feeling it all come back clearly. How hard it'd been to resist kissing Hitch. How she'd realized things had gone past writing practice. Early on she'd made it about the orgasm instead of the kiss:

I pull you up before you can make me come. I'm so wet, so ready for you. But I say when I orgasm. Not you. I take a step back from you—even though I know you want to kiss me. I can see it in your eyes. I point to the bed. Go lie down. I want to ride that strap-on of yours until you come.

She felt turned on all over again. How had she been so brazen? Could she ever be like that in real life? She'd never ordered anyone around in the bedroom. Never put herself first in the way she'd done with Hitch. That was part of why she'd felt like the online sex wasn't real. It wasn't who she was.

"Not who I've ever been, anyway."

Spunk brushed past her leg, making a purr-meow sound. She closed the computer and picked him up. He settled into her lap with a contented sigh.

"I wonder what you'd think about Ty," she mused, scratching his cheek.

With Spunk happily purring, and thoughts of going to her bedroom to pleasure herself now gone, she opened the laptop again and forced herself to pull up the DeCosta contract. Once more she repeated the same words she'd said over and over again that past year. "I need to focus on work."

Where had that gotten her?

"I'm making more money than ever," she murmured. Was that all? She had a new car and had nearly paid off her house.

She'd considered buying a bigger, nicer house, but this one was comfortable. It was home. The problem was, home felt lonely, even with the cats. "Maybe that's the problem? Maybe I need to get out of the house more?"

She felt guilty for the thought when Spunk looked up into her eyes. "I'd still love you even if I went on a vacation." She'd tried to think of where to go on said vacation—mostly on her office assistant, Kaitlin's, insistence—but hadn't come up with anything that sounded worth the time and money.

"I wonder if this is what a midlife crisis feels like."

Spunk turned his head to stare at her, his purr faltering for a moment.

"Do you think so?"

He blinked once, then yawned and pushed his head into her hand.

"You think I'm boring. I get it." She smiled. "Well, maybe I'll take up horses and be more exciting." She could work on getting over her fear at least, and it'd be something different. What she really wanted, though, was to take up Ty.

CHAPTER FOURTEEN

"I thought this was only a lesson," Zoe said, hands on her hips. "Why are you dressed up?"

"I'm wearing clean jeans and a shirt that isn't ripped," Ty argued. "This doesn't count as dressed up."

"It's a collared shirt, which counts as dressed up for you."

"Whatever." Ty wished Zoe would take Polaris for the ride she'd said she was going on. Leslie was due any minute and the idea of reintroducing Zoe to Leslie wasn't sitting well.

"What time is she supposed to be here?"

"Ten minutes ago." Ty ignored Zoe's look of disapproval. "She texted me to say she was running late. She had a closing on a house take longer than expected."

"You gave her your number?"

"She asked for it." Ty caught Zoe's eyebrow raise and added, "So we could talk about the plan for the lesson."

"Fine. We can pretend this is only her coming over for a lesson. Do you know what's up with the waffle iron?" Zoe motioned with her chin to the "kitchen" area of the barn. "Is Paige making waffles for the chickens now?"

"Little healthy waffles with cracked corn?" Ty smiled. "I could see that."

Paige took the barn animals' nutrition more seriously than her own—and admitted that freely. In addition to a wall of treats and supplements, she had a mini-fridge filled with more supplements and vitamins, a counter for mixing up rations, and a high-end blender. But the waffle iron wasn't Paige's. "Actually, it's from our house. I brought it."

"Why?" Zoe scrunched up her nose. "Are you thinking of moving in? Having breakfast in the barn?"

"It's a long story." And one Ty didn't feel like admitting. Zoe would definitely tease them for it. "Weren't you taking Polaris out? It's getting late if you want to get a good ride in."

"I want to give us both more experience in the dark."

"Where are you riding to?"

"The water tower. But I'm taking the long loop."

"You'll get plenty of time in the dark even if you leave now. I want to be home by eleven. I've gotta work tomorrow."

"So, if I'm not back by ten, you're coming to find me." Zoe stuck out her tongue. "Back to the waffle iron."

Ty knew Zoe would get the truth eventually. "Leslie mentioned she loves having waffles for her birthday."

"You're making her waffles for her birthday—even though this is *just* a horse lesson."

"Well, it's her birthday and this is the only thing she's doing. I figured after the ride, if she wants…" Ty's voice trailed. "Maybe it's a dumb idea. But I already made the mix and chopped up the strawberries. And I bought whipped cream."

"Oh, Ty." Zoe stepped forward and wrapped her arms around them. "It's not a dumb idea at all. You're so fucking sweet."

"Get off me," Ty said, laughing as they pushed Zoe away.

"This woman better not break your little heart." Zoe wagged her finger at Ty.

"I know what I'm doing."

"Do you really? We both know you're the pro when it comes to horses. But women?" She shook her head. "I've probably dated more women than you and I'm only twenty-three."

"You want a medal?"

She narrowed her eyes. "How many relationships have you had? Everyone in the house thinks you're this Casanova but I know you're always sleeping in your own bed by morning."

"That doesn't mean I'm not having sex."

"How many *real* relationships?"

Ty met Zoe's gaze. Did online count? It had felt real, but maybe it hadn't been. "Two."

"Two?" Zoe's tone was incredulous. "That's worse than I thought."

"Are you trying to make me feel bad?"

"No. I'm trying to make you see that you have to be careful. Leslie's not some nobody from those dating apps. You're already way too into her."

"Making waffles on her birthday doesn't mean I want to propose."

"You sure?"

Ty rolled their eyes. "I'm sure I don't have time for a relationship and I'm sure she doesn't want one either."

"She's told you this?"

Ty hesitated. Girl-Monday had said she didn't want a serious relationship. There was no reason to believe Leslie would feel any different. "I know if anything happens, it'll only be sex. And I'm not saying that will happen but—"

"You need to date someone who wants more than sex." Zoe's expression was set. "Someone who's interested in the long-term. Someone you can fall in love with. You hold yourself back and keep your heart in a box. You don't spend the night because you don't want anyone to see the real you. But the real you deserves to be loved."

"Can I say the same thing back to you but with Hallmark music playing in the background?"

"Asshat, I'm trying to be serious." Zoe laughed and shoved Ty's shoulder.

Ty stuck out their tongue but sobered a moment later. "It's not as easy for me as it is for other people. You're right. I don't spend the night and I'm used to keeping my heart in a box. But that means you have nothing to worry about. I'm not going to get too attached and let Leslie break my heart." That had already happened once.

"Okay. Maybe you're right. Maybe you know what you're doing with Leslie. But I'm going to say this again—she seems a lot more mature than you. I'm sure she's had more experience."

Ty ran a hand through their hair. "What are you saying I should do? Not make her waffles? This isn't even a date. I'm only being nice cause it's her birthday."

"We both know it's more than that." Zoe reached out and patted Ty's hair down, then sighed. "I can't stop you from falling for her, but I don't want you to get hurt. Also, selfishly, I need you to be on your game for Tevis. It feels like time is slipping away and I'm starting to freak out."

"I'll be on my game for Tevis. No matter what." Ty forced a smile. "What if I only make her waffles and skip the marriage proposal?"

Zoe shook her head. "I love you, cuz. Just keep your heart in that little box, okay?"

Ty made a square with their fingers and held it over their heart. "Happy?"

The sound of a car pulling up to the barn got Ty's attention and Zoe immediately piped up with, "Does she know she has to ask me for my blessing?"

Zoe was only mostly joking. "Weren't you leaving? If you want to take the long loop—"

"All right, fine. I'm going." Zoe took one step and then stopped. "It's sweet you're making her waffles. But I don't think you're ready to have sex with her."

Ty pointed to the paddock where Polaris was waiting. "Go."

Sex definitely wasn't in the plan. Ty was already too nervous about the evening. They went out to Leslie's car still debating the waffle idea. Would it come across as sweet or as too much? They waited for Leslie to open the door, wondering if a handshake or a hug would be more appropriate. What they really wanted was to kiss Leslie. Instead, they stuck their hands in their back pockets and only smiled. "You made it."

Leslie returned the smile. "I did. It was dicey there at the end, but my clients signed and we did the walk-through already so I won't have to do that in the morning." She got out of the car and exhaled. "It's good to be done with the day. Hope I didn't keep you waiting too long."

"Not at all." Ty scanned Leslie's outfit and wondered—okay, hoped—she'd brought a change of clothes. As nice as she looked in strappy sandal heels and a pencil skirt, it was completely the wrong attire for horses. "Did you want to change clothes? Or are you okay if that outfit gets dirty?"

Leslie glanced down at her shirt and then pressed her hand to her forehead. "I had a bag packed and I completely forgot it."

"Any chance you have other shoes in the car?"

"No. You must think I'm a total idiot."

"I'm thinking you've had a lot of other things on your mind and shoes weren't the important part." Ty smiled. "Happy birthday, by the way."

Leslie's face softened. "Thanks. You're the first person who's said that to me today."

"Seriously?"

"Don't worry. It's fine. Seren and I are going out tomorrow to celebrate—which will be nice. And my parents will remember at some point. But, more importantly, I successfully avoided telling anyone at work. Which meant no one sang to me and I didn't get one of those office cards with the dumb joke about getting older but not funnier."

"Is now a bad time to tell you I got you one of those cards?"

Leslie tilted her head. "I don't think I believe you, but…"

Ty laughed. "I didn't get you a card, but I may have a surprise for you later. It's small, I promise. And I won't sing if you don't want me to. Although I was planning on it."

Leslie smiled. "Thank you."

"For singing or not singing?"

"For making me feel special on my birthday." She held Ty's gaze for a moment. "I'm not sure what to do about my footwear, however."

"Right. That." Ty glanced at Leslie's sandals. They didn't have any old boots at the barn, but Paige might have something in the house that would fit. They reached into their pocket and pulled out a set of keys. "Paige decided I needed a house key. Maybe we could find you a pair of Seren's boots that will fit?"

"Too bad Paige didn't give you that key a week ago."

"No kidding. But she told me I'm now free to open the door for any ex-cheerleaders who are trying to climb in through her bathroom window."

She laughed and reached for the keys. "Give me a minute. I know right where Seren keeps all her shoes. I may borrow some pants too."

"If you're not ready to ride tonight, the skirt's fine."

Leslie arched an eyebrow. "I do remember you like me wearing skirts."

Ty felt heat shoot up their neck and settle at their cheeks. Fortunately, Leslie turned to head to the house and didn't see. A whistle behind them made Ty realize Zoe was still waiting in the barn. Probably she'd overheard everything.

CHAPTER FIFTEEN

The truth was, she had packed a bag with horse-suitable clothes. But she'd entirely spaced on needing boots. So maybe it was for the best that she could simply claim she'd forgotten the bag. At least she didn't have to explain how all week her mind had been taken up by the thought of the lesson and only a few times she'd remembered there'd be a horse.

When she had thought about it, she'd immediately pictured Nellie. The old mare's wary look struck a chord in her. She was drawn to her, even if it made no sense to try befriending a horse that was scared since she was scared too. But if she was going to have any chance with horses in general, let alone win over Nellie, she needed to rein in her hormones where Ty was concerned.

As soon as she'd seen Ty standing next to her car and looking like they wanted to reach for her but holding back, everything else blurred. Which is why she decided to keep the skirt on even if it looked a little ridiculous with Seren's boots. She could say it was a statement, but when she passed by the mirror in the hallway, she stopped short. Words Ty had written to her came back like she had the screenshot in front of her again:

My hand slides up your thigh. Under your skirt. I wait for you to nod. Then I push your underwear aside and find what I need.

The part at the end—*and find what I need*—was what had really gotten her wet. Now her clit pulsed with the memory and a blush rose up to her cheeks.

"Horse lesson," she said to her reflection. "I'm here for a horse lesson. Focus."

Ty was waiting for her on the back porch. She smiled and hoped the pink on her cheeks would be mistaken for her rush.

"That was quick. You found boots."

"I did."

"Great." Ty held up a rope. "We're gonna start at the beginning, if that's okay with you. This is a lead line. You can call it a rope if you want, but it's not a leash."

No kinky thoughts. "Lead line. Got it."

Ty clicked a halter onto the end of the lead line. "And this is a halter. I was thinking we could start with you learning how to put it on."

"On the horse."

"Yup. On the horse." The corners of Ty's mouth lifted almost imperceptibly. "You ready for the horse part?"

"I think so."

Confidence oozed from Ty, and when they looped the end of the rope, Leslie wanted to catch their hand and pull them toward her. She wanted to press her lips against theirs and find out if Ty was burning up with desire as much as she was. All the times they'd kissed online and she'd had no idea how much she'd really want it in real life.

"I promise this is gonna be easy," Ty said. "Archer's in the pasture. We'll go meet him there."

Ty led the way, bypassing the barn and cutting through the orchard. A big tree with a gnarled trunk and branches laden with green apples stood like a sentry next to the pasture gate. Sunlight filtered through the leaves but there was enough shade to make it a perfect spot to stop—and a perfect spot to second-guess the horse thing. Maybe they could simply talk about horses?

Ty whistled, and in the distance, a horse whinnied.

"I kind of thought everything would happen in the barn." At least at first. With the horse safely in a stall.

Ty glanced at her but didn't say anything. She felt her pulse quickening as she watched the horse-shaped object in the field get closer until she could clearly recognize the brown-and-white pattern.

"He's moving kind of fast, isn't he? I thought you said he only walks."

Ty nodded. "He's trotting. He won't do that if anyone's riding him, but he's excited to see us."

Great. "He'll stop before he gets to us, right?"

"Archer won't hurt you. He's as gentle as can be. And there's a fence between you and him."

She swallowed, knowing Ty had stopped at the gate for her. Knowing she'd be too frightened to go into the pasture. Maybe Archer was gentle, but he was coming up fast. She focused on breathing in through her nose, reminding herself of the fence.

"He's slowing down now. See it?"

Ty's words made her look at the horse. He had slowed down. He was still about fifty yards off but ambling now. Still, he was aiming right for her. "I'm worried he'll know I'm scared like Nellie did and react to that."

Ty shook their head. "You could have a full-on panic attack and he'd just stand at your side looking at you funny."

"That wouldn't help my panic attack." She watched the horse coming closer and when Ty murmured, "Breathe," she forced herself to do so. Thirty feet away. Twenty feet away. He stopped ten feet away and sniffed at a clump of dry weeds.

"Maybe don't think of him like a horse," Ty said. "Honestly, he's more like a brother to me. Or a fun weird uncle that chews on grass."

Leslie smiled. She couldn't help it. "So this is basically like meeting the in-laws?"

"The in-laws of the person you were having kinky sex with online. No pressure."

Leslie laughed, then met Ty's gaze. "You went there."

"I did."

She glanced back at Archer, picturing him in a little bowler hat because for some reason Ty's uncle in her mind would be sharply dressed and wear a bowler. Ty touched her arm. "You're doing great," they said. "Remember, I'm giving you the lesson this time. It's kind of like we're switching roles. You get to relax."

She wasn't relaxed at all with Ty's hand on her arm but at least she wasn't thinking about the charging horse. She wanted to turn to Ty when their hand slipped off her arm.

"Want to try opening the gate?"

"I'm not ready for a charging horse."

Ty's lips rolled into a tight line like they were holding back a smile. "Charging?" They pointed to Archer, who'd come another five feet closer only to lift his tail and let out a noisy fart.

"He was almost charging."

Archer opened his mouth wide, sticking out his tongue, and yawned. She couldn't help smiling. "I think he's making fun of me."

"Only a little. Here." Ty held out a baby carrot. "Palm open, like last time, and call his name. We'll keep the gate closed."

Leslie took the carrot and stepped up to the fence, heart pounding. She held out her hand and Archer came forward. His lips touched her palm and the carrot was gone a moment later, but he didn't step back. Instead, he stretched his neck over the fence and sniffed her shirt, then her face, then her hair. She'd tied her hair back low at her neck so he had to inch close until he was practically standing on top of her to get a good sniff. Thank god for the fence. When he didn't move away, she looked over at Ty. "Is this normal?"

"Archer's not exactly normal. But for him? Yeah."

She almost laughed when he sniffed the top of her head, his muzzle ruffling her hair. "I feel like I'm being inspected."

"You are."

But she wasn't scared. Or worried he'd bite. Something about Archer's almost clumsy forwardness made her forget all that.

"I think he likes how your hair smells."

Archer leaned forward another inch and rested his chin on her shoulder. She sucked in a breath. "This part's normal too?"

"That's how he gives hugs."

"Hugs?" Archer sighed and when she looked up, his eyes had closed.

"Want me to get him off you?"

"Well...no." Archer was too chill to really be afraid of. "Your weird uncle smells good."

"I think so too." Ty grinned. "He likes you."

She glanced at Ty, then back at Archer, not able to hold in her own smile. "I think I like him too."

"Ready to try opening the gate?"

She was. Archer took a step back politely, letting her and Ty into the pasture, then stood still, clearly waiting on her.

"Want to put the halter on him?"

At the question, Archer nosed the rope, then the halter.

"Can you show me how to do it the first time?"

Ty took the lead line and halter and ran through the steps, rope over the neck first, then halter held up to the nose. A moment later the latch was secured.

She squinted at the halter. "You make it look so easy."

"I've been around horses forever." Ty finger-combed a burr out of Archer's mane. "Archer's my third horse. Before him, I had my dad's old horse, Chico. And before Chico, there was Diva."

"Diva?"

"She was my brother's pony before she was mine and she was a total diva...I think I was four when I started riding her. I can't remember not riding, not being around horses." Ty took the halter off Archer and handed it to Leslie. "But this is your first time, so go easy on yourself."

Getting the halter on with Archer helping was easier than she'd anticipated, but she begged out of leading him to the barn. When they passed Nellie's stall, she had a moment of regret for not pushing herself more. If she was going to work with a scared horse, she needed to be the brave one.

Ty looped the rope around a post and patted Archer's shoulder. "Don't untie that, okay?"

"You have to tell him?"

"And he rarely listens. Want to say hi to Nellie while I clean Archer's feet? There's some more carrots in the fridge."

She went to the fridge and found the bag of baby carrots. "I hate that I get so nervous. I know that makes it worse. Any advice?"

"Try to act calm even if you don't feel that way. And don't move too fast or talk too loud. That makes any horse anxious."

She nodded and went over to Nellie's stall. The wary look was in Nellie's eyes again. Leslie glanced back at Ty, who had one of Archer's feet lifted off the ground and was busy cleaning out the hoof. "I don't think she trusts me."

"Probably not yet." Ty paused, setting Archer's foot down. "But she wants to. See how she's looking at you? She's hoping you're a friend."

And she wanted to be. She tried to transmit that thought to Nellie as she took a step forward. Nellie didn't approach the stall door, so she had to reach into the stall with the carrot in her palm.

"Want to be friends?" she asked softly.

Nellie studied her for a moment, then looked at her outstretched hand.

"Please don't bite."

"I don't think she will," Ty said. "Some horses do bite. Especially if you give them too many treats."

Leslie pulled her hand back and eyed Ty. "Are you serious or joking?"

"Serious." Ty moved to clean Archer's next hoof. "Too many treats can turn them into nippers, but you're trying to build Nellie's trust. One carrot or a cookie when you come to the barn won't be too much."

"I wish I wasn't scared."

Ty didn't look up. "Everyone's scared of something."

"What are you scared of?"

Ty finished cleaning Archer's hoof and straightened. Their brow furrowed like they were thinking hard. As the seconds stretched, Leslie said, "Okay, so, we've established you're fearless and I'm a wuss."

"No, there's lots of things I'm scared of."

"Not sure I believe you."

"I'm not scared of animals—unless they're trying to eat me or kick me or whatever—but I'm scared of plenty of other things."

"Uh-huh. What's one thing?"

Ty hesitated for a moment, then said, "I'm scared I'll fail out of vet school. I'm scared that if I do pass, I'll be a terrible doctor. Want me to keep going?"

She shook her head, stopping herself from blithely saying neither of those things would happen. By Ty's expression, there was no doubt what they'd admitted were real fears. Her heart seemed to fill her chest. There was no façade with Ty. Nothing hidden.

"Now I feel silly worrying about getting my finger bit off."

"You've got nice fingers. It'd be a shame." Ty lifted Archer's next foot without making eye contact and Leslie turned back to Nellie. The mare was standing in the same spot watching her. She thought of Ty's comment about her fingers as she stretched out her hand. Nellie came forward to sniff and she reminded herself to breathe when whiskers tickled her palm. The carrot was gone a second later.

"Good job," Ty said. "Now you can brush Archer."

From one test of nerves to the next. "Does he like to be brushed?"

"He loves it."

Archer bobbed his head up and down and Leslie smiled. "I think he's listening to our conversation."

"He does that." Ty got a brush, showed Leslie where to start, and then stepped back. "The problem with him—and most mustangs—is they understand a lot but that doesn't mean they'll do what you want. Mostly they do whatever they want."

Ty watched Leslie for a moment, scratching under Archer's neck. "How do you feel?"

"So far so good." She was nervous but she focused on the dust coming up from the coat. She knew Archer could startle at any moment, but his eyes were half-closed and he seemed even calmer than Ty, who at the moment was distractingly sexy, leaning against the tie post watching her.

"How'd you pick Archer?"

"I didn't pick him exactly." Ty shifted their gaze from her to Archer. "My dad had a friend who rescued mustangs. They'd brought in a big herd after a fire and all of the horses were in bad shape.

"Most went right to a kill lot. But there was this one colt my dad's friend was looking for someone to foster. I overheard my dad talking to the guy and I started begging. I just had this feeling..." Ty stepped forward and touched a scar on Archer's shoulder. "Archer was only a year old then. He was so skinny and covered in ticks. Full of cuts. My dad told me, 'Don't plan on him making it a month.' But he made it. I knew he would."

"What's a kill lot?"

Ty's face tightened. "Wild mustangs get rounded up and auctioned off. The ones that don't get sold at auction end up in other places. Not good places."

Leslie looked at Archer again, feeling sick at the thought that any animal—but especially one so intelligent—could end up in a place called a kill lot. "Why are they rounded up at all?"

"The big herds can be really destructive. Ranchers hate them. And when there's droughts or fires, there's nothing to eat. Horses starve to death."

"That's awful."

Ty nodded.

"How'd he get the scar on his shoulder?"

"My guess is he pissed off a bigger horse and got bit. It was a fresh wound when I first met him." Ty traced the scar. "As it healed, I thought it looked like a bow and arrow. I started calling him Archer, and it stuck."

"Your tattoo, that one," Leslie said, pausing to point at Ty's right forearm. "Is that the Archer constellation?"

"Good guess. Most people can't figure it out."

"I've been thinking about it for a week now." Leslie smiled. "The other one's harder."

Ty turned over their left hand, exposing the underside of both forearms and making the muscles tense under the tattoo. "I got the Archer first. When I was eighteen. My parents almost disowned me." They looked up and grinned. "Good thing they didn't know about the queer thing back then. This other one is the constellation for the Little Dipper and this last star here"—they pointed to the dot nearest their wrist—"is Polaris. The North Star."

"My parents still don't know about my tattoo." As soon as the words were out of her mouth, Leslie realized what can she'd opened. Ty's gaze swept up and down her body and then met her eyes.

A hot flush followed as she realized Ty must have imagined her body every time they'd had sex. Like she'd imagined Ty's. Even if it was virtual, they'd both thought about each other naked. She quickly looked at the horse, trying to ignore how her body buzzed. "Is this side brushed enough?"

Ty nodded. "Good job, by the way. It's like you're not even scared."

"I don't feel scared around Archer."

"Hang around him long enough and you might turn into a horse person."

"I'm starting to think that might be possible."

Lots of things seemed possible.

CHAPTER SIXTEEN

"Ready to get out of here?"

"Let's do it." Leslie smiled as Ty grabbed their cowboy hat and set it on their head. "You look good in that hat."

"Thanks." Ty's grin was sheepish. "So, we should talk about horse language."

Horse language… It was a quick deflection, but Leslie's mind didn't want to make the jump. She wanted to run her hand over the brim of Ty's hat. Trace the lines of their tattoos. Unbutton their shirt. Unbuckle their belt.

Ty led the way out of the barn, listing the signals horses gave. With the cowboy hat, dark blue jeans, a collared plaid shirt with the sleeves rolled up to the elbows, and boots, Ty was perfect fantasy material. Like their choice of pronouns, Ty really did seem to fall between the genders. It didn't seem to be a matter of sometimes being more like a guy, or sometimes being more like a girl, but simply fitting a space in the middle of the two extremes. Questions swirled about Ty's path to figuring out they were nonbinary.

"And when they swish their tail or stomp their feet. Although sometimes that's just flies."

"Flies?"

Ty looked over at her and smiled. "Am I talking too much?"

"No. Not at all." She stopped short from saying how much she loved the sound of Ty's voice. "Sorry, keep going. Flies."

Ty launched back into horse signals as they led the way through the orchard to the back pasture. When Ty unlocked the gate out to the trail, they paused for a moment and said, "How you doing?"

"Good." Perfect, in fact. "It's a lovely evening. Maybe the whole day was nice, but I missed it being in meetings and hurrying around..."

Ty smiled. "Or maybe this is the best part and you're here for it."

Ty's look more than words caught her. The whole scene was one she wanted to commit to memory. The sun sinking low on the horizon, Ty and Archer holding the gate for her to pass through, and golden hills behind them dotted with dark green oaks. Birds called to each other and the sound of branches snapping in the brush made her think of little animals scurrying home for the night. "I think you're right," she said.

"It doesn't happen often," Ty joked, leaning against the open gate. "You coming?"

Once they left the boundaries of Paige and Seren's ranch, they took a trail following a dry creek bed. It wound through a cluster of oak trees and then headed uphill. Since it was only a footpath, Ty suggested Leslie take the lead, but when the path widened Leslie slowed so she could walk alongside Ty again.

"It smells so good out here." She took a deep breath. "And the view's even prettier." The path had opened up on the crest of a hill and rolling hills stretched out in front of them. She looked down at herself. "I feel kind of silly in this outfit, but these boots are surprisingly comfortable. I might get myself a pair."

"You shouldn't feel at all silly in that outfit," Ty said, looking at her with a sidelong smile. "Besides, it's your birthday. You get to wear whatever you want."

She laughed and bumped against Ty's shoulder. "This is not what I'd pick for a birthday outfit."

"Birthday suit?" Ty grinned.

"We're not going there."

Ty sighed. "Yeah, probably for the best."

Leslie wanted to ask if Ty meant it but stopped herself. She gazed again at the view. "I can see why people hike."

"You don't hike?"

"In case it wasn't obvious, I'm not a rough-and-tumble girl." Ty laughed.

"Too obvious?" She smiled and smoothed her skirt. "I did buy a pair of hiking boots once. For a date."

"How'd the date go?"

"Let's just say the boots still look new."

"Hmm. Is walking a horse more fun than hiking?"

"Definitely more fun. The company's better too."

"Archer is good company," Ty said, deflecting again. "Ready to try leading him?"

Leslie bit the edge of her lip.

"Watch this." Ty swung the lead line over Archer's neck. The horse didn't move. Ty walked ten feet up the path and made a clicking sound. Archer looked first at Leslie, then walked past her to stand next to Ty.

She felt ridiculous being nervous around a horse that was so clearly tame. A toddler would probably be safe walking him. "He won't suddenly take off running?"

"Once upon a time he was the fastest horse on the trail. Now that trot you saw earlier is about as fast as he can go."

Leslie walked over to where Ty and Archer stood. "Okay. Teach me how to hold his leash."

"Lead line."

If she hadn't been watching, she would have missed Ty's quick smirk. "Right. That."

Ty reached for the rope and stepped up to the horse. "You stand on his left side like this. And hold the lead line in both hands, with the one end looped, like this."

Leslie took the rope from Ty, pushing away the impulse to take a step closer to them.

"Remember, the rope goes in both hands," Ty said. "And you gotta stand right next to Archer."

Leslie inched closer to the horse and looked down at the rope. How had she already forgotten how to hold it?

"Closer."

Leslie glanced at Archer. His eyes were closed so she pushed herself to move a half step nearer.

"Is it okay if I move you into position?"

Leslie nodded, trying to pretend she felt nothing when Ty stepped right in front of her. She met their gaze and her body tingled with anticipation. *No thinking about kissing.*

"You okay?"

She nodded again.

"Try to relax." Ty settled their hands on Leslie's hips. "You need to be this close." Leslie held her breath as Ty's hands guided her body. "Right alongside him."

Ty had to feel the energy zipping between their bodies, but they didn't move away. "Got it?" they asked softly.

"Mm-hmm." Ty had reduced her to head nods and grunts.

"Okay, then move your hand up the lead line so you're closer to his head." When she didn't move, Ty let go of her hips and reached for her hand.

Ty's hands on her hips may have short-circuited her brain, but when Ty's larger palm covered hers, rough calluses against her smooth skin, she knew she was in more trouble. Ty loosened her fingers and moved her hand into position, and all she could think of was how much she wanted to be in their arms. Their movements managed to be gentle even as they completely overpowered her defenses.

"You're holding your breath," Ty said.

She took a deep breath and exhaled. "Sorry."

"You don't need to apologize. Does this position feel okay?"

"It feels...complicated."

Ty cocked their head. "Complicated?"

She wanted to let hormones take over and couldn't believe she was thinking of going for a kiss while standing next to a horse.

"Maybe I can make it easier." Ty glanced at Archer and then back at Leslie. "Do you ever go dancing?"

"Not lately. Once upon a time."

"Leading a horse is kind of like dancing. Archer's your partner. You gotta pay attention to your partner—like when you're dancing with someone—and you gotta stay close enough to sense his movements."

"Do you dance?"

The question seemed to surprise Ty. They hesitated for a moment and then said, "I used to dance—or kind of jiggle my body, you know. At nightclubs when I was trying to pick up women. I'm not very good."

"At dancing or picking up women?" She smiled.

"Yes." Ty laughed and then said, "Don't stand too close or Archer might step on your feet. Like a distracted date." They reached for her hand again. "You moved your hand again. It's gotta be right here. Nice and close so you have control."

Ty's hand lingered on hers but they sounded all business when they said, "Your hand on his lead line is the same as when someone's hand is on the low of your back. You're the one giving direction. Leading."

She swallowed, wanting to feel Ty's hand settle into position on the low of her back. Archer, however, yanked her attention back to the moment by shifting on his feet. "I don't really like my hand this close to his face."

"You have more control that way. He won't bite. I promise." Ty stepped back. "When you feel comfortable, start walking."

She took a deep breath and looked at Archer. She had to trust him. And Ty. The weird thing was, she did.

CHAPTER SEVENTEEN

The meadow loop only took an hour, and they were home before Ty was ready. But dusk was settling in and Leslie had gotten quiet after taking Archer's lead. She was either too nervous to talk or wasn't having a good time.

When they got to the barn, Ty flicked on the lights and took Archer's lead line. They looped his rope around the tie post and handed Leslie a brush.

"More brushing?"

"Usually we do it after we take off the saddle as kind of a 'thank you for the ride,' but he expects a grooming even if he doesn't give anyone a lift. If you need to go, though, you can."

"Oh, no. I want to do all the things."

Leslie started brushing Archer and Ty wondered again about the waffle idea. *Maybe waffles are too much?*

"Thank you for tonight," Leslie said. "Walking a horse was a perfect way to spend my birthday." She smiled at Ty, then murmured a thank-you to Archer.

"Maybe next time we'll get you in a saddle."

Leslie rocked her head. "Let me think about it. I might just like walking a horse. All that stuff you were saying about horse communication...I didn't really take it in until I was holding the lead line. Then I started watching him more closely. And listening to him. He gives all these signals. It's like he's talking without saying anything at all."

"You got all that your first time? Pretty amazing."

"I think I've got a good teacher." Leslie stopped brushing and glanced toward Nellie's stall. The mare had her rump to them but her ears showed she was listening to the conversation. "After I get more comfortable with Archer, I really want to try working with Nellie."

"She might be a handful at first, but I know it'd be good for her." Ty glanced at Nellie and then back at Leslie. "Can I ask you something off-topic?"

Leslie's hand stilled. "Sure."

"Did you have waffles for breakfast?"

"I did not see that question coming." She smiled. "Sadly, I didn't have time. I was running late for my meeting and had to make do with yogurt and a fruit cup."

"How do you feel about waffles for dinner?" Ty went over to the makeshift kitchen and held up the waffle iron. "With strawberries and whipped cream? It's possible I'll sing 'Happy Birthday,' but I'll do it really quietly."

Leslie's smile spread across her face. "You're making me waffles here?"

"If you want—and if it's not too weird."

"It's sweet, actually."

"Good." Ty lowered their voice and sang, "Happy birthday to you..."

A blush rose up on Leslie's cheeks. "Wait. If you're going to make me embarrassed, I want to be eating waffles while you do it."

With coaching, Leslie led Archer back to his stall and Ty set about making waffles. The first one came out perfect. Crisp and golden brown.

Ty heaped on the strawberries and whipped cream, then carried the paper plate with the whole concoction over to where Leslie was sitting—on a hay bale with her legs stretched out in front of her.

"This smells amazing." Leslie sat up straighter and took the plate.

"Those are three words rarely heard in a barn."

"I love the smell of barns. This place in particular."

"The things I learn about you." Ty smiled, then went back to the waffle station and poured batter into the iron. "It's funny. We messaged each other so much but I feel like there's so many things I don't know about you."

"Yet," Leslie said. She seemed almost embarrassed and quickly added, "And same. We'll get to know each other better if you keep giving me lessons."

Get to know each other as friends? Online it would have been easy to ask. Or easier, at least. Other questions had been hard. Ty thought of how it'd taken weeks of messaging—and doing lots of other things—before they'd been brave enough to type: *Can I kiss your lips?* Leslie's response had been immediate: *About damn time.*

"You gonna try the waffle?"

"I was waiting for you," Leslie said.

"You're the birthday girl. Try it."

Leslie smiled, then forked a bite into her mouth. She closed her eyes and moaned. "Okay, I was going to say it was delicious no matter how it tasted, but this is perfect."

Ty watched her take another bite. She added another moan and Ty grinned. "That good, huh?"

"Better."

Ty wanted to kiss her then. Not a big romantic thing. Just a little kiss. A happy birthday kiss. A can-we-try-being-friends kiss. An I-missed-you-in-my-life kiss.

The thought of kissing Leslie warred with Zoe's advice. Truthfully, Ty was worried about getting close. As much as they wanted to feel Leslie in their arms, to press against her lips, the memory of having their heart stomped on hadn't faded completely. They were torn between knowing they could handle another rebuff and not wanting to go through the pain again.

Leslie got another bite loaded onto the fork and held it toward Ty. "You gotta try it."

"I'm making one of my own, you know."

"It might not be as good as mine."

Ty smiled. "Okay, fine." They leaned close and caught a faint scent of Leslie's perfume. They had to focus to take the bite, alarm bells ringing like a fire station between their ears. Leslie watched them chew and Ty tried to act nonchalant. "It's good, but I think you were hungry. It's not so good I'm ready to start moaning."

"Yeah, well you're the quiet serious type." Leslie shook her head like she hadn't meant for the thought to come out loud. After a moment she said, "I know this is too forward, and might not be fair to say, but I keep thinking about kissing you."

It wasn't a fair thing for her to say at all. But it was the best thing Ty had heard all day. They didn't know how to respond and instead went to the fridge and pulled out a bottle of beer. They'd bought extra to replace the ones of Paige's they'd drunk earlier—and for tonight. They popped open the bottle, took a long sip, and then handed it to Leslie.

After she had a drink, Ty said, "Considering all the things we did together, where's the line between too forward and not forward enough?"

"Good point." Leslie got another bite on her fork but then paused. "Do you ever think about the things we did? I mean, like after we stopped messaging. Did you reread some of the things we'd written to each other?"

"I thought about it plenty, sure. But everything we wrote was deleted after each session and you didn't want to exchange emails."

"I may have taken screenshots of our conversations." Leslie smiled almost self-consciously.

"Damn, why didn't I think of that?"

"I could text you some of the screenshots if you'd like. There are a few that are particularly good."

"I can't believe you kept them." Ty was more dumbfounded than upset. Actually, they weren't upset at all. Strangely, they felt proud. But they wanted to razz Leslie a little. "After telling me to forget your name, forget I ever knew you?"

Leslie ate the bite on her fork, then motioned with her fork to Ty's head. "That pretty head of yours didn't forget my name, so we're even."

"Pretty, huh?"

"Pretty. Handsome. Fucking sexy? All the above. When I think of how you used to start our conversations by dropping to your knees in front of me, and then I'd run my hands through your hair…I look at you now…" Leslie paused. "Real life's better than my imagination." She shook her head and added, "I can't believe I'm telling you all this."

"You used to say I made you drop your inhibitions."

"Hence me breaking my rules and calling you that night." She sighed and pushed another bite of her waffle onto her fork. "Apparently I didn't learn my lesson."

Ty wondered what to say. One minute Leslie seemed to be saying she missed what they'd done. Maybe even wanted it in real life? Then the next she was saying it'd been a mistake.

"I've been thinking of you being a writer. It makes a lot of sense. I always felt like my responses to things you'd say weren't adequate. You'd have all these descriptions and I'd have my hand down my pants and barely manage, 'mm, that feels good.'"

Leslie laughed, then met Ty's eyes and laughed harder. "You'd play with yourself while we were messaging?"

Ty wondered if she was serious. "That was the point, right? Didn't you?"

Leslie laughed again. "Only after we'd finish the conversation. I'd read everything over and then, well, you know. My vibrator was your tongue, or your hand or your strap-on." She stopped, looking as if she'd gone too far.

"That makes me feel better. I always wondered how you could type that fast with only one hand."

"Even if I could, I'm not good at relaxing while I write. I have to focus too much on what I want to say. And I second-guess every sentence. That's why I finally gave up on writing that realtor-sleuth story." She paused. "Don't get me wrong. When I told you I was wet, I wasn't making that up. And when we'd message each other, you helped me let go more than I ever could."

That was something at least.

"I think the other waffle's burning," she said, pointing to the makeshift kitchen counter.

"Oh, shit." Ty scrambled to get the waffle out while smoky steam puffed in their face. It was too late. The whole thing was a scorched mess. With a few more curses, they unplugged the waffle iron and carried it over to the chicken coop, scraping out the charred remains for the chickens. Even though it was past dusk, the hens rustled awake for the treat.

When Ty returned, Leslie patted the hay bale next to hers. "Sit. We'll share mine. This waffle's huge and you put half a pint of strawberries on it. By the way, when are you going to sing to me?"

Ty smiled, taking a seat. "You ready? Because I can do it whenever."

"I'm ready." Leslie held up a perfect bite—waffle with a slice of strawberry topped with a tuft of whipped cream.

Ty cleared their throat and then sang. When they'd finished, Leslie smiled. "That might be the best rendition of 'Happy Birthday' I've heard in a long time."

"I practice the song in my spare time." A moment later they added, "I'm kidding."

Leslie laughed and held the bite out for them.

"That's your bite. It's perfect and it's your birthday."

"It's perfect and I want to share." Leslie tilted her head, waiting.

Ty met her eyes, heart thumping fast in their chest. "I'd rather kiss you."

"I know. And I want to kiss you back. Which is why you should eat this bite instead." Leslie held the fork higher. "I haven't figured out if us kissing is a good idea or not."

Ty wasn't sure either. They took the bite, hardly tasting it as the possibility of a kiss hung in the air.

"When's Zoe getting back with her horse? It's getting dark." Leslie took a sip of the beer and passed it to them.

"She wanted to practice riding at night to gear up for Tevis— the big endurance race she's doing." Ty didn't want to talk about Zoe, didn't even want to think about horses. "If she's not back by ten, she knows I'll go looking for her."

"She has to do a race in the dark?"

"Part of Tevis is at night," Ty said. "You start at five in the morning and go until you finish the hundred miles—unless you get pulled."

"What do you mean by getting pulled?"

"Eliminated. There's mandatory vet checks and places where you have to rest your horse along the route. Most often teams get pulled out of the race because a vet's worried about the horse. But sometimes it's the rider who can't finish." Ty stopped and looked over at Leslie. "You know I'd rather be talking about other things."

"I know. I'm keeping us from making a mistake one of us might regret." She held out her hand, palm up.

Ty stared at Leslie's hand for a moment. "You want to hold hands while we talk about endurance racing?"

"I don't want to talk about endurance racing at all. I want to kiss you. Holding your hand is a consolation prize."

Ty placed their hand over Leslie's. As soon as their palms touched, a rush went through Ty. Leslie's fingers curved to grip their hand, her eyes tracking up to find Ty's. Neither of them moved and Ty didn't want to breathe. Leslie's hand fit so perfectly in theirs.

"This isn't bad for a consolation prize," Ty murmured.

Leslie held out her other hand and Ty clasped that one as well. Time seemed to slow. Neither of them spoke, but Ty realized there was nothing to say. Not now. They both had to figure out if there'd be a next step.

Archer's shrill call broke the silence. The sound of hoofbeats and Zoe's voice followed.

Ty pulled back their hands and Leslie dropped her gaze.

"I should go. It's late and I have to meet with a client first thing in the morning." She glanced around the barn but her gaze came back to Ty. "Thank you for the birthday waffles. They were perfect."

"You're welcome."

"Can I text you about another lesson?"

Ty nodded. It wasn't a date, but it was close.

CHAPTER EIGHTEEN

Seren looked up from her corner table and smiled, then stood to hug Leslie. "You look amazing. I love the dress."

"Thanks. You look good too. New tank top?"

"It's a nursing tank top." Seren made a sour face. "And I look like I haven't slept in months and forgot how to put on makeup. But I'm happy, so there's that."

"You're beautiful. And I'm not the only one who thinks that. Speaking of, where's your adoring entourage?"

"Adoring entourage, huh? I might start calling them that. Paige took Olivia for a walk around the block. She was getting cranky waiting. By the way, we already ordered drinks so you'll need to catch up."

"What are we drinking?"

Seren held up her glass. "I'm drinking a virgin mojito, but you should order whatever you want."

"How is it?"

"Actually, not bad. Wanna sip?"

The waiter came and Leslie decided to order the same. After he'd left, she turned to Seren. "I'm sorry you're not getting much sleep. Is it because of Olivia or Bea?"

"Both." Seren waved it off. "But I'm fine. Happy birthday, by the way." She handed Leslie a gift bag. "This is for you. Before you open it, I want to know how yesterday went. I chatted with Ty this morning and they seemed excited about you wanting another lesson."

Since Ty boarded at Paige and Seren's ranch, Leslie was going to have to get used to Ty being connected to more than one part of her life. Still, it caught her by surprise. Partly because she was still reeling from the moment she'd left Ty. She'd never wanted to kiss someone more and yet known at the same time she wasn't ready. "The lesson went well. I think there's a chance I might get over being afraid of horses."

"Ty said you did finally relax."

Leslie smiled. "Lots of things go better when we relax."

"Are we already making sex references?" Seren laughed and checked her watch. "It's that time in the evening?"

"I wasn't really thinking about sex, but since you brought it up…" She thought of what Ty had said about being okay if Seren knew what they'd done together. Hopefully, they meant it. "I need some advice."

"You need sex advice from me?" Seren sounded more than a little skeptical. "We both know you've had more experience, but if you want to talk about the perils of breast play while lactating—"

Leslie laughed. "I'm happy to know you and Paige are back at it."

"Back at it and then some." Seren sipped her drink with a smug look.

"This is more of a general 'should I have sex with someone or not' question." Leslie glanced around the restaurant. Fortunately it was still early and only a few tables were filled, none near theirs. Still, she shifted closer to Seren and lowered her voice as she asked, "Do you remember that group I told you about? The online anonymous sex thing?"

"How could I forget? If I didn't have Paige keeping me happy in that department, I'd be joining that group myself. Although I'm no writer."

"You don't have to be a writer. It's online sex. There's a low bar for spelling and no grammar rules. Basically if you can type 'I want you to suck my blankety-blank,' you'll have people messaging you back."

"Love it." Seren laughed. "And it's queer, right?"

"Queer and mostly women." Leslie paused. "A few trans men and some folks who are nonbinary." She was stalling, questioning whether she really should tell Seren more. But when she'd mentioned Hitch months ago, Seren hadn't acted weird. "There was this one person I got kind of caught up with. We were messaging all the time for a while."

"I remember. Lots of dirty talk and tying each other up." Seren waggled her eyebrows. "And sticking all sorts of things into all sorts of holes."

"Shh, you." Leslie laughed but checked to see if anyone at the other tables were looking at them. No one was, but her cheeks burned with a blush.

"Sorry." Seren lowered her voice and added, "Was it the sticking things in holes or the tying each other up part I shouldn't have shouted across the room?"

"It's a good thing I love you."

"What was the name of the person you were so hot on? It was something odd…Fetch?"

"Hitch." Leslie felt a rush simply saying the name aloud.

"They were nonbinary, right? Like Ty?"

"Yeah." She steadied herself. "And Hitch is Ty."

"Wait. Are you saying…" As Seren's voice trailed, Leslie nodded. Seren's mouth dropped open. "Did you know?"

"No."

"When did you figure it all out?"

"The night you and Paige went down to Stanford. When I was babysitting."

Seren leaned in closer. "Are you two still having sex online?"

"No. That all stopped that time we were going to have phone sex."

"When you called and forgot to block your ID! I remember that fiasco."

She still felt like an idiot. "Anyway, Hitch—Ty—remembered my name. And still was nice to me even after I screamed horrible things to them. It was not my best moment. At all."

"Honestly, I would have freaked out too." Seren pursed her lips. "Although I'm not sure I would have gone for phone sex with a stranger in the first place."

"Hitch wasn't a stranger. We'd been messaging for months." She shook her head. "I'd told them all these things. Secret sex fantasies, you know?"

"Kinky stuff."

"Yes. And then suddenly they were real and knew my identity."

"I'd have been nervous too. You never know about people you meet online."

"Hitch would never have said anything to anyone. I know that now. But in the moment, I panicked. It took me three days to calm down. By then, I couldn't apologize because Hitch—Ty—had dropped out of the group."

Seren whistled under her breath. "And now you're taking horse lessons with them."

"While trying not to imagine *doing* all the things we've already done."

"Wow. Okay. So you want to do sexy things with Ty?"

Leslie held up her hands. "I don't know. I think so."

"When you're with Ty do you feel a spark?"

"More like a fucking bonfire."

Seren laughed.

"I'm serious. I look at them and want to strip off their clothes. And every time they get close to me, I want to kiss them so much I can't think. It's bad."

"Then just have sex. You're overthinking this."

"But sex is going to be complicated now. The things I asked Hitch to do…" She stopped and shook her head. "And I shut them down hard after that phone call. I know I hurt them. Plus, I have no idea what I even want beyond sex. Do I want to play once and get them out of my system? Or do I want a real relationship?"

"You really don't know?"

Leslie lifted a shoulder. "I know I've been missing Hitch for months. I thought I'd get over it, but I didn't. And knowing Hitch is Ty…and that real-life Ty is sweeter and more attractive than I ever imagined Hitch would be?" She shook her head. "And I hurt them once and I'm worried I'll do it again. Especially since I don't even know what I want. I'm not in a position to date. You know my schedule absolutely sucks. And I'm not good in relationships. I've got issues. Plus Ty starts back in vet school in a month. I think their schedule is going to be even worse than mine soon."

"Your issues really aren't that bad. But the time thing could be a problem. Still, I'd like to see you happy, and Ty's a sweetheart."

"Tell me about it."

Seren's smile was full of sympathy. "You once told me that after you'd made 'realtor of the year' you'd cut back your hours. Maybe a relationship would make you cut back and take time for other things?"

"Maybe." Leslie sighed. "I do want to do other things besides work."

Seren pointed to the gift bag still on the table. "Open your present."

Under the tissue was a notebook with a glittery purple cover. "It's for you to write down story ideas," Seren said. "If you want. Or you can use it for your grocery list."

Leslie opened the journal and on the first page were the words: *One dark and stormy night...* She ran her finger over the words and smiled.

"Remember that game we used to play? I loved the stories you'd come up with."

Back then, she'd been sure she'd be a writer one day. In a dramatic voice, she said, "One dark and stormy night...I went to the grocery store for a turnip."

Seren laughed. "You always came up with the best first lines. After we talked the other night, I couldn't stop thinking about that novel you were working on. With the realtor-sleuth. Someday I want to read that story." She handed Leslie a business card. "The notebook is only something pretty that reminded me of us in high school. This is your real gift."

Leslie read the name on the card, not recognizing it, and then the title under the name. "Writing consultant?"

"She looks over outlines, reads drafts, and helps with the whole process. She described herself as a life coach for stories. I've arranged for you to have three sessions with her. She knows agents too." Seren tapped the journal. "I know you're thinking that publishing is a far-off dream, but I know you. You make things happen when you want them bad enough."

Leslie eyed the card again, feeling a mixture of hope and uncertainty. "Thank you. It's a perfect gift."

"Did I miss the food?" Paige asked, appearing at their table. Olivia was sound asleep in the baby carrier strapped to her chest.

"We haven't even ordered yet," Seren said, standing to kiss Paige. "Thanks for getting her to fall asleep." She looked lovingly down at Olivia and sighed. "She's so much work but so damn cute."

"This time she didn't fall asleep until we got to the park."

"But she's asleep without chewing off my nipple." Seren kissed Paige again. "Once again, you're magical."

"Hi, Paige," Leslie said. "I think you're magical too, but I'm not going to kiss you."

"Happy birthday anyway." Paige sat down carefully, managing not to wake Olivia. "Thanks again for babysitting last week."

"It was nothing."

Paige and Seren looked at each other and then at Leslie. "Sure," they both said.

She laughed. "Okay, it was a ton of work and I was exhausted, but it was also nice. I liked spending the afternoon at your ranch and slowing down for a change."

The waiter came back with Leslie's drink and after he'd taken their orders, Seren turned to Paige and said, "We do have a nice little ranch."

"The more time I spend there, the more I realize why you two love it," Leslie said.

"Speaking of, I hear you might want to lease Nellie?" Paige asked. "If you're serious, I'd love to have someone work with her a little more."

"I'd only do it with Ty's help."

"Of course," Paige said. "Ty's great with horses. Amazing, really. You'll learn a lot from them."

Seren met Leslie's gaze with an arched eyebrow. Yes, it was messy.

Paige continued, "I know Nellie's lonely. I've tried convincing her to hang out with the other horses but she won't. Cows are so much easier."

It was no secret how much Paige loved cows. Leslie didn't quite understand it, but Seren seemed smitten too. "I'm nervous about working with her but I want to try. And Ty will be there. They said they can give me lessons twice a week, at least until they start back in school."

"Once that happens, you won't see much of them," Paige said. "Between classes and work, they'll hardly have time to sleep. I can barely get them out to help me finish the barn projects now. In a few weeks? Forget it."

She couldn't help feeling disappointed. Even if Ty gave her two lessons a week for the next three weeks, it wouldn't likely be enough for her to feel comfortable handling Nellie alone. She'd assumed Ty would be able to work with her at least occasionally once school started. But if their schedule was as intense as Paige suggested, that wouldn't be happening. And then there was the question about dating. "Maybe leasing Nellie is a bad idea?"

"We won't hold you to anything," Paige said. "She'll appreciate whatever attention you can give her."

Seren tapped her glass against Leslie's. "Things work out in mysterious ways."

CHAPTER NINETEEN

"Would you relax? She's not even here yet." Zoe handed Polaris's headstall to Ty. "Make yourself useful and oil that for me."

Ty grumbled but reached for the oil cloth anyway. Having something to do would at least keep them from worrying about how the afternoon would go. "Polaris is looking good. I think that supplement you added is putting on some weight."

Zoe brushed a hand over the mare's withers with a critical eye. "She's still skinnier than I'd like."

"She looks good, Zoe." Polaris's coat shone from all the loving care Zoe had been giving it these past few weeks and muscles rippled under her skin. "Want to talk about who we're going to add to your crew with Johnny dropping out?"

"Did you actually think he'd come? I love your brother but he's a flake—like most of our relatives." Zoe shook her head. "I'll be fine with you and Paige."

"Paige can't spend the night and she's only available for one checkpoint."

Zoe shrugged. "And you'll do the others."

"What about asking that guy you were dating a while back? The one whose parents live in Truckee."

"I'd rather skip a checkpoint."

"What about Holly? Or Allie?" Between the housemates and all the vet students that hung out at their house for the Friday night parties, someone had to be available. "I bet one of them would be excited to help. Not many people get to crew for Tevis."

"You know who was excited to help? Jenna. But before you jump into overprotective cousin mode, I already told her no thank you."

"Why?"

Zoe dropped her shoulders. "Because I like her. I know you think she comes on too strong and dating someone who's my housemate would be hard. Mostly I agree with you."

Ty wasn't entirely surprised by Zoe's admission. Since the last party, they'd noticed Zoe and Jenna hanging out in the kitchen or on the couch more and more together. "If she really wants to help—"

"I don't want her help. It'd make things too complicated. I need to be focused on Polaris. I don't want anything pulling my thoughts off her, or the ride."

Ty couldn't argue with that.

"Besides, I really don't think we'll need anyone else. Plenty of riders do Tevis without a crew."

"Riders who think they can cowboy it alone are usually the ones whose horses end up getting pulled." Technically it was possible to run the show with only two people crewing, but the logistics and potential risks weren't insignificant. "If we had one more person… It would have been nice to have Johnny's help moving the trailer at least."

"I'll think about who else to ask." Zoe pulled Polaris's headstall out of Ty's hands. "In the meantime, can you stop pressuring me about it? I'm already stressed enough as it is. I can't believe it's in less than two weeks."

"You're ready," Ty said. "It's logistics at this point. How's your knee?"

"All better," Zoe said, not meeting Ty's gaze.

Ty studied her. She'd dropped more weight but she'd been running sections of the trail alongside Polaris. "You sure about your knee?"

"I'm sure." Zoe met Ty's gaze. "I'm not going for a win. I only want a buckle that says I finished."

Ty wanted the same for her and Polaris, but Zoe's competitive spirit had made them think they wouldn't be satisfied with that. "I know you can do it."

"I can't stop obsessing about things I might forget." She met Ty's gaze with a seriousness that wasn't usually Zoe and said, "I'm scared something like what happened to you and Archer will happen to me and Polaris. I don't think I'll be able to save Polaris like you saved Archer."

"Archer saved me, not the other way around." The sound of a car pulling up to the barn broke the silence. "That's Leslie." Ty put a hand on Zoe's shoulder. "I know you'll do everything to keep Polaris safe. And I know you're both ready for Tevis."

Zoe rested her hand over Ty's and took a deep breath. "Go have fun with your non-girlfriend so I can obsess quietly over my horse's gear."

Non-girlfriend. The phrase repeated in Ty's mind as they walked out of the barn but was gone with one look at Leslie. She wasn't in work clothes this time. Instead, she wore a black tank top with a pair of jeans that hugged her curves. The tank top dipped low and Ty couldn't help noticing her cleavage. They forced their gaze away from Leslie's chest and managed a greeting. "New boots?"

"I bought them yesterday. What do you think?" Leslie stretched out her leg, ostensibly to show off the shiny new black boots.

"They look good." Ty felt their cheeks get hot as they imagined running a hand up Leslie's legs.

"I wasn't sure if they were the right kind of boots for horses. The place I got them from mostly sold sexy country stuff."

"Sexy country stuff?"

"You know, for going to country music bars. Frilly blouses with rhinestones."

"Oh." Ty scratched their head. "Do you go to those places?"

She laughed. "No."

"I don't either."

"Somehow I'm not surprised." She laughed again. "You really think these boots will work?"

"They're perfect." Ty needed to stop staring at her legs though. "I talked to Paige and she's happy we're going to try taking Nellie out. I told her I'd be the one leading. You're okay with Archer, right?"

"By myself?"

"I'll be right next to you the whole time."

Leslie didn't seem completely comfortable with the plan, but she didn't argue as they made their way to the barn. Zoe had Polaris saddled and looked ready to head out on the trail, but Ty guessed she was taking her time waiting for them.

"Thought you'd already be on the trail by now," Ty said.

"Hi, Leslie," Zoe said, ignoring Ty and flashing a big smile at Leslie. "I hear Ty's convinced you to take up horses."

"They didn't have to try hard."

Zoe raised her eyebrows at Ty.

"What I mean is, I've always liked horses and I wanted to get over my fear."

"Riiight." She drew out the word, making Ty want to strangle her. Then added, "You look hot in those boots."

"Thanks." Leslie's cheeks colored.

"Weren't you leaving?" Ty asked.

"On my way out." Zoe winked at Ty—not at all subtly—and hopped into the saddle. Polaris pranced in place, every bit of her ready to run. "I'm going to let her go all out on the long stretch by the fire trail. I'll see if I can catch up to you two on the cooldown loop." She signaled Polaris and the horse shot forward.

In the blink of an eye, Zoe grabbed a shovel, swung it forward to knock open the barn door, and tossed it to the dirt. Polaris slid through the opening and the door clanged shut behind them, leaving only a swirl of dust.

Leslie's mouth hung open. "Does she do that often?"

"She's showing off for you," Ty said. "You should see her with a rifle."

"I don't know that I want to?"

Ty grinned. "She's more of an adrenaline junkie than I've ever been. Polaris and her are a good match."

"You don't worry that she'll get hurt?"

"Oh, constantly. Loving Zoe is the same as worrying about Zoe."

"Have you two always been close?"

"She moved in with my family when she was two. I was fourteen and didn't think I liked little kids. She won me over quick." Ty smiled. "Her mom was a total loser and her dad was even worse. But she was sweet as could be. Back then. Then she got older."

Leslie laughed.

"I thought I was a rebel as a teen," Ty said. "I had nothing on Zoe." They glanced at the shovel Zoe had discarded in the middle of the barn's center walkway and went to move it back to where it belonged with the other tools. "Some days she has so much energy, so much love for life. But other days she won't get out of bed. And she stresses about everything. Like things she said to people two years ago and…I don't know. Species extinction."

"I get it," Leslie said. "This world can be a lot."

Ty wondered if Leslie meant she understood the anxiety part or the depression part. Maybe she understood both. There'd been times when they'd messaged online that Leslie had hinted at depression being something she was dealing with. Their conversations had never really dived into that much, though, and Ty hesitated asking now.

"She's gotten better this past year. She started on antidepressants after she moved in with me. A little over a year ago."

"Meds can really help."

"She's way better than she was. But I don't know what part is the meds and what part is everything else. She's completely changed her life." Unfortunately, it was impossible to forget how bad things had gotten before she made the changes. "Zoe dropped out of college two years ago. She'd been living with my folks in Reno and working at a diner. Then, long story short, she got into drugs and her world kind of spiraled. My parents kicked her out. I tried to get her to move in with me, but she wouldn't. A year later she ended up in the hospital on a suicide watch."

"Shit."

"Yeah." Ty sighed. Archer made a similar sound, then pushed at his stall door. Ty walked over to him and rubbed his head. "You agreeing it was bad, huh, old man?"

Ty took a minute to rub the gelding's head before continuing, "She called me from the hospital and said she wanted to turn her life around. I think she was scared of what she'd almost done. I told her I had a horse for her to ride while she figured her life out."

"Polaris?"

Ty nodded. "She's always loved horses—grew up riding like me—and Polaris needed someone who had extra time. I didn't know how it'd go at first. For a while, she slept in my room on the floor in a sleeping bag and Polaris was the only reason she left the house. But she's got a job and she's back in school now. And she's happier than I've seen her in a long time."

"From the outside, she's doing amazing."

"Turned out, her and Polaris were good for each other." Ty stopped petting Archer. "That was probably too much information."

"As long as you think Zoe is comfortable with me knowing, it wasn't too much. And I promise you can trust me not to talk about it with anyone else."

"I know, but you came for a lesson and then I lay all this heavy stuff on you."

"I can handle the heavy stuff."

Ty held out Archer's halter and lead rope. "Can you handle the heavy stuff and getting Archer out of his stall?"

"I'm getting him out?"

"You wanted to make sure those boots were legit, right?" Ty smiled. "You got this. Just open the stall door, throw the rope over his neck, and put on his halter like you're the boss."

"Like I'm the boss." Leslie took the halter and lead rope but then stopped, eyeing Archer.

"If you want, you can watch me with Nellie first."

Leslie quickly nodded. "Yes, please."

"I've had her out every day this past week and she's been coming along nicely. Getting braver each time. Even walked as far as the back pasture fence last night."

"You've been working with her every day?"

"I wanted to make sure she was safe for you." Ty walked over to Nellie's stall and clicked. She looked up and gave Ty a little nicker. As soon as they opened the gate, she nosed their pockets for a treat. "No freebies today."

"It's sweet you've been working with her."

"She wants attention." Ty haltered her and led her out. She followed, more willing than ever. "I think maybe she's not as old as Paige was told. She's stiff from standing around in her stall, but I think she's closer to Archer's age."

"How old is Archer?"

"Twenty-two."

Nellie walked right up to Leslie and sniffed the halter she was holding, then searched her hands for a treat. "Good job not being afraid," Ty said.

"I'm terrified. I'm just pretending I'm not."

"I was talking to Nellie."

Leslie smiled and met Ty's eyes. "Of course you were."

"You're doing a good job too." Ty winked. "Ready to get Archer?"

"Yes." She turned toward Archer's stall and squared her shoulders.

Ty led Nellie over to the tie post, then watched Leslie. They studied her profile as she unlatched Archer's stall gate. Her dark brown hair was pulled back in a ponytail showing off the curve of her neck and the smooth tan skin of her cheek. Her snug jeans and boots may have been made for a country bar but were sexy as hell in a barn.

Ty looked away from her long enough to focus on Archer. He was trying to help, first pushing the gate farther open when Leslie hesitated, then nuzzling the halter when she stood frozen in his stall.

"Want help?"

Leslie shook her head. "I want to do it on my own. But it might take a minute."

"Take all the time you need. I don't know about you, but I've been looking forward to this lesson all week."

"Me too," Leslie said, not looking back at Ty. She took a step into the stall and Archer pretended to ignore her. "I'm going to put this rope around your neck, Archer, and then put on your halter. Deal?"

She walked up to him and swung the rope. Instead of going around his neck, the tip of the rope smacked Archer in the side of the face and then fell to the ground. "Oh, shit, I'm sorry."

Another horse would likely have thrown up their head, but Archer only opened and closed his mouth like he was unimpressed, then dropped his head to sniff the rope.

"Try again," Ty said. "But this time maybe just set the rope on his neck."

It took Leslie a while to get Archer haltered and out of his stall, but she seemed quite proud of herself when she tied the knot securing him to the post. "Don't untie that knot," she said, wagging her finger at Archer.

Ty smiled and held out a brush. "Here you go, boss."

"I think you make me brush Archer so much because it makes me less nervous around him. It's not about making him clean."

"Yup."

She shook her head and took the brush. "It's fine. I like brushing him."

"Good. You're gonna be brushing Nellie starting next week."

Leslie eyed Nellie. "How's she been doing with the grooming part?"

"Not bad, but I use a wash rag on her right side instead of a brush." Ty held up the rag. "I do think something happened to her—some old injury or someone whipped her. Nothing seems to hurt. It's more like a memory of the pain."

"Memories are hard to shake," Leslie said, giving Nellie a sympathetic look.

"Yeah, and it means more work for us to earn her trust." But Nellie was one group project they wouldn't turn down. Not considering who else had signed up.

CHAPTER TWENTY

Leslie agreed to lead the way on the trail. It was mostly Archer showing her where to go, but she didn't hesitate opening any of the gates and seemed almost confident walking at his side. Ty wished they could simply enjoy the view of Leslie and Archer but Nellie was a handful as soon as they passed the ranch's perimeter fence. She threw her head every few strides, balked at every shadow, and tried rearing when a sound startled her in the brush. She got more testy, even crow-hopping a few times, when they crossed onto the fire trail. When they finally reached the meadow, Ty decided she needed a break.

"Let's stop here and let them graze." Ty loosened Nellie's line and she lurched for a tuft of grass.

Leslie glanced at Nellie and then at Archer. He hadn't tried to go for any of the weeds, only eyeing her with one ear cocked back listening for a cue from Ty.

"You have to unclip his lead rope. I trained him not to eat if someone's holding his rope."

"Won't he run away?"

"Nope." When Leslie only pursed her lips, Ty added, "He won't go anywhere without us."

Ty sat down on a fallen log and slackened Nellie's line. She'd relaxed some with grass to think about but still twitched at every noise.

Leslie unclipped Archer's rope and then stepped back, seemingly ready for him to bolt. He looked at her, flicked his tail, then reached for the grass. "Huh."

"You surprised?"

"A little." She looked at the log, clearly considering whether she dared to sit on it.

"Don't ask how many bugs live in this thing. Or spiders."

She scrunched up her nose. "You had to say that, didn't you?"

Ty patted the log. "Most of the bugs don't bite."

She hesitated another moment, then gingerly sat down a foot away from Ty. "It's nice to sit for a minute. My morning spin class kicked my ass and I was putting out fires all day." She sighed and gazed out at the clearing. "This is peaceful. I can almost imagine why people like doing outdoorsy stuff like camping."

"You don't camp?"

"No. Terrible lesbian, I know. No hiking, no camping. I figure since I'm bi I get a pass."

"Zoe's bi and she loves camping. Well, technically she identifies as pansexual. But my last girlfriend was bi, and she loved camping. More than I did."

"Probably I should call myself pan too. It's more accurate." She looked over at Ty. "But I'm not happy you took away my good excuse about why I don't camp."

"You can tell people the truth—that you're scared of bugs. Wait, hold still." Ty reached over and pretended to brush something off her knee.

She stiffened and looked down at her leg, then back at Ty. A moment later she caught Ty's smile and laughed, swatting their shoulder. "You!"

"Ouch." Ty rubbed their shoulder.

Leslie's eyes widened. "Did that hurt?"

"No." Ty grinned. "But even if it did, you know I'd come back asking for more."

Leslie was quiet for a minute, watching the horses, and Ty wondered if the joke had been taken wrong. Right when they decided to ask, Leslie said, "I wasn't going to bring it up but...is there anything I did that went too far? When we were messaging, you know."

"Not at all. I loved every minute. Right up to the end."

Leslie looked up at the sky. "If that had been real life—"

"It wasn't," Ty said. "It was a fun game."

Leslie nodded slowly. After a moment she said, "I told you why I joined that group. Why did you?"

Ty pushed a rock with the toe of their boot, wondering how to answer. "I heard about it through a friend. Someone I knew back in college. She's into the kink scene and had been in TryItOnce for a while. She said it was a little too vanilla for her tastes."

"I think it depends on who you connect with. But that doesn't answer why you tried it."

"No. I guess not." Ty met Leslie's eyes. "I don't know if I want to tell you."

"Do you not think you can trust me?"

"I trust you. I'm maybe a little embarrassed is all." They couldn't lie, as tempting as it was to come up with an answer that wouldn't make them seem naive. "I wanted more experience having sex. It's not like I hadn't had any at all…I had a girlfriend in college for two years but we mostly cuddled. She wanted to do more but I always felt awkward in my body and I didn't really like how she touched me."

Ty chewed the inside of their cheek, keeping their gaze trained on Nellie and Archer. "I used to bind, but not at night and she was always wanting to touch my breasts. She loved to play with my nipples. Loved to tell me how pretty I was. Loved to tell me how I was so feminine and soft even though I acted tough. When I told her I didn't like those things about my body, she said I had to find a way to love myself. And when we had sex, I was fine if I was touching her but when she touched me, well, I remembered what parts I had, if that makes any sense."

"It makes a lot of sense. And I'm sorry."

"It's not a big deal." Not anymore anyway. "I spent a while trying to figure out what was wrong with me."

"Nothing's wrong with you."

"I know that now. It took me a while." Ty smiled. "A few years later I met Micah. I told myself it was going to be different—that I'd be able to tell her how I wanted to be touched and would be happier having sex. I think it might have been. The problem was she lived in London and neither of us had any money to travel."

"Not a lot of opportunities for sex?"

"Exactly. We were only in the same time zone a handful of times. But she also liked thinking of me as a woman. She'd only been with men before and she'd just come out as queer. She wanted to say she had a girlfriend, you know? And wanted to think of me that way. Especially when we had sex."

"So you joined the group to have sex the way you wanted it?" Leslie guessed.

"To have sex as me." Ty felt their cheeks get hot but pushed on. "I wanted to feel confident in my body. And I wanted to be the same person on the outside that I was on the inside. Nonbinary."

"You know, this makes me feel a lot better." Leslie smiled. "I thought I was the only one who had an ulterior motive."

"You needed to learn how to write sex and I needed to learn how to like sex." Saying it aloud, Ty realized that wasn't quite right. "It wasn't that I hated sex or anything. I just never felt completely comfortable. But with you, I did. The first time we messaged, you didn't tell me 'I want to see your breasts.' You said, 'I want to put my hands on your chest.' I realized then things were going to be different. I could relax and be myself."

"Your chest is fucking sexy, by the way. And you in a cowboy hat and those jeans? Mm." Leslie gave Ty a look that sent a warmth through them. "And I know saying that may make other things more complicated between us, but you might as well know I love how androgynous you are. I'm sorry the women you've dated in the past haven't appreciated you for that."

"Thanks for teaching me to like my body." Ty felt a lump form in their throat. They took a minute to steady their emotions and then said, "Since you said you liked my body, am I allowed to tell you how fucking sexy you are? Because when you stretch out those legs…"

"I already know you appreciate my body. You don't hide anything." She laughed and pushed the brim of Ty's hat down over their nose.

Ty grinned and adjusted it back into place. "You sure you don't want to hear all the things I find sexy about you?"

"I'm sure that would make it even harder for me to not kiss you." Leslie cleared her throat. "I want to ask you something, but you don't have to answer. Do you still bind?"

"No. I had top surgery a few years ago. Best thing I ever did for myself." Ty hesitated and then added, "I'd show you my chest, but that might make things more awkward between us."

"Maybe you should. It's really not awkward yet."

Ty laughed and Leslie joined in. The horses eyed them; Nellie looking judgey, Archer slightly amused. After a minute, both went back to their grass.

"You know what's hard?" Leslie asked. "There's no starting at the beginning with us. In some ways, I barely know you. In other ways, I already like you way more than I should."

"You like me, huh?"

Leslie rolled her eyes but the smile on her lips buoyed Ty's heart.

"Maybe starting at the beginning is overrated," Ty said. "Neither of us have time to go on dates, right? That's what we both talked about from the start. That first night you told me you didn't have time for a relationship. And I thought to myself—perfect. Me neither."

Leslie nodded, her gaze on the horses. She uncrossed her ankles and held out her hand. "Can I try holding Nellie's lead rope?"

"Sure."

She sat for a long moment simply holding the rope and watching Nellie, then stood. "I want to pet her. If I mess up and she spooks—"

"You got this," Ty said.

Leslie breathed out, then walked up to Nellie, clicking to get her attention. Ears flicked back in her direction, but the mare didn't stop munching the grass. Leslie rested one hand on Nellie's shoulder, the other holding the rope. She scratched Nellie's withers and then glanced at Ty. "It's the boots," she murmured.

"Those boots are legit," Ty joked.

Leslie smiled back at them, then gave Nellie another rub. "Okay. That's as long as I can handle being brave." She walked back to the log and handed off the rope.

"Good job facing your fears."

When Leslie sat back down on the log, she picked a spot close to Ty. Her arm bumped Ty's and she murmured an apology but then shifted closer, her thigh settling in alongside Ty's. When she leaned her head against Ty's shoulder, it felt entirely too good.

"You trying to make this hard for us?" Ty asked.

"What's hard is not touching you," Leslie said. "But tell me if I should stop."

"I'm not complaining." No complaints, but lots of questions. Starting with, how much restraint did Leslie think they had?

"You know, I didn't see it at first, but you and your horse are kind of alike."

"How's that?"

"You're both easy to trust." Leslie brushed a bit of dirt off her jeans and added, "Never in a million years would I have been okay taking a horse for a walk—and being the one in the lead—but you tell me I'll be fine and I believe you for some reason. And I look at Archer and I know he's not going to all of a sudden take off. Why am I trusting you two?"

"Maybe you shouldn't," Ty teased.

"I know I can. Which is weird...but also nice." Leslie shifted back against Ty and set her hand on their thigh.

Ty's whole body thrummed. "I thought you were gonna say Archer and I were alike because we're so good-looking."

"Polaris is the real looker," Leslie said. "That horse could win a beauty contest."

"Don't tell Zoe. She already thinks that mare's worth a million bucks."

Leslie turned to look at Ty. "Is she?"

"No. She's maybe worth five thousand. Not that Zoe would sell her."

Leslie turned back to face the horses, her hand not leaving Ty's thigh.

"I'd really like to kiss you," Ty said softly.

"I'd like to kiss you back."

Leslie's simple statement made resisting all the more difficult. "One of these days we should decide if kissing's a good idea or not."

"It feels like a good idea, doesn't it?" Leslie was quiet for a moment, then said, "We could kiss once and leave it at that."

Ty's heart thumped in their chest. They took a risk and stroked their knuckles down the side of Leslie's cheek. Her skin was impossibly soft, and when she turned into Ty's hand, her mouth brushed their fingers.

Ty didn't want to breathe. Leslie held their gaze for a long moment and then pushed past their hand to close the distance between them.

As soon as Leslie's mouth was on theirs, Ty thought they must have already kissed a hundred times. Leslie's lips fit perfectly against theirs, asking for more with exactly the right pressure, and parting at just the right moment. Yet at the same time it was all new. They slipped their hand behind Leslie's neck, giving in to the desire that had been bottled up for too long.

When they both pulled back for a breath, Ty searched Leslie's face, wondering if she'd say the kiss had been nice but couldn't happen again. She didn't say that, though. Instead, she murmured, "I hope you're not done, because I'm not even close," as she moved to straddle Ty's lap.

The next kiss was even better than the first, full of a hunger that couldn't be contained. A low moan escaped Leslie's mouth and she shifted closer to Ty, opening for them to deepen the kiss. Arousal raced through Ty, and it was impossibly hard keeping one hand on Nellie's lead line. If Leslie never wanted another kiss, it would crush them, but having her in their arms now was worth whatever came later. This wasn't a first kiss. This was coming home to the woman they'd fallen for months ago.

CHAPTER TWENTY-ONE

Ty's hand slipped under Leslie's tank top. Fingertips grazed along her ribs, Ty's touch a light caress at first, then with more pressure, giving away how much they wanted her. She moved into a deep kiss, parting for Ty's tongue. Gone was any thought of holding back. Ty's unmistakable desire made her own need impossible to contain.

She was about to pull off her tank top when she felt Ty tense. Ty broke away from their kiss and looked at Nellie. The mare's head was high, ears pricked toward the brush-filled cluster of oaks. A heartbeat later, she spun, wrenching the lead line taut.

"Easy, girl," Ty murmured, seemingly calm but shifting Leslie off their lap. They stood, not quickly but deliberately, and repeated, "Easy, girl."

A bird shot out of the brush and Nellie reared. Leslie got to her feet, wondering if she should climb behind the log or go to Archer. Before she'd decided, Ty led Nellie away from the log and then in a circle.

Nellie didn't seem to be able to settle. She kept her head high, pivoting from one direction to the next with the whites of her eyes showing.

Leslie looked to Archer and realized he hadn't bothered to even lift his head from the weeds. Drama apparently wasn't his thing. She took a deep breath, silently talking her own anxiety level down a notch. Ty had control of Nellie and Archer wasn't bolting anywhere, which left her to sort out what had nearly happened. She'd been one breath away from pulling off her tank top even as she wondered if she was taking things too fast and all without a plan.

Ty circled Nellie again but as soon as they stopped, she pawed the ground. "I hate to say it, but I don't think I'm going to get her to relax again."

"Do you think we should head back?"

Ty glanced at the log and sighed. "Yeah, probably."

Leslie had no doubt what Ty was thinking. *Talk about bad timing, Nellie.* But maybe it'd been a good thing they'd been interrupted before clothes had come off. They could both probably use a moment to regroup.

Were they ready to have sex? Her body had certainly thought so. She'd been more sure when Ty had deepened their kiss. A pulse had started between her legs and she was wet still. But did she want more than sex? And what did Ty want?

She had feelings for Ty already—complicated by grieving how she'd messed up and lost Hitch. She'd berated herself for not recognizing when she'd slid too deep into that relationship, and she didn't want to repeat the same mistake. And Ty had only mentioned two girlfriends. If that was all, she was almost embarrassed to admit the number of relationships she'd had.

She clipped Archer's lead line onto his halter and met Ty's gaze. "Should we talk about what just happened?"

"Did you not want to kiss me?"

"I literally jumped you."

"Then I think we're okay." Ty started walking Nellie toward the path. The mare had quieted enough to stop trying to wrench her lead line out of Ty's hands, but she still had a wild look in her eyes.

"I don't mean to shut you down," Ty said. "What part do you think we should talk about?"

Leslie appreciated Ty stepping back and trying again, but she wasn't sure what to say. "I think we need a bed if that happens again."

Ty smiled. "My place or yours?"

"The thing is, I'm not sure we're ready. I mean, I want you to come home with me, but we don't have anything figured out."

"Do you usually have everything figured out before you take someone home?"

The directness in Ty's voice stopped Leslie. "Honestly, it's been a while since I've had someone over. I used to jump into things, but I made a lot of mistakes."

"Does this feel like a mistake?"

"No." It didn't. At all. But she still felt like she ought to be the responsible one. "Maybe we should talk about what we're doing."

"Full play-by-play? Like old times?"

Ty's cocky tone melted her last resolve. She stepped close enough to push the brim of Ty's hat down. "You."

Ty repositioned the hat, then reached for Leslie's hand and pulled her into a kiss. Ty's forwardness and their hard kiss made her forget any hesitation. When Ty stepped back, they said, "Still not sure I'm on board?"

"I have no doubt that we have…shared interests."

Ty laughed.

She smiled too, but doubts pushed forward. "The problem is we haven't talked about expectations or what we want out of this."

"If you want to talk about all that, we can, but don't worry about me. I don't need to have everything figured out." Ty tipped their cowboy hat. "Tough cowboy, remember?"

"How'd you know I was worrying about you?"

"Because you hurt me once. You're worried about doing it again."

Ty's words slammed into her. It was one thing knowing the truth in her heart. Another thing entirely hearing it from Ty. "I'm sorry."

"Me too. But I learned a few things about myself that I needed to learn." Ty paused. "After we stopped messaging each other, I joined a dating app."

"Did you meet someone?" Leslie steeled herself for Ty's answer.

"I met lots of someones." Ty looked almost guilty. "My housemates started to tease me for being a Casanova. But it was only hookup sex. And I know that sounds bad, but it worked for everyone involved."

"Worked, as in past tense?"

"I stopped after a couple months." Ty seemed to focus on the trail for a moment, leading Nellie through a stand of straggly oaks. "I needed to focus on my classes."

"Why are you telling me then?"

"I can handle a hookup," Ty said. "Maybe I like you more than all those other women, but honestly all I want to do now is have some fun. And there's a few things you told me to do once that I'd really like to try for real."

Ty gave her a sly smile and Leslie thought of the times she'd ordered Hitch onto their knees and what had happened next. Or when she'd told them to strip, sit down, and keep their hands to themself while she sat in their lap touching whatever she wanted to touch... When she met Ty's gaze again, she knew their thoughts had followed a similar track. "Which things would you like to try?"

"Maybe you'll find out if you keep kissing me."

Ty sidestepped when Leslie tried pushing their hat again. The confident smile they flashed made her think she was worrying for no reason. It also made her realize she might not be calling all the shots later.

"You're walking on the wrong side of your horse, by the way," Ty said.

Leslie looked at Archer and realized the mistake. "Sorry. I was distracted."

"Archer doesn't care. I just thought you should know." Ty reached for her hand.

Leslie loved how Ty's grip felt—strong and sure but gentle at the same time. Like their touch on her skin had been earlier.

Hitch had let her start every encounter, let her decide how far things went, and she'd been comfortable taking the lead. But that had all been virtual. And now she knew Hitch deferring to her had been partly inexperience. She thought of Ty's hand slipping under her tank top and guessed that things would be different in real life.

"I like how you kiss," Ty said. "I can't wait to find out what else you're good at."

Ty caught her eye, and desire seemed to build in the space between them. "You sure this is a good idea?"

"Completely."

Ty gave her hand a light squeeze. Their smile was so easy, so carefree, that she had to laugh. "Okay."

"Okay meaning you decided you want to have sex?"

A buzz of excitement took hold. "Yeah. Why not?"

Ty laughed then too and she let herself relax into the idea that what happened next could be a no-pressure thing. Maybe, for once, something that felt simple would turn out that way.

After a few minutes, she looked up and realized she'd lost track of where they were. Maybe a half mile from the ranch? The sun had set and the real heat of the day had ebbed. A light breeze swayed the treetops and Ty hadn't let go of her hand. For a moment, she focused on the sounds—the horses plodding down the trail, the squirrels chattering to each other, and the birds settling in for the evening.

She bumped against Ty's shoulder and said, "You were right. Walking horses is nice."

"I'm glad you like it."

For some reason, Ty's comment made her relax even more. She'd been surprised when she'd connected so quickly with Hitch—and connected so well she'd let go of her inhibitions. Partly it was because of the promised anonymity and that she'd told herself it was all a game. But she knew a bigger part was simply because of who Hitch had been. Easy. Comfortable. Someone she could relax and be herself around.

Maybe she should feel self-conscious for everything she'd told Hitch to do. She didn't. Instead, she felt as if she had nothing to hide now. But the scenarios and scenes she'd played out with Ty had only been virtual. They weren't starting from zero, but she couldn't exactly buy a pair of cuffs and expect no one would get hurt.

CHAPTER TWENTY-TWO

When they got back to the barn, Ty let go of Leslie's hand and walked Nellie over to her stall. Leslie led Archer to a tie post and looped his rope the way she'd watched Ty do it. While Ty mixed up a bucket of Nellie's special feed, she picked out a brush and started working on Archer's coat. She'd teased Ty earlier for making her brush Archer more than necessary, but the truth was, she liked it. She focused on making the white patches shine against the warm reddish brown that nearly matched Ty's hair.

The space between her and Ty held a dozen questions, and every time she glanced at them she considered asking one. But then she'd draw the brush over the old gelding's side, hear his contented sigh, and she let the question go.

While Nellie ate, Ty ran a brush over her coat as well. They didn't seem focused on the task, though, and every time Leslie looked their direction, they averted their eyes as if she'd caught them staring. The realization that Ty couldn't help looking at her made her smile. She could say she didn't mind being checked out. In fact, she liked it. But she kept the secret, enjoying how she made Ty distracted.

"Do you think Nellie will be sore tomorrow?" Leslie asked.

"Maybe. We kept it slow, but she did dance around a lot when we first started out." Ty came out of Nellie's stall, as if they'd been waiting for the excuse. "I'll text Paige and ask if she wants me to give her some pain meds. She did well on the walk back."

"I noticed," Leslie said. "I think even I could have walked her home."

"Listen to you sounding all cocky." Ty leaned against the tie post opposite Archer's, hooking their thumbs in their front pockets. "You're a fast learner. Do you want to ride Archer next lesson or try leading Nellie?"

"I want to work with Nellie."

"Good."

"Though if I got to pick from Archer, Nellie, or you…" The words *I'd ride you* were on the tip of her tongue. It was a line she would have had no trouble typing, but saying it aloud, with Ty's gaze hot on her, was a different thing altogether.

"Who would you pick then?"

She swallowed. Hitch hadn't challenged her the way Ty did. Hitch hadn't made her as wet, either. "I think you know."

Ty unhooked their thumbs and came forward. They reached for the brush Leslie was holding, letting their hand linger over hers for a moment, eyes locked on her, then tossed the brush in the bucket with the other grooming supplies. "You passed the grooming test."

"What comes next?"

Ty's look was enough answer. Arousal raced through her and she had to remind herself to breathe when Ty led Archer into his stall. The gelding pushed his head toward them and Ty paused to give him a scratch and then a kiss on the white strip that parted his forehead. Ty murmured, "You're the best horse," and he made a contented sound like, *Humph, of course I am.*

"You two are sweet together."

"I love my horse." Ty stepped out of the stall and tossed an armful of hay into his trough.

"I can tell."

Ty looked from Archer to the empty stall next to his and then straightened. "I want to go home with you, but I gave Zoe a ride. I always wait for her and Polaris to get back when they go out at night. She'll be back before ten but maybe not much earlier."

Leslie tried not to let her disappointment show. "I've got a morning meeting at seven. Maybe you could come over tomorrow night?" Even if she didn't like it, she knew it wouldn't be a bad idea to take things slow. "It'd give us some time to think."

"Do you need time to think?" Ty came forward to where she stood, stopping a foot away and waiting for her answer.

"No."

"Me neither." Ty's hands settled on her hips. The light pressure of their thumbs on her hip bones made her melt into the touch.

How could she possibly take things slow?

She shifted forward a step and Ty's mouth claimed hers, taking her breath and ramping up her desire. She didn't resist when Ty helped her out of her tank top, their hands sending shivers of anticipation as they grazed over her bra. She undid the hooks herself, enjoying the look on Ty's face when she reached for their hands and pushed her breasts into them.

"What do you want to do with me next?"

"So many things." Ty drew a light line over one nipple with their thumb. "And everything all at once."

"Don't hold back on my account."

Ty had cupped her breasts lightly, but at her words they grabbed hold, drawing a moan from her lips. They pinched her nipples, making them ache with need. "You sure?"

She nodded, not trusting her voice.

"I'm stronger than you. I want you to say you're sure."

Leslie tried not to squirm with Ty's hands on her breasts, alternating between gentle caresses and grips so tight her knees went weak. She set her hands on their shoulders, feeling Ty's muscles tense under their shirt. God, she wanted Ty naked. And on her. She wanted to feel Ty everywhere. "I'm sure."

Ty let go of her breasts and slid both hands behind her neck, pulling her into a deep kiss. One long kiss and then another as Ty's hands roamed up and down her. Over her breasts, up her ribs, then down again to undo her jeans. Each kiss made her feel more dizzy than the last and she welcomed the solid surety in Ty's body, knowing when she pressed against them that her weight was nothing to them. She managed to unbuckle Ty's belt and work loose the top button of their jeans, but then she was being pushed backward.

Ty pulled away from her lips. "Give me a sec." They picked up one of the big hay bales like it was a paperweight and set it down next to another bale, pushing the two together. After they tossed a saddle blanket over the hay, they turned back to her. "Now where were we?"

Ty took a step toward her, looking cocky and sexy as hell. "Oh, yeah. Here." Their hands settled on her hips again and her mouth was taken up in a kiss.

She felt desire surge with each deep kiss. She was wet and ready for Ty to find out how aroused she was. Ready for her own overwhelming need to be sated finally. When Ty pushed her back a step, she didn't resist. She let them guide her until she was pressed against the hay bales. The next thing she knew, she was on her back on the saddle blanket. Rough wool scratched at her skin and the smell of horse and sweat and the sight of Ty looming over her was all she wanted. She kicked off her boots and Ty helped her out of her jeans.

She almost complained when Ty didn't take off her underwear but then they ran a finger lightly under the waistband and all thoughts were replaced with one. She wanted Ty between her legs.

"This okay?" Ty asked. "Right here?"

In the middle of a barn, legs spread wide, her clit pulsed with a longing so strong she knew she'd soak her panties. "Right here is good." She pushed up her hips to bump Ty's hand, wanting to beg them to hurry up and put their fingers inside her.

"I like feeling how much you want me." Ty traced along the inside seam of the underwear, the silky black cloth a perfect contrast to their rough fingertip.

She couldn't hide her need, so she decided to give Ty the pleasure of knowing how much they turned her on, pushing herself toward their hand again. "I want you inside."

"We'll get to that," Ty promised, only stroking lightly over her underwear as they peppered her belly with kisses.

She moaned and dropped her head back on the hay bale as Ty caressed her legs. "You like making me wait?"

"Maybe." Ty kissed her inner thigh and finally moved on top of her.

"Mm. That's better." She savored their weight while wishing she could feel skin against skin. "Will you take off your clothes? I want to feel you."

Ty's kisses slowed for a moment. "That's a change. You not telling me to strip." They kissed her cheek, then smiled and pressed a finger to her lips. She parted to take Ty's finger into her mouth, loving the hungry look in Ty's gaze. Ty pulled the finger out of her mouth and she feigned a pout.

"Please?"

"I think I'll stay dressed and have you like this," Ty said. "What do you say to that?"

Instead of answering, she caught Ty's hand and sucked their middle finger deep into her mouth. Ty's low moan was exactly what she wanted. She knew she had Ty's full attention when another finger was pushed to her lips. She opened for that and took both inside, sucking deeply and loving the feel of Ty's other hand on her breast as she worked. After a moment, she turned her cheek, letting Ty's fingers slip out of her mouth. She looked up and her breath caught. Raw desire made Ty's eyes as dark as the midnight sky.

"You don't know how much I want you."

She knew. And she loved it. "I want you to call the shots tonight. You know what I like." Her heart raced as Ty drew a line down the center of her underwear. "I want you in charge."

"I've learned a few things since our first night together," Ty said, their voice a low gravel.

"Show me."

"I might not be able to go slow." Ty kissed her neck, then grazed teeth over her throat. She settled back on the saddle blanket but didn't feel at all relaxed. She didn't want Ty to go slow. She wanted hard and fast.

Ty pushed her panties to the side. "You're already wet."

"Your fault." She shifted her hips, trying to get Ty to dip their fingers into her.

Ty held her in place, a knowing look on their face. "I thought I was the one in charge."

She tipped her head. "Please?"

In the next moment, Ty's fingers thrust into her. She gasped, and clutched at their arm, then started to sit up, only to be pushed down again. "Fuck, I like your aggressive side."

"I know you do," Ty said, pumping deeper into her.

She had no choice but to fall into their rhythm. Her center clenched in ecstasy. She told herself to relax even as she raked Ty's arms with her nails. When she looked down, Ty's forearm, muscles tensing under the constellation tattoo, pumped between her legs.

She couldn't control her panting breaths or the twitch of nerves as Ty's thumb rode against her clit each time their fingers thrust in and out. She tried to take off Ty's shirt but only got the cloth pushed midway up their torso before she had to give up. Her fingers couldn't seem to grip. All she could do was let Ty have their way with her. Which was everything she wanted.

"I want to get you off," Ty said.

She thought of telling them that it would take more than thrusting but she felt too good to want anything to change. Then Ty shifted up to her lips and kissed her, gentle at first brush of lips, then harder. She stole breaths between the kisses, parting her lips and welcoming Ty's tongue. Every time Ty pulled back, she wanted them again.

"I want you naked," she said. Her voice sounded needy, annoying her. Ty ignored the request anyway. She reached for their shirt again, thinking she could manage to get that off at least, but Ty pushed deep into her then, adding another finger when she wasn't expecting it. Pleasure rolled through her.

Ty's roughness brought a fresh surge of wet arousal. She drenched Ty's fingers as she bucked against them, but Ty only pressed her more firmly against the saddle blanket. The thought crossed her mind that she couldn't push Ty off if she tried, couldn't stop what was happening. A moment later she reminded herself that one word was all that was needed. They'd talked about safe words months ago. Never had she thought she'd use a safe word in real life. It had only been part of the game she'd played with Hitch. But never had she felt so taken, so at risk of not being able to hold her own. Ty had her pinned on a dirty saddle blanket and she was completely at their mercy.

And I love it.

She wouldn't tell Ty, but it was true. She wanted everything that was happening in this moment. She wanted Ty dressed while she was completely naked. She wanted jeans rubbing her inner thighs with every thrust, wanted her chest crushed under Ty's weight. She wanted to be taken advantage of because Ty couldn't wait a second longer for her.

She pushed up her hips every time Ty stroked into her, asking for more. Ty didn't stop, didn't slow down, and she was lost to their hands, lost to their rhythm. Still, the pulse in her clit had gotten insistent.

"I need…"

"You need more," Ty said. "Don't think I won't give it to you."

They shifted off her, then pulled her to the edge of the hay bale and finally tugged off her underwear. Ty pulled her legs over their shoulders. "Remember when you taught me this move?"

Before Leslie could answer, Ty's head dipped and in the next moment, their tongue slid between her folds. She sucked in a breath, reveling in the pleasure Ty brought with every stroke and lash against her swollen clit. When Ty sucked her between their lips, all the sounds she'd been trying to hold broke lose. She couldn't control her body's response and knew the orgasm was coming. She started to say as much, but when she opened her eyes the sight of Hitch, face buried between her legs, was too perfect. Ty. But Ty was Hitch and it was all she'd imagined. All that and more. She let her head fall back on the saddle blanket and gave in to what her body wanted.

Ty thrust once more and her climax hit. She moaned out her pleasure, then shuddered and tensed. Ty held her in place, fingers deep in her and tongue still cornering her clit. It was too good. Too good for a first time. But it wasn't really their first time. It was months in the making and Ty was no beginner now. She let the orgasm wash over her, and a moment later Ty shifted their hand, sending a second tremor through her.

Only when she fully relaxed did Ty get up from between her legs. She rolled onto her side, squeezing her thighs together to hold on to the last wave of the orgasm. Ty settled against her back, one arm wrapping around her.

"You're so damn sexy," Ty murmured. "I never thought I'd really be able to touch you—that it could be real."

She tugged Ty's arm closer to her chest as their words repeated in her mind. Same, she wanted to say. But she couldn't speak. Emotions overwhelmed her. She felt perfect in Ty's arms. Like she'd never belonged somewhere as much.

Tears welled but she squeezed her eyes against them, trying to explain away their presence. This moment had been months in the making. All the fear when Hitch said her real name aloud, all the anger at her own mistake, then the unexpected grief the day after when she realized what she'd lost, and now the longing for this not to be an end but a beginning.

"You're amazing," Ty said, kissing her neck softly. "I knew you would be but…damn."

Minutes passed and Ty slowly eased their grip on her. She accepted a gentle kiss on her cheek and then another on her lips before opening her eyes.

"You're shivering."

Was she?

"I'd offer you a jacket, but I don't have one. Do you want my shirt?"

"I'm not cold." She pulled Ty against her again. "Though if shivering is what I have to do to get you naked…"

Ty chuckled and kissed her neck. "Did it bother you so much that I wasn't naked?"

"Yes. And no. Next time I want to feel your skin against mine."

Ty caressed her cheek. "I like hearing you want a next time."

"I want more of you. More of that."

"Thank god."

She laughed softly, then turned so she could meet Ty's gaze. "Were you honestly worried that once would be enough? I still haven't even had my hands on you."

"You had your hands all over me."

"With you all the way dressed," she complained.

Ty opened their mouth to say something, but Archer interrupted, whinnying from his stall. They glanced at Leslie. "I hate to say this, but you should probably get dressed. He only calls like that if it's Polaris coming home."

"Polaris and Zoe?"

"Well, Polaris better be with Zoe. It's not ten yet, but—"

"Shit." She sat up, feeling more out of it than ever. She was entirely naked in a barn where anyone could walk in at any moment. At least she knew Paige and Seren were gone for the evening, but she didn't want Zoe to see her in her present state. Unfortunately, she also couldn't completely control her muscles.

Ty handed her the bra and tank top that had landed on a neighboring hay bale. "I really don't want you to get dressed."

"I don't even want to move, but I also don't want to explain this to your cousin." She hurried to fasten the bra at the sound of a not-so-distant whinny. Polaris—and Zoe—were close. As she slipped on the tank top, she scanned for her underwear. "Maybe you can meet Zoe outside and distract her for a minute? I'd like to finish getting dressed and get over the shock of how much I liked being fucked in a barn."

"No problem." Ty leaned down and kissed her. "Thank you for letting me do that, by the way. It was exactly what I wanted."

It was exactly what she wanted too. Which worried her more than a little.

CHAPTER TWENTY-THREE

Polaris burst through the clearing between the apple tree and the shed. Ty lifted a hand, but before they could say anything, Zoe said, "I know I have to take her on a cooldown loop. But I have to poop."

Zoe launched out of the saddle right as Ty caught Polaris's reins. "Key?"

Ty fished Paige and Seren's key out of their pocket and Zoe was gone a moment later, racing toward the house.

Polaris circled around Ty, whinnying for Zoe. "She'll be back." Unfortunately, that meant there was no chance of slipping to the barn to be with Leslie. Ty let Polaris pace, their mind spinning with one thought: they'd had sex with Leslie.

It didn't seem possible but it'd definitely happened. Every muscle seemed to vibrate, wanting more of Leslie and needing a release. They felt like they'd been plugged into a charger and only barely used.

Ty looked at Polaris, who was prancing in place. "You just getting warmed up too?"

According to Zoe's Garmin GPS monitor that she'd left hooked on the saddle, Polaris had run fifteen miles. She tugged her reins as if asking for another fifteen.

"I get it, Polaris." If for different reasons, they understood each other.

Ty led the mare in a wide circle in front of the barn, studying her movements and trying to keep their thoughts occupied on something besides how much they wanted to be back with Leslie.

Her scent was still on their hands and when they closed their eyes, they could picture her under their body. The look of bliss on Leslie's face when she'd climaxed had felt surreal. Leslie had let them do what they'd fantasized about for months. But they'd only had a little taste of what they desperately wanted more of.

Polaris yanked the reins and looked back at the trail. "It's hard stopping when you want more, huh, Polaris?"

"More of what?"

Ty glanced over their shoulder at the sound of Leslie's voice. "Hey. Didn't see you come out of the barn."

"If I was holding that horse, I don't think I'd notice an avalanche coming at me."

"Polaris is high as a kite," Ty admitted. "She had a good run and wants more."

"Mm. I understand."

Leslie's words and the look of desire still in her eyes made Ty's arousal burn hotter. They struggled to keep their attention on Polaris even as she danced around them. "I need to take her on a loop around the orchard. Want to join me?"

"Sure. Where's Zoe?"

"She went up to the house to use the bathroom. She'll be back soon."

Leslie came forward a few steps and then stopped and eyed Polaris. "I get what you mean about the half wild part now."

"She'll calm down in a minute." Ty started toward the orchard and Leslie fell in next to them, keeping a good distance from Polaris. "She won't hurt you."

"She's just…a lot."

"She is. All she really wants to do in life is run. And then run some more. It took her a long time to understand she can have more fun running if she stops long enough to listen to us humans once in a while."

"She does that?"

Ty lifted a shoulder. "Sometimes."

"She seems so different from Archer. She's like how I would imagine a racehorse and he's…calm."

"He's also old," Ty said. They walked for another few minutes, passing the row of peach trees and then the apricots. Stars had begun to pop in the night sky, but the moon hadn't risen and the shadow-filled light made it hard to read Leslie's expression. Ty wanted to ask what she was thinking but stopped short of saying the question aloud.

Plenty of questions filled their mind. Could they really only have sex and not get attached all over again? They'd felt a lot more confident about that plan an hour ago. Now the thought of another goodbye pressed down on them like a weight.

"I know you have to give Zoe a ride home, but do you want to come to my place after?"

"I thought you had an early meeting." Ty had to be at work early too, but sex with Leslie definitely took priority.

"I'm willing to go without sleep."

"Then yes, please."

Leslie smiled. "The *please* is really not needed."

"If I leave the house right after I drop her off, Zoe will ask where I'm going."

"I don't care if she knows," Leslie said. "What I didn't want was her to see me stretched out naked in the barn."

"It was a good look. You could definitely work it more often."

Leslie playfully batted Ty's shoulder. A moment later she sidled up closer and hooked her arm with Ty's. "I have some ideas about good looks for you, too. How do you feel about wearing chaps?"

Ty stopped. "I read that in a message once, but it's a thousand times better when you say it in real life."

"Am I quoting myself?" Leslie laughed. "Sorry. It may be an actual fantasy of mine."

"Seriously?"

"Yes." She laughed again. "And I can't believe I just admitted that."

"There's a lot of things you've already admitted wanting."

Leslie arched an eyebrow. "You're thinking of things Girl-Monday wanted from Hitch."

"Damn. You're right." Ty only pretended to be let down. They knew from Leslie's tone that her real desires weren't that different than her online persona. "Wait, so only Girl-Monday wants to call me dirty names while she rides my biggest cock, wearing nothing but a cowboy hat?"

Leslie covered her mouth as she laughed.

"Because I was really hoping we could make that a reality," Ty continued. "And the spanking thing—"

"I'm not ready for that in real life," Leslie interrupted, still laughing.

"Not yet?"

"I think we need some regular sex first before we jump into kink." Leslie's words were definitely a rebuff but her tone was gentle and the look of playfulness stayed in her expression.

"I could use some more regular sex right about now."

"You're the one with the responsibilities," Leslie said, loosening her hold on Ty's arm. "I don't want to bring it up again, but are you sure we aren't going too fast? We're talking about fantasies and kink like we've been together for months and…I don't want one of us to regret we didn't think things through."

Ty knew she had a point but they didn't want that to be a reason for them to stop. "We're both adults. I think we can handle it. And maybe it's better we both can't do a serious relationship." Better in theory, anyway.

Leslie looked as if she wanted to say something but Zoe's voice interrupted, "Ty? Where'd you go?"

"Over here," Ty called.

Zoe met them as they rounded the last apple tree. "Gorgeous night, isn't it?"

"It is," Ty and Leslie said in unison.

Zoe looked between them. "You two are like Paige and Seren answering questions in stereo." She took the reins and rubbed Polaris's neck. "Barely sweaty."

Ty glanced at Leslie, wondering what she'd been about to say before they were interrupted. Maybe she'd only wanted to agree that it was better not trying a relationship.

Polaris pushed at Zoe's hand affectionately and Ty took a deep breath, trying to refocus. "How was the ride? You got home faster than I thought you would."

"Thanks to this one," Zoe said. She let Polaris rub against her even though the horse had been trained not to do that while wearing a bridle.

Zoe must have caught Ty's disapproval because she wagged her finger at Polaris and took a step back. "Naughty mare. You're not supposed to let Ty see you do that." She winked at Ty, then leaned closer to Polaris and added, "But I love you and you're perfect and you can do no wrong."

Ty chuckled. "I feel like we've talked about the whole consistency thing."

"Once or twice." Zoe kissed Polaris's cheek and then looked over at Leslie. "So how'd it go with you two?"

"Um..." Leslie opened and closed her mouth and Ty knew she wasn't thinking about the horses.

"It went well," Ty said.

"You got Nellie to leave the ranch?" Zoe asked.

When Ty nodded, Zoe looked at Leslie like she was trying to figure out if she was missing something. After a moment, she said, "Huh. You never know about mares. Leslie, I told Ty they really need to get you in a saddle. It's nice leading a horse, but there's nothing like a good ride."

Leslie glanced at Ty, and there was no doubting where her thoughts had gone.

"You do want to ride, right?" Zoe pressed.

"I guess I'd like to ride, but I want to work with Nellie more."

"Why not do both? Work with Nellie and ride Archer. You're in good hands with Ty, and I'm not just saying that because they're my annoying cousin." Zoe patted Ty's cheek, clearly trying to be the more annoying one. "Ty's seriously good with horses."

"I do feel like I'm in good hands," Leslie said. Her wink Ty's direction was subtle. "Really, I'm up for whatever. But I see you with Polaris, and Ty with Archer, and I feel bad that Nellie doesn't have someone like that for her. I know Seren and Paige would love to give her more attention if they weren't so busy."

"You should lease Nellie!" Zoe excitedly launched into all the benefits of exercise for aging horses. And all the benefits for people of being around horses.

She rarely talked long to anyone she didn't know well, and to hear her go on now was both heartwarming and annoying. They'd made another loop around the orchard and stopped again in front of the barn. If only they could say goodbye and let Zoe drive herself home.

"I know you already know this, Zoe, but your horse is gorgeous," Leslie said. "Ty told me not to tell you that because apparently you already think she's worth a million bucks."

"Two million at least," Zoe said, laughing. "Maybe more if we win Tevis."

"You'd never sell her," Ty said.

"Never ever," Zoe vowed, kissing Polaris again.

"Tevis is that big ride that's coming up?" Leslie asked.

"Yep." Zoe sounded more pumped about it than she had in the last few weeks. She was probably on the same adrenaline high as Polaris. Her wide smile was bright even in the starlight. "A hundred miles on some of the most beautiful—and most challenging—trails in the world. With some of the best endurance horses and riders ever. Do I sound like a commercial for the ride? Because I feel like one."

Leslie laughed. "Only a little."

"Did Ty tell you they almost won it a few years back with Archer?"

"I didn't know that." Leslie glanced at Ty.

"More than a few years ago now," Ty said.

"They came in second and less than a minute behind the rider who won," Zoe said. "But the guy who won shouldn't have."

"You don't know that," Ty chided.

"The next day his horse couldn't walk. Archer, on the other hand, went on to race another three Tevis Cups after that. Plus a bunch of other rides. How many times have you and Archer been a top-ten finisher?"

"Doesn't matter. That was a different lifetime."

Zoe stuck her tongue out at Ty. "In case you didn't know it, Leslie, Ty is basically famous in the endurance world."

"Not true."

"True," Zoe argued. "Has Ty told you they got recruited by this Arabian prince to race one of their stallions in Brazil?"

"Um, no." Leslie arched an eyebrow at Ty. "What other secrets are you keeping?"

Zoe continued, ignoring Ty's head shaking. "Ty even had a sponsor who paid for Archer and them to travel to a bunch of rides on the East Coast."

"That was luck. And thank god for it. No way could I have afforded any of it."

"It wasn't luck. You were on fire back in the day." Zoe turned back to Leslie. "And after they won a bunch more races in the States, Ty got offers to ride horses all over the world."

"She's exaggerating," Ty said. "It was two offers."

"Two people with lots of money and lots of horses." Zoe looked at Leslie and added, "They finished on all of the horses they raced on. Which is a big deal. Ty, how many races did you win?"

"Again, doesn't matter anymore," Ty said.

"Fine. Be that way," Zoe grumbled. "But what was the name of that horse you rode in Brazil?"

"Khahil. He liked to run as much as Polaris. He wasn't as smart though." Ty glanced at Polaris and felt a swell of pride. It wasn't simply that she was in top condition and race ready. It was how far she'd come. They looked over at Leslie and added, "Now I leave the racing to my cousin."

"Why?"

Leslie's question surprised Ty. They weren't ready to tell her the whole story and certainly not tonight. Everything felt too good tonight to bring it down with memories. Zoe bit her lip, eyeing Ty like she knew they didn't want to answer.

"Long story," Ty finally said.

"Do you miss it?"

"I can't say I don't have moments of missing it, but I've got other things I want to focus on. That was a phase."

"Phase, my ass," Zoe said. "You still love it."

"I love parts of it. Like being able to ride amazing horses in beautiful places. I don't love racing anymore."

Ty didn't want to discuss it further and it was a relief when Leslie said, "Well, it sounds like Tevis is going to be a fun experience, Zoe."

"I hope so." Zoe patted Polaris. "I've got a kickass horse and the world's best crew."

"A crew of basically one," Ty said. "Paige can only drop supplies at one checkpoint, and she texted me saying she'll have Olivia with her so she's not going to be able to take care of Polaris. It'll be up to you. And you're going to be running on fumes by then."

"I run my best on fumes," Zoe said. "Anyway, I really can't think of anyone else to ask. I'm sorry, Ty. I spent most of tonight's ride trying to think of anyone I know—and haven't pissed off—who might be around. I got nothing."

"Anyone you could ask for what?" Leslie asked.

"To be on my crew and help during the ride," Zoe said. "There's checkpoints and mandatory rest stops along the race route. I can't carry supplies for me and Polaris for the whole hundred miles. It'd be too much weight."

"So," Ty said, cutting in. "Most riders have a crew of three or four people who can drop supplies at the stops, and, ideally, take care of the horse so the rider can get a break. You're going to have basically me, Zoe. And I can't be everywhere all at once."

"When's Tevis again?" Leslie asked.

"The first weekend in August," Ty said.

"It changes every year because they time the ride over the full moon," Zoe added.

"I'm not working that weekend. I could help if you'd like—though I'm not sure how much I could do."

Ty didn't know what to say. They glanced at Zoe. Her eager nod and wide smile made it clear how she felt.

Leslie continued, "My office assistant decided I work too much and scheduled me a mandatory weekend off."

"You don't have any plans for the whole weekend?" Zoe asked.

"No. I thought about booking an Airbnb up in Tahoe but never got around to it."

"You know what's a lot like an Airbnb in Tahoe? Camping in the Sierras." Zoe grinned and bumped Ty's shoulder. "Right, Ty? It's lovely this time of year."

"Crewing for Tevis is nothing like staying at an Airbnb in Tahoe." Ty could tell Zoe was thinking they'd want Leslie there. As amazing as it sounded to share a tent, especially after what had happened in the barn, Ty wasn't sure they were ready for a weekend together. "Didn't you say you didn't like camping?"

"I've never camped but that doesn't mean I couldn't try it." Leslie shrugged like there was nothing different about camping than ordering something new on a restaurant menu.

"If you're serious, it'd be amazing to have your help," Zoe said. As Zoe fell to describing what would happen—camping the night before the race, spending the next day driving between checkpoints with supplies, moving the trailer to where the race ended, and finally camping the next night at the fairgrounds in Auburn—Ty wondered if Leslie understood it wouldn't be the party Zoe made it sound.

When Zoe finished, Leslie smiled. "Sounds fun."

"It is a lot of work," Ty said.

"Well, yeah, but we'll have fun too," Zoe said. "Most of the work is moving supplies and setting up camp—which isn't awful when you're in a beautiful spot. And the race is way more exciting if you aren't in it. There are so many gorgeous horses. Plus, Ty brings the best junk food and knows all the camp songs."

"Camp songs and junk food, huh?"

Leslie smiled at Ty, and they couldn't help feeling a bump of excitement. Maybe Leslie would have a good time. But what if she didn't? What if she was miserable camping? Their focus had to be on Zoe and Polaris. "Crewing can get boring. And hot. It's a lot of standing around at checkpoints waiting."

"I don't mind the heat. And I don't think I'll be bored." She met Ty's gaze. "Besides, this will mean I can finally tell people I've tried camping."

"Everyone needs to try camping at least once," Zoe agreed. "I promise you won't be bored. Ty's done a million endurance rides and forgets how exciting it is the first time."

"It really does sound fun."

Zoe bounced on her toes. "What do you think, crew boss? Can Leslie join the party?"

Ty looked from Leslie to Zoe and then back to Leslie. So many questions filled the space between them. But Ty could only say one thing. "Welcome to the crew."

CHAPTER TWENTY-FOUR

Leslie knew it might be a disaster. She wasn't a spontaneous person. At all. And Ty seemed nervous about her coming. In truth, she wasn't sure how much help she'd be. She knew pathetically little about horses and even less about camping. But the timing felt like kismet.

"Do you have a sleeping bag?" Zoe asked. "We could probably find an extra tent…"

The feeling of kismet vanished. Of course she'd be in her own tent. And in her own sleeping bag. Which she didn't have.

"Don't worry," Ty said, apparently reading her expression. "I'll give you a list of what you'll need and get you anything you don't have."

Ty's tone was all business—clearly in crew boss mode—and Leslie wondered again if she was making a mistake. Maybe it'd be better that she'd have her own tent. There were still so many questions about what Ty and she were doing. Before she had time to overthink it, a car pulled up to the barn, parking between Ty's Jeep and her Mercedes. Ty visibly tensed as the driver got out.

"Why's Jenna here?" Ty asked.

"She called when I was on the ride," Zoe said, giving a half shrug like it was nothing. "She wanted to meet Polaris and had the night off. I knew you had to work in the morning and figured this way you wouldn't have to wait for me."

A woman with pale skin, an asymmetric cut to her purple-black hair, and lots of piercings stepped out from between the cars, raising a hand in a wave.

Ty's jaw clenched. "She doesn't even like horses."

"Can you not make a big deal about this?" Zoe said, mostly under her breath.

"Fine." Ty's expression didn't change but their voice softened. "You want Jenna to give you a ride home?"

"Yeah." Zoe's eyes met Ty's for the briefest of moments and Leslie wondered what passed between them. Whatever it was, Ty's shoulders dropped.

Jenna reached their group a second later—Polaris prancing again, Zoe with a hesitant smile, and Ty looking sullen. Leslie stepped forward and held out her hand. "Hi. I'm Leslie."

"I'm Jenna. Nice to meet you. Though I feel like I already know you." She smiled and raised her eyebrows at Ty as if there was some inside joke.

The dread of what Ty might have told this woman came like a blast of cold air. Before Leslie could think of what to say, Zoe said, "Jenna lives with me and Ty, and I may have put your business card up on our fridge. With a little heart magnet. But only because it was either a heart or a cat butt magnet right on your face."

"I hear you make amazing cookies," Jenna said.

"She thinks that because I used a heart magnet and may have said I wanted to marry you for your cookies, I have a crush on you." Zoe rolled her eyes.

The tension left as fast as it had arrived. Leslie smiled. "Thank you for not putting a cat butt right next to my face."

"You do make really good cookies," Zoe said. "I would almost marry someone just for that."

"If you're trying to get me to bake a batch just for you, it's working." Leslie laughed.

"Ooh, could you bring cookies to Tevis?"

Zoe's cookie enthusiasm was hard not to love. "You got it."

"Maybe now would be a good time to talk about crewing and go through what you'll need," Ty said.

Leslie waited until Zoe and Jenna had left with Polaris for another loop around the orchard before turning to Ty. "So why do you hate your housemate? She doesn't seem awful."

"I don't hate Jenna," Ty said. "But Jenna likes Zoe. And, I guess, Zoe likes Jenna. I'm trying to get used to the idea of them dating but I know it won't work out. I hate knowing Zoe's going to get hurt."

"You can't always keep people from getting hurt. Also, you're kind of adorable in protective cousin mode."

"I know."

"You know you're adorable?"

Ty rolled their eyes.

"Your cousin does a better eye roll." Leslie smiled and stepped forward, reaching for Ty's hand. "But you're way more my type, crew boss."

"Lucky for me."

Leslie felt the fire that had been embers for the past half hour flicker back to a flame when Ty brought her hand up to their lips. "Mm." She moaned softly, thinking of where Ty's hand had been an hour ago. "I have to ask you something before I get distracted."

"Uh-oh."

"It's not a big deal, but it's something I need cleared up." She saw the trepidation on Ty's face and quickly pushed on. "Are you really okay with me joining you on the camping trip and crewing and all of that?"

"I am." After a moment, Ty added, "I'm maybe a little worried it won't be as much fun as Zoe makes it sound."

"Ah. So, it turns out I'm a grown adult and fully prepared to suffer the consequences of my decision."

"I know, but—"

"I might hate camping," she said, interrupting Ty. "But I want to try it. I want to get a little peek at the endurance racing world too."

"It's not nearly as exciting as Zoe makes it sound."

"Me having a good time and being happy is up to me. Not you."

"Sometimes happy is a group project."

"True. *And*, I don't want you to worry about making me happy when you'll be worrying about Zoe and Polaris. If I come, can you still focus on what you need to do?"

Ty exhaled. "Yes."

"Good." Leslie shifted closer. "I'm glad we got that out of the way. Now. There's something else we need to discuss."

Ty cocked their head.

"I think you should follow me home."

"Hmm. Okay." Ty stepped in front of her. "Why?"

Leslie slipped a hand behind Ty's neck. "Because I want more of this." She shifted forward and pressed her lips against Ty's.

The kiss raced through her body. God, the things she wanted to do with Ty. All the things she'd written about. All the kinky things they'd done together. For once, her fantasies could become real. She felt a thrill at the thought, promptly followed by a swell of misgiving. How far could she go? And could she really keep from hurting Ty again?

She stepped back and Ty's eyes stayed closed for a moment like they were savoring the kiss. Her heart skipped a beat. *I can't let either of us get in too deep.*

"Damn," Ty breathed out. "You sure know how to convince someone to go along with what you want."

"I have a few skills." For Ty's sake she had to be careful with how she used those skills. But that didn't mean they couldn't enjoy each other.

Ty walked her to her car and then kissed her again. A light kiss but full of the promise that things weren't over.

"Don't get in an accident. I want you in my bed in thirty minutes." She gave Ty a light push toward their Jeep.

"Yes, ma'am," Ty said.

"Watch it. I might make you pay for the ma'am comment."

"Like you used to make Hitch pay every time they called you ma'am?" Ty grinned and hopped in the driver's seat of the Jeep. "How fast do you drive?"

Not fast enough, she thought. The possibilities of payback danced in her mind as she waited for Ty to start the Jeep's engine. She pulled out of the driveway first with Ty following down the gravel road. She was wet. Again. And knowing she'd have to wait to have her needs met only made the sight of the Jeep's headlights in her rearview mirror all the more distracting.

CHAPTER TWENTY-FIVE

When the road dipped before the cutoff to the water tower access road, Leslie eased the pressure on the gas pedal. A moment later, she tapped the brakes, then stopped completely and let the Mercedes idle. The Jeep cruised to a stop behind her. She eyed the access road and then the Jeep again.

"Fuck, what am I thinking?"

She was thinking she wanted Ty now. The half hour to get home suddenly felt too long. She hit the turn signal, then turned onto the access road. Since when had she become spontaneous? Since when did she agree to go camping or let someone have her in a barn?

She didn't go far before stopping again. This time she turned off the ignition and got out. Ty hopped out of the Jeep with a look of concern.

"Something wrong with your car?"

"No. I just want to be in yours." She took a shaky breath, wondering why she was all nerves now. "Is it okay if we don't go back to my place?"

Ty's brow furrowed. "I think I'm missing something."

"I don't want to wait."

Ty smiled. "That changes everything."

Leslie stepped forward and met Ty's lips. They responded with a thorough kiss that left her breathless. When Ty pulled back, she had to stop the whine that rose up.

"The water tower isn't far," Ty said. "And it's a nice view."

She didn't care about the view, but she let herself be led to Ty's Jeep. As soon as she'd settled into the passenger seat, her thoughts zipped to what she wanted next. Ty got in and she set her hand on their thigh. "Do you know how much I want you right now?"

"Didn't have enough earlier?"

"You weren't naked. And you called me ma'am, so you better be ready for some paybacks."

Ty smiled but she sensed some hesitation. Maybe she was pushing too hard. Before she could decide how to ask if kink talk was okay in real life, Ty said, "You might want to put on your seat belt. It's a short drive but it won't be smooth."

As soon as she clicked the buckle, Ty hit the gas. The Jeep bounced off the road to swerve around her Mercedes. Leslie laughed, jostled again when the Jeep pulled back onto the road. "Did you do that on purpose?"

Ty grinned. "Nope. Welcome to an off-road ride."

"This is my first time in a Jeep. Go easy on me." She'd seen some Jeeps that were plush but Ty's had nothing fancy about it. She glanced over her shoulder at the back. The rear seats were folded down, and judging from the bits of hay scattered about, she guessed a hay bale had recently filled the space.

"I've got some blankets we can spread out," Ty said. "But there's not a lot of room back there."

"I'm not worried." Not about the space, anyway. The only thing she was worried about was how fast she wanted to take things. "It's more room than we had the first time."

"We can say we're making our way up to a real bed."

It was a joke, but Leslie wondered if there was some truth to it. She didn't ask, though. Instead, she reached her hand across the drive shaft and set it back on Ty's leg. Ty smiled. "Your hand feels good there, but it won't last long."

One moment later, the Jeep bumped over something and her hand bounced up again. She pulled back, laughing.

"You signed up for a rough ride, right?"

"Apparently." She laughed again, loving the way Ty looked her up and down with a cocky smile.

Several bumps and bounces later, the water tower came into sight. The only thing visible beyond the tall tower and a cluster of oak trees were faint lines of rolling hills in the distance. When Ty switched off the headlights, a sea of stars flickered into view.

"Wow, that's gorgeous."

"Perfect night," Ty said.

"It is. I bet this place is even prettier in the daytime."

"We'd be more likely to get caught then." Ty hopped out, went to the back, and opened a storage compartment.

Leslie watched as Ty spread what looked like a picnic blanket across the back of the Jeep. Not a bed, but she was more than a little ready to push Ty down on it. She got out and walked around to glance up at the sky. With no clouds in sight and the town far enough away, the stars glowed brighter than she'd ever seen them.

"There's Polaris," Ty said, coming up next to her and pointing to a distant star. "Not that you needed me to point that out."

"Actually, I did. I don't spend a lot of time looking up at the stars," Leslie admitted.

"Why not?"

"Too busy, I guess." The reality made her unexpectedly sad. She forced a smile when she realized Ty was studying her instead of the stars. "And I don't have a Jeep to take me places like this."

"Hang out with me and I'll take you all sorts of places."

"I'm getting that feeling." She turned to face them. "But right now I want to take you somewhere."

"Where's that?"

"On a wild ride."

Ty grinned. "I get the feeling you want to be calling the shots this time."

"Mm-hmm. I do. Think you can handle that?"

Ty reached for her hand and then took a step back, pulling Leslie with them. "Maybe. But I'm gonna tell you now, I may not be as obedient in real life as I was online."

"I like a challenge." She slipped her hand free of Ty's and placed it on their chest. "And I know how to convince you to do things for me."

She let her hand slide off Ty's chest and walked to the back of the Jeep. Ty followed, watching her as she eyed the makeshift bed. "This should work."

"You sound like you have a plan."

"Oh, I do." She smiled when Ty laughed. "You don't think I'm serious?"

Ty opened and closed their mouth, then shook their head. "I should know you're serious."

"You should. It's hot tonight. You okay with me taking off my clothes?"

Ty smiled. "I've read that line before somewhere."

Leslie shifted between Ty and the Jeep. "I'm not sure I quoted myself perfectly, but your next line is: 'If you're okay with me taking off mine.' Remember?"

"I remember."

She slipped her hands under her tank top and pulled it off, then undid her bra. "I feel like I've already done this once tonight."

"It's even better the second time going slow." Ty licked their lips, and the desire in their gaze only amped up Leslie's arousal.

"Your turn." Leslie reached out and tugged Ty's T-shirt. "Fair is fair." She shot Ty a playful look but read the hesitation on their face.

"In real life, I usually keep my clothes on."

"Why?"

Ty lifted a shoulder. "I don't like showing off my scars."

From their tense expression, she knew they were serious. She let go of the shirt hem and lightly kissed their lips, then took a step back. "I want to play, but I won't push you to do something you don't want to do."

"Wait." Ty blew out a breath. "Fuck. I wish I could be Hitch right now."

"Hitch was fun, but I like Ty better." She also knew what she needed to do. It wasn't what she'd planned on, but it was what Ty needed. And now she wanted it more than any game. "I want to make you feel good. And I wasn't kidding about liking a challenge. You want to keep your shirt on?"

"I know it's not fair and I'm sorry that—"

She shook her head, stopping Ty's apology. "Don't apologize. Tell me what's okay." She set her hand on Ty's wrist, waited for a nod, then traced a finger over the Polaris constellation tattoo. Slowly she moved up Ty's arm, outlining the curve of the muscles. She rested one hand on Ty's shoulder. She loved how solid Ty felt. "You have nice shoulders."

"Thanks. You have nice perky nipples."

Leslie smiled. "It's still a warm night, but I'm maybe ready to be…warmer." She moved her hand to the center of their chest. "Is this okay?"

Ty nodded. They set their hand on top of Leslie's, pressing it tighter against their chest. "I want to take off my shirt."

"Forget what I said about things needing to be fair." It might be torture not feeling Ty's naked body but she could handle it. It was more important to her that Ty was comfortable with what happened.

Ty gripped Leslie's hand and then stepped back. They tugged off their shirt and stood for a moment as if questioning the decision, then tossed the shirt into the back of the Jeep. Their eyes met hers.

"I haven't had my shirt off with anyone since my surgery." They reached for her hand and set it back in place in the center of their chest. Their jaw clenched like they were holding back their emotions.

"How's my hand feel on your skin?" Something way deeper than desire held her eyes hostage on Ty's.

"Nice. No…Fucking amazing."

"Good." The two scars were so faint she could hardly see them in the dim light. What she did see was gorgeous. Smooth skin, perfect pecs. She ran her hand from one side of Ty's chest to the other, loving how Ty moved into her touch. "You are so damn sexy." She'd never meant the words more. "I want to feel you all over me."

"Tell me what to do. Like you used to tell Hitch."

"I want you to get me off." She brushed a fingertip over Ty's jawbone, the sharp line catching the starlight. "And after, I want you to let me get comfortable between your legs. I want you to lie on your back and let me taste you…" Her voice trailed and she waited for a signal from Ty. "You have no idea how much I want it. Would you do all that?"

"Fuck," Ty breathed out.

"Is that a yes?"

"Yes, ma'am." Ty shifted forward and kissed her. One light kiss and then a deeper kiss before pushing her against the Jeep. She let Ty unzip her jeans but didn't try to take off theirs. It wasn't easy having restraint but she knew Ty was already letting her have more of them than they were maybe ready for. When Ty lifted her into the back of the Jeep, she kicked off her boots and shimmied her jeans down the rest of the way.

Ty moved between her legs, kissing from her mouth to her neck, between her breasts and across her belly. Their lips and their hands seemed to be everywhere at once, and she let herself be taken away by the dance of Ty's body on hers.

"God, you feel so good," Ty murmured. "I wish I had my strap."

"You had to say that, didn't you," she said. "Just to make me want what I can't have."

"We could do this again in an actual bed and I can show up prepared." They kissed Leslie's cheek, then her lips. "In the meantime, I can still make it feel good."

When Ty's mouth was on hers, she couldn't argue. She didn't want to argue, either, when Ty moved lower, sucking her still-tender nipples. But her body was getting impatient. She reached for Ty's hand and brought it between her legs.

"I want you here."

Ty nipped at her breast, then shifted their position and kissed her lips. "If you insist..."

Ty's fingers slid into her wetness. They filled her, then pulled back and stroked again, roughly brushing over her swollen clit. She pushed into their hand. "Fuck, you feel so good."

"That's my line." Ty sounded more than a little pleased. "I can't believe you're letting me do this in the back of my Jeep. You're so damn hot."

"Give me more."

Ty pulled out, then touched a wet fingertip to her lips. She licked it, holding their gaze.

"I'll give you so much more," they promised.

Ty pulled their hand away from her lips and spread her legs. Desire surged in her. "You like being able to do what you want with me, don't you?"

"So much."

When Ty entered her again, she felt a spasm of pain followed quickly by a rush of satisfaction as her body clenched on Ty's hand.

"More?"

She dipped her chin, barely managing a nod.

They shifted, spreading her farther, and slid in another finger.

"Oh, god."

Ty held her firmly in place then, one hand pinning her to the bed of the Jeep as they thrust in and out. Did Ty have four fingers in her? It was too much and yet exactly what she wanted. She let her knees go slack, giving herself to Ty's rhythm. She was already a little sore from the first time in the barn but deliciously wet. She loved having no choice but to give herself over to Ty's desire, not able to do anything more than grip Ty's forearm.

"Don't stop."

Ty leaned close and kissed her, not easing up on the rough strokes in and out of her body. "All night if that's what you want me to do, ma'am."

She closed her eyes, feeling the tingly beginnings of an orgasm. She pumped her hips faster, struggling to keep up, then let go of Ty's forearm. The climax was close. *So close.* Ty knew what they were doing and her body loved their touch.

"You want to come, don't you?" Ty's voice was husky. "Will you let me do this again after I get you off?"

She couldn't answer. Her swollen clit was taking a bruising under their forceful thrusts but she wanted every second of it. She couldn't take Ty's whole hand, but when Ty turned their wrist, pushing deeper, she begged for more.

She rode the line between pleasure and pain for two more thrusts, moaning and twisting under Ty. She didn't want it to end but she couldn't hold back the climax. When it hit, she let loose all the sounds inside her. No one was around so she didn't have to hold back, and she wanted Ty to hear all of it.

CHAPTER TWENTY-SIX

Ty was covered in sweat. So was Leslie. They couldn't seem to get enough of her, though, and even after she came they wanted to ask if they could do it all over again. Before they could say anything, Leslie pushed up on her elbows and scooted back on her butt.

"Wow."

Ty smiled. "I agree."

"No, but really." Leslie ran a hand through her hair. "My body likes you a lot."

"Same."

"I want to ask you something."

"Okay." The last thing Ty wanted to do was talk, but they waited for Leslie to go on.

"I know Hitch was like an alter ego. But was it a part you liked playing?"

"One hundred percent."

"So when I told you to do things...there weren't times where you felt like I pushed too far?"

"Never."

Leslie nodded slowly, then studied Ty for a long moment.

"Do you not believe me?"

"I'm sorry. I totally believe you. I was staring at your chest and all of your muscles and I got distracted. You are distractingly sexy."

Ty laughed. "You're the one who's sexy. I'm just…me."

"Am I pushing too much asking you to take off your pants?"

Ty shifted to their butt and sat up. They scrubbed their face, then looked back at Leslie. "Okay, truth? I do feel a little pushed. But maybe I need it. I think part of why I liked being Hitch was because I could feel you were really into me. I can tell the real-life Girl-Monday is into me too."

"I'm glad I'm making it obvious. You should also know that I'm trying to be patient but I'm fucking dying of thirst over here."

"I have a water bottle—"

"I don't need water." Leslie arched an eyebrow.

"Oh." Ty chuckled. "You want me to take off my pants."

"I want you to want to do it," she said. "But yeah. I really, really, want to taste you." She paused. "I can handle not getting that, though, if you're not ready. The last thing I want is to make you uncomfortable."

"I feel comfortable with you." Ty met Leslie's gaze. "The thing is, my parts don't completely fit how I feel on the inside. I mean, I like having a clit but…when I say I'm nonbinary, I feel that way all the way through my body. Like, I wish I had both parts."

"Now that would be fun."

"Best answer ever." Ty grinned. "You know, I've never told anyone that."

"Thanks for telling me." Leslie reached over and set her hand on Ty's. "I've been with women and men. More women lately, but I like all the parts. Mostly I like this part." Leslie let go of Ty's hand and tapped their forehead, then ran her hand through Ty's hair.

"My hair?" Ty joked.

She narrowed her eyes. "You know what I meant. Your hair is a mess right now, by the way." She finger-combed Ty's hair for a moment, pushing strands into place, then met their gaze. "I want to make you feel good. Whatever that means for you."

Ty pictured Leslie between their legs and knew they wanted that. *In theory.* The problem was, they hadn't been naked with anyone for a long time. They always wore a strap-on or boxers or both—along with a T-shirt. Would they even be able to relax enough to enjoy it?

"It's been a while since I've let anyone go down on me."

Leslie nodded slowly. "What if you don't think of it that way? Can you picture your body the way that feels sexy to you? Then picture my mouth on those parts."

Ty looked down at their jeans. They flicked open the button and toyed with the clasp on the zipper. Could they picture it? They'd done so a thousand times alone.

Leslie set her hand on Ty's crotch, covering the zipper. "You can leave it zipped if you want. I've got some other tricks."

"I know all about your tricks." Ty forced a smile. "Fuck, I feel ridiculous. I'm thirty-five years old and don't know how to be in my own body." They looked up at the stars, trying to fight the swell of emotion. "I want to try being naked with you, but I might change my mind halfway in."

"You can change your mind anytime."

Ty trusted Leslie but knew they'd be embarrassed if they had to stop her. "I wish I didn't have so much baggage."

"It is a nice night to pretend you don't have baggage," Leslie said. "I'm quite enjoying it myself."

"You have baggage about your body? But it's perfect."

Leslie's hand moved off their crotch and settled on their thigh. "I'm a cisgendered female. Yeah, I have baggage about my body. It's different than yours, but it's baggage all the same. And I've got baggage about sex too. Well, I wouldn't call it baggage. More like issues. And issues about life in general." She sighed, then scrunched up her nose. "So don't go thinking you're special."

Ty smiled. "Wouldn't dream of it."

"Good." Leslie winked. "I do like it that you help me forget about my issues. And the baggage too."

"I wish you could see yourself the way I see you. You really are gorgeous."

"You should see me in lingerie."

"I'd like that. But it wouldn't be better than this." Ty held her gaze for a moment, desire rippling through them. They moved Leslie's hand to their zipper.

"Are you asking me to take off your pants?"

Ty nodded. They watched as she slowly tugged the zipper, heart pushing up in their chest. When their pants were off, Leslie touched the waistband of their boxers and their throat went dry. Were they ready to be naked?

"I don't know if it makes any difference or not, but you're doing me a big favor here," Leslie said.

"I'm doing you a favor?"

"I've been thinking about how you would taste for way too long. It's been driving me a little wild being close to you and not getting to try you." Leslie drew a line over the seam of their boxers, then continued the line upward. Her light touch coursed over Ty's belly button, between their scars, over their throat, and stopped at their lips. She took away her finger and replaced it with her lips.

When she pulled back from the kiss, she said, "I really want to suck you off." She settled between their legs, her hands lightly roaming up and down Ty's chest, then stopping again at their boxers. "Can I?"

Ty barely suppressed a whimper. They were so hard for Leslie. And still nervous.

"It's okay to tell me no."

"I want to say yes." Ty swallowed. "But can you...I don't want anything inside."

Leslie nodded. "What else?"

The press of Leslie's fingertip on the seam of their boxers made them feel drunk with need. It'd been so long since they'd had a woman between their legs. All of their fantasies started with that and now they wanted it more than anything.

"Can you pretend my clit is a cock?" Ty felt a blush push up their neck just saying the words aloud.

"I used to do that with Hitch sometimes."

"Really?"

She nodded. "I thought it was hot that you were nonbinary. It has me even more turned on at the moment. But everything about you has me turned on."

Ty moved Leslie's hand lower on their boxers. "I want your mouth here." They shifted up, pushing their sex into her palm and feeling a pulse of warmth spread out.

Leslie moaned, eyes closing as Ty rubbed against her hand. "So much better than the screenshot."

Ty wasn't sure what she meant, but before they could ask, Leslie shifted and pressed her lips against theirs a second time. One deep kiss and then another. They stopped thinking. Leslie's lips were too distracting.

Ty was dimly aware of Leslie's hands moving up and down their chest, stroking their arms, pushing their boxers down an inch. Only when Leslie stopped kissing their lips and began kissing everywhere else, did they open their eyes. Leslie's dark hair fanned out on their chest. She kissed her way over their belly and then tugged the boxers down another inch. Ty tensed and she looked up at them.

"You want me to stop?"

"No." Ty licked their lips. How many times had they imagined Girl-Monday dropping to her knees to suck them off? But instead of the nondescript face of a stranger, now it was Leslie in the fantasy. And she was more beautiful than Ty could have imagined. Sculpted features, soft curves, and gorgeous dark eyes. "Don't stop."

Leslie took off Ty's boxers and settled between their legs, slipping an arm under each thigh like she had every intention of staying for the night. Her chin hovered over Ty's pulsing center and her lips parted. "May I?"

Ty pushed into her mouth. One second they had everything under control. The next their mind was complete chaos.

"Fuck." The word came out involuntarily. Ty gasped, pulled away from Leslie's tongue that had sent a rocket exploding through them, then immediately pushed back into her. The sensation was overwhelming. Every nerve fired at the same time. They twitched as Leslie's tongue skirted over their swollen sex again, jerking away once more only to be pulled back by a magnet they had no ability to resist.

Leslie's grip on their thighs tightened. "I knew you would taste good," she murmured. "I want every drop of your cum."

Ty opened their mouth, caught between another gasp and a moan. Leslie knew what she was doing with her tongue, and by the sounds she was making, she was enjoying it. But no way could she be enjoying it as much as Ty.

Leslie stroked and circled and sucked, sending their mind to oblivion with waves of pleasure. They climaxed once but Leslie only let up long enough for them to ride it out before her tongue and her lips were right back to work.

The second orgasm wasn't as strong as the first but seemed to last longer. Tremors passed through them, making their toes curl. Ty covered their groin with their hand, squeezing their legs together and slurring an apology to Leslie as they crushed her between their thighs. Their brain didn't seem to work anymore but their muscles were on strike as well. When they finally relaxed enough to take a deep breath, Leslie said, "Can I go for three?"

Ty pulled her up to their lips. Leslie tasted like sex. They breathed it in after the kiss, then wrapped her tight against their chest. Her naked body felt even more petite now in their arms.

"That felt unbelievably good," Ty said.

"Is that a yes to one more time?"

Ty smiled. Even that took effort. "I don't know if I can handle another orgasm."

"You don't know until you try," Leslie said. "Please? I didn't get enough of you."

"How did you not get enough?"

"I don't think I'll ever get enough of you."

Leslie's tone was so serious, Ty opened their eyes and looked at her. She seemed to be waiting for them.

"I made a mistake once with you, Ty. I'm scared of making another one." She held Ty's gaze. "This feels like something perfect. I don't want to screw up."

"We both know what we're doing."

"Do we?" She shook her head and shifted down on Ty's body, settling again between their legs. "I don't want to think. I just want more of you."

Ty pushed into Leslie's mouth.

CHAPTER TWENTY-SEVEN

"I took off my shirt."

Zoe looked up sharply from the topographical map. "I'm sorry, what?" The map had taken up the entire kitchen table and Skittles dotted a trail. She shook her head slowly, like she was trying to make sense of what Ty had said. "With who?"

"Leslie."

"Leslie?" Zoe squinted at Ty. "When?"

"Last night."

"Dammit, Ty." Zoe slapped the table, sending the Skittle candy markers scattering.

"Why are you upset? You're the one who told me I needed to go to counseling to learn how to open up to people."

"Having sex with someone isn't opening up to them."

"Well, yeah, but the reason I told you I took off my shirt is because that's me opening up."

"To someone you hardly know."

"I've known her for a long time," Ty argued.

"What really happened with that online thing between you two? I know it's more than you've told me."

Ty shook their head. "I can't talk about it. I made a promise."

"It's two weeks to Tevis. Couldn't you have waited two weeks to fuck her?"

"Are you mad at me for starting something with Leslie because you're jealous? Or because you're scared? I won't let you down for Tevis. You know that."

"Fuck you. I'm not jealous. Or scared. I just know that I need you and I don't want you distracted."

"I can run your crew distracted. I'm not the one in the race." Ty hadn't wanted to bring up things with Jenna, but they went for it. "It's kind of annoying that you're chewing me out for being distracted when I saw you coming out of Jenna's room this morning and you clearly weren't in your bed last night."

Zoe closed her eyes and dropped her head, cussing softly. When she opened her eyes, she didn't look at Ty. Instead, she picked up one of the red Skittles and slammed it onto the Auburn campground. The finish line. "All I'm saying is that you could have waited two weeks to start a relationship."

"We're not getting into a relationship. We had sex. That's it."

Zoe muttered, "Sure," as she shook her head. "For your information, Jenna and I didn't have sex last night."

"What'd you do all night? Cuddle?"

"Why don't you like her? She's smart, she's got her shit together, and she's a nice person. What more do you want?"

"She *seems* like she has her shit together. She's as much of a mess as the rest of us. Honestly, I think more. But that's not point. You and I both know that she pressured you once and—"

"She came on to me and I turned her down because I wasn't in the right headspace." Zoe exhaled. "Not that you asked, but the new meds I'm on have really been helping. I'm starting to feel like I could date someone and actually be...me." She held up her hand. "But before you say it, no. I'm not ready to date Jenna."

Zoe pushed the Skittles around on the map, not looking at Ty. "After we came back from the ranch, we hung out talking in the living room. She's been stressed about applying for an internship and stressed about getting the residency her mom wants for her." She stopped talking for a moment and pushed the red Skittle south of Auburn. "Anyway, she wanted someone to talk to but Holly came home looking exhausted so we went to Jenna's room so we wouldn't keep Holly awake. We watched old episodes of *Lost* and I fell asleep."

"You've liked her for a while."

"Yeah." Zoe plucked a yellow Skittle near Tahoe off the map and popped it in her mouth. "And I want to sleep with her. But I'm not ready yet, so it didn't happen. You were the one who told me it was dumb to have sex with people you like if you weren't prepared for the emotions that came with it."

"No counseling at all and I came up with that?"

"Sometimes you're actually smart." Zoe stuck out her tongue.

"I'm sorry for jumping to conclusions with you and Jenna."

"And?"

Ty sighed. "And I trust you to do the right thing." They came around to Zoe's side of the table and moved a green Skittle into place at Robie Park—the start of the ride. "I didn't want you and Jenna hooking up if you both didn't think it through. But you think everything through and I should know better."

"You should. If anyone is going to overthink something, it's this girl right here." Zoe jabbed her thumb at her chest.

"It's going to be a long year for all of us. And it'd be harder for everyone if you two hook up and then decide it doesn't work. You'll still have to live together—and share a bathroom. But if you're really not feeling pressured, maybe you two would be good for each other."

"Now you approve of us fucking?"

Ty closed their eyes. "Can we not call it that? You know you're basically my little sister. I don't want to imagine Jenna all over you."

"Fine. But you should know it was me this time, not Jenna. I tried to get her to kiss me last week after the party. She was drunk. I was sober." Zoe popped a Skittle in her mouth. "I'll spare you the details because fair is fair and I don't want to think about what you and Leslie did last night."

"I want you to be happy more than anything." They bumped Zoe's shoulder with theirs. "And Jenna's not awful. Maybe I want someone better for you but I'm not your parent."

"Even though you sometimes act that way."

"Me?" Ty mocked a look of surprise and Zoe nodded a little too emphatically. "I just don't want you to get hurt."

"I know." Zoe wrapped an arm around Ty's waist and leaned against them. "*And* I don't want you to get hurt with this thing with Leslie which is most definitely going to become a relationship."

"Neither of us has time for that." Ty reached for another Skittle, but instead of moving it onto the trail line, popped it into their mouth.

"I think Polaris and I could finish in the top ten."

"I thought you were only aiming for a buckle."

"I am. But you've seen how good she's looking lately." Zoe pushed one of the scattered Skittles into line. "Maybe not this year, but one of these years, I know she could win."

"It takes two to win. But I know you both could do it."

"Only with you crewing." Zoe pushed away from Ty and studied the section of the map near Goat Rock. "How'd it feel when you took off your shirt?"

"I was scared. But when Leslie touched my chest, all these things happened at once. Her hand felt so good on me and I felt sexy as fuck and strong and—"

Zoe held up her hand. "I get the picture. You liked it."

"I loved it."

"Good. It's about time you had someone appreciate you." Zoe shook out another handful of Skittles onto the map and then passed Ty the rest of the bag. "So, I guess we don't need to find Leslie her own tent." She reached for her Tevis notebook and checked "extra tent" off the to-do list.

"Polaris and you could win. You and I both know it. If you want to go for it this year, I won't stop you."

Zoe didn't say anything, only stared at the map and then at her to-do list.

"Also, the digital version of the trail map is—"

"All right, this conversation is over. Get out of here. You know how I feel about my maps."

Ty laughed but Zoe waved them off as if they'd already left the kitchen.

"Goodbye, see you later. Go call Leslie or something. I want to obsessively plan out every last mile of this ride."

Ty rolled their eyes but it was only for show. There was something adorable about Zoe's love for planning and love of paper maps. There was also something amazing about Zoe on meds that worked for her. The difference from even six months ago was undeniable. But Ty knew it wasn't only the meds. She'd decided to turn her life around and gone for it.

Ty hung in the kitchen a moment longer, feeling a swell of affection. Cousin had never been quite the right word to describe their bond. They'd do anything for her. Including giving her a horse who truly had the potential to win a race they'd always dreamed of winning.

Zoe's dark blond hair fell over her shoulders as she peered at the space between Tahoe and Auburn. It wasn't much distance really. Only a hundred miles. And yet so much could go wrong. They offered up a silent prayer to whoever was listening that Zoe and Polaris would make it to the last Skittle on the line without getting hurt.

"Hey, Zoe."

She didn't look up from the map. "What?"

"I love you."

A soft smile curved her lips but she kept her gaze trained on the map. "You say that like I don't know it already."

"Still love you."

"Love you too, cuz. If I didn't know why you were acting weird, I'd ask. But clearly it's because you got laid last night."

"Whatever." Ty couldn't argue. The last twenty-four hours had been a strange hurricane of emotions. The uncertainty, the fears, the highs with Leslie, and then the lows at work.

They'd taken over a patient that morning that the night tech had worried would likely be euthanized. A big, beautiful Thoroughbred with two severed flexor tendons. He was in perfect condition and it'd been a freak accident. His owner had been hosing him down after they'd won a cross-country jumping event. Something had spooked him. No one knew exactly what happened because the owner had been taken to a different hospital. She'd been crushed under him.

If something like that happened to Zoe and Polaris... Ty pushed away the thought and headed to their room. Penelope was sound asleep in the middle of the unmade bed and the rest of the room was a mess. They ignored the piles of laundry and sank down next to the Chihuahua. When they pet her head, she opened her one eye, licked their palm, then curled up tighter in the little cinnamon-roll way she slept. Calamity Jane, Holly's border collie, had gone with Holly down to her folks' place in San Bernadino, which meant the other animals in the house were doing as they pleased. For Penelope, doing as she pleased meant napping.

Ty pushed a pillow under their head and reached for their phone. They eyed Penelope, knowing by her perked ears that she wasn't truly asleep. "Think Leslie will answer if I call?"

Penelope made an annoyed groaning sound but opened her eye and crawled closer to Ty's leg. She rested her muzzle on Ty's thigh when they pet her head.

"You know, you drive Jenna crazy when you sleep in my room instead of hers."

Penelope closed her eye, clearly not intending on responding.

"Fine. Be stubborn." Ty glanced at the phone and then at the Chihuahua. They hadn't actually talked to Leslie on the phone since the one time. Everything after had been texts.

Ty stared at the number on the screen until the phone timed out and the screen went dark. They tossed it on the mattress next to Penelope and closed their eyes.

Instantly, they were back at the water tower and Leslie's hand was on their chest. "Fuck. I want to talk to her." They reached for the phone again and Penelope's look was definitely judgey. "You gonna tell me I'm making a mistake?" It was too late. The phone was ringing.

Leslie answered before Ty had thought of what to say. "Hi."

"Hi." Leslie didn't sound mad, but her tone was curt. "I'm in a meeting but we were just wrapping up. Can you give me a minute?"

Ty's heart hammered in their chest as they listened to Leslie excuse herself from said meeting. They should have texted. What were they even going to say? That last night had been amazing and they wanted some confirmation that it'd really happened?

"Hi again." Leslie's voice sounded warmer this time. More friendly.

"Should I have texted?"

"Calling is fine. I might not always be able to answer but—hang on, I'm stepping into my office."

Ty tried to picture Leslie's office and fit the sounds that came through the line into the image. A door opening and closing, then a faint rustling that might be papers. "Are you sitting at your desk?"

"Maybe I am. If you ask me what I'm wearing, I won't be able to answer seriously."

"What are you wearing?"

Leslie laughed. "As much as I'd love to answer that, I've got big windows and the blinds only partly close."

Ty smiled, knowing what she was thinking. "Don't worry, I wasn't calling you for phone sex. This time."

Leslie laughed again. "I'm not saying you couldn't now. But I'd prefer not to be hot and bothered at work." She paused, maybe drinking something. "You sound sleepy. Where are you?"

"On my bed. And I am sleepy. I was thinking of taking a nap, actually. I couldn't sleep last night."

"Really? I went home and crashed. Can't remember the last time I slept so well."

Ty couldn't help feeling a swell of pride. "You're welcome."

"Yes, thank you," Leslie said, taking on a proper tone that made Ty laugh. "Why couldn't you sleep?"

"I was too wired, I think."

"Sounds like I didn't do my job right."

"No, you were perfect." Maybe too perfect. "It was all me."

"Hmm. You could come to my place later and I can try some other methods to help you relax."

"Other methods, huh?" Ty chuckled.

"I know lots of methods. And I have the best bed."

Ty glanced at the time. They'd worked a ten-hour day on no sleep but the thought of being with Leslie again was enough to stir up a second wind. "You inviting me for a sleepover?"

"I am. Unfortunately, I've got a client I have to take to dinner at seven but I'll be home by nine."

"Text me your address."

"You're going to laugh when you find out where I live."

Leslie ended the call and Ty waited for the text. The address blinked on their screen along with a winking emoji and Ty couldn't help smiling. Leslie's place was only three streets over.

They quickly texted back: *I can't believe you live on Tiber.*

Leslie: *Small world, right?*

Ty had never gone down Tiber Avenue on their runs, though they'd passed it too many times to count. They'd never driven down it either because it was the opposite direction from the vet school. But even if they'd passed Leslie on the street months ago, they never would have guessed she was Girl-Monday.

Ty pushed away the question of whether a sleepover was a good idea and set an alarm for a quarter past eight. Thinking could happen later.

CHAPTER TWENTY-EIGHT

"Ty, turn off your alarm." Jenna's voice jostled Ty awake. "I can't take any more noise. I had to recover two huskies from surgery and there was a hound dog in ICU that wouldn't stop baying."

"Sorry." Ty reached for the phone, turning off the wake-up song that reliably got them out of bed each morning. Penelope was gone. Ty guessed she'd slipped out of the room to eat dinner. They rubbed their eyes, staring at the time and hoping it wasn't true. "It's not really eight forty-five, is it?"

No one answered.

Ty cursed and hopped out of bed. They hardly had time for a shower but they weren't showing up at Leslie's still smelling like work. No one wanted a hookup date that smelled like the equine barn.

Five minutes after an icy shower brought them fully awake—and too long spent wondering if they really could manage not getting attached to Leslie—they were hurrying into clothes. Nothing fancy, just jeans and a T-shirt. After a minute of indecision, they dug through their dresser for the boxers that had an O-ring for a strap-on. Ty had worn them before with the women they'd met from the dating app. Each time they'd put a condom on the strap-on and kept the boxers on the entire time, along with a tank top or a T-shirt they never took off. They'd argued it was about safe sex, but the staying dressed part was more about keeping their heart safe. That had gone out the window with Leslie last night.

They tossed a change of clothes and a dildo into a backpack, trying not to think about the fact that if they stayed the whole night, it'd be the first time in years they'd slept with anyone. "That's assuming sleeping happens," Ty murmured.

Leslie opened the door with a plate of cookies in hand.

"You baked?"

"I did. My client canceled last-minute so I came home and baked. I thought of calling you to join me but you sounded like you needed some sleep."

"I did," Ty admitted. "Even slept through my alarm. Thirty minutes of Britney Spears's 'Oops I Did It Again' on repeat."

Leslie looked dubious. "Is that your usual pick?"

"You don't love Britney?"

"I..." Leslie's hesitation was answer enough. When Ty pretended to turn around and leave, she reached out and caught their shoulder. "Get your butt back in here. We can talk about all my failings later."

Leslie's hand on Ty's shoulder was impossible to resist. Not that they wanted to resist. They met Leslie's gaze and their heart bounced up in their chest when she smiled. "It's good to see you."

"I was thinking the same thing." Leslie held out a cookie. "Snickerdoodle? This recipe is one of my favorites."

Ty took a bite of the cinnamon-sugar-covered cookie. Butter, sugar, vanilla, and cinnamon all seemed to take center stage. "These might be better than those double chocolate ones."

"I'm going to bake a few different kinds and freeze them for Zoe. I want her to have some variety."

"She's gonna love that."

"I hope so. I'm taking this crew thing seriously. I've got a crew boss I want to impress." Leslie opened her door farther. "Come on in."

Ty finished the cookie in another two bites, then took off their shoes and set them by the door along with their backpack. The boots Leslie had worn last night were lined up next to a pair of heels, sandals, and one pair of running shoes.

Ty straightened and smiled. The place was exactly what they would've imagined for Girl-Monday. Sparsely decorated but tasteful and organized. One glance and they knew Leslie wouldn't have a chair in her bedroom filled with unfolded laundry. All the books on the shelf were perfectly aligned and the artwork was carefully framed. The furniture in the front room was clearly high-end, and the plush carpet immaculate. Even the sleek black cat that studied Ty from under the coffee table seemed to fit with the décor and have an assigned spot.

"Something wrong?"

"Not at all. I was thinking this place fits you. Smells amazing and it's all put together and fancy."

Leslie rolled her eyes. "I think you know I'm not always put together. Or fancy."

"But you always smell amazing."

"Did you practice that line?" She shook her head, laughing, and added, "I almost believe that you're serious, though, which makes me want to let it slide. Here, have another cookie." She waited for Ty to take one and then gestured to the living room. "See if you can make yourself comfortable in my fancy house. I'm going to make us drinks."

Ty didn't ask what Leslie was making. They ate the second cookie as they read through the titles on the bookshelf, wondering which ones Leslie liked and if she'd read them all, then checked out a framed painting of a cat sitting in a window. The cat looked suspiciously like the black cat hiding under the coffee table.

"Is this you?" Ty asked, peering under the table.

The cat met their gaze, then pointedly looked away.

Ty walked over to the second painting. It was on the wall over the sofa. A solitary horse in a red rock desert background. The horse painting was done in an impression style and Ty looked for the artist's name.

"Do you like that one?" Leslie asked, handing Ty a tumbler glass.

"I love it."

"Me too. But now when I look at it, I think of Nellie being alone for so long." She sipped the tumbler she was holding. "I found it in a little studio in Santa Fe. There was another painting that went with it. I thought the second one was too busy—it was of the rest of the herd looking back at this one here."

"And now you think this one looks lonely?" It did, in a way. "You could go back to Santa Fe and buy the other painting. There's enough room on the wall for two."

"I tried. Someone else bought the second painting and the artist didn't have any others." Leslie lifted a shoulder. "It taught me to jump on art that I like."

"I've noticed you don't only do that with art."

"Very funny." She stepped forward and brushed a light kiss on Ty's lips. When she pulled back, her expression made Ty want more than a kiss. "Thanks for coming over. I know it's late and you probably have work tomorrow."

"So do you, right?"

"Yes, and if I'm as distracted tomorrow as I was today, my office assistant is going to ask questions." Leslie arched an eyebrow. "I'm trying to decide how to explain you."

Ty wished Leslie didn't need to think of an explanation. Wished that it could be simple. But it wasn't. They weren't dating; they'd met online at an anonymous sex site, and they'd already broken up once. No one would believe that a relationship would work. It wasn't that bothering Ty so much, though, as the fact that Leslie had her whole life together while they were still in school and stressing about the cost of groceries.

"Did I say the wrong thing?"

"No, I was just thinking." Ty shook their head. "Maybe overthinking."

"You're not the only one who does that. What is it?"

"Last night you mentioned having all these issues. But you seem so together. You have a job you like, a beautiful home. Cute cats. Friends. And you're amazing and—"

"Sometimes you don't see the issues right away," Leslie said.

Ty held Leslie's gaze as she took a deep breath and set down her drink.

"You told me Zoe was on meds for depression?"

Ty nodded.

"I'm on meds too." She sighed. "I like to pretend it's not a big deal, and at this point, most days it isn't. I've figured out how to manage. But it took me a while to accept I needed help and a lot longer to find a medication that worked—and didn't have side effects I hated.

"I was on antidepressants at first but now I'm on something for anxiety. The depression got better with therapy and, well, life changes. But I've promised my therapist I'll let her know if it becomes a problem again."

Leslie spread her hands. "See? Issues. And I seem almost normal, right?" She made a face like she clearly didn't put much stock in the word.

"It's okay to need meds."

"How would you feel if you knew I had to take two of my anxiety pills yesterday instead of one because I knew work was going to be stressful and I still wanted to see you and have a horse lesson?"

"I'd feel thankful you trusted me enough to tell me," Ty said. "And I'd admire that you've got yourself so well figured out."

Leslie smiled. "I tell you I'm on meds and you honestly sound impressed. Who are you?"

Ty smiled back and took a sip of the drink. "This is good. What'd you give me?"

"Gin and tonic."

"It goes well with snickerdoodles."

Leslie glanced at her own drink but didn't reach for it. "Maybe we need to slow down and hang out tonight. Want to watch something?" She motioned with her chin to the television screen.

Ty had no desire to watch anything but murmured, "Sure."

Leslie reached for the remote and sat down, patting the sofa next to her. "I can tell you'd rather do something else, but sit down anyway. I'm on episode five of *Is It Cake?* If you've seen this one, don't tell me which one's the real cake."

Ty sat down on the sofa but focusing on the show with Leslie so close was impossible. She had her hair down and the dark locks fell in soft waves over one shoulder. At the other shoulder, a cherry-red bra strap peeked out from under her loose gray shirt.

Leslie bumped her knee against Ty's. "You're supposed to be watching the show, not me."

"Right." Ty looked back at the TV. They lasted maybe five minutes—long enough for the stress of the baking and decorating to make them glad they weren't a contestant. Their gaze tracked back to Leslie. She wasn't wearing shoes and her shorts stopped mid-thigh, leaving a long distance of smooth tanned skin for Ty to imagine under their hands.

"How was work?" Ty asked.

"Fine," Leslie murmured, not looking away from the screen. "When I couldn't focus on contracts, I decided to work on my story."

"That novel you were writing? The one about the realtor detective who finds the dead body?"

Leslie nodded. "It's been in my head more lately...I finally wrote the kissing scene."

"Can I read it?"

"No way. Not a chance."

"Why not?"

Leslie seemed to watch the show but Ty could tell she was stalling on answering.

"Is it a straight kissing scene?"

"No. It's two women who fall in love. Well, they might fall in love. I haven't decided that part yet. I also haven't completely decided on the killer."

Ty grinned. "Sounds fun. Why don't you want me to read it?"

"I'd be too embarrassed. The whole story is probably terrible. I can't handle anyone reading it."

"Not yet? Or not ever?"

Leslie reached for one of the throw pillows and hugged it to her chest. "Probably not ever. I kind of regret telling you I started working on it again. Apparently, I'm in an oversharing mood."

"I'm not going to make you show me the story. But you already know I like your writing. Your kissing scenes especially."

"This is different." Leslie blew out a breath and lowered the pillow. Instead of looking at Ty, she stared at the screen. The show announcer was trying to cut through a bowl of tortilla chips.

"Not a cake!" he said cheerfully.

"Okay, truth?" Leslie turned and met Ty's gaze. "I want someone to read the story. I mean, someday, I maybe even want to try publishing it. I love reading—anything, really, but especially fiction." She gestured to the bookshelf. "That's only a quarter of my books and you should see my Kindle. I love when a writer completely takes me away, you know? Like I forget that I've lived my entire life in Davis and instead I'm working at a research facility in Antarctica. Or having sex at a Halloween party in the Castro."

Ty laughed.

"Books are amazing, right?" She smiled, then added, "And I love it when I read a sentence and feel like someone else understands me. Like maybe I'm not alone, you know?"

"You make me want to read more." How long had it been since they'd picked up a fiction book? Too long. "Maybe you could give me some recommendations? Although mostly I just want to read your writing."

She pursed her lips. "I was in that writers' group and I never shared my stuff."

Ty held out their hand, palm up. When Leslie clasped their hand, they said, "Do you know how scared I was last night?"

Leslie's shoulders dropped. "I'm sorry if I pushed you—"

"I wanted the push," Ty said. "And sitting here, right now, I know I had nothing to be scared of. I can be myself and tell you exactly how I'm feeling. Which is the weirdest thing ever. But also I love it."

"Thanks?"

"I know I sound like I'm joking but I'm serious. I don't feel comfortable opening up to many people. There's Zoe, but no one else really. And I'm not saying this to make you feel like you have to say or do anything in return. Only thought you might want to know that I won't judge you, or your writing, at all. And I love that you don't judge me."

Leslie looked down at their interlaced fingers. She took a shaky breath. "What if I promise you can read the story first? When I'm ready."

"You don't have to promise me anything."

"I want to make the promise."

"Then I'll tell you a secret. I can't wait to read the kissing scenes. How hot is the realtor-sleuth?"

"Very hot."

Ty grinned, already picturing Leslie as the realtor-sleuth. On the television screen, cheering broke out as the announcer yelled, "Not a cake!"

"Can I ask you a question that you totally don't have to answer?" Ty asked.

Leslie nodded.

"When Zoe started on meds, she said she didn't want to have sex. She broke up with her boyfriend over it. Well, that and other things. But I think she's feeling different now on the new meds she's taking. Do you feel—" Ty stopped short, suddenly worrying if the question was too much.

"I think I know what you're wondering. The first antidepressant I tried made me feel nothing at all when my ex touched me. I couldn't orgasm." She paused. "On the plus side, I didn't care as much that she thought I was broken?"

Leslie smiled, clearly trying to keep the conversation light. "I went on another med and gained a bunch of weight. Which meant my boobs and my butt got bigger but so did my waist and I had to buy new clothes. I hated that I constantly had to think about everything I ate. Sorry you asked?"

"Not at all. As long as you're okay telling me all this."

"I am." After a moment she said, "I think it helps that I know you have problems too."

"Me?" Ty pretended to be surprised.

"Yes. You." She stuck out her tongue. "Honestly, therapy helped a lot. I figured out anxiety was a bigger issue than depression. I think about sex more than ever, and as you might have noticed last night, it feels amazing when it happens."

The announcer interrupted, calling out, "Cake!" The crowd cheered and Leslie reached for the remote, hitting the off button.

"Now that I know which one was cake," she said, moving to straddle Ty's lap, "I want to know what's in that backpack by the front door."

"You invited me to spend the night. I had to bring scrubs for tomorrow."

"That's all you brought?"

Ty knew Leslie guessed the truth. "I may have brought something else."

"Good. Oversharing makes me want sex."

Ty laughed. "The things I learn about you."

"Buckle up, there's more to learn." Leslie shifted forward and met Ty's lips with a deep kiss. She pulled back and leveled her gaze on Ty's. "I want to tell you to go grab what you brought—which is something I'd never tell someone to do."

"Why not?"

"Aside from the role-playing with Hitch, I'm not used to asking for what I want. I'm used to going along with what other people want."

"In this case it's what we both want."

"Yeah…but…" Leslie combed her fingers through Ty's hair, seeming to need a moment to think about what she wanted to say.

She could take all the time she wanted. Her fingers had Ty's attention completely, nails lightly scraping their scalp as strands of hair were tugged and then tousled. When her hand strayed to the back of their neck, toying with the shaved section like she enjoyed the feel, Ty closed their eyes.

"You make me feel like I can go for what I want. Like it's okay that I want things."

Ty opened their eyes and saw the worry in Leslie's expression. "Of course it's okay that you want things. And I want you to go for what you want. That's how it's always been with us."

"Maybe that's why it feels right now? Because that's how I was when you were Hitch and I was Girl-Monday?"

Maybe they'd fallen into the same pattern of how they'd been when they were together online? Was that what she was worried about?

"But I think it's more than that. You make me feel like the things I've always wanted are okay to want."

"How do you feel about that?"

"I like it. A lot." She moved her hand from Ty's hair down their shirt. "Can I take off your shirt?"

Ty nodded, pulse quickening. Leslie's hands had been all over them last night but it'd been dark. Now they were sitting in a fully lit room and Ty was giving up control. So many times they'd stopped other women. Was it different with Leslie because she was Girl-Monday and they'd long ago gotten used to her calling the shots? Or was it something more?

Leslie kissed Ty as her hands slid under the shirt. As she pushed up the material, her fingers brushed over Ty's nipples, sending shivers through their body.

"God, I want you," Ty said. The words slipped out but the smile that came to Leslie's lips made it worth it.

"I know." She kissed Ty again, nipping at their lower lip. When she pulled back from the kiss, she took Ty's shirt all the way off and then ran her hands over their shoulders. "I'm already wet thinking of how much you want to fuck me."

Ty tried pulling Leslie closer, but she shifted off their lap and stood.

"I want a bed tonight. Come find me in my bedroom when you're ready."

CHAPTER TWENTY-NINE

One look and Leslie knew Ty hadn't been expecting lingerie. Ty's hand hadn't left the door handle and their mouth still hung open.

"Like what you see?"

"A lot." Ty nodded. "I like it a lot."

"I like what I see too." Leslie raised an eyebrow. Ty without a shirt on was a gorgeous sight. Ty packing something that would feel amazing between her legs was even better.

Ty let go of the door handle and came into the room. After a few steps, though, they stopped again. "You told me Girl-Monday wore red lacy things, but…damn."

"Didn't think I was telling the truth?"

"Reality is better than my imagination."

When she'd worn lingerie in the past, she done it because it made her feel sexy. This time it was more about Ty. She'd wanted to give them something more than a hookup. Whatever it was they had together, it deserved more than hookup sex.

Ty's reaction to the red sheer teddy and matching panties was better than she'd hoped for, and even from across the room she could feel how eager they were to have her in their hands. "Come here."

Ty closed the distance between them. As soon as their lips were on hers, she felt the temperature in the room spike.

"The things I want to do to you." Ty moaned as they slid their hands along the seams of the teddy. "You're all dressed up and I know I should take my time but…" Their words trailed as they kissed her neck. Ty nipped her shoulder and shifted closer. "I don't know if I can go slow."

This was when she usually went quiet and let her lover have their way. But something made her want to rewrite her usual script. Maybe it was Ty. Or the mood of the evening.

"What if I make you?"

Ty pulled back, a half-smile on their lips. "I'd ask if you're serious but—"

"You know I am." She pressed a hand on their chest, pushing them back a step. "So, tell me, Ty Sutherland, what would you like first?"

When Ty moved to kiss her lips again, she shook her head. "Sometimes you have to ask for what you want in life. I'll tell you what you can have."

Ty opened and closed their mouth, then laughed. "You turn me on so hard." They glanced at the bed. "Can I pick you up and put you on that bed and fuck you exactly the way I want?"

Ty could do all of those things and she knew it. She also knew Ty would never do anything without her permission. "You can nicely ask me to lie down for you."

Ty dropped their chin. When they looked up, their arousal was so palpable Leslie wanted to give up on the game and simply spread herself. She bit her tongue and waited.

"Will you lie down for me?" Ty asked. "Please?"

Leslie went to the bed and stretched out on her side, adjusting the teddy. "What would you like to do with me now?"

Ty approached the bed. Leslie resisted staring at Ty's midsection until they stopped right in front of her. Once she let herself look, desire pulsed between her legs. She wanted Ty on top of her. She wanted to feel them thrust into her, wanted the curved shaft filling her…

"What are you thinking?" Ty asked. She considered the truth but Ty quickly added, "Or is asking your thoughts off-limits?"

She swallowed. "It was your turn to answer a question. What would you like to do with me?"

"I'd like to touch you. You're unbelievably sexy in lingerie. May I?"

She tipped her head and Ty caressed her arm, sweeping loose locks of her hair over her shoulder. They ran a fingertip along the lacy parts of the teddy, then reached for her hand, lightly kissing her knuckles. "May I join you in bed?"

"I'd like that."

Ty settled in next to her, adjusting themself. She almost reached for their strap-on then but stopped short. As she debated the benefits of waiting, Ty set their hand on her thigh. She tensed at the light touch.

"Off-limits?"

"Not off-limits." She closed her eyes as Ty's hands skimmed down her leg, then slowly up along the inside of her thigh. When she opened her eyes, Ty was watching her. She tried to keep her breathing in check, tried not to gasp when Ty's thumb grazed the edge of her panties. The material was already wet. She was so ready for them.

"I don't know how you're single. If you were mine, I'd never let you go."

Ty's words were nothing compared to the look on their face. There was no doubting they meant what they'd said and she couldn't hold back a rush of emotion. Complicated, messy thoughts that made her throat tighten. She wanted someone to want her the way Ty did, to look at her the way Ty was looking at her now. Before her heart could get tangled in what-ifs, she channeled Girl-Monday and tried for a coy smile. "I could be yours for the night."

Ty caressed her cheek, then drew a soft line across her lips. "Will you be all mine?"

"That depends. Will you show me what you can do with this?" She touched Ty's lips, then traced a line downward until she'd reached the cock.

Ty smiled. "Not my lips, huh?"

She circled the tip, drawing a light moan from Ty. "I like your lips, but I want this between my legs."

Ty touched her chin, tilting her face up to theirs. "I'll show you what I can do if you let me taste you first."

"Are you bargaining with me?" She laughed.

"Yes," Ty said, eyes creasing with their smile. "Please?"

She nodded, only feigning annoyance. Even hot and bothered, she liked their game and waiting made her more wet.

Ty kissed her. One deep kiss before they tugged off her panties and then moved on top of her. She loved being under Ty but only got to enjoy it for a moment before Ty shifted down on her, settling between her legs. They pushed up the teddy to kiss the space below her belly button, then looked up and caught her eye.

"I like the butterfly tattoo."

"It's cliché, I know. I was nineteen."

"It's pretty," Ty said. "You found a good artist."

She sucked in a breath when Ty rubbed their thumb lightly over the monarch's wings. The tattoo was just below her right hip and the spot always felt exquisitely sensitive.

"Wanna tell me why you got it?"

"No. I want to tell you to focus."

Ty chuckled, then moved from the tattoo to her center. "So difficult," they murmured, peppering kisses over her belly. They shifted lower and parted her slit. "And so wet for me."

As ready as she was, she still gasped when Ty's tongue lashed over her clit. She moaned, pulling her knees up. "Mm. I think I want one thing and you make me want something else instead."

"You taste so good. I could stay here all night."

She ran her hands through Ty's hair as she pushed up her hips. Ty licked and sucked until she nearly forgot what she'd wanted earlier. Nearly. But when she felt the rising wave of a climax, she wanted Ty inside her even more.

She wrenched away from Ty's mouth and struggled to catch her breath. Ty moved up to kiss her lips, one hand slipping under the teddy to circle her nipple. When she didn't object, Ty moved to the other nipple. Her clit throbbed, reminding her of her need.

"Did you forget you were going to show me what you could do with this?" She gripped the strap-on, drawing a groan from Ty.

"I didn't forget," Ty said. "But I may have gotten distracted."

"I have to keep you in line."

"You can try keeping me in line," Ty said. "But I may turn the tables." They pinched her nipple, sending shock waves through her.

She was still recovering when Ty stroked a finger into her opening. "You're dripping wet."

"I need more than a finger." She made a sound that was one part whine and one part moan and Ty bruised her lips with a hard kiss.

"I know," Ty said. The tip of their cock nudged her opening.

Clit quivering, she had to beg. "Please."

"For you, anything."

With the next breath, Ty thrust into her. She cried out at the sudden entry, then wrapped her arms around Ty's back to hold them in place. "Fuck."

"Too much?"

"Just right." She licked her lips, her center rhythmically clenching on Ty. "Give me more."

When she parted her legs farther, Ty thrust deeper, filling her completely. As Ty pumped into her, she tried to hold on, tried to keep pace. But Ty's kisses were everywhere at once and their hands roamed all over her body.

She let herself be taken by Ty's desire. Ty's hands slid under her hips, moving her into a better position and thrusting faster, and she only followed their lead. She was no longer in control, but her body wasn't complaining.

When Ty paused between thrusts to ask, "Will you let me take you all the way?" all she could do was nod. She was covered in sweat and the throbbing between her legs was needy and incessant, but she doubted she'd get off. Still, she didn't want Ty to stop.

"I'm gonna turn on the vibrator, okay?"

She nodded again but didn't really register Ty's words until she felt the vibrations. One click and the game changed. Ty fell back into the thrusting but their sounds left no question that the vibrations affected them too. She felt her orgasm building fast. She couldn't fight it.

Ty didn't stop and didn't slow down. When they stroked her clit, she knew she was going to come hard. But Ty's panting breaths made her realize they were close too. "I want to hear you," she said.

The sound of Ty's climax filled the room. They only went slack for a moment, though, then went right back to thrusting, hard and fast. She let Ty hear her mounting pleasure, knowing it would drive them equally wild, then heard herself asking for more even as she felt the first wave crash through her body.

The climax spread through her. She squeezed her legs together, trying to hold Ty in place as stars danced under her eyelids. She couldn't say the words to stop Ty and a second wave crashed into the first. Her fingers and toes tingled and she couldn't get a deep breath before another orgasm claimed her. Finally, when she didn't think she could take any more, she heard Ty's second orgasm break. They tensed, then shivered, groaning low and full of satisfaction. When they collapsed on her, she wrapped her arms around them as they rode out the last of the wave. Tears slid down her cheeks. Completely satisfied, can't-take-another-round, and never-felt-this-good tears. She swiped them away as she exhaled a deep breath.

Ty switched off the vibrations but didn't move to pull out of her. She gripped their body tighter, wanting to hold them in place. After a long minute, Ty shifted and kissed her cheek, murmuring, "Well, that felt good."

She laughed. "Um, understatement, but yes."

"It's an understatement, but if I say what I'm really thinking…" Ty's voice trailed. "I'm going to pull out now, okay?"

She nodded, trying to relax the muscles still clenching. When Ty came out, she rolled onto her side, feeling the emptiness all the more acutely as one thought ran through her mind. *Hookup sex never feels that good.*

CHAPTER THIRTY

Ty was more than a hookup. More than something casual. She couldn't pretend her heart wasn't on the line as she held them close. Ty, naked and sweaty, one arm draped over her, was everything she wanted.

It wasn't simply the afterglow. She knew there was more to it. All those months with Hitch and opening up to Ty without hiding anything. Instead of feeling anxious about how much she'd exposed, she only wanted to take more risks.

"I want something."

Ty kissed her cheek. "I'll give you anything."

"I want to know how spanking feels in real life." She trembled saying the words but rolled onto her belly.

"Now?"

Yes, now. She knew she should only want cuddling and for a moment she worried what Ty would think. "Please?"

"My pleasure." Ty sat up in bed. "I have to tell you I've fantasized about spanking you, but I didn't think it'd really happen. Not in real life." They traced a line down her backside. "I need you in the right position."

She shivered when Ty's hands circled her ankles. Not from cold but from anticipation. In the next second, Ty pulled her halfway off the bed. Her knees had hardly settled on the floor before Ty's palm seared her butt cheek. She gasped and her center clenched as an aftershock raced through her.

"Fuck. Yes."

Ty hesitated for only a moment. The second time stung more than the first but it excited every nerve. Ty's lips brushed over the spot their palm had struck. The kiss was so gentle, Leslie didn't hold back the tears.

"You want more?"

"Say something dirty." She couldn't believe she'd said the words aloud and heat flared up her neck.

"You're the one with all the dirty thoughts," Ty said in a low tone. "You like me looking at your ass, don't you?" They stroked their hand over the place they'd spanked, then parted her cheeks. "I know you want someone to take you from behind."

She shuddered when Ty pushed against her.

"You want it bad, don't you? Even after everything we just did, you want more."

Her breath caught when Ty leaned over her, brushing a kiss on the low of her back. Ty pulled back and spanked her again.

Pleasure spread from her butt cheek to her clit. The next spank threatened to push her over the edge. She was still reeling when Ty took her up in their arms, their chest against her back, their strap-on pressing against her butt. "So dirty. And all mine tonight."

She loved being in Ty's arms, loved knowing Ty didn't think her desires meant something was wrong with her. She reached behind her and gripped the cock. "I want this again."

It was going to hurt, but she wanted it all the same. She moved her knees apart but Ty pushed her farther, then fingered her wetness. They nudged the tip of the cock against her dripping opening.

"I can't believe you want more. You are so damn hot."

Ty pushed in with one smooth stroke. It was everything she needed. She clutched at the sheets as spasms of pain crashed against pleasure. Ty pushed her down on the mattress and got to work. She didn't stop herself from calling out Ty's name, didn't stop herself from moaning loudly and asking for more.

Minutes passed and Ty didn't let up, riding her hard and fast. Her mind seemed to drift in and out of being present with her body and hovering above watching it all play out. It was true she'd imagined it, but this was better than her fantasies.

Ty orgasmed and she savored their climax, thinking she wouldn't come again herself but not caring. She might be past the point of an orgasm, and would definitely be sore later, but when Ty started to ease out of her, she gripped their forearms—the only thing she could reach. "Don't."

"More?"

When she nodded, Ty started thrusting again. Slow deep strokes. Their hand slipped under her and fingered her clit, and she felt a weak tremor but told herself again she was too far gone.

"More."

Ty shifted and fucked her harder. She panted, struggling to keep up. Every thrust was pure bliss, but she was exhausted. Finally she let go of the sheets and fell into Ty's rhythm.

It seemed impossible, but another climax built. She tried to ignore it, wanting nothing to stop Ty, but she couldn't hold it back. She moaned as the orgasm took over.

Ty gave one last thrust, then collapsed on her. The moment was perfection. Ty, filling her, their sweaty chest against her back. She could hardly breathe but she didn't want to move. When Ty finally pulled out, she knew her body had taken all it could.

Ty brushed a kiss against her butt cheek, then spanked her.

"Fuck." She broke down and sobbed out her pleasure.

Ty wrapped her in an embrace, kissing her tears. They held her tight as she cried, then eased her onto the bed with a tender kiss on her lips. Slowly she got ahold of her emotions, and with a shaky breath, curled against Ty's chest.

Warmth enveloped her as Ty pulled the sheet over them both. They lay together quietly for a long stretch of time before Ty stroked her cheek. "You okay?"

She nodded, not able to form any words. She was more than okay. She'd been satisfied in a way she'd only dreamed about.

Ty kissed her forehead. "I don't know what I did to deserve that, but thank you."

"You're welcome," she murmured. The words fell far short of how she felt, but sleep took her in the next breath.

CHAPTER THIRTY-ONE

Ty coaxed Nellie to lift her swollen leg, then eased it into the bucket. As soon as she felt the water, she yanked her foot back up, sloshing Betadine solution everywhere. "I don't know about you, but I don't have anywhere else to be," Ty said. "We can keep doing this all day." Not that they wanted to try soaking a stubborn horse's leg for hours.

Paige appeared at the stall door with Olivia strapped to her chest in a baby carrier. "Sounds like your patient isn't being too compliant."

"We're working on understanding that we have the same shared goal."

Paige laughed. "There's a reason you get all the tough patients. You sure you don't mind soaking her leg?"

"It's no problem at all. I soak Archer's bad leg all the time. I'm a pro."

"You're definitely better at horse medicine than me. Give me all the cows and kitty cats and I'm happy." Paige swayed side to side when Olivia rustled. She yawned but didn't open her eyes. Paige watched her for a moment and then continued, "Are you ready for classes to start back up?"

Ty's thoughts went right to Leslie. They'd been at her house every night and still hadn't broached the subject of what would happen when school started up again. "Not even a little bit."

"I never was ready either...I know you said you were worried about your grades last semester, but all you have to do is pass, you know? A C still equals DVM."

"Heard that line before." Ty sighed. "But who wants a doctor who barely scraped by?" They asked Nellie to pick up her foot again, wishing Paige had more confidence in their ability to get better grades. But why would she? Ty had admitted they'd gotten two Cs the last term. Gingerly, Ty lowered Nellie's leg into the bucket. The mare seemed not to notice for a moment, then yanked it back out again.

Ty sighed. "Remember, Nellie. I got nowhere better to be."

"You're as stubborn as she is."

"Nope. Way more."

"Which is why you're going to get through this next year. I won't tell you second year is easy. It isn't. But after that the fun begins. Junior surgery and all the real medicine courses...You're going to be awesome at those. You already know so much after teching for so long." Paige paused. "Can you see a cut on the leg?"

"Not yet." They placed Nellie's leg in the bucket again and waited for her to pull it out. She didn't. Ty reached for a rag and started massaging the leg. A flap no bigger than an inch peeled open right at the fetlock. "Found it." Fortunately, Nellie was already on pain medication. Paige had noticed her favoring the leg but hadn't been able to touch it earlier to look for a wound.

"How bad?" Paige asked.

"I don't think it needs to be sutured. Let me clean it a little more and you can have a look."

"I trust you," Paige said. "We both know you can run circles around me when it comes to horses."

"I'm just glad it's not an old injury flaring up now that she's getting some exercise." That had been Ty's first worry when Paige called to tell them the leg was swollen.

"I saw her kick the fence," Paige said. "The heifers were playing, pushing each other around wanting to be first in line at the feed trough and she got annoyed. Honestly, it was nice to see her move that quick. She's gotten more lively these past few weeks."

"I know she likes going on the walks with Leslie."

"How's that going, by the way?"

"Leslie and Nellie?" Or Leslie and them? The answer that came right to mind to the second question was "unbelievable" because it was. Everything felt perfect. Too perfect to believe. "Good," they said finally. "Here, take a look." They hefted Nellie's leg up so Paige could see the laceration.

Paige nodded. "And what's your recommended treatment plan, Dr. Sutherland?"

"I'm not a doctor yet," Ty said.

"Close enough. Go on. I want to hear what you think."

Ty knew Paige was entirely serious and there was no use trying to wriggle out of answering. "I'd recommend wrapping it. Daily Betadine soaks. I can give you some ointment to use…"

"Do we need to suture the wound?"

"It's been a day since it happened, right?"

Paige nodded. "Yesterday at feeding time. Twenty-four hours exactly."

"I think it's best if we leave it to heal with second intention then. What do you think?"

"I think I'll follow my horse doc's advice," Paige said. "Thanks for the consult, Dr. Sutherland."

Ty shook their head. "I'm not ready to be called that yet."

"You better get ready quick. Before you know it, you're the one who has to make all the decisions." Paige glanced down at Olivia, still asleep. "You know, Nellie hollered for Archer when I sent him and Polaris out into the pasture this morning."

"I really want her to have a herd," Ty said, dunking Nellie's fetlock in the Betadine bath again. "Unfortunately, now we're stuck until this heals."

Nellie had gone on a handful of walks with Archer, and Ty had seen an improvement each time. More confidence and more eager to leave her stall. Leslie had gotten more confident too.

Olivia woke up with a start, crying so loud Nellie startled away from Ty. Paige announced it was time for a bottle and hurried off while Ty calmed Nellie down. The barn door had hardly swung closed before it opened again for Leslie. She came right up to Ty and Nellie, worry lining her face.

"What's wrong with her leg?"

"You got my text?"

"Yes, but you only said it was swollen. What happened?" She looked about to cry and went right to Nellie, holding an apple out for the mare. Doubtless she'd bought the apple just for the horse. Ty had realized quick that Leslie was prone to spoiling and had to smile at how she cooed to Nellie now.

"Oh, sweetie, I'm so sorry," Leslie said. Nellie chomped the apple, completely unperturbed.

Leslie turned to Ty. "Do you think it was something I did? Was our last walk too much for her?"

"Paige saw her kick the fence last night. The heifers were being rowdy and she decided to be a mare and tell them who was in charge." Ty lifted Nellie's leg out of the bucket once again and examined the wound. "She's got a little cut, but—"

"Oh, god, is it infected?"

"I've cleaned it up," Ty said. "And I'm gonna wrap it. It doesn't look good now, but that's mostly because of the swelling. She'll need the bandage changed daily at first because it might swell a little more as she moves around, but she'll be fine."

"Are you sure?"

"I'm sure." Ty was more surprised by their own confident response than by the question. Paige's words about being the one who'd have to make all the decisions came back to them. What if they made the wrong call on not trying to close the wound now? But they hadn't. They might have barely passed biochemistry but they could wrangle wounds with the best of them. "Anything can happen when it comes to a horse and a wound, but I know what I'm doing. Sadly, I have plenty of experience with horse injuries."

"Can you show me how to take care of it? If she's going to need daily bandages, I want to help."

"All right. Get in here."

It didn't take long to show Leslie where to stand and how to coax Nellie to have the foot soaked. After that, they cleaned the wound and had Leslie apply the ointment and then the wrap. Ty made her redo the wrap twice but she didn't complain at all. When they finished, Leslie went right to the grooming supplies, grabbed a brush, and started working on giving Nellie a good brush down while chastising her for kicking the fence.

Ty left them and went to get Archer. Convincing Leslie to try riding instead of only walking a horse had been something they'd been working on for days. With Nellie injured, it was the perfect time. When they got back with Archer saddled up and ready for a ride, Leslie was still chatting away to Nellie.

"Ready for a change of pace in our lessons?"

Leslie looked up at Ty. "I don't want to leave Nellie in this condition."

"She's got a two-centimeter laceration on her fetlock. It's clean and wrapped and she's on pain meds. She'll be fine."

Leslie glanced between Nellie and Ty. "But…"

"She probably would appreciate taking a nap anyway. We've been messing with her for a while now and she's an old lady."

"An old lady who decided to kick a fence and cut herself." Leslie looked over at Archer and then at Ty. "I'm not sure I'm ready to ride."

"You're ready for Archer. Trust me."

Leslie took more coaxing to put her foot in the stirrup than Nellie had needed to put her foot in the bucket. But once she was sitting astride Archer, she couldn't hide her wide smile. Ty took Polaris and they rode all the way to the water tower without any incidents. Leslie asked a million questions about riding, which Ty found entirely adorable. The truth was, they could have set Olivia in the saddle and Archer would have done the rest.

Unfortunately, Polaris insisted on jogging instead of walking, which meant Ty had to loop circles around Archer and Leslie. But when they all stopped to watch the sunset, the evening felt perfect.

"Want to let the horses graze for a minute?"

Leslie nodded. With some coaching, she slid out of the saddle. She gave Archer a pat and then turned to Ty. "Guess what? I rode a horse."

"You did. How do you feel?"

"Amazing."

Leslie beamed and Ty's heart took way too much notice. If only a real relationship could be in the cards for them. Ty shook away the thought, knowing the risks of going down that path.

"What? You surprised I liked riding?"

"No. Not at all. I was just thinking…I still can't wrap my head around how you're single."

"Oh. That." Leslie laughed. "Issues, remember? You could ask one of my exes, if you really wanted to know all the reasons. Or we could say I'm perfect and my exes were the ones with problems."

Ty laughed. "I'm sure that's the case."

"Me too. Except..." Leslie made a cringey face. "I may have dated a lot of people and they all decided I had too many issues."

"Lots of people can be wrong."

"Thanks for saying that." Leslie looked at Archer and then sighed. "My last ex didn't think I had my life together because I needed meds."

"Are you kidding?"

"I wish I was. It was a whole thing. She thought people could either choose to be happy or choose to be sad. And she thought I made up my panic attacks. Turns out, I had a lot fewer of those after we broke up." Leslie gave Ty a wry smile. "She also hated that I didn't want to move in with her—and that I never suggested she move in with me."

"Why didn't you?"

"I couldn't relax around her. I didn't want to live always on my toes. In some ways, I can't believe I stayed with her for three years. But she was my boss and everything was complicated."

"She was your boss?"

"Yeah, and I almost married her."

Ty couldn't hide their surprise. "You almost married someone you couldn't live with?"

"She was beautiful and crazy successful. What can I say? I'm drawn to determined people who are good at what they do. Especially the sexy ones." She bumped Ty's shoulder. "It's not always a bad thing. I almost turned you down when you suggested this ride because after watching you take care of Nellie, I was thinking that I'd really like to ride you instead."

Ty laughed. "And you only tell me this now?"

Leslie's eyes sparkled. "Something for you to think about." Her dark brown hair caught the sunlight and red highlights showed. "You're coming to my house again tonight, right?"

Ty didn't want to spend even one night away. "If the offer stands."

"The offer definitely stands. And if you show up with your strap, you know I'm going to be all over you."

"You don't have to answer this, but...aside from spanking, are there other kink things you want to try?"

"All the things." She smiled. "But maybe not all at once. You're helping me build up my confidence in asking for things though."

After a moment she added, "Before Hitch, I hadn't really done anything kinky. My last ex would have freaked if I'd even suggested a vibrator. Then again, sex with me was a low priority for her."

"With you? Meaning what?"

"She had another girlfriend on the side."

"Wait, this is the woman you were going to marry?"

"Yeah. Technically, she did ask me if we could open up the relationship. I said no but she did it anyway. It was hard on my ego, but I realized we had bigger problems. Between the meds and, well, everything we disagreed on, it was a huge relief when she ended things." Leslie's eyebrows bunched together. "That sounds bad, doesn't it?"

"Sounds honest."

"I think most of my exes wouldn't have been comfortable with kink. I know I wouldn't have been able to ask." She paused. "Until Hitch, I kept that part of myself closed off. I pretended I only wanted the things women are supposed to want. I felt like if people knew what I really liked, they'd be disgusted." She clenched her jaw and looked up at the skyline.

"I wish you didn't feel like you couldn't open up to the people you've dated in the past," Ty said. "But also I'm glad. If you were married, this watching the sunset together while I imagine you sticking your ass in the air for me to spank would be awkward."

She laughed and swatted at Ty's backside.

Ty caught her hand when she tried again and pulled her into an embrace. "I love the kink side of you. And I know there's more than spanking that you want to try. When you're ready, I want to play out some of the scenes you have in your head."

Leslie pursed her lips but didn't answer. She turned her gaze to the sunset. They stood together for a long moment before her hand slipped under Ty's shirt. Her fingers were light along their ribs. "Asking you to spank me was a big step."

"And it paid off." After the first time, Leslie had asked to be spanked nearly every night. It clearly turned her on and it amped up Ty's arousal more than they'd ever imagined. "No pressure, but I'm ready to try other things when you are."

She nodded slowly. "I've been thinking about role-playing."

"Yes!"

She laughed at Ty's enthusiasm. "I haven't even told you what roles I'm thinking of."

"I'll play any role for you."

Leslie smiled. "I'm not quite ready but I love that you are. I also love that I don't have to hide anything with you. Once you get used to hiding one part of yourself, it's easy to hide other things too. And it's so hard trying to be perfect when you aren't."

"No one's perfect."

Leslie moved her hand higher up Ty's chest, grazing over nipples and then stroking their muscles. "If I asked you, would you take off your shirt right now? No one else is around and I'd love to see you in this light."

Aside from the night at the water tower, and under cover of darkness, they hadn't taken their shirt off outside. But Leslie was right. No one else was around. Ty's nipple hardened with Leslie's attention and their center pulsed.

"I shouldn't probably ask," Leslie said. "Here I am admitting I'm not ready to try all the kinky things and I ask you to strip so I can appreciate your body." She shook her head. "Forget I asked."

"I don't want to forget."

Ty stepped back and peeled off their shirt. A warm breeze played on their chest and the setting sun seemed to kiss their shoulders. They straightened and glanced at Archer and then Polaris, both grazing quietly. Behind the horses, the horizon was streaked with color. Ty exhaled, feeling a calmness take hold. They looked back at Leslie and smiled. "Feel free to take off your shirt too. I recommend it."

"You are so sexy," Leslie said, touching Ty's arm. She moved her hand to the center of their chest and then leaned close for a kiss. When she pulled back, she said, "I wish I was brave enough to tell you all the things I think of when I look at you. And I can't believe I'm going to do this, but…" She stepped away and pulled off her own shirt, eyed Ty again, laughed, and took off her bra next.

"Dammmn," Ty said, drawing out the word. "I like you half naked."

"I can tell." She smiled and stepped forward to kiss Ty again, her palm returning to their chest.

Leslie's hand felt good, but when Ty deepened the kiss she moved closer, letting her breasts brush their skin. "Mm. Even better."

CHAPTER THIRTY-TWO

"Am I catching you at a bad time? You sound out of breath."

Seren's voice was so cheery that Leslie didn't want to say it was a bad time. "I'm packing but I can multitask."

"The camping trip! I forgot that was this weekend. And I'm checking in on your cats."

"Yes, please." Leslie had planned on calling Seren to remind her.

"Are you excited?"

"I am. I'm also maybe a little nervous."

"You'll be fine. Just watch out for poison oak. Especially when you pee."

"Didn't need that image." She wondered if she should admit that she wasn't exactly sure what poison oak looked like.

"And don't forget a flashlight. Getting lost in the dark is even worse than getting a rash on your lady bits."

"Why am I going camping again?" She laughed but she knew the answer. *Ty.* The closer it'd gotten, the more she'd been looking forward to the weekend. She eyed the backpack she'd nearly filled and the cooler of food, wondering if she'd remembered all the items on Ty's list. It'd seemed too short, but she'd kept to it. "Do you think I should bring bug spray?"

"Maybe for mosquitos? Otherwise you'll be fine as long as you have a couple spiders in the tent. They get the bugs first."

"Please tell me you're joking."

"Speaking of tents," Seren said. "I hear you won't be needing ours."

Leslie bit the edge of her lip, knowing what was coming. "Yeah. Ty said their tent has enough room for two."

"Uh-huh. And when were you going to mention you two were sleeping together? Paige told me Ty blushed quite a bit when they said you'd be sharing their tent. She tried asking how serious things were but Ty clammed up fast, apparently."

She should have been the one to tell Paige and Seren. They were her best friends, and she realized now that she'd put Ty in a hard spot. Probably Ty had worried that if she hadn't said something, it was because she didn't want them to know. Which wasn't the case. "I've been meaning to call you. I promise. But these past two weeks have been a blur. Ty's been at my house every night."

"Every night? Damn, girl!" Seren cheered and Leslie couldn't hold back her smile. "I told Paige things had to be going well because I hadn't heard from you at all—which happens if you've hooked up with someone you actually like. You drop off the face of the planet."

"Sorry."

"Don't apologize. I love that you and Ty are a couple. It's perfect."

"I don't know if we're technically a couple yet. We haven't had that conversation." She'd considered bringing it up with Ty more than once. The topic was starting to feel overdue, in fact. Partly, she'd been hoping that Ty would bring it up first but partly she worried about their answer.

"I'm trying not to overthink things. It's just been nice. Really nice." Even if it meant she'd had to step back a few things at work because she was spending her evenings with Ty, she didn't want to change anything.

"Paige says you've been making a lot of progress with Nellie. I'm sorry I keep missing you. I've been over at Bea's every evening. Olivia loves her grandma time and we've been bringing Bea dinner."

"How's Bea doing?" Leslie felt a pinch of guilt that she'd entirely forgotten Paige's mom was still rehabbing from her surgery.

"Better. It's so sweet to see her with Olivia. But I want to see you and Nellie. You'll have to tell me the next time you're coming over."

"I'm falling for Nellie big time. She's the best horse." It hadn't taken long, really, for Nellie to warm up.

"I heard you went on a ride, too."

"I did. It was...amazing." She smiled, remembering the break they'd taken at the meadow to watch the sunset. The night that followed made her hot all over again. She'd straddled Ty's legs and told them they couldn't stop fucking her until she told them to. Then she'd admitted to wanting things that still made her feel shaky. She knew she wasn't ready for all the kinky things Girl-Monday and Hitch had done together, but the little tastes she'd had so far were better than she'd imagined. "I know it's too soon, especially since we haven't even talked about a relationship, but...I think I'm in love."

"Oh, I could tell that from your voice. I honestly wasn't sure if it would work—Ty's so different from the people you've dated—but I really think you two are perfect for each other. I mean, who would have thought that Leslie Brandt would be going camping with horses?"

"Even a month ago, I'd have said no way." But one month could change everything. *And one month from now?* What would things be like? Ty would be back in school and she'd be back to her regular work schedule. Ty had agreed to keep Monday and Friday nights for lessons and she'd manage to carve out time to work with Nellie then. But she knew they'd both have less time together and she worried about what that would mean for their chances at something serious.

The doorbell rang and she glanced at the time. It was already a quarter to ten. "Shit, I think Ty's here. I'm not done packing."

"I'll let you go," Seren said. "Have so much fun—and don't forget to look under your butt when you squat to pee."

She ended the call and went to answer the door. Ty stood on her doorstep, cowboy hat on and a one-eyed Chihuahua in their arms. "Um...did you just find a dog?"

"This is Penelope. It's a long story, but don't worry, she's not coming camping with us."

"Not a camper?"

Penelope snuggled closer in Ty's arms and seemed to give Leslie an accusatory look with her one eye. "She's more of a house dog. But she's not on the lease. Our landlord told us last minute that he wanted to do an inspection this weekend."

"But Penelope's not yours?"

"She only thinks she's mine." Ty shook their head. "Penelope belongs to Jenna, who's at the barn with Zoe right now."

"Jenna—the roommate who you don't want Zoe to date?"

"I didn't say that."

"You didn't need to." She liked that she could read Ty easily. "You look really cute with a Chihuahua, by the way."

"Don't tell anyone." Ty kissed Penelope's head. "I've never been a Chihuahua person."

"Uh-huh. I see. But you brought her with you instead of leaving her with Jenna at the barn."

"She's scared of horses," Ty said. "I think Jenna hoped she'd turn into a cattle dog as soon as she got to the ranch. I felt bad for her."

"You're a softie."

"I have my moments." Ty grinned. "Ready for our adventure?"

"Almost. I have to pack the cookies in the cooler."

"I could help."

"Mm. I know your type of help." Leslie wanted to kiss Ty but Penelope didn't look like she wanted to share. Fortunately, the dog wasn't going to be in the tent later.

Even with Ty distracting her, it didn't take long before everything was loaded in the back of the Jeep. Leslie made one last sweep of the house, promising her cats that Seren would check in on them tomorrow, and then settled into the Jeep. Penelope hopped out of Ty's arms and right into her lap.

She looked down at the Chihuahua, trying to figure out if she could move her to buckle her seat belt. "Huh."

"Not a dog person?" Ty asked.

"I used to have a dog, but it was a dog-sized dog, you know?"

"Penelope grows on you." Ty turned on the ignition. "What type of dog did you have?"

"A pit bull mix. Bubbles."

"Bubbles?" Ty laughed. "Did you name her when you were five?"

"Try twenty-three." Leslie grinned back at Ty, scooting Penelope out of the way enough to buckle the seat belt. "Now, focus on the road. I've had a taste of your off-roading skills and I don't want Penelope to get car sick."

"Fine." Ty sighed and turned their attention to the road. "Tell me more about Bubbles."

"She was the best dog." Leslie glanced down at the Chihuahua curled up in her lap and remembered how Bubbles would try to do the same but was too big. "She loved to cuddle. Whenever I had a bad day, Bubbles knew and she'd climb into my lap. She totally didn't fit but it was sweet anyway."

Leslie pet Penelope's head and thought of how close she'd been to Bubbles. The first year after she'd lost her had seemed so empty and off-kilter. Still, she hadn't wanted to get another dog. She'd convinced herself she was happy with her cats. Which she was. Mostly. But now after spending more time with Nellie, she realized she was happier with more animals around.

"I got Bubbles from the shelter. She was a stray and someone at the shelter had named her Bubba because they thought she looked tough. She wasn't tough. At all." Leslie smiled, remembering how Bubbles used to pick her way delicately around puddles. "I decided the name didn't fit her but she'd been at the shelter for a month and had gotten used to the name. Bubbles was close enough."

"Bubba didn't fit her but Bubbles did?"

"Completely. She was always so happy. Tail constantly wagged."

Ty looked over and grinned. "I'm trying to picture you with a pitty named Bubbles. You're such a cat person in my mind."

"There are things you still don't know about me. Even after two weeks of being in my bed every night." Leslie arched an eyebrow.

"Clearly I've been enjoying myself too much in your bed," Ty said. "Guess I need to start asking more questions."

"You should if you want to get to know me in other ways."

"Oh, I do."

Leslie laughed but the truth warmed her all the way through when Ty nodded almost solemnly.

"I feel like we do know each other better than two weeks of dating—or whatever we're doing," Ty quickly added. "I mean, it's only been a few weeks in person, but it was three months online."

"We weren't trying to get to know each other then."

"Speak for yourself."

Leslie studied Ty for a moment, thinking she had gotten to know them as Hitch. *In some ways.* But she'd been reluctant to share too much about herself and stopped herself from asking questions. Now she didn't want to hold back. She wanted to ask all the questions. Even as she considered that, though, Ty's words "dating—or whatever we're doing" repeated in her mind.

"Open the glovebox. I got you something."

Leslie maneuvered Penelope so she could open the glovebox. A wrapped present was on top of papers and an old owner's manual. She picked up the present and then glanced at Ty. "For my first camping trip?"

"For your first time crewing. Don't get too excited. It's nothing big."

It was sweet that Ty had thought to get her something. She stared at the silver paper for a moment, then ran a finger under the tape.

She pushed the tissue paper aside and felt coarse bristles against her hand. She lifted the brush out of the box and smiled. A curry comb and hoof pick were under the soft brush along with a washcloth. "My very own grooming kit! And you got Nellie her own washcloth?"

"Until she gets braver about being brushed on both sides. I decided you two needed some of your own equipment. Plus, I figured you could try that brush out this weekend."

"I do need a job on the crew team. Official groom?" Leslie held up the brush and smiled.

"Sexiest groom ever."

She laughed, then reached over and set her hand on Ty's leg. "Thank you. I love the present."

"You're welcome. Thanks for giving up your weekend of relaxation for Tevis."

"Who needs relaxation when you can have an adventure? Maybe I'll become one of those outdoorsy-types and start wearing cargo pants with pockets for all my gear." She held up the hoof pick. "Do I look tough enough?"

Ty grinned. "Yes. And I'd love to see you in cargo pants."

"You'd love to see me in no pants."

"True." Ty glanced back at the road. "Mostly I just love to see you."

Leslie wanted to say the same words back. Her throat tightened as she looked out the window at the passing cars. Did Ty want a relationship as much as she wanted it?

CHAPTER THIRTY-THREE

As usual, it took longer than Ty would have liked to load all the supplies and get Polaris and Archer in the trailer. Then Jenna wanted to talk to Zoe alone. Ty tried not to get annoyed at the delay or worry about how Jenna might be a distraction. Zoe was already a ball of nerves which helped no one—especially Polaris. Thankfully, Archer was as steady as always.

"Remind me not to get you mad," Leslie said.

Ty met Leslie's gaze. Penelope had decided she liked Leslie and hadn't wanted to get out of her arms. "I'm not mad."

"I know. And you a little ticked off is already intense."

Ty exhaled. "The horses are loaded up. I want to be on the road."

"And we're going," Zoe said, appearing with Jenna's hand in hers. She turned to kiss Jenna on the cheek and murmured, "See you tomorrow."

"Good luck, babe," Jenna said. She took Penelope from Leslie, thanking her more than was necessary, and headed to her car.

As soon as Jenna drove off, Ty looked over at Zoe. "Babe?"

Zoe held up her hand. "I don't want to talk about it. Tomorrow night you can tell me all the reasons I shouldn't date Jenna. For the rest of today, I only want to think about Polaris and Tevis. I'm already so stressed I vomited everything I ate this morning."

Ty dropped their shoulders. "Zoe, I'm sorry—"

"Don't apologize. Just get us to Robie Park in one piece."

Zoe headed right for the truck's back bench, leaving Leslie shotgun. Ty settled into the driver's seat, feeling Leslie's eyes on them. Fortunately, no one wanted to talk. Ty checked the mirrors, making sure Polaris and Archer were ready, then pulled out of the driveway. As they rumbled down the gravel road, Ty picked one of Zoe's favorite playlists, hoping the music would change her mood.

"You like EDM?" Leslie asked.

"It's not my favorite," Ty said, hoping for a neutral tone.

"They're playing it for me," Zoe said. "They're hoping this will chill me out. Which it won't. But it's sweet because I know Ty hates this music and they're trying to be nice."

"Not untrue."

"I like EDM," Leslie said.

"Really?" Zoe and Ty said at the same time.

"Really." Leslie smiled, then turned halfway round in her seat and started quizzing Zoe on different songs she liked. By the time they'd reached the main road, they'd both pulled up their favorite songs on their phones. Leslie decided then she was taking over the music in the car, proclaiming herself DJ.

"You'd make a cute DJ," Ty murmured. "I'm still surprised you like EDM. You haven't played anything like that in the last two weeks."

"It's my morning jam music. I play it when I go to the gym and when I'm driving...or if I need to de-stress after work." She lifted a shoulder and added, "It's just not what I'd pick for sex—which is the music you've been hearing."

Zoe laughed. "See, Ty? EDM is awesome. Even your smart girlfriend agrees with me. Also, pay attention to the road and stop looking at her so much."

Leslie gave Ty a perfect side-eye. "Keep your eyes on the road, crew boss."

Ty wanted to banter back, but Leslie had already turned back to face Zoe. "I love that shirt. Where'd you get it?"

Zoe launched into a description of the street artist who'd turned to selling his art online. Ty could tell Leslie was trying to distract Zoe from overthinking tomorrow's ride—and it was working. Ty wanted to thank her but instead focused on the highway. Due east they could make out the hazy line of the Sierras. If everything went well, they'd be there in two hours. Then the check-in process, getting camp set up, the welcome banquet, and trail debriefing. But after all that, they'd have Leslie to themself in their tent.

Leslie hadn't seemed upset that Zoe had called her their girlfriend, but Ty wondered if they should apologize later or simply let it go. They didn't want to start the conversation of what would happen after the weekend.

After covering art and music, Leslie quizzed Zoe on endurance riding and other races she'd done. The hour passed without Zoe once mentioning Ty's driving and still it was the most Ty had heard Zoe talk in one sitting. Somehow, Leslie knew exactly how to pull Zoe out of her shell.

"So you learned how to ride on Archer too." Leslie smiled back at Zoe. "He's a sweetie but almost too good, you know what I mean?"

"Completely!"

"I think that's why I like Nellie. Apparently, I need a horse with at least one issue." She glanced at Ty and winked.

"Polaris has maybe a few too many issues but I love her anyway," Zoe said. "Did Ty ever tell you the story of how they got her?"

"No."

Zoe swatted Ty's shoulder. "What have you two been doing? Just having sex?"

"Um…"

"Basically," Leslie said, smiling at Ty.

"That's what I get for asking." Zoe chuckled. "Anyway. Ty knew this woman, Najima, who was big in the endurance world. She'd won Tevis twice and dozens of other races—always on Arabs. But she decided to breed one of her stallions to a mustang mare. She wanted to try a half Arab, half mustang. The mare she picked was wild. Smart, but too wild for anyone to handle. She hoped the foal would take after the stallion."

"But Polaris took after her mom?" Leslie guessed.

"Bingo." Zoe leaned forward, bumping Ty's arm. "Take this next curve slow. It's a tighter turn than it looks."

"I know this road, Zoe." Ty shook their head.

"So, Ty decided to buy Polaris?" Leslie asked, glancing between Zoe and Ty.

"No. I didn't want another a horse."

"Najima, the woman who owned Polaris, didn't want to sell her," Zoe said. "At least not at first. She tried a handful of trainers but they all decided Polaris was too much like her mom. So Najima called up Ty and asked if they'd be willing to train her."

"You trained Polaris?"

Ty nodded. "Najima knew I loved mustangs. We'd raced together a few times and she had to put up with me gushing about them."

"After a month with Ty, Polaris was a different horse," Zoe said. "I saw her when Najima dropped her off that first day and thought Ty was crazy taking her on. She wouldn't stop rearing up and she trashed her stall. But she completely changed with Ty."

"And I fell in love with her," Ty admitted. "When Najima came to pick her up after I'd finished the month of training, I broke down crying."

"So then you bought her?"

Ty shook their head. "I couldn't afford a second horse."

"It's actually a really sad story," Zoe said. "Najima broke her neck. She got thrown off and hit a fence…"

"Wait, she was on Polaris?" Leslie said, sounding panicked.

"No. She was on a different horse," Zoe said. "And she ended up being okay after months of recovery—and having vertebrae fused in her neck."

"That's awful."

"Completely," Ty agreed. "No one blamed Najima for giving up riding. She sold all of her horses except one of her favorites who she kept as a pet. And Polaris. She knew how much I loved Polaris. She called me, told me what had happened, and asked me to come pick her up."

"Wow." Leslie shook her head. "Okay, Zoe, I need you to tell me a happy horse story now or I don't think I'm letting you ride tomorrow."

"I've got lots of happy ones." As Zoe launched into a story about the first time she rode Polaris, Leslie broke out a Tupperware of peanut butter cookies with little chocolate kisses in the middle.

Once they reached the mountains, everyone quieted down. Ty's attention was solely on the road. They slowed on all the curves and kept one eye trained on the side mirror, making sure Polaris was handling the trip. The rig bent around one gorgeous vista after another, each with a frighteningly steep drop-off, and they tried to ignore the gasps from Leslie and Zoe, mentally clocking the miles. They were almost to Robie Park.

The story of Najima's accident bounced back and forth in their head. Zoe had left out a lot of the details but the reality remained. Riding any horse could be dangerous. Ty glanced back at Zoe. She had a serious look on her face that Ty recognized. Her mind was on Tevis.

CHAPTER THIRTY-FOUR

They reached the campground ahead of schedule. While Ty and Zoe signed in for a campsite, Leslie got out of the truck to stretch her legs. The spot was beautiful, campsites all spread out along a narrow dirt road that skirted the crest of a mountain, and the air smelled unbelievable, like fresh pine mixed with a morning rain. Which, she realized, was likely because it'd clearly recently sprinkled and pine trees were everywhere.

The place was nice enough to make her think she'd been ridiculous to worry about how she'd fare roughing it. When she spotted a bathroom, she almost cheered. No portable toilet, no peeing behind a bush.

Ty met up with her after she'd used the facilities. They'd dropped Zoe off at the registration tent and had a tense expression on their face. Leslie had noticed the lines on their forehead for most of the drive through the mountains but now she guessed it was more worries about Zoe.

"Ready to go find our campsite?" Ty asked.

A lot of the spots closest to the main road were already taken and some folks looked as if they'd been set up for a while with paddocks in place for multiple horses and clothes drying on lines above tents or between campers.

They drove down the dirt road, slowing at every opening between the thick cover of pines. Horses and people were everywhere.

"People are serious about this."

"You have no idea," Ty said, stopping the truck and leaning out the window to holler at someone who was waving at them. "Hey, Martina."

"Hey, stranger. Figured you'd show up here again one of these years. You want to make me and my horse look slow again, huh?"

"I'm not riding. My cousin, Zoe, is gonna have all the fun."

"Little Zoe? She can't be old enough to drive!"

"She's not so little anymore." Ty smiled. "Picante's looking good. So are you."

The older woman patted the brown-and-white spotted horse she was brushing. "You hear that, Picante? Ty thinks we're going to win." Martina pointed at another horse tied up near Picante—a dark gray horse a few inches taller than Picante. "I got a new baby who's here learning the ropes. He's too young for Tevis this year but I'm hoping Picante will show him how it's done."

"He's handsome."

"Right? My Antonio Banderas." She laughed. "I named him Banderas and my husband asked if I was trying to tell him something." She laughed again. "I'm hoping one day he'll be as smart as he is good-looking."

Ty laughed too. "That's what we always hope about our horses. Hey, you need any help with supplies at the checkpoints?"

"Nah, the whole family is coming to crew for me. They think it's a party!" She shook her head. "I'll keep an eye on Zoe. Wish you were riding with us tomorrow. Not that I'd see much of you—you always left me and Picante in the dust." She lifted her hand in a wave.

They hadn't gone more than two campsites past Martina when more people were recognizing Ty and calling out hellos. Ty didn't stop again but kept one hand out of the truck to wave and shouted back "good luck tomorrow" and "have a good race" each time.

"I'm starting to think Zoe was right."

"About what?" Ty asked.

"You're a little bit famous."

Ty kept their gaze on the dirt road, breaking over a dip. "The endurance community is small—you get to know everyone—and Archer and I did Tevis five years in a row. Along with a lot of other races." Ty didn't say more until they came to a clearing no one had claimed. "What do you think about that spot?"

"You're asking me?"

"Thought maybe you'd want to pick your first campsite." When she hesitated, Ty added, "Think of it like picking a spot to build a house. Ms. Brandt, best-selling realtor, would you recommend I build a house on that lot?"

She smiled and eyed the clearing. "Okay, when you put it that way..." The campsite wasn't as big as some of the others, but they didn't have a camper or an RV and their horse trailer was a lot smaller, not to mention less fancy, than most of the others. The other bonus was that the space was too small for anyone else to try to squeeze in next to them. "I think it's perfect. Once you have your house built, can I come visit?"

"Oh, you'll be building the house with me," Ty said, maneuvering the truck and trailer into the space. "Gotta learn how to set up a tent to officially say you've camped."

Getting Polaris and Archer settled was the first order of business. Ty set up a set of ropes between trees and then attached each horse's lead line, allowing them room to pace back and forth. Next, Ty brought out water and feed buckets. Leslie watched, marveling at how efficient Ty was, unloading supplies and setting the site up like a machine.

"I feel like I should be doing something to help..."

"In a minute, we'll get the tents."

Ty slipped around the far side of the trailer and Leslie eyed Polaris, knowing the horse was anxious and wishing she could calm her.

Polaris would stand still for a few seconds then stomp, dig at the dirt, reach for a bite of hay, drop it, and let out a high-pitched whinny. Each time, some horse in the distance would answer. Archer ignored it all, content with his bucket of hay.

Leslie wondered if Archer recognized where they were. Ty had said the race always started at the same point and she guessed Archer must have some memory of the place. Was that why he seemed so comfortable? Or maybe he knew he wouldn't be racing tomorrow.

Zoe had called Archer "Polaris's security blanket." The mare did keep one ear trained on Archer and she'd likely be even more anxious without him. But she'd have to leave him behind in the morning. Leslie wondered then how Archer would act. Would he long to be on the trail with the others? That question made her wonder how Ty was feeling.

Polaris let out another whinny and pranced in place, kicking the feed bucket and making the water bucket splash.

"I could brush you," Leslie said, voicing her thoughts aloud. "I kind of don't want to get close to you when you act wild like that, but...I think it might help calm you down." She considered it for another moment, reminding herself she'd doubled up her dose of anxiety meds for a reason. "Would you like to be groomed?"

Ty appeared with a bin of supplies. "You're talking to a horse. You know that's a sign you've become a horse person. And, yes, she'd loved to be brushed."

Now that Ty had heard, she didn't want to back out. She went to the truck to get the new brush, then approached Polaris.

The mare's head was high, her neck arched. Her ears twitched to scan in every direction. Leslie took several deep breaths, in and out, slowly. "Hey, Pol. I'm going to try brushing you."

She took another step closer and Polaris held still. Leslie stroked the brush over her coat, trying not to think about how her hand trembled.

"A couple weeks ago, you'd have been too scared to do that," Ty said.

"I'm still scared."

"But you're doing it."

She nodded, proud of herself but not willing to let down her guard. She'd only groomed Polaris at the barn once and the mare had been decidedly calmer then. Now, she twitched at any little sound and pawed the dirt every other minute. Between each outburst, however, she nosed the brush, asking to be groomed.

"I'm impressed," Ty said, coming up to stand next to Leslie.

"That I haven't gotten myself killed yet?" She backed away when Polaris startled again.

"That you're trying. Anyone would be scared of Polaris right now."

Leslie knew Ty was telling the truth, not simply trying to make her feel better. "Thanks."

Ty rested a hand on Polaris's withers and murmured, "Easy, girl."

Polaris gave a half shudder and lowered her head. Ty pushed the feed bucket under her nose, and she started eating.

"One touch from you and she's a different horse."

"The brushing helped," Ty said. "I wasn't joking about being impressed. You've gotten braver with all the horses but especially Polaris."

"I've had a good teacher."

Ty met Leslie's gaze, a smile on their lips. "These past few weeks have been such a high. I can't remember ever feeling this good for so long. Come Monday, I'm gonna miss sleeping at your house every night."

"I do have a nice bed."

"You do. But that's not what I meant."

"Oh, you meant the sex?" Leslie said with mock surprise.

Ty smiled but their expression clouded a moment later. "At this point, I wish it was just the sex I was going to miss."

"Turns out we can still have sex even if you're not at my house every night."

"Yeah…" Ty's voice trailed. They looked from Polaris to Archer and then walked over to the gelding and gave him a scratch on his withers.

A long minute passed, and Leslie knew there was something Ty wasn't saying. She debated asking, then wondered if she was making a big deal out of nothing. Things seemed so perfect five minutes ago. "Want to let me in on whatever's going on in your brain?"

Ty glanced over their shoulder at her. "It's nothing."

"*Nothing.* Now I know it's a big deal."

Ty turned to face her, leaning against Archer who sighed contentedly. "It's my own issue."

Leslie titled her head. "So this issue has nothing to do with me?"

"It has something to do with you, but I don't want to bring it up."

"If it's about me, I'd like you to bring it up." Sunlight slanted through the pine trees, making dapples of light on Ty's cheeks and nose. Leslie wished she didn't feel the thrum of attraction in the same moment her gut was sending up warning flares.

Ty pushed away from Archer, scrubbing their face. They straightened and met Leslie's gaze. "I know we aren't in a relationship, but it feels like one. And I told myself I would keep feelings out of this, but...I'm kind of failing at that. I fell in love with you once and I don't want to go through it again."

"You don't want to fall in love with me again or you don't want to break up again?" Leslie felt like her own heart was in free fall as the question hung in the air. She placed a hand on Polaris's neck, needing something to balance against. The mare, for once, was something steady.

"I know this was only supposed to be fun. We promised each other that's all it'd be. And neither of us has time for a relationship." Ty shook their head. "So it's my own issue and I'm going to deal with it. On Monday. All I'm saying is I don't want to face reality yet."

"You didn't answer the question. The reality of breaking up?"

"We aren't dating, right? We're just fucking around." Ty jammed their hands in the pockets of their jeans and gave a half shrug. "Like what Hitch and Girl-Monday used to do."

Ty's words made her feel hollow and cold. Before she could think of what to say, Polaris nickered.

"Hey, party people," Zoe said, her excited voice seeming too loud as it cut through the campsite. "I'm all registered! I have to take Polaris down for the pre-ride vet check but there's a line so I figure I'll wait a bit. Great spot, by the way." A moment later she added, "Am I interrupting something?"

Ty glanced at Leslie with a look that tore at her heart. They dropped their gaze and said, "We were just talking."

She felt sick. Ty acted like they'd been discussing the weather. *Nothing serious.* Maybe that was what Ty wanted. If what they had together was nothing serious, they could both walk away unhurt.

Ty cleared their throat. "You're right on time to set up the tents."

Zoe looked at Leslie and it was obvious she knew more was going on. "I could take Polaris down to the vet check now?"

"She's finally eating," Ty said, nodding at the mare who was contentedly chomping her hay. "Leslie got her to relax."

"She loves being brushed," Zoe said, coming up to stand at Leslie's side.

Leslie hadn't noticed how she'd twined her fingers through the horse's black mane, or that she'd subconsciously been petting the mare while Ty had talked. She loosened her hold and shifted away, murmuring, "She does."

"You okay?" Zoe asked.

Ty had gone to the truck and was sorting through bags. Leslie looked at them, wondering how to answer. When Ty straightened, two bundles in their arms, she felt her chest tighten. She hadn't meant to fall for someone who wasn't emotionally available. Or soon even physically available. But it had happened all the same. She was most definitely, painfully, in love.

"I'm fine. Just working through something." She forced a smile.

Zoe nodded. "Tevis can be a lot even if you aren't the one in the race."

CHAPTER THIRTY-FIVE

Ty did most of the work getting the two tents up but let Leslie help enough that she didn't feel simply in the way. Zoe helped too, though mostly she talked. She was brimming with news. During check-in she'd run into several people Ty knew and had loads of gossip. She managed to thank Leslie and Ty for getting Polaris settled—in between telling them the drama between other riders and the news of a portion of the trail being rerouted.

Ty nodded often but didn't say much, adding a few bits of advice and mostly listening. Leslie wondered if their somber mood was because of worries about how Zoe and Polaris would do tomorrow, whether some part of them wanted to be racing too, or if they were still thinking about the conversation Zoe had interrupted.

She didn't have a chance to ask. Even if their campsite seemed far from the others, more trailers streamed in, and as the afternoon slipped away there was a constant line of people and horses walking past. Nearly everyone seemed to know Ty and Zoe, but anyone who stopped to chat included Leslie in the conversation as soon as they heard she was part of the crew. It was strange having membership in a group she barely understood. But both Ty and Zoe acted like she belonged so much that part of her felt like she did, though watching Ty get clapped on the back and hugged dozens of times made her realize how much this was Ty's world. And after their earlier conversation, she was more aware than ever how temporary her presence was.

"I am so ready for dinner," Zoe said. She eyed her watch and then Polaris, who'd apparently done well for her pre-ride vet check and was back to eating. "Ty, I know how you feel about showing up early for the buffet, but can we go early anyway? I don't want to miss the race announcements."

"They always do those after."

Zoe gave Ty a frustrated look. "I guess I could go by myself."

"Martina will be there. She'll keep you company."

Zoe complained about not wanting to be a tag-along but when it was clear she wasn't convincing Ty to go early, she finally left.

Once they were alone, Leslie asked, "Do you have something against buffets?"

"Everyone's always keyed up before the race. And I swear each time someone starts telling a story of some rider who got bucked off and is still in the hospital...or a horse who broke a leg." Ty shook their head. "You get this many adrenaline junkies in the same place and people do stupid things and everyone loves to tell the stories after."

"So I shouldn't hope that you were begging out so we could talk?"

Ty shrugged. "We can talk if you want. I don't really know what more there is to say."

"I think there's a lot we could say." Leslie pushed on, trying not to get mad at Ty's shrug. "I know things are going to be different next week when you start back at school. And I can tell you're stressed about that. But deciding things are over simply because we won't have as much time to see each other is dumb."

"Dumb. Okay."

"I'm not saying you're dumb. I'm saying I don't like your plan." She exhaled. "It doesn't have to be all or nothing for us."

Ty cocked their head. "Is there an us? You said you didn't want a relationship and I've spent the last couple weeks wondering what the hell we're doing. Are we fuck buddies?"

Before Leslie could get in a word, Ty continued, "I didn't want to bring it up tonight but I knew I was going to have to be the one to say something first. I feel like I have to work to get you to tell me what's going on in your head. What you're feeling. It's like you don't really want me to know you." Ty ran a hand through their hair. "Which is fine, I guess. You're a private person and you have every right to not want to open up, but…is it because you don't trust me?"

"Ty, what are you talking about? You know more about me than anyone I've ever dated."

"I know what you like sexually and I know you're on meds and all that but I feel like there's all these gaps. Things you don't share. I don't know anything about your family. I don't know if you have siblings. I don't know where you went to college. Or what you studied. I didn't know you liked the same music as Zoe, and until today I had no idea you had a dog who was clearly so important to you that you were tearing up talking about her.

"I get that maybe you never open up to people, but I hate feeling like I have to pry information out of you. Is it because you don't want to get close?"

She didn't know what to say. Ty was right—she didn't open up easily. And yet she had opened up to them, which made their accusations hurt all the more.

"Look, just forget it. I don't want to start a fight," Ty said, shaking their head.

"It's a little late to say that."

Ty seemed to wait for her to go on, but when she didn't, they said, "I get that you didn't want Hitch to be part of your real world, but I can't help thinking you don't want me to be part of your real world either. Paige acted like she had no idea we'd gotten together, and you said Seren and Paige are your closest friends. It's not like I need you to tell people we've been fucking around, but—"

"Ty, stop." Leslie felt tears press at the corners of her eyes when Ty's jaw clenched. "You're right. I am a private person and I'm not used to letting people in. I hadn't talked to Seren or Paige these past couple weeks because I've been spending every free minute with you. But I talked to Seren this afternoon—before you came to pick me up—and I told her how happy I was with you." She wasn't going to admit the other things she'd told Seren. "I never said I didn't want a relationship. I said I didn't have time for one."

Ty's brow furrowed. "I'm not sure what the difference is."

"The difference is, I might not have the time but I'm willing to make the time." She paused. "Yeah. I've got issues. You knew that already. I don't open up easy. I've got anxiety. I live in my hometown because I'm scared I'd never make it anywhere else." She took a shaky breath. "But I'd like to change. And, honestly, you make me think I could." Until that afternoon, she'd convinced herself she was different. "I'm sorry about how I was with Hitch in the end. I don't know what to say except I panicked. But now I know I can trust you and I'd tell anyone who asked that we were together.

"Maybe I'm not an open book." She lifted a shoulder. "Maybe I've gotten too used to worrying about scaring people away. But if you wanted to know something, you could've asked." When Ty only held her gaze, she knew she had to ask the question that felt way too risky. "Do you want there to be an us?"

Ty took a moment before answering. "I want it, but I don't know how I could make it work. I love spending time with you and if you're serious maybe we could try, but…everyone says the second year of vet school is the hardest. I feel like I barely got through the first. I had to study for hours every night. This next year won't be any different. Plus, I'm scheduled to tech every weekend. And I've gotta keep up with mucking stalls and helping Paige with projects. She's giving me free board as long as I do my share."

"That means you'll still be coming out to the barn."

"Yeah, of course. And I want to keep giving you lessons but I don't know if I'll be able to swing twice a week. I know I promised but I'm stressed about how much time I'll have."

Leslie knew it shouldn't feel like a letdown. Unfortunately, it did. Ty was willing to make time to give her a lesson but not to think of ways they could make a relationship work. "One minute I think you're telling me you want to break up because I didn't make this about more than sex and didn't open up to you enough, and the next I think you're telling me that you don't have time anyway. Which is it?"

Ty held her gaze. "All those things. I'm sorry. My head's feeling kind of a mess right now."

"Thanks for being honest." She clenched her jaw, determined not to give in to her emotions. Not yet. Ty wasn't saying they wanted to break up, and she could sympathize with feeling like a mess. "What do you want? After this weekend, do you want there to be an us or not?"

"I've been trying not to think past this weekend."

Leslie felt a weight press down on her chest. "If you don't even want to think about it, I guess that tells me what I need to know."

"That came out wrong."

She waited for Ty to try again, feeling nauseous at the thought that nothing they could say would change reality. Once again, she'd fallen for someone she shouldn't have. She should have kept Ty as a friend. Love was a game she had no business playing. She always lost.

"I wish I could promise I'd be able to make time for a relationship, but I know when school starts, I won't have anything left to give. Vet school has to be my focus."

"I get that, and I wouldn't want you to not focus on vet school. But you assume you'd only be giving me something. And that I wouldn't give you anything in return. Which is pretty shitty. I'm not sure if that says more about me or about you."

"I didn't say that. I—"

"There's ways we could make it work, ways we could spend time together without making your life harder. Do you know how much I'd love to give you a back rub after a long day? Or make you dinner while you were studying? Or meet you at the barn to walk Archer and Nellie?" She shook her head. "I know you haven't been in a lot of relationships, but next time you want to end something, don't start out blaming the other person. Figure out your own shit first."

She knew from the look on Ty's face that the words had hit like a belly punch. It hurt her to say it too. Still, she was pissed.

"Wow. Okay."

"I know that was a crappy thing to say—"

"But it's true."

Someone driving down the path called Ty's name, waving enthusiastically. Ty waved, seeming to force a smile. They called back a hello to some guy named Brent. Brent railed on Ty for being late to the banquet, laughing as he did, and Ty only nodded.

When Brent had finally gone, Leslie said, "Maybe we should go to the banquet. I think we both need to eat." She knew she was hangry. Maybe Ty was too and that's why the conversation had gone so wrong. But it didn't change what had been said.

"I'm sorry for starting a fight," Ty said. "I don't want to be fighting."

"Me neither." She wanted to wrap her arms around Ty but she crossed them instead.

"I wasn't joking when I said I've been on a high these last two weeks. I really wish it didn't have to end."

"You're not moving to Antarctica. If the 'us' thing were important to you, you'd have been thinking about how we could make it work."

"You're right." Ty sighed. "I clearly suck at relationships."

She met Ty's gaze. The words "I love you anyway" wanted to slip out. How typical. When the cards all fell, her heart was still completely invested. "Let's go eat."

CHAPTER THIRTY-SIX

The banquet buffet was much like Ty's description. The food was better than tolerable but everyone swapping stories of injuries and fears of trail issues meant no one seemed to be enjoying it much. Least of all Leslie. The conversation with Ty spun round in her mind and she knew the spaghetti dinner wouldn't sit well.

Someone's horse had slipped getting out of the trailer that afternoon and torn a ligament. A runner had gone to test out a questionable section of the trail and ended up sliding down a sheet of rock and needing to be rescued. One of the vets was already checking on a colicky horse, and the debate on whether or not a new path around an erosion spot was safe had everyone on edge. Especially Ty and Zoe.

Leslie thought of asking Ty if the new section was as risky as several people suggested, worrying about Zoe and Polaris, but decided against it. She couldn't pretend things were normal between them while everything Ty had said circled round in her mind. Was she truly in love with Ty, or caught up in the amazing sex and the unexpected connection?

After the announcements, Zoe wanted to stay to talk to a woman who'd tried out the new section of trail. Ty worried about leaving the horses alone for long, or at least used that as an excuse, and Leslie headed back to the campsite with them.

Dusk had set in, and under the heavy cover of pine trees it felt late. The temperature had dropped quickly as well. Leslie wished she'd thought to bring warmer clothes. Ty's list had included a jacket and a sweatshirt, but since she'd packed on a ninety-five-degree day in Davis, she'd decided a windbreaker would be enough. That was a mistake. She considered saying she was tired—the warm sleeping bag would feel good, she knew—but going to bed early with Ty would be complicated now.

"I keep trying to think of something to say to make things okay between us," Ty said.

"Maybe there's nothing to say." There was no reason to talk about it more if Ty wasn't interested in thinking about how they could go forward.

"Girl-Monday would say there's always more to say," Ty said, holding back a branch for Leslie as they cut through the trees to the campsite.

She passed Ty and murmured, "Girl-Monday didn't have patience for bullshit either."

Her comment shut Ty down. As intended. She felt terrible about everything that had been said. Like gut-wrenching, worried-the-spaghetti-wouldn't-stay-down terrible. Instead of trying to smooth things over, though, she silently helped Ty check on Polaris and Archer, then gathered the stores of food that needed to be kept in a bear-proof container. Whether Ty needed the help was hard to say, but she felt better keeping busy.

"I think I might go to bed early. Where do we wash up?" She'd used the outhouses a few times now, and while they didn't smell awful, there was no sink.

"Right here. I'll heat up some water if you'd like. It'll only take a minute to set up the camp stove."

She nodded, mumbling, "Thanks," and tried not to let on how cold she was as she watched Ty work. Discreetly rubbing her hands together didn't do much good, and she was full-on shivering before the little pot of water came to a boil on the burner.

"I'd brought cocoa and marshmallows thinking we might watch the stars come out, but I don't know if you'd want to do that now…I also have a bottle of rum tucked away in the supply bin if you want that instead." Ty glanced at her and their brow furrowed. "Are you cold?"

"I'm freezing," she admitted.

Ty studied her like this was surprising news. How was Ty not cold?

"I can loan you some more layers. Want a sweatshirt? There's gloves and a hat in the supply bins too."

"Do you have a heating blanket and a warm bed?" She was mostly joking and broke a smile when Ty apologized that they didn't have that. "In that case, I'll take the cocoa. With the rum, please. And your warmest sweatshirt."

"You got it. Go ahead and use this pot of water to wash up. I'll start another pot for the cocoa after I grab you a sweatshirt."

While Ty started another pot of water boiling, Leslie took off the windbreaker, washed her face and hands quickly, then toweled off, still shivering so hard she couldn't stop her chattering teeth. She pulled Ty's sweatshirt on, enjoying the faint scent of Ty on the thick material. Ty handed her a knit beanie and, although tempted to turn it down on pure aesthetics, she pulled it on and was happy she did.

"Better?" Ty asked, handing her a mug.

She took a sip and the combination of cocoa and rum warmed through. "Better."

"Did you miss me?" Zoe asked, appearing at the campsite flushed with excitement.

"Not really," Ty said, their ribbing comment earning them a smack from Zoe.

"I was talking to Polaris." Zoe peeked over Ty's shoulder at the pot on the stove. "Ooh, are you making cocoa?"

"Already made." Ty motioned to a mug. "Yours isn't spiked."

"Thanks." Zoe reached for the mug and took a deep sniff of the cocoa, murmuring how much she liked camping. She walked over to Polaris and swung an arm over the horse's neck. "As much as I like Ty's special cocoa, I wouldn't drink it tonight. I'm not doing anything to mess up our chances tomorrow."

"You can go to bed early if you want," Ty suggested. "Polaris seems pretty relaxed. I think Archer must have finally told her to chill out."

"Who needs sleep?" Zoe kissed Polaris's withers and said, "Guess what, Pol, tomorrow's our first Tevis."

Ty glanced from Zoe to Leslie. "Zoe, if you're gonna stay awake, would it be okay if Leslie and I took a walk?"

"Go have fun. I need to tell Polaris all the reasons she's amazing."

"You up for it?" Ty asked Leslie.

"Sure." Taking a walk in an unfamiliar forest in the dark brought up about a dozen possible ways to die, but if Ty wanted to talk more, she wanted to give them a chance. Her heart wanted to give them fifty chances.

Ty grabbed a flashlight and their mug of cocoa, then waved to Zoe. As they started down the path, Leslie debated bringing up the earlier conversation. She couldn't pretend she wasn't still upset but she wanted to know if Ty had really made up their mind. If so, nothing she said would matter. She focused on the bobbing halo of light on the path ahead until she realized how she couldn't clearly see anything beyond that halo.

"I'm not used to being in places where it's so dark. No lights anywhere…"

"It makes it easier to see the stars," Ty said.

She thought of the night at the water tower and the constellations Ty had pointed out. Everything about that night had been so distinct. Details ingrained in her mind that she knew she wouldn't forget—the stars overhead, the warm night air, the cool metal of the Jeep. How vulnerable and yet strong Ty had looked when they'd first taken off their shirt. How sexy she'd felt. How amazing it'd been to settle between Ty's legs, knowing Ty trusted her and wanted her, but knowing too they were nervous.

Ty stopped walking and Leslie realized they'd reached a clearing. Ty flicked off the flashlight. Instead of noticing stars, her eyes tracked right to the moon. It shone over the peak of one of the nearest mountains, big and almost orange. "The moon's gorgeous."

"I don't know why I didn't think about the moon being full…" Ty said. "We won't see many stars with that big flashlight up there."

"It's still gorgeous." Leslie shifted closer, wanting to put an arm around Ty but holding back. The conversation about next week and all the weeks after fought against the memory of the night at the water tower.

"Can I ask you something?" When Ty nodded, she pushed herself to ask the question that had been on her mind for a while. "Why aren't you riding Polaris tomorrow?"

"I don't race anymore." Ty didn't meet her eyes.

"You've said that, but why? Zoe said you still take Polaris on long rides when she can't. And I know how much you love Polaris— maybe not quite as much as Archer, but you can't hide how you feel about her."

"It's a long story."

"I don't know about you, but I've got some time on my hands. Earlier today I was hoping for tent sex, but after our conversation…I don't think I'm up for it."

"I'm sorry."

She shrugged. "We've been complicated and messy from the beginning." That was the truth. "If you really don't want to tell me why you aren't the one doing Tevis, I won't push."

Ty aimed the flashlight at a boulder with a flat surface. "Is it okay if we sit down?"

She sat down, leaving a few inches between her and Ty, trying not to think about how much she wished she could simply lean against them and have everything back to the way it was.

"I wonder how many spiders are hiding around this rock."

"Too many to count," Ty said. "Welcome to camping." They smiled but it seemed forced.

Something skittered in the bushes and Ty swung their flashlight toward the sound. Everything went quiet for a moment, then from somewhere above an owl hooted. A chill went up Leslie's spine. "All of a sudden I'm realizing there's probably lots of things watching us right now that we can't see. Are there bears here?"

"Yeah, and mountain lions. Bobcats too. And lots of raccoons, but you don't have to worry about them unless they have rabies."

"Lovely." She crossed her arms and legs, hoping nothing would crawl up her clothing.

"We could sit closer, if you want."

She hesitated but a moment later scooted over and leaned against Ty's warm body. Her own body practically cheered. When Ty wrapped an arm around her, she felt entirely too good. In that moment, she could almost believe she was theirs. And Ty was hers.

She swiped away tears that welled, thankful for the dark. Ty didn't need to know how much her heart had gotten involved.

"The good news is I'm a slow runner."

Leslie squinted at Ty. "What are you talking about?"

"If something attacks, you only have to run faster than me. And you like to jog. I know you're in way better shape."

"Thanks for trying to make me feel better."

"Sounds like it didn't work."

She sighed. "I'm feeling a little out of my element." Too many unknowns, like if she'd end up alone and if she could really be happy that way now. And too many knowns, like the fact that Ty didn't want to make the sacrifices for a relationship and wouldn't be in her bed come Monday. She didn't completely blame them even if it hurt. "I think I spend too much time in Davis."

"It's not a bad town."

"No. And I love it. But it's probably good to get out of town more than I do."

"Where would you like to go?"

She considered her answer. "Anywhere would probably be good for me. Aside from the trips I've taken to see my dad in Florida and going to Santa Fe where an old friend lives, I haven't gone anywhere since my ex and I broke up. Even then we rarely went anywhere. We were both focused on work…I say I don't have time to travel, but I know it's an anxiety thing. I've always wanted to go to New York, but I know I'll never go."

"Why not?"

"It's too overwhelming. The planning, the place itself. All the people. Figuring out taxicabs and subways. I'll probably never see a show on Broadway or walk down the street in Manhattan."

"I think it's totally reasonable to feel anxious about a trip like that. What if someone else did all the planning?"

Leslie stopped herself from asking if Ty was volunteering. "The problem is, I like the option that's safe. The option that means I don't have to go out of my comfort zone. So I convince myself I'd have a terrible time in New York." She glanced at the moon and felt a swell of loneliness. She felt so good wrapped in Ty's arms, but knowing it wouldn't last made her feel worse. "I wish I could go for the things I want in life."

"What are the things you want?"

She thought of all the things she'd wanted over the years and how they all came down to one thing. "You owe me an answer first. Why aren't you riding Polaris tomorrow?"

"The truth is, I'm too scared to compete anymore. I don't want to ruin another horse like I did Archer."

"What do you mean ruin Archer?"

"The last Tevis we did together. Our last real ride." Ty stopped and the moonlight reflecting in their eyes showed a sheen of tears. "Zoe and everyone else you ask would say it wasn't my fault, but they weren't there.

"Archer and I were so close to the end. Only a few miles from the finish. There was one horse ahead of us. I knew the rider was pushing his horse too hard. He wasn't the type of guy to condition his horses and he'd blown through a couple of the vet checks, barely giving his horse time to catch his breath. I kept thinking he was gonna fall back and then Archer and I could slip into the lead. I had all my attention focused on that. Waiting for a break.

"Archer was in such good shape back then. I think he knew he could win. He kept inching up on the other horse, wanting to pass. I made him hold back and he wasn't happy with me." Ty laughed softly. "He was so full of himself.

"It wasn't a clear night like tonight. The moon kept slipping behind clouds and I had to rely on Archer to see the path. The closer we got to the end, I was focused on chasing the other guy and his horse. All of a sudden, the guy pulls his horse up short. Instead of just stopping, his horse stumbled and fell. Right in front of Archer. Before I could even think, Archer jumped past them. But there was no trail to land on. We started sliding down a ravine."

"Oh shit."

"Somehow we'd missed one of the trail markers and gotten on a little deer path. I should have been paying closer attention, but I was only thinking of how close we were to winning." Ty met Leslie's gaze. "It felt like we were sliding forever. Tree branches kept hitting us and Archer kept scrambling to get a foothold but he couldn't. I can still hear the sound of us crashing down that hill."

"That's awful." She pictured the scene, sweet Archer, likely terrified, and Ty clinging to his back.

"When we stopped sliding, I got off and fell down on my knees crying. I thought we'd both be dead when we hit the bottom, but we were alive." Ty paused, looking up at the moon again. "The climb out of the ravine took hours. Literally. When we were on level ground again, I realized Archer wasn't placing any weight on his back left leg."

Ty had mentioned Archer's injury several times before but never any details on how it'd happened. Leslie waited for them to go on, but they didn't. "That was a freak accident. It wasn't your fault Archer got hurt."

"I wasn't paying attention. I wanted to win and I wasn't looking out for my horse. It was completely my fault."

Leslie reached for Ty's hand. "It was an accident. I could see how you would blame yourself for getting off the route, but—"

"I know it was my fault," Ty interrupted. "You don't need to try and make me feel better. I've relived the whole thing in my head about a thousand times. There's no changing what happened or what I did wrong. Which is what I finally realized—I couldn't change the past. All I could do was change the direction I was going.

"I knew I couldn't race Archer anymore, but I stopped racing other horses too. I put all my time and energy into rehabbing Archer and getting into vet school. I want to help other horses after injuries like that. And maybe stop some injuries before they ever happen."

"Will you forgive yourself then?" When Ty didn't answer, Leslie pressed on. "After you get through vet school and start helping other horses, other riders, will that be enough?"

A tear slipped down Ty's cheek. They squeezed Leslie's hand but didn't respond.

"You won't, will you?" She reached out and touched Ty's cheek, catching the tear. "We all make mistakes."

"I know." Ty cleared their throat. "Anyway. Tevis always happens around a full moon. They plan it that way so it's easier to see the trail."

"Ty." Leslie waited until they finally met her gaze. "I know if he could talk, Archer would say he forgave you a long time ago."

"Do you think I'm chickenshit for not wanting to race anymore?"

"Chickenshit is the last word I'd use to describe you. You live every day completely yourself, not hiding anything. You took on training Polaris when no one else would touch her. I bet you've done a hundred other things like that and I just don't know all the stories yet." She paused. "And with endurance riding, you recognized you weren't in the right headspace to do something inherently dangerous—something that puts a horse's life at risk as well as your own—and took a step back. That's fucking brave."

"It doesn't feel brave."

"Well, it is."

The sound of an approaching car cut through the quiet of the night. A moment later, headlights flooded the clearing. A voice called out, "Have you seen a loose horse come this direction?"

"Shit. No." Ty stood. "Whose horse?"

"Dunno," the driver said. "But it tore through the registration area and then someone thought they saw it run this way." They didn't wait to say more, hitting the gas and backing out of the clearing.

"Do you think it could be Polaris?" Leslie asked.

Ty was already in motion. "We need to get back to camp."

CHAPTER THIRTY-SEVEN

Archer. Polaris. Zoe. Ty counted off each one and felt a flood of relief.

Zoe stood up from the camp chair she'd positioned next to Polaris, holding her Kindle out at arm's length. "Why the hell are you running?"

Ty threw their arms around her. "There's a loose horse. I thought if it was Polaris and you'd taken off after—" They struggled to catch their breath. "Damn, I'm out of shape." They paused and looked behind them. Leslie had been right at their side...

Ty spotted her a moment later and reached out for her hand. She seemed surprised but clasped it. "Fuck, you're not out of breath at all."

Leslie smiled. "You can come jogging with me anytime."

The next moment, Archer let out a high-pitched whinny. A warning. Ty knew the sound and a shiver went up their spine. They let go of Leslie's hand and shone the flashlight the direction Archer was looking. A moment later, a gray Arab tore into view. The horse's eyes looked wild, panicked out of his mind.

Polaris reared up, knocking over Zoe's chair and trampling the canvas in the next step. Ty reached for Leslie, pulling her toward them. Thank god Zoe was out of the way. *Thank god Zoe wasn't sitting in the chair.*

Before Ty could grab a rope, the gray Arab threaded between the tents and in the next breath was gone. Hoofbeats pounded the dirt road. Ty swung the beam of light to see which direction he'd taken but there was nothing save the dark green pines set close together and the empty dirt road.

"Was that Martina's new horse?" Zoe asked Ty.

"I'm almost sure of it. Banderas."

Zoe shook her head, trying to quiet Polaris as she cussed under her breath. Archer met Ty's gaze and then looked toward the road where it turned south.

"Even if it isn't Martina's horse, I think I should go after him," Ty said, following Archer's gaze.

"How would you catch him?" Zoe asked.

Leslie's grip on Ty's hand tightened. Her signal was as clear as Archer's. But Archer was asking to follow the horse. Leslie wanted Ty to stay.

"You could take Polaris," Zoe said. "Follow him until he gets tired?"

"I'm not taking Polaris," Ty said. "But I don't think Archer could catch up to him."

"What if we took the truck?" Leslie asked. "Do horses want to get in carriers like cats do when they're scared? We could follow the road until it ends and see if he'd come up to the trailer."

Ty hadn't expected the "we" part or the look in Leslie's eyes like she was sure they needed to do something.

"There's no way a scared horse would get into a trailer. Not when they're spooked like that," Zoe said. "Especially a trailer they don't know."

"We could try anyway," Ty said. "If Archer's there…"

"You seriously think it would work?" Zoe was incredulous. "Which way did he even go?"

"That way," Leslie said, pointing the same direction Archer's ears were angled.

That sealed the deal. Ty turned to Zoe. "If it were Polaris, wouldn't you want someone to go after her?"

Zoe's shoulders dropped. "Yeah, of course."

"And you know how Archer is with other horses. He can get anyone to trust him." Ty was already untying Archer from the highline, trying not to weigh the likelihood of the plan's success. "Leslie, will you come with me?"

"Wait, what about me?" Zoe asked.

"You're staying with Polaris." Ty handed Leslie Archer's rope and went to get a spare halter and lead. "If you can get in touch with Martina, tell her we're going after Banderas."

Archer didn't bat an eye about being loaded up. Ty pulled out of the campsite, heading south with the brights on. They passed several campsites with everyone awake and clearly unsettled.

"Did you see a loose horse? Gray Arab?" Ty asked. Heads nodded and hands pointed in unison. "Guess we're going the right direction." They pressed on the gas.

"Where is he?" Leslie asked, shining the flashlight on both sides of the path and leaning out the window to see. "He could have taken one of the paths between the trees instead of staying on the road."

"Maybe. But horses usually take the easy route." Ty glanced at Leslie. "Thanks for coming with me. I don't know if we'll be able to catch him or what will happen to him…"

"We have to try." There was no doubt in Leslie's voice.

They reached the end of the road with no horse in sight. The tents and RVs clustered at the turnaround didn't show any sign that anything had disturbed the occupants, and the horses at each spot looked half asleep. Ty idled for a moment as Leslie shone the flashlight along the sides of the road.

"There!" Leslie pointed at the trees and a flash of gray appeared a moment later.

The horse leapt out into the clearing, eyes wide, then bolted across the road and onto another narrow trail. There was no doubt it was Banderas. "Guess that boy doesn't take the easy route."

Banderas was headed for a section of the campground that had been closed off. A fire block had been cut and logs had been left behind to help with erosion. There was a forest service trail through the area, but last Ty had heard it wasn't closely maintained, and of course Banderas picked the most dangerous direction—the route that went straight downhill.

The thought of Archer trying to navigate the steep path made Ty sick. At least the downed trees would slow Banderas down. Maybe he wouldn't get himself killed.

"Do you think he'll turn back? We can't go any farther, can we?"

Ty shook their head. "This is the end of the road." They pulled the trailer off to the side, trying not to think about what they had to do next. "Wait a minute…" The image of Zoe's map covered in Skittles came to mind. "That trail he took crosses the Tevis path. I'm almost sure of it."

Ty took one last glance at the spot where the horse had disappeared and then turned on the ignition. They pulled back onto the road and looped the truck and trailer around in the turnabout.

"You're not going to try following him?"

"It's too risky. But I think Archer and I can cut him off."

When Ty pulled the truck to a stop at the Tevis trailhead, they couldn't help but think that in mere hours the space would be filled with horses and riders all dreaming of a buckle. Or a first-place finish that came with a shiny cup.

Ty pushed away the reminder of what could have been and hopped out of the truck. Archer willingly came out of the trailer. He looked at the trailhead, then back the direction they'd come, sniffing the air as if saying, "You know that gray horse went the other way, right?" Ty rubbed his neck, hoping he'd figure out the plan quick enough. If anyone could bring the other horse back it was Archer, but taking a different path might throw him off.

Ty looped Archer's lead line around his neck, fashioning reins, and then swung astride him. Leslie passed them the flashlight.

"You sure this is a good idea?"

"No." Ty forced a smile. "But Archer won't let me do anything too crazy."

Leslie handed Ty the extra halter and lead line. She turned to Archer. "Bring Ty back in one piece, okay? I have some things I need to talk to them about and they aren't getting out of the conversation by getting themself killed."

"We'll be back. Promise." Ty wanted to kiss her but held back. "Can you drive the truck back and let Martina and Zoe know the plan? Tell them to give me an hour. Shouldn't take longer than that if I'm remembering the map right."

She nodded, taking the keys from Ty. Her lips formed a thin line as she glanced at the truck. "You realize I have no idea how to drive that thing, right?"

"You didn't know how to ride a horse until last week either."

"You're on a mission to get me out of my comfort zone, aren't you? Okay. I'll figure it out. Go on, before I get mushy. And, I swear to god, you better come back alive."

"I will. I know we're in a fight—and I know it's my fault—but there's three words I want to say right now."

"If you want to figure out a way forward, I do too." Leslie reached for Ty's hand. She squeezed it lightly once and then let go. "Dammit, now I want to say those same three words. Hurry up and find that horse."

Ty didn't need to cue Archer. He heard Leslie and seemed to assume the message was for him, setting off at a trot. Ty had to pull him back to a walk, and when they looked back, Leslie raised one hand in a wave as the other swiped away tears. Ty wanted to say something to assure her but their own heart pounded in their chest. *Three words.* The same three words that had been tangled up in their chest for weeks.

It didn't seem fair. Finally they'd met someone they could be completely themself with, finally they'd fallen in love. But how could they concentrate on a new relationship at the risk of everything they'd worked for and dreamed of? Then again, could they really walk away if Leslie wanted to try to make something work?

"What I'm really worried about is getting my dumb heart broken again." Archer's ears flicked back at Ty's words. He gave a snort and Ty knew what he was thinking. *Some things were worth the leap into the unknown.*

CHAPTER THIRTY-EIGHT

After the fourth try, and subsequent fail, Leslie abandoned the idea of turning the truck and trailer around on the narrow dirt road. Backing up was the only option—and a terrible one at that. Unfortunately, channeling her focus on not hitting a tree, and actually staying on the road while the truck crept backward, didn't mean she couldn't worry about Ty and Archer.

It felt like a week at least before she'd backed up as far as Martina's campsite. Likely it was closer to ten minutes, but ten minutes of barely breathing. She spotted Polaris and Zoe standing next to the brown-and-white paint Martina was going to ride tomorrow. The horse looked like a younger, slimmer version of Archer. The gray horse who'd been tied up next to the paint was of course missing. Martina was being comforted by a man Leslie assumed was her husband. A younger man stood off to one side, looking pale even in the moonlight. All four faces turned to her when she hopped out of the truck.

"Any news?" Zoe asked.

"We saw the horse—"

"Is Banderas okay?" Martina interrupted.

"He looked okay, but we couldn't catch him. We saw where he went though. Ty took Archer and is going to try to cut him off from a different trail." She wished she'd thought to ask the trail names. At least she could show the others where Ty had gone. Still, she ached with worry. "Ty thinks Archer can handle the trail in the dark and can catch Banderas."

"I bet he can," the man hugging Martina said, nodding vigorously.

"I'm sorry, Mom," the younger man said. Closer up, Leslie realized he was probably no older than fourteen or fifteen. Tall and skinny and scared. "I didn't think Banderas would bolt like that."

"It wasn't your fault." Martina shook her head. "Those idiots who decided to tear down the road on those motorcycles...They're not even allowed here. Thank god they didn't hit you or Banderas." She held out her hand and brought the teen into a family hug. "Ty will find him. We'll get him back before he gets hurt."

Her last sentence was said more like a prayer. Leslie added her own to that. *Please don't let Archer or Ty get hurt either.*

Martina's husband kissed his wife's head and straightened, seemingly only then noticing the truck and trailer positioned the wrong direction. "How far did you drive that rig backward?"

"From the trailhead." Whatever the name of the trail was.

Zoe opened and closed her mouth. "You backed up the whole way?"

"I never want to do it again." She felt like a drama queen complaining about having to drive backward, but before she could say it was really no big deal, Martina let go of her husband and son and stepped forward to give her a hug too.

"Thank you. Thank you for helping us tonight." She pulled back and her warm eyes had so much sincerity that Leslie's heart ached all the more for her. "Emmanuel can take the rig up to the turnaround and then back to your campsite."

Leslie was more than happy to give the keys to Martina's husband. Then Martina decided she and her son would go wait at the clearing where Banderas had disappeared in case he turned back—though no one believed that would happen—and Leslie and Zoe agreed to go wait at the trailhead Ty and Archer had taken.

Everyone exchanged numbers and promised to text with any news, then Leslie, Polaris, and Zoe headed back to the trailhead.

Most of the campsites they passed had people still awake—sitting in camp chairs chatting in subdued tones or fussing with their horses and last-minute to-do items.

"I think people assume that the loose horse has already been caught," Leslie said, eyeing a group of two men and two women laughing as they clinked beer bottles together over a cooler.

"Or it's not their worry," Zoe said. "Some folks here only care about being able to say they've done Tevis. They don't care who else is on the trail with them."

"I take it you don't feel the same way?"

"No." Zoe half covered her mouth as she stage-whispered, "I'm following Ty's example, but don't you dare tell them that."

Leslie smiled. "I won't."

"Speaking of you and Ty…"

Zoe's tone left no question what she wanted to know. Leslie decided to save her the trouble of asking. "I love your cousin. I think they love me too. But we haven't said those words. And earlier tonight…"

"What happened? I knew you two were arguing back at the campsite."

"Ty basically said we should break up. Not that we're officially dating."

"What?" Zoe shook her head. "Are you sure? They took off their shirt with you."

"Ty told you that?" Leslie felt her cheeks get hot and was glad that the moonlight wouldn't show her blush.

"It was a big deal for them. I haven't even seen Ty's chest. They never take off their clothes around anyone. Like, literally, no one."

"I think we have a connection that's important to both of us, but I don't know that they want a relationship. Ty said they needed to focus on vet school."

Zoe stopped walking and brushed a hand down Polaris's neck. "Vet school is important to Ty—I know that—but, also, Ty is totally in love with you. The thing is…Ty hasn't had many relationships. I don't think they know what they're doing. And I think they're scared of getting any closer."

And getting hurt if things didn't work out. Leslie felt the same fear. From the beginning, she'd known Ty was more of a heartbreak risk than anyone else she'd dated before. They were so easy to get close to, so easy to love. Which was why a relationship felt worth the risk. She knew that, but she didn't want to have to convince Ty. If they didn't feel the same, maybe it was better things ended now.

Zoe had started walking again. "I'm not saying inexperience is an excuse. And you should do what you need to do to take care of yourself. But Ty has never really been able to be themself around anyone, and I see them with you and I know they're finally able to do that. It's really nice to see."

Leslie let the words sink in. She loved that she could be herself with Ty too.

"Honestly, I was worried it'd be you who didn't want a relationship and Ty would end up with a broken heart," Zoe said.

"If we stop now, I think we'll both have broken hearts." Leslie swallowed, feeling the weight of that reality. "I love Ty and these past few weeks have felt almost too good to be true. You ever just know you're hugging the person you're supposed to be with?" Tears sprang to her eyes. "That the person for you finally showed up?"

"I can imagine it." Zoe looked at Polaris. "Don't laugh, but that's how I felt the first time I rode Polaris. Like I belonged with her—even though she's technically Ty's horse. I cried when Ty said I could have her if I got clean. It's the only thing that shook any sense into me. But people are harder to connect with...I think I feel that with Jenna but I'm not sure? And I don't want her to have to deal with all of my shit."

"Maybe Jenna can handle it. People surprise you. The only way to know is to open up to her and see what happens." Leslie paused. "By the way, I'm glad you got clean and I'm excited for you and Polaris. You two are perfect together, and in case I forget to say this tomorrow, I hope you both have fun."

"I'm not sure it will be fun," Zoe said. "Probably most of the ride I'm going to be thinking, *all of this* for a damn belt buckle?" She flashed a smile. "You know Ty has a whole collection of buckles and never wears even one. What a waste." She laughed. "But a year ago I needed something to shoot for and here I am. I don't need to win—even if I think Polaris could win. I just want to finish. I want to prove to myself that I can follow through on something hard."

"You aim high."

"Yeah." She caressed Polaris's cheek. "But I know we can do this."

"After you get your buckle, can you convince Ty to wear theirs too? I'd love to see that. I'd probably make you two take a picture." She smiled, but a moment later wondered if she was being foolish. Ty might be in love with her, and she might know her own heart, but that didn't mean they'd be able to work things out.

"I don't know what will happen after tomorrow, but thanks for letting me crew for you. Also…Ty mentioned you've had to really work to get your head in a good space—and that you're on meds. I am too, and I get it. If you ever need someone to talk to, you can text me or call whenever. Whatever happens with me and Ty."

"Thanks." Zoe exhaled. "I kind of hate that I need anything but I'm definitely happier on drugs. The legal kind."

"Same. In fact, I'm not sure how I'd be handling tonight if I wasn't on something."

Zoe's smile was full of understanding. "Thanks for the offer to talk. As for Ty, I hope they get their head out of their ass and realize a relationship with you is worth it. You're kind of amazing."

Leslie met Zoe's gaze, feeling a press of tears. "Thank you. The thing is, I can't argue with Ty on them wanting to focus on school. It hurts that they won't consider options for how we could be together, but maybe this is how it has to be." Her heart felt heavier than ever. They'd reached the spot where she'd left Ty and Archer and she pointed to the trailhead. "That's the trail they took."

"That's the same trail Polaris and I will be on tomorrow morning. This is the spot where our hundred miles starts." Zoe gazed down the path, trees arching over it and the moonlight casting only a weak glow.

Leslie glanced at her watch. "I'm going to send Martina a text to check in."

The minutes passed slowly. After sending the text and getting the report back that Martina had no news, Zoe dropped to the ground and settled up against a tree. Polaris kicked up a back heel and half closed her eyes. Leslie couldn't sit or relax. She wanted to pace, but instead she got out her phone and started a game of solitaire.

After losing two games, she turned off the phone. Her brain wouldn't be distracted from worrying about Ty and Archer and she hoped to see them coming up the trail with every sound—twigs crunching, voices in the distance, the shuffle of leaves. She thought about how Ty and Archer had fallen down the ravine and then wondered if Banderas would have the same fate. Or what if the whole story was repeated? What if they couldn't catch Banderas at the spot where the trails connected and Ty decided to race after the horse?

Suddenly, Polaris lifted her head and snorted. Zoe's gaze tracked right to the horse. "What is it, girl?"

The horse swung her head toward the trail marker, the whites of her eyes showing. When she whinnied, the sound was answered a moment later by a high-pitched call. "Archer?"

Zoe got to her feet, nodding. "Let's hope he's got Ty and Banderas with him."

CHAPTER THIRTY-NINE

"It's not as bad as it looks," Ty said, knowing by how Leslie and Zoe rushed forward that they were both worried. "He's got a bunch of little cuts on his forelegs and a gash on his right hip, but he's been sound the whole walk back. I don't know how he didn't break anything coming down that hill at the speed he was going, but—"

"You goof," Zoe said, pulling Ty into a hug. "We weren't half as worried about Banderas as we were about you. And Archer."

Polaris, who was loosely tied up at a post by the trailhead, nickered in agreement. Leslie added, "It's true." Instead of hugging Ty, Leslie hugged Archer. "Thank god you're all safe."

Considering how the night had gone, Ty didn't blame her for going to Archer. Still, it made the ache in their chest all the worse. As they'd searched for Banderas, they'd had time to think about everything they wanted to say. Now they looked at her and wondered if any of the words would come out right.

"I'll call Martina," Zoe said. "No bad injuries, right?"

"No. Tell her I think he needs fluids and he'll need the gash on his hip sewn up for sure. The sooner the better. The legs can probably be wrapped."

As Zoe phoned Martina, Leslie asked, "How'd you catch him?"

"It was mostly Archer. We waited at the spot where that forest service trail meets the Tevis route. You should have heard Archer chewing out Banderas when he showed up. Snorting and huffing at him. Banderas was so distracted it was a cinch to throw the rope around his neck." He was also exhausted and dehydrated, which made him even easier to cajole.

"Martina's on her way," Zoe announced. "Her husband's bringing their trailer here. They parked ours back at our campsite."

"You and Polaris should head back," Ty said. "You two need to try and get some rest."

Zoe looked from Polaris to Archer. "How about I take Archer too? Polaris won't really rest until he's at her side."

After Zoe left, it didn't take long for Martina to show up with her husband and son in tow. There was a quick conference about the wounds, and lots of hugs, before her husband volunteered to take Banderas to the vet. Martina couldn't seem to stop crying as she hugged Banderas and Ty and then Leslie. Her husband and son followed suit, not hiding their own tears of relief.

When they'd finally gone, Martina back to the campsite to stay with Picante—although it was up in the air on whether or not they'd be racing in the morning—and her son and husband off to the vet with Banderas, Leslie and Ty headed back to the campsite.

"You saved the day," Leslie said. "Good job."

"Funny, I spent the past couple hours thinking how I messed up the whole day."

"You didn't mess up the whole day. You brought up something we needed to talk about. Just maybe not the best way."

Ty thought of all the words they'd planned to say but nothing came to their tongue except *I'm sorry* and *I love you*. Leslie wasn't even walking close, which didn't bode well. At least they had separate sleeping bags.

"I'm not sure how—" Ty started to say, while Leslie said, "It's so bright out."

Leslie looked over at Ty and said, "Sorry. I cut you off."

"It is bright," Ty said. They looked up at the moon, directly overhead now and perfectly full. There was no need for a flashlight. "It could almost be dusk." But the campsites they passed were all quiet and Ty knew it was well after ten.

"What were you going to say?" Leslie asked.

"I love you." Ty shook their head. "I know I shouldn't start with that, but I've been wanting to say it for so long. I can't hold it in anymore. And you don't have to say anything in response. I just need to say it. I love you."

When they looked over at Leslie, she only met their gaze, waiting for them to go on. Ty pressed on. "It isn't true that I haven't been thinking about what happens after this weekend. What happens with us, I mean. I've been thinking about it nonstop. I *want* to make it work. These past few weeks you're all I've wanted to think about. I love the things we do together. The things you want to do in bed…and your lingerie." Ty stopped and risked a smile but Leslie's gaze was on the road ahead of them.

Maybe in the past hour Leslie had decided she didn't want anything more to do with them. Ty knew they'd behaved like an ass, and she had every right to want to walk away. Still, the thought alone made them feel desolate.

"The truth is, I love the other parts just as much. Waking up with you. Being at the barn together. How you make me feel when I walk in the door and you ask, 'How was your day, hun?'"

Ty hoped Leslie would look their direction then, but she didn't. "I don't want this to end," Ty continued. "I think about not seeing you again and feel sick. But I don't know how we can keep going. And I'm scared, honestly, that real life will mess up what we have. That we won't have enough time to connect and one of us will get mad and blame the other. I want a relationship with you—I want to try for an 'us'—but I honestly don't know how I could make it work."

Leslie nodded and Ty wondered which part she was agreeing with. They walked together for another minute, not saying anything. Pine branches arched overhead, cutting out the moonlight, and Ty wished they could reach out to Leslie. The space between them seemed to widen the longer Leslie took to respond.

Finally, Leslie's steps slowed. "Ty, how often do you ask for help figuring things out?"

"Not often."

"Mm-hmm. I can tell." She caught Ty's hand and gave it a squeeze. "You're cute, but you're a pain in the ass."

Ty looked from Leslie's hand up to her eyes, hope brimming over.

"And, no, that's not a compliment." Leslie smiled, then shifted closer so her shoulder bumped Ty's arm. "Want to ask if I have any ideas on how we could make things work?"

"Do you have any ideas on how we could make this work?"

"Actually, I do. Thanks for asking." She stuck out her tongue at Ty. "One idea is that you could spend the night at my house a few times each week. Maybe not the same nights we're at the barn."

Ty nodded, taking in the words and the meaning. Leslie still wanted to give the relationship a chance. A cautious happiness filled them. "The thing is, I have to study every night."

"I've got a plan for that." She tapped her temple. "I want to write when you study. I want to actually finish that novel I started. These past few weeks I've mostly figured out how to get all my work done on the day job before dinner—which was your fault, and thank you very much for that. So I was thinking…what if I use your study time to write?"

"You wouldn't get mad at how much time I'd have to study?"

"Would you get mad if I became a famous author?"

Ty smiled. "Not one bit."

"It might not be a perfect solution but it's a starting place. I honestly like the idea of having a writing schedule and you keeping me to it." She paused. "And the other days of the week we go back to being Hitch and Girl-Monday and send each other dirty messages—as long as it doesn't take too much time away from your studies. I really do want you to be able to focus on vet school."

"I don't know if you're serious about Hitch and Girl-Monday, but I'd love to bring them back."

"I'm totally serious."

They walked another few steps and then said, "Okay."

"Okay?"

"Okay, I want to try your plan." Ty felt a rush when Leslie smiled back at them. "I want to try for an us. And I feel crazy lucky that you want there to be an us too." They brought Leslie's hand up to their lips and brushed a kiss over her knuckles. "Will you tell me what you want?"

She squinted. "What do you mean?"

"Earlier—before I told you about why I'm not riding tomorrow—you were going to answer the question of what you want in life."

"Oh. Yeah." She looked up at the moon and then at Ty. "Right now I want you."

"In a tent?" Ty grinned.

"Yes, please."

Ty laughed. "But big picture. What do you want in life?"

"I want to do more of the things I've held myself back from doing. Like traveling. And taking days off work to go on an adventure. And I want to finish the novel I started. But more than any of that..." She blew out a breath. "Damn. This is hard to say aloud."

Ty looked at her, waiting. After a moment they said, "You don't have to tell me."

She started walking again, and it was a long minute before she said, "I want someone who wants to spend their life with me. It's cheesy, I know, and I've said I'm fine alone. And truly I am. I'd rather be alone than with the wrong person. But I'm happier not alone." She met Ty's gaze and added, "I'm happier with you. I like sharing things with you."

"Like morning kisses?"

"Like all the kisses." She smiled. "I wouldn't mind a never-ending supply of kisses."

"I could handle that." Ty paused. "I love you."

Leslie stopped walking. "You said that before and I didn't say anything because I was scared there'd be a *but* after it."

"I shouldn't have said that other stuff about loving your lingerie or loving what we did in bed because that's not the important—"

Leslie stepped forward and pressed a finger to Ty's lips. She pulled it away a moment later and then stared at them for a long moment. "I love you, Ty. All the parts of you. I love you so much. Why do you think I was so mad earlier?"

"I'm sorry." Ty was. More than a little.

"You're forgiven." Leslie paused. "I know this started out...not like most relationships, and I know we still have a lot to figure out. But you're the first person I've ever wanted to ask to move in with me."

"Really?"

"Don't look so surprised. You're kind of amazing."

"You're the amazing one." Ty closed the distance to Leslie's lips. The kiss raced through them, confirming everything they'd known. There was no doubt in their heart. When they pulled back, Leslie had a pensive look on her face. "What is it?"

"Does this mean Hitch and Girl-Monday are officially dating?"

Ty laughed. "Yes. And Girl-Monday better get ready for so many kisses."

"Oh, she's ready."

Ty kissed her again. When they pulled back, Leslie's eyes were still closed. Ty wanted to memorize the moment, feeling in their heart how important it was.

Leslie sighed softly as she opened her eyes. "Yeah, I could get used to that."

CHAPTER FORTY

"It's not going to be easy sharing a tent with you," Ty whispered. Leslie's eyes narrowed. "Why's that?"

"Neither of us are good at being quiet." Ty let go of Leslie's hand as her lips turned up in a smile. They pulled back the rain fly, then unzipped the mesh and held the door open.

Leslie squeezed close as if to slip into the tent but then pressed her lips to Ty's ear. "I could be very quiet if you make me."

Ty's mouth went dry. They lifted their index finger to their lips and Leslie tipped her head. Unfortunately, they both would need to be quiet. By all indications, everyone else was asleep. Zoe's tent flap was zipped, the campsite was dark, and both horses were snoozing.

Boots came off first as they bumped together in the tent's front section, both taking turns shushing each other, then jackets. Leslie slipped into the tent ahead of Ty and turned back to whisper, "So, who's on top?"

"You aren't quiet when you're on top," Ty whispered back.

Leslie smiled impishly. She reached for Ty's hand and pulled them through the tent entrance. In the next moment, she pushed Ty onto their back and pressed into their lips with a hard kiss. She pulled back and whispered, "I could be quiet."

"Could you really?"

She considered it for a moment and then shook her head. Ty smiled and flipped her. The sleeping bag material crinkled noisily but offered no resistance. On her back, Leslie opened her mouth in mock surprise.

"How'd you do that so fast?"

"I got moves." Ty grinned. "Tonight I want to show you all my moves. I love you so much."

They leaned down to kiss Leslie but she stopped them with a finger between her lips and theirs. "You don't need to be on top to show me that." She pulled away her finger and accepted Ty's kiss.

Her lips parted and Ty deepened the kiss, feeling warmth spread through them. One kiss moved into another and another until Leslie broke away to say, "Also, I can still give orders lying on my back. Now strip."

Ty pressed a hand over Leslie's mouth. "You're supposed to be quiet. Remember?"

Leslie nipped at Ty's fingers, then let out a half moan when they moved to cup her breast. Ty found Leslie's nipple through the layers of her clothing.

"You'd look good in a leather harness," Ty mused.

"So would you," Leslie returned.

"There's no way either of us would stay quiet wearing leather."

Leslie shifted up on her elbows for another quick kiss, then dropped back on the sleeping bag and said, "I still want you naked. Now, strip. Please."

"Since you said please." Ty winked, then sat back on their heels and tugged off their shirt. Before they could take off their pants, Leslie's hand went to their chest. She traced their scars and then met Ty's gaze.

"Thank you for showing me it's okay to be myself. That I don't need to hide things." Her voice caught but she added, "You have no idea how much I've learned from you."

"I think it's the other way around," Ty said.

Leslie shook her head. She sat up and wrapped her arms around Ty, then kissed them again and whispered, "Keep stripping. I want to feel you all over me."

Ty had no problem obliging that request, even as emotions made all the next steps blur. Clothes came off and Ty's gaze never left Leslie's. They tumbled together, skin against skin, and Ty sent up a silent thank-you to the universe. Leslie was everything they wanted, everything they needed.

When Leslie's hands moved over their body, her lips whispering against their ear, "You are so sexy," for once, they felt it.

With Leslie, they didn't feel embarrassed by their body, or by their wants or by their needs. She knew everything and wanted them still.

"I love you," Ty murmured.

"Show me," Leslie said, playfully pushing her sex against Ty's thigh. She was already wet.

"I want to show you all night."

Ty shifted between her legs and Leslie let her knees go slack. Her glistening pink folds and swollen clit beckoned Ty's tongue. Ty kissed the inside of each thigh, then the rise above Leslie's sex.

"You feel so good," Leslie murmured. Her head fell back on the sleeping bags, now all pushed out of place, and her fingers combed through Ty's hair as her eyes closed. "I love you."

Ty savored the three words, wanting to hold them in their mind. They bent their head, breathing in Leslie's familiar musk, and they wanted to hold the sight in front of them in their mind as well. They loved that they knew how to please Leslie, loved how much she wanted them. Their chest ached with the thought of how impermanent it had all felt before and how many possibilities stretched before them now.

"I love you for more than sex," Leslie continued. "But I also really love having sex with you."

Ty grinned. "Same."

"So are you going to get to work or not?"

Ty laughed, remembering too late that they had to be quiet.

Leslie's eyes seemed to dance as she teasingly hitched up her hips to bump Ty's chin. "I'm dripping over here."

"I noticed." Ty caught a drip on their finger, then slowly traced the outline of Leslie's opening, enjoying how she writhed and moaned in response. They pulled away from her, their breath catching at the sight of Leslie's naked gorgeous body spread out for them. "But this won't be work. This is all pleasure."

Ty parted Leslie, then drew their tongue over her clit. Leslie tremored and arched up, gasping.

"Oh, fuck."

"Shh." Ty pressed a finger to her lips. "Let me show you how much I love you."

Leslie's chest heaved with a panting breath. She pushed past Ty's finger to kiss their lips and then fell back on the sleeping bag. Ty bent and licked her swollen clit again. Leslie's responsive twitch made Ty's own arousal push up, eager for notice. *Later.* For now, they only wanted to pleasure Leslie.

They licked and sucked as Leslie tugged at their hair. She pushed her hips up rhythmically, pressing into Ty's mouth as she dug her nails into their shoulders. Her panting increased as she got closer. Still, it was the quietest sex they'd ever had even when Ty slid a finger inside her.

"More," she said, her voice barely more than a breath.

Ty slid in another finger and started thrusting faster.

"More."

Leslie's wetness dripped into their palm as they slid in a third finger. She pumped into their hand, mouth open but no sound until Ty found her G-spot. When she let out the quietest of moans, Ty sucked her clit between their lips. She clutched at their arm, and in the next thrust came in a hard rush. As the climax coursed through her, she clenched her thighs together and Ty's own center responded. She trembled under Ty, pulled herself roughly away from their mouth, then a moment later pushed back into them. When she pumped her hips again, she gasped as a fresh orgasm raced through her.

Aftershocks followed and Ty kept pace, emotions overwhelming them. Only when Leslie had finally exhausted herself, dropping back on the sleeping bag and letting out a shaky breath, did Ty ease their fingers out of her, pressing their palm against her when she shivered and squeezed her legs together. Ty moved alongside her, wrapping an arm around her chest and kissing her cheek.

"Damn," Leslie whispered. "I like camping."

Ty chuckled softly. "Me too."

"And I love you." Leslie pulled Ty closer, kissing their lips.

CHAPTER FORTY-ONE

"We'll see you at Robinson Flat." Ty wrapped Zoe in a hug. They didn't bother fighting back the tears that rolled down their cheeks.

"And we'll have cookies for both you and Polaris," Leslie promised, stepping up to be next in line for a hug. "As well as all the electrolytes and healthy stuff you can handle."

Zoe didn't seem to be able to speak but she nodded and clasped Leslie tight as soon as she'd let go of Ty. Polaris was full of herself, jogging in place and she hadn't even gotten to the starting line.

Ty held Polaris's reins below the chin strap. They placed a steadying hand on the mare's neck. "Listen up, Pol, you get yourself and my cousin to Robinson Flat safe, okay? That's only thirty-six miles." But the most treacherous terrain of the day.

Ty had seen horses topple off the trail at the first set of cliffs and plenty of riders lose their nerve at Cougar Rock. Some horses got pulled out of the race at the first vet check—which would happen before Robinson Flat—and some riders gave up on a buckle long before they'd made it to the halfway point on the elevation gain. Then again, things didn't get easier after Robinson Flat.

Tevis might only be a hundred miles, but that included over fourteen thousand feet of elevation gain and twenty thousand feet lost. There was no telling how many riders and horses broke down at the first rock scramble through the Olympic Valley. Getting to Robinson Flat was an accomplishment and yet only the first step. Then came the grueling up-and-down trek through the canyons at midday with the temperatures expected to peak at a hundred and five. Typical August.

Another horse passed them, nickering as he tossed his head. Polaris squealed and yanked at the reins. Ty looked at Zoe and her expression mirrored their thoughts. She was gonna have her hands full.

"Martina's in your group with Picante. See if you can get Polaris to stay at their pace at least until the first checkpoint." Given how amped up Polaris was, that alone would be a monumental effort.

Ty turned back to Polaris. "I know you feel cool now, Pol, but you're gonna be burning up later. Take all the time you need in those water crossings and remind Zoe to keep her bandana wet."

"Don't worry. We got this." Zoe swiped at Ty's tears before kissing their cheek.

Before Ty could respond, Zoe vaulted into the saddle. "Wish me luck," she called over her shoulder.

Ty barely forced out the words, "Good luck." It was too late for all the other advice that rushed into their mind. They watched Zoe line up with the others in the "pen" waiting area she'd been assigned. There were always too many hotheads, both horses and riders, to have everyone start together, but Zoe and Polaris wouldn't have long to wait. Their group assignment was being called up second.

Ty rubbed away tears but more sprang to their eyes. They struggled to keep their breathing in check. Was Zoe really prepared for what came next? Could she hold Polaris back? Was Polaris too wild to have any business skirting cliffs with thousand-foot falls?

If something happens to either of them, I'll never forgive myself.

"Hey." Leslie touched Ty's shoulder.

When Ty turned to look at her, they knew she could see how much of a mess they were. "I'm sorry. I'm just…I don't want either of them to get hurt."

"This is where Zoe and Polaris both want to be. You got them here, but what happens next is up to those two." Leslie motioned to the second pen and the blur of horses and riders. "You have to let them try."

"I know but…" A lump formed and Ty couldn't finish the sentence.

"Come here." Leslie opened her arms and Ty stepped into her embrace.

Leslie let Ty break down on her shoulder. She held them tight as the first group set off and Ty only pulled away when the call came for the second pen to line up. *Zoe and Polaris.* Ty straightened, watching as the rope around the second pen was opened. As soon as the first horse stepped forward, a chestnut Arab, Polaris reared and tried to shoot to the front. Zoe got her under control, but not before Polaris annoyed everyone in the group.

"Fuck," Ty murmured. "Polaris isn't ready for this."

"You said she's better conditioned than any horse you've ever raced. Maybe her head's not ready but that's where Zoe comes in, right?"

Ty knew Leslie was right, but the knot in their stomach only seemed to tighten as they watched Zoe fight with Polaris over who was in charge of the bit. Ty could almost feel the burn of the reins in their own palms as the second group jostled forward, Polaris managing to cut ahead of the others despite Zoe's best efforts.

"Pol's gonna sprint ahead. She's going to use up everything in the beginning and Zoe's going to waste energy trying to slow her down."

"Then that's what happens."

Ty glanced at Leslie.

"This is Zoe and Polaris's race," Leslie said. "You gave Zoe a chance to get her life back on track. This is all part of it. She needs this—everything that happens today. And you got Polaris here too. When no one else could. It's pretty damn impressive. But now you have to let them run on their own."

Leslie's words settled over Ty as the signal sounded for the second group. The horses and riders leapt into motion, and in seconds the only thing remaining was a cloud of dust.

Ty exhaled and looked away from the starting line. "Damn. I didn't think that would be so hard."

"You do hard things, but you do them well." Leslie caught the front of Ty's jacket and pulled them to her. She kissed their lips. A long tender kiss.

When she pulled back, Ty returned the kiss with one of their own. As they parted, Ty said, "Thanks for being here."

"There's no place I'd rather be." Leslie hooked Ty's arm with hers. "Should we go check on Archer?"

"Yeah." Archer was probably listening to the hooves pounding the trail even from his spot back at camp. He'd know when they came back without Polaris that the race had gone on without him. Ty scrubbed their face, taking away the last of the tears. "It's gonna be a long day."

Leslie pulled Ty closer as they walked away from the race. "I'm looking forward to it. Although, not as much as I'm looking forward to being in a tent with you again tonight."

Even starting at five, the morning passed quickly. They cleared the campsite at Robie Park and trailered Archer down to Auburn where the race would end. Once Archer was set up in a stall, they backtracked to Robinson Flat. Ty kept tabs on Zoe and Polaris's GPS coordinates and knew they were making good time. Possibly too good. But Leslie reminded them it was out of their hands. And it was. Until the first checkpoint.

Polaris wasn't one of the first horses to arrive at Robinson Flat, but she was well ahead of the time Ty had expected. They'd hardly set up a smorgasbord of treats—both for Zoe and Polaris—when Leslie pointed out a rainbow bandana on a rider a few hundred yards up.

"Isn't that Zoe?"

"Thank god. Yes." Ty exhaled. The next breath in felt like the first full gulp of oxygen they'd had all morning.

"What sweet hell did I sign up for?" Zoe asked, sliding off Polaris and thrusting the reins at Ty. "Fuck me. How did you do this ride five times, Ty?"

"You ready to call it already?" Ty joked only because they knew Zoe was definitely not to that point.

"No," she grumbled. "But seriously? How insane am I?"

"Just as insane as your cousin, apparently," Leslie said, flashing a smile at Ty before handing Zoe a bottle filled with an electrolyte solution. "Now sit and drink. We'll do the rest."

Polaris hardly needed the break and acted antsy to keep going. With a little convincing, however, Ty got her to drink a good bit of the electrolyte water along with some grain and mash while they gave her a quick rinse down and checked her pulse.

"Think she's good to keep going?" Zoe asked.

"If you want to keep going, I know she is."

Zoe stood up from the camp chair where she'd been chomping on a double chocolate chunk cookie. "Hell yeah I want to keep going." She smiled at Leslie. "I just needed a cookie." She went over to Polaris and kissed the mare's muzzle. "You are a rock star. Want to head down to the valley with me? I hear there's a party at the campgrounds in Auburn tonight and we've only got another sixty-four miles to go."

"Rock and roll," Ty said, grinning. "All you gotta do is clear the vet check. Want me to go with you?"

"Nope. We got this." Zoe patted Polaris's neck. "My horse is amazing. The most amazing horse ever."

Ty had never felt more proud of Zoe—and of Polaris. They'd both gotten themselves through so much and were so much braver than even a year ago. "See you at Forest Hill?"

"Oh, we'll be there all right," Zoe said, throwing a wave over her shoulder.

Forest Hill was the two-thirds mark and a mandatory one-hour hold. If Zoe and Polaris made it that far without getting pulled from the ride at any of the next vet checks, they'd need the hour rest. Ty remembered the first time they'd done Tevis and reaching Forest Hill only to collapse on the ground. It'd been Martina's family who had taken care of Archer then. They'd needed the help more than they'd realized. Zoe and Polaris would need it too.

Leslie tapped Ty's arm. "Good job, crew boss."

"You too. We make a good team—you taking care of Zoe and me taking care of Polaris."

"We do make a good team." Leslie's gaze went to the vet check station where Zoe and Polaris were waiting. "You think they'll make it to Forest Hill okay?"

"I do, but if Zoe thought she just went through hell, she's about to enter Tartarus."

"The inner depths of hell?"

"Exactly. The canyons are so damn hot and it's all up and down, over and over again. You finish climbing one hill and realize you've gotta climb another. When you're in the canyon, you just cook. It'll be over a hundred in some of those spots and the sweat pours off you. But if you drink too much water, you'll cramp up and won't be able to move. You gotta fill your helmet with water at every water crossing and drench yourself—and your horse. Or you both wish you were dead."

"Lovely." Leslie shook her head. "And you willingly did this ride how many times?"

"It was a phase. I think Archer and I had something to prove back then."

"Now you two don't need to prove anything," Leslie said, leaning close for a kiss. She pulled back after a quick peck and said, "I was thinking...do we have time for a break somewhere shady and out of the way?"

"Sure. Like for a little picnic?"

"Or a quickie in Paige's truck."

Ty opened and closed their mouth, then laughed. "I have to say, I could get used to this version of Tevis."

"The version where you have lots of sex instead of riding a hundred miles on a horse in the blazing hot sun?"

"I mean, it doesn't sound awful."

Leslie smiled. "Maybe you've entered a new phase."

It didn't take long for them to clear up the rest stop and make room for the next crew. Ty knew from the GPS tracker that Polaris had cleared the vet check. Paige had promised to bring supplies to the next vet check and would take care of Zoe and Polaris—she had a vet friend working the ride and was planning on hanging out there for the day with Olivia. She'd get to wave to all of the horses and Paige promised she was looking forward to it. Ty had felt guilty having someone else step in, but when Leslie took their hand, murmuring about all the things she'd like to do to Ty, the guilt vanished.

Tevis was still theirs, even if they weren't in the race. Even if they weren't at every checkpoint. It was a trail they could picture with their eyes closed. They didn't need Zoe's map with the Skittle candy markers. It was an experience they'd shared with Archer five times over. Endurance riding and all the races they'd gone on, with all the different horses they'd been lucky enough to ride, had changed their life. But now life had changed.

They shifted closer to Leslie. "When I'm a vet and I'm working Tevis, doing exams on all the horses, will you hang out with me?"

"I'd love to."

"It gets hot and boring and it's a long day but—"

"I'll be with you." Leslie smiled. "It won't be boring. Nothing with you is boring."

Ty clasped Leslie's hand, a tingly happiness spreading through them. "When you're a published author of a cozy mystery series that's flying off the bookstore shelf, can I be at your book signings?"

Leslie laughed.

"I'm serious."

"I know. And it's amazing to have someone believe in me as much as you do." She exhaled. "Yes. I'd love to have you at my side. For the signings and for everything else." Her gaze dropped to their entwined hands. "I feel so lucky I got to meet you in real life. And that we got a second chance." She looked up and her eyes were wet. "I love you."

Ty met her lips with a deep kiss. Love had never felt so real.

EPILOGUE

The barn door swung open and Ty strode in, a big smile on their face. "Someone looks happy," Leslie said, smiling back at them. "Does that mean final exams went well?"

"I don't even care. I'm done for the summer." Ty gave Leslie a quick kiss, then went to Archer and gave the horse a hug, exhaling deeply.

She knew Ty did in fact care about their final exams. They'd studied for hours and hours, then worried they'd never be able to know enough. But she also knew they were overdue for a break. Since Ty had officially moved in over winter break, she'd realized how much time went into their studies. So much more than she'd imagined. Yet that hadn't stopped Ty from wanting to snuggle every night—which Leslie loved.

"I'm so ready for a ride," Ty said. "Thanks for grooming Archer for me. He's looking very handsome."

"That's what Nellie thinks too." Leslie finished tying Nellie's braid, then gave the mare an affectionate pat. "She started flirting as soon as I brought the two of them in from the pasture."

Ty chuckled. "Mares."

Leslie watched Ty fit Archer's saddle in place. As they looped the cinch, she came around to Archer's side of the hitching rail. "Congrats on finishing your second year of vet school. Can I call you Dr. Sutherland yet?" When Ty shook their head, she tousled their hair. "Fine. Be that way."

She started to step away, but Ty caught her hand and brought her close. "Hey."

Her pulse thumped in her ears, and she wondered at how a year later Ty could still make her breathless with one touch.

"Thanks for saying yes to a ride today," Ty said. "I need to decompress with some horse time. And I'm sorry I've had my attention on school so much lately. But I fully intend on making it up to you all summer long."

Ty closed the distance to her lips with a deep kiss. Her whole body responded as she shifted into Ty's arms. She definitely wouldn't mind Ty being amorous for the next three months if this was a hint of what was in store.

"Do you two ever go an hour without having your hands all over each other?" Zoe's voice interrupted. "This is a barn, not a hotel room, you know."

"And no one would ever make out in a barn." Ty winked at Leslie as they stepped back. "Hi, Zoe. How was your psych final?"

"Fine. I think I passed." Zoe's brow knit together. "When you say make out, you two haven't had sex in here, have you?"

Leslie looked at Ty, who bit their lip in response. Zoe groaned, then turned to Archer and Nellie. "You two were supposed to be chaperoning. What happened?"

Archer looked at Nellie, who only stomped at a fly.

"Useless," Zoe muttered. She turned back to Ty and Leslie and said, "Full disclosure, I've had sex in here too."

"You did?" Ty's mouth dropped open. "This didn't happen when you were supposed to be house-sitting for Paige and Seren, right?" Leslie elbowed them and they quickly said, "You're an adult and I'm sure you were being responsible."

Zoe and Leslie both laughed at Ty's quick backstep. Most likely it had been the time Zoe and Jenna were house-sitting. Their relationship had lasted several months and the ending had surprised everyone. Ty especially had worried what the breakup would mean for Zoe's mental health. But it was Jenna who'd shown up at Leslie and Ty's house bawling. Zoe seemed to weather it better, focusing her energy on her college classes and endurance racing.

Zoe went to the tack room and came out with Polaris's saddle slung over her shoulder. "You two heading out soon?"

Leslie and Ty nodded. Ty had suggested the plan—a celebratory ride after their last final and then a whole weekend off together. As much as Leslie had been looking forward to the reconnecting time, she felt bad not including Zoe. "We were planning on riding to the water tower. Want to come with us?"

Zoe shook her head. "I know how slow Nellie and Archer go. Polaris won't have the patience. But maybe we could all have dinner tonight? I feel like it's been weeks since we've hung out."

Ty glanced at Leslie, and she knew what they were thinking. Zoe wouldn't ask unless she needed company. "Dinner tonight would be perfect," Leslie said. "Maybe I can finally get that picture I've been wanting."

"What picture?" Ty asked.

"Funny you should ask." She arched an eyebrow. "Don't move." She went to the tack room and came out holding the belt she'd brought from home. Zoe clapped her hands together and Ty scrunched up their face.

"Remember your promise?" Leslie handed Ty the belt with the Tevis buckle attached. It was only one of many buckles in Ty's collection—none of which they ever wore.

Zoe gave Ty's shoulder a shove. "No getting out of this now, cuz."

Zoe didn't often wear her Tevis buckle either—Leslie had only seen it on her at Seren and Paige's Christmas party. But that didn't change the fact that she and Polaris had finished ninth in their first Tevis race, which meant a buckle and a listing in the top ten finishers. Everyone said it was an amazing accomplishment for two first-timers. Leslie had no doubt that was true because Ty's smile hadn't left their face for weeks after.

"I guess I can wear it for one picture." Ty's cheeks had a hint of red but they smiled down at the buckle.

"See you two later tonight," Zoe said, already heading out of the barn. "And, Leslie, thanks for making more horse cookies. Polaris loves them."

Polaris was in the pasture being frisky with the new horse—a young gelding Paige and Seren had agreed to foster mostly because of Ty. He was a rescue mustang with baggage and fit in perfectly with the herd. All he needed was to find his long-term human.

As soon as Zoe had gone, Leslie turned to Ty. "So, are you strapping that on for me or not?"

"This won't be as much fun as my other strap-ons."

"I could think of some fun role-plays," Leslie said, waggling her eyebrows. "Please? Just a sneak peek?"

Ty threaded the belt through the loops of their jeans and then fastened the buckle. Once they'd adjusted it in place, they held out their arms. "I look silly, right?"

"Not even a little silly. But you are missing one thing." She went over to where Ty's cowboy hat hung from a hook above Archer's tack. She set it on their head and then took a step back, narrowing her eyes. "Mm. Yes. That's nice."

Ty laughed, clearly embarrassed at the attention. They took off the hat and shook their head.

"Um, did you forget about our deal?" Leslie stepped forward and placed the hat back on Ty's head. "Not the one about the picture. The other one—about how after you finished finals, we'd go for a ride and then you'd be all mine for the weekend?" She paused a moment, letting her intentions sink in. "All. Mine."

Ty grinned. "Am I in for some kink fun?"

The hopeful tone in Ty's voice boosted her confidence. "I may have plans for you."

Kink had gotten them together in the first place, and while it wasn't the only glue that kept their relationship going, she loved that it was part of what they shared. "You know that time Hitch said they'd be my house servant and do chores naked? Our house really needs to be vacuumed."

Ty's smile spread across their face. "Yes, ma'am. Anything else?"

"Oh, I have a list."

Ty stepped toward her, the smile still creasing their eyes. "You are so damn sexy." They took another step and then pressed into her lips.

After a long kiss, Ty pulled back but kept their hands settled at Leslie's hips. "As much as I'd like to go right to naked vacuuming, thank you for agreeing to dinner with Zoe. It means a lot to me that you'd be willing to change our plans for her."

"I didn't want her to be alone tonight." Zoe had become like family to her. In fact, she was closer to Zoe in some ways than her own sister and loved her just as much.

Ty motioned with their chin to Nellie and Archer. "Look at those two."

Leslie smiled at the two horses standing close together, then realized they were so close because Archer had untied his rope. He'd moved next to Nellie and his chin rested on her withers. Nellie closed her eyes and sighed contentedly.

Leslie's heart filled with pride. Nellie had grown and changed so much in the past year. She loved that she'd been responsible for some of it. "Lovebirds."

"Speaking of lovebirds, how'd your writing session go today? Did the realtor finally kiss the neighbor?"

"Yes." She took a deep breath. "And I ended with two words I'm quite happy with."

"Which two words?"

"The End." She couldn't hold back her smile saying the words aloud.

"Seriously?" Ty's eyes lit up. "That means I get to read it now, right?"

"Mm, yes." Nervous excitement filled her.

"Yes!" Ty pumped a fist in the air, then did a happy dance.

Ty deserved to be the first to read the book. She wouldn't have finished without all the ways they'd encouraged her. Ty's enthusiasm for her project—along with the fact that they had to study every night—meant she'd kept writing even when she'd doubted herself.

"We should do something to celebrate," Ty said. "Did you tell Paige and Seren?"

Leslie shook her head. "I didn't want to tell anyone but you. And we've already got the plan for celebrating. A horse ride and kinky sex."

Ty laughed. They kissed Leslie, then pulled back and said, "As much as I want kinky sex all night, it's gonna be hard waiting to read your book."

"You can read it tomorrow. We can stay in bed all day reading and having sex."

"That sounds amazing."

It sounded perfect to her too. Leslie gave them one last kiss. "But first—horses."

She walked over to Nellie and let her sniff her outstretched hand. When she pet Nellie's head, the mare shifted closer to her.

Ty went to Archer and rested a hand on his neck, then looked back at Leslie. "Do you think it'll be this good forever?"

Leslie knew Ty was serious despite their light tone. "I think there'll be ups and downs." Even if the past year had felt like an endless high, she knew the bumps would come. "But you're the only one I want to try forever with."

"Same," Ty said. They met her gaze and smiled. "You're my forever person."

Bella Books, Inc.

Women. Books. Even Better Together.

P.O. Box 10543

Tallahassee, FL 32302

Phone: (800) 729-4992

www.BellaBooks.com

More Titles from Bella Books

Mabel and Everything After – Hannah Safren
978-1-64247-390-2 | 274 pgs | paperback: $17.95 | eBook: $9.99
A law student and a wannabe brewery owner find that the path to a fairy tale happily-ever-after is often the long and scenic route.

To Be With You – TJ O'Shea
978-1-64247-419-0 | 348 pgs | paperback: $19.95 | eBook: $9.99
Sometimes the choice is between loving safely or loving bravely.

I Dare You to Love Me – Lori G. Matthews
978-1-64247-389-6 | 292 pgs | paperback: $18.95 | eBook: $9.99
An enemy-to-lovers romance about daring to follow your heart, even when it's the hardest thing to do.

The Lady Adventurers Club - Karen Frost
978-1-64247-414-5 | 300 pgs | paperback: $18.95 | eBook: $9.99
Four women. One undiscovered Egyptian tomb. One (maybe) angry Egyptian goddess. What could possibly go wrong?

Golden Hour - Kat Jackson
978-1-64247-397-1 | 250 pgs | paperback: $17.95 | eBook: $9.99
Life would be so much easier if Lina were afraid of something basic—like spiders—instead of something significant. Something like real, true, healthy love.

Schuss – E. J. Noyes
978-1-64247-430-5 | 276 pgs | paperback: $17.95 | eBook: $9.99
They're best friends who both want something more, but what if admitting it ruins the best friendship either of them have had?

CPSIA information can be obtained
at www.ICGtesting.com
Printed in the USA
JSHW080733170223
37883JS00001B/2

9 781642 474398